DAYS OF TRIAL AND TRIBULATION

DAYS OF THE APOCALYPSE, # 3

MARK E. FISHER

Extraordinary Tales

Publishing

Days of Trial and Tribulation (Days of the Apocalypse, #3), By Mark E. Fisher

Extraordinary Tales Publishing, LLC
@ExtraordinaryTalesPublishing.biz

First Extraordinary Tales edition April 2023

Print Book ISBN: 978-1-950235-16-2
eBook ISBN: 978-1-950235-15-5

Cover art purchased from 123rf.com
Cover design and interior formatting by Booknook.biz
Editing by Deirdre Lockhart of Brilliant Cut Editing

To learn where to buy this book or for more information about this and the author's other books visit: MarkFisherAuthor.com

Library of Congress Cataloging-in-Publication Data:
Fisher, Mark E.
Days of Trial and Tribulation (Days of the Apocalypse, #3) / Mark E. Fisher 1st ed.

Printed in the United States of America

CONTENTS

CAST OF CHARACTERS

THE PRINCIPALS

- Brianna—Now fifteen years old, she was orphaned when a bear killed her parents shortly after the vanishing. Caleb and Tanya have taken her in.
- Caleb Turner—Brother to Dylan and Chelsea and a Minneapolis native. Before the vanishing, he was a budding author and blogger. His brother, Dylan, arranged his escape from a Unitum Imperium prison, after which he flew back to Chicago and escaped to Minnesota's Northwoods.
- Chelsea Turner—Sister to Dylan and Caleb, she's the daughter of Adam Turner, the head of the Unitum Imperium's Ministry of Truth. Chelsea is personal secretary to Davato.
- Dylan Turner—Brother to Chelsea and Caleb, Dylan helped arrange the release of his brother and other prisoners from one of Davato's underground prisons. He's part of the Nazarene Friends, a group fighting against the Antichrist. He's in love with Margot Durand.
- Margot Durand—A Belgian woman whom God directed to paint visions of the coming Rapture and Tribulation. When the CSA came after the Nazarene Friends, they captured her and took her to a death camp.
- Tanya Baranov—A Chicago resident and granddaughter of the previously raptured Uri Baranov, the famous author. She accompanied Caleb in fleeing to Minnesota's Northwoods.

THE NAZARENE FRIENDS

- Angelo—A former Truth Squad member who defected to the Nazarene Friends after they captured him in the Paris restaurant altercation.
- Pasqual Berger—Founder and leader of the Nazarene Friends, some call him their pastor.
- Danielle DuBois—Rescued from Marseille, she's a good friend of Victor.

- René LeClerc—Former spy and a friend of Sergei, the spy who helped Dylan and Margot escape from Chicago, René has become the unofficial leader of the Nazarene Friends.
- Victor Marceau—Tech wizard and guitar player.

THE UNITUM IMPERIUM

- Adam Turner—Former CEO and founder of Turner Enterprises, he's father to Caleb, Dylan, and Chelsea. Recently, he was promoted to head the Ministry of Truth, below whom is the feared Central Security Agency.
- Carlo Scutari—Davato's personal aide and bodyguard.
- Davato—The Antichrist and ruler of the Unitum Imperium, the man of lawlessness, also called the beast. He is part of Satan's unholy trinity and his representative on earth.
- Dino Castiglione—Head of the Central Security Agency under Adam Turner.
- François Desroches—Vice Imperator of the Unitum Imperium.
- General Eric Hofmann—Supreme Commander of all Unitum Imperium forces and head of the Ministry of Peace.
- Grady Wilson—A Jew from New York City who served on the Raleigh-Burke class destroyer, the USS *Avenger*, Chaim (Cam) Weinberg assumed the identity of Grady Wilson, his deceased lieutenant. He's now the ambassador from the US President to Davato in Jerusalem and New Babylon.
- Sebastien Rey, the Prophet—Green-eyed false prophet sent to corrupt the message of God, part of the unholy trinity of Satan.

THE ISRAELIS

- Ariel Geller (aka Big Matza)—Head of a large black-market operation in Tel Aviv that helps refugees escape Unitum Imperium tyranny.
- Baruch Abramovich—Leader of the Great Assembly, a group of 144,000 men chosen by God to bring the message of Christ to all who would believe during the Tribulation. Dylan, Margot, and Chelsea recently freed him from a Unitum Imperium prison.
- David Benjamin—Jewish friend of Baruch Abramovich.

THE FREEZER TRAWLER

- Altin Tolan—An Albanian crewman working for Fabio Caruso.
- Enzo Rivera—An Italian Christian who's taking passage on the *Am Albahr* from Haifa to Venice.
- Fabio Caruso—The Jewish sea captain of the *Am Albahr*, a freezer trawler out of Haifa, Israel.

THE SWISS SKUHAUS

- Jakob and Emma Huber—They manage the farm down the road from *Das Ländliche Skihaus*.
- Klaus Martin—Ex-spy and friend of René LeClerc.

THE AMERICANS

The Northshore
- Andy and Mary Hart—Owners of the Intrepid Moose General Store and Sandwich Shop in Tofte, Minnesota, and friends of Caleb.

Camp David
- Alex Reed—Ambassador from the Province of North America after Grady Wilson's promotion.
- William Cole—President of the United States, residing at Camp David after nukes destroyed Washington DC.

The Village
- Bradley—An elder of the Village church who lives in and guards the storehouse.
- Frank—An elder of the Village church who lives in and guards the storehouse.
- Heather—Free-spirited Village greeter and guitar player.
- Damon—Founder and leader of the Village Church in Redwood Falls, Minnesota.

Currie, Minnesota
- Henry Adams—Henry preaches at the Currie church.
- Jack and Linda May Manson—Part of the Currie church, they arrive at the Shetek Park group camp to welcome the newcomers to Currie.

The Scientists

- Ben Smiley—An astrophysicist working at the McDonald Observatory in West Texas.
- Jeffrey McPherson—An astrophysicist at the Mauna Kea Observatory on the Big Island of Hawaii.
- Randy Foster—A volcanologist with the University of Utah's Department of Geology and Geophysics.
- Sally Stewart—An assistant to Ben Smiley at the McDonald Observatory.

PREFACE

This series is about the end of the world as we know it. It's about God's judgment on a sinful, unrepentant world and the end of Satan's rule in the hearts of the people. And it's about the conclusion of the Church Age and the events leading up to Christ's one-thousand-year reign on earth.

Jesus warned us about the signs of the end and told us to watch for them—wars, rumors of wars, famines, plagues, earthquakes, increasing chaos and lawlessness, a coldness infecting the hearts of the people, a turning away from God, and finally, apostasy in Christ's church. As we look around us, all these signs and more are with us. And they're increasing daily.

The nations, one and all, have abandoned God and turned their backs on him. All act as if he doesn't exist, creating plans for humanity that embrace every kind of evil. With stunning arrogance, they have built towers of godless ideology perhaps worse than the Babel of old.

What will be God's response? From Isaiah 2:12, 17–19, 21b–22 (NLT):

> For the LORD of Heaven's Armies has a day of reckoning. He will punish the proud and mighty and bring down everything that is exalted. . . . Human pride will be humbled, and human arrogance will be brought down. Only the LORD will be exalted on that day of judgment. Idols will completely disappear. When the LORD rises to shake the earth, his enemies will crawl into holes in the ground. They will hide in caves in the rocks from the terror of the LORD and the glory of his majesty. . . . They will try to escape the terror of the LORD and the glory of his majesty as he rises to shake the earth. Don't put your trust in mere humans. They are as frail as breath. What good are they?

The God who gave us free will wanted better than what we gave him. He wanted us to turn to him with all our hearts. He planned the beginning, and knowing how we would go astray, he planned the end. Now events are converging, gathering in greater numbers than ever before, foreshadowing the events leading us into the end-times.

No era of history compares with this one—not the Dark Ages, not World War I, not World War II. In no previous historical period have so many signs of the end converged, worldwide, as they have today.

Note what Jesus said in Matthew 24:8: "*All these events* are the beginning . . ."

It's not just one thing; it's all of them. It's the convergence—the sum total, the simultaneous occurrence of events happening everywhere across the planet in a way we have never before seen—that tells us we stand on the brink.

Jesus said we won't know the day or the hour. But we *should* look for the signs of the times. And from everything this author sees, the unprecedented accumulation of portents, signposts, and warnings points to the approaching Rapture of the Church and the second coming of Christ.

The Bible lists approximately 2,500 prophecies, of which 2,000 have been fulfilled. Those that remain relate to the end times. So think about it: If God predicted the future, recorded in the book he sent us through his prophets and apostles, and if what he already predicted came to pass, then so will the prophesied end-times events.

But now one might ask: Why should I read about such things? Why is the author writing about it? Because Revelation 1:3 (HCSB) says this: "The one who reads this is blessed, and those who hear the words of this prophecy and keep what is written in it are blessed, because the time is near!"

Not only is the time near, given the unprecedented accumulation of signs, the time may now be upon us.

We should also read about it because we have friends, relatives, and neighbors who do not know the truth about Jesus and need to wake up.

Because eternity is knocking at the door, and we need to be ready. We need to know what's coming. We need to strengthen our faith and look, not to the plans of a fallen world, but to Heaven.

The first book in this series tells the story of the Rapture and the coming of the Antichrist.

The second book describes the opening of the first five seals in the months and years leading up to the Tribulation midpoint.

This novel, the series' third, tells the story of the months immediately before and after the crucial midpoint, the opening of the sixth seal, and the terrible consequences of the first four trumpet judgments.

So read and take heed. When the Rapture comes, no one wants to be left behind. No one wants to live through the seven terrible years of the Tribulation.

How can you escape it?

Believe in Jesus as the Son of God.

Follow him, and God promises you a way that leads to a blessed, happy eternity in the presence of an all-loving, all-powerful, all-knowing God.

What better message could one hope for in troubled times such as these?

Mark E. Fisher
February 2023
Rochester, Minnesota

The shadow of the Tribulation already darkens our world. Know what's to come, stay true to the faith, and seek refuge in Christ. Subscribe to Mark's newsletter and receive two free gifts:

1. 10 Reasons Why the End Times Could Come Tomorrow
2. How the Green Agenda Prepares the Way for Earth Worship and the Antichrist

Go to: www.MarkFisherAuthor.com/newsletter

THE THIRTY-SEVENTH THROUGH THE FORTY-SECOND MONTHS

APPROACHING THE MIDPOINT

CHAPTER 1
DYLAN

Marseille, France – August, Year 4

The planet has flipped upside down, Truth Squads darken every alley, and we are on the run. Everything that once was is no longer. Or else it's changed so much, I don't recognize it anymore. Out on the streets, people are racing toward oblivion. They're blind to what's happening, willfully ignoring the truth, clinging to a hard-hearted immorality, bewitched by a man who is evil incarnate, a monster leading them to eternal death. And no one understands that time is running out.

While the world spirals ever downward, I lie here in this ramshackle hotel, mocked by the cries of seagulls, shaken by the rumbling of freight trains and the blasts of tugboats, wondering when we'll flee to another hideout. We always do.

They've taken the one I love, and I swim against a whirlpool of despair. They've sent her to a death camp, and I have no idea how or when or if I will ever get her back. I am wracked by such a sense of loss. And of loneliness. And of sadness. I am sprawled over our threadbare couch, counting the mold spots on the wall, watching the paint flaking off, surrounded by my companions, and still, I am lonely. Am I selfish to feel this way? Shouldn't I feel something more honorable? I don't know.

I am a water barrel, and someone has punched an awl through the rotten wood at the bottom. Now all that I am, all that I have ever been, is leaking out, drop by drop, into the dust. If you look hard, you can watch me seeping into the earth. But maybe that's the way I should feel because I realize now how much I loved her, and that's what love does to a person.

Did I say "loved"? Has my heart given up so easily?

René says that if we can find a new base where it's safe, where the squaddies can't find us, maybe we can start the search for her and somehow get her out. He spends his days in the community of former spies, most of whom now refuse to work for the Unitum Imperium. They are no lovers of government.

Pasqual's faith is like a rock, and he tries to comfort the rest of us. I envy him. We call him Pastor, but he denies the title. Everyone came to faith too late, all except one—this miserable soul who begged God to be left behind.

Angelo keeps me company with his own quiet desperation, regretting what he did for the Unitum Imperium. But you must forget what you can never undo. If you're always looking back, trying to change what can never be changed, it will eat you alive.

Victor is a cipher, quiet, hard to read, focused on what he can do with what little we salvaged of his computers, oscilloscopes, and techy tools. He and Danielle are a pair. We miss his guitar we left at the farm.

The farm. It seems a lifetime ago. Was it only a dream? We barely escaped with our lives.

René won't let Danielle go out onto the streets. It's simply too dangerous for a woman out where the refuse of humanity covers the walls with graffiti and lies in wait, guns loaded, seeking the unwary, the weak, or anyone having anything worth taking. In her own way, she's beautiful. She and Victor spend hours alone in her bedroom, but Victor tells me all they do is talk. When he's out, she mopes about like a lost puppy. I see now how much her friendship with Margot had grown.

And me? I'm losing patience and hope, flirting with despair, wandering the streets scrapping for food—as are we all—and otherwise, finding pictures in the mold spots on the wall.

Meanwhile, the clock hands go round, and Margot's in a camp where they kill people. From his time with the squaddies, Angelo says they spare a lucky few and put them to work. But was she one of them?

Luck. Now there's a word for those with little faith. If God is in control, there's no such thing as luck, is there? I hope he is in control, that he still has a plan for Margot and me. We thought he did. But right now, I can't see it.

The world is ending, I am caught up in the Apocalypse, and, God forgive me, I don't know any more how to hold on to faith and hope.

Can she hold on to hers? Is she even still alive? Such thoughts keep me up at night.

Without her, how can I ever again accomplish anything good for God? Before the vanishing, I begged the Lord to leave me behind, and he answered my stupid prayer. But have I saved another living soul? I don't know. Did I make a mistake? Did God? Without her, I don't know how to serve Jesus or, for that matter, anyone.

Only after she was gone did I discover these things. How stupid is that?

Somewhere outside, gunshots echo through the streets. It happens several times a day. Next time I go out, there will be bodies. The Tribulation's harvest, I guess. A reminder that our time here is running out, that any of us could be next.

We are all rootless, wandering souls, waiting for, but perhaps fearing eternity, grasping for something here on this earth to hold on to before the end. It should be faith. I want it to be faith. But maybe for me, it is now love, a love who's been taken from me. How wretched am I!

Lately, it's not only Margot who occupies my thoughts, it's also Chelsea. Last I saw her, she was desperate to find a way out but didn't know how or if that could ever happen. She's in a bad place, a really bad place, working for evil itself, and again, I can't do anything to help my sister. I am useless to anyone, even to myself.

As if that weren't enough, lately, I've been wondering about Caleb. Is it possible my brother got out before the missiles struck? Why am I seized with this strange, irrational feeling, this impossible glimmer of optimism that he might still be alive? Or is that, too, just wishful thinking, a desperate grasping for the wisps and vapors of hope before they fade between my fingers? I don't know.

What little I know for sure is indeed grim knowledge:

We are on the run.

Hydrogen bombs have obliterated Chicago.

Chelsea works for the Antichrist.

And Margot is in a death camp.

CHAPTER 2
ENCROACHING DANGERS

Joel 1:15, 19–20 (HCSB): Woe because of that day! For the Day of the Lord is near and will come as devastation from the Almighty. . . . . I call to You, Lord, for fire has consumed the pastures of the wilderness, and flames have devoured all the trees of the countryside. Even the wild animals cry out to You, for the river beds are dried up, and fire has consumed the pastures of the wilderness.

Tofte, Minnesota – August, Year 4

Each day, the western smoke roiled ever blacker and thicker over the cabin. Each night, the wolves became ever bolder and more aggressive, gathering in the yard and throwing up an eerie, skin-crawling howl until the horses in the garage whinnied in terror, until Brianna raised a worried glance and Tanya pulled a whimpering Nika to her side, until Caleb opened the cabin door, aimed his M16, pressed his finger to the trigger, and released three or four of his precious bullets, blowing out the brains of enough beasts to drive the pack away.

And each morning, Caleb didn't know what to do next.

This afternoon after the ride from the cabin, he clutched a mug of homemade beer provided by his friend Andy Hart and lifted his glance past the rocky shoreline to Lake Superior and the whitecaps beyond. A cool breeze, heavy laden with woodsmoke, so familiar and harsh in his nostrils, washed the patio where he and Andy now sat.

Dangers were closing in on Tanya, Brianna, and the refuge he'd made for them in the Northwoods.

And he didn't know what to do next.

"So, Caleb, what're you going to do next?" His black-bearded friend, dressed in a plaid wool shirt and light khaki windbreaker, clutched his brew, and his wooden rocker creaked back. Andy managed the Intrepid Moose General Store and Sandwich Shop, the last remaining purveyor of general merchandise for miles up and down this section of Lake Superior's coast. But the sandwiches Mary now served to random travelers were wolf meat wrapped in garden-grown lettuce with onions, peppers, and homemade mustard.

"I don't know."

"I'm telling you: You should take one of these new solar phones they started dropping at my place since you were here last. That's how I learned about the fire's extent."

Caleb glanced at the shiny device waving in Andy's left hand. "Won't they be able to track me with that?"

"Maybe. But it will give you satellite images of when the Priest Creek Fire will arrive at your place. You've got to get out of there, Caleb."

"I know. When I return tomorrow, we're leaving. Until today, I had no idea the fire had spread so far, so fast."

According to Andy, Caleb had three, maybe four, days before the blaze engulfed the cabin. If it weren't for the wolves, he'd start for home this instant. But it would soon be dusk. That's when they came out. He didn't have a chance against the wolves after dark.

"It's burning everything in a line a hundred miles wide, north to south. We might lose the entire Superior National Forest and Boundary Waters Canoe Area."

"But if we left the cabin, where would we go?" He brushed hair away from his forehead.

"Come to the shore. There's the abandoned Johnson place down the road."

"But Mary says the fire will burn right down to the shoreline."

"Mary is a fearful woman. The Johnson place is right next to the water. Even if the fire got into the trees by the house, it'll be all right. It's got a tin roof. And it's a nice house. If it wasn't so darn much work, Mary and I would move the store there."

"I don't know." Caleb had to find someplace safe for his family, well out of the fire's path. He faced Andy, the only other Christian and like-minded soul for miles and his best friend these last three years. Even the folks at the Bluefin Bay and the Lutsen Sea Villas—or what was left of them after that first-year gang attack—had packed up and left. "Even if we moved there, what about the wolves and the Silver Bay squaddies?"

"You and I can take care of the wolves." Andy patted the leather holster with its Glock 17 strapped to his waist. He never went anywhere without his pistol.

"You haven't seen how bold they've become. The fire has been driving them east for weeks. They've lost all fear of humans, even though I've shot three, maybe four, dozen. They are now our main source of meat."

"See!" He slapped Caleb on the shoulder. "There's some good in this. I wouldn't worry about the wolves. You've no idea the firepower Mary and I have hidden away, and I've seen how much ammo old Vernon left you. Between the two of us, we can take care of the wolves."

"Maybe. What about the squaddies?"

"The squaddies, yes." Andy frowned. "You didn't know Fred Wellstone, did you? Before you came, he was our county tax assessor. Not too bad a fellow back then. If he upped your assessment, you could always argue him down with a beer or two. Well, he became a squaddie—funny how that passing wayfarer dropped that term on us. Anyways, once he began showing up with that black armband and that hexagram patch with the lightning bolt and skull, he was a different guy. Nastier. Full of himself. Started to bully folks. He tried to bully me into giving him freebies, and I pulled out my shotgun, shoved it at his chest, and told him where he could go. Hasn't bothered me since. There are other squaddies, of course, but all of the same ilk. How did these people ever get control? You'd think it wasn't our country anymore."

"The squaddies don't bother you, Andy, because you deliver their phone tracking devices for them. I wouldn't have the same protection."

"If Fred did come around, sticking his nose in your business, just shove a pistol in his face."

Caleb laughed and sipped his beer. That was the ex-marine talking.

Andy took a different phone from his jacket pocket and held it up. "This one's for you. Take it, and it'll be just like before V-Day. Ever since I got mine, for the first time in three years, I know what's going on in the outside world. I don't have to rely on rumors from travelers, what's left of them. That's how I discovered there's a new government running the country in league with this Davato fellow. Take it, and we can talk—

anytime. We don't have to wait for you to make the half-day trip on horseback. A good four hours in the sun, and this thing'll give you a half hour of service. There's no monthly charge, of course—who has a bank account nowadays?—but you do have to register it."

"And if I register, they can track me wherever I go."

Andy shrugged and took another draught from his mug.

Caleb didn't trust anything coming from the new government. For some reason, President Cole had cozied up to Davato, the man Dylan was convinced was the Antichrist. Cole had even brought Davato's Truth Squads up here to the North Shore—part of the same group that had followed Caleb, Baruch, Margot, and Dylan from Florence to Paris.

And now there was a squaddie nest down in Silver Bay.

"You want to contact your sister and brother, don't you?" Andy continued waving the phone. "Well, take one of these, and you can call them."

"You've got a point there. Let me see that thing."

Andy passed it to him, and Caleb turned it over. How many hours hadn't he spent with one of these stuck to his ear? How often hadn't he wished he could talk to Dylan and Chelsea? Were they even still alive?

Taking it would put him at risk. And yet the phone had given Andy information about the fire that could now save his life and the lives of Tanya and Brianna, their adopted daughter. And if they left the North Shore for the road, internet access would be a great help.

"Okay. I'll take it." He slipped it into his shirt pocket.

Andy nodded and leaned further back, creaking the chair. A gust carried the harsh scent of burning trees across the patio. Waves broke on the rocks below, shooting up geysers of spray, the repetitive motion lolling.

Then Andy scratched his beard. "I've been thinking lately about the Sanctuary. If what we heard was true and if my roots weren't so deep here, I might consider going there."

"It's just a rumor. And no one knows where it is."

"They say it's in the Black Hills of South Dakota. Nearly every passing traveler mentions it."

"They also say it's in Montana. And in Colorado. And in Utah. Face it: It's just a myth."

"I don't know. So many folks know about it. A place hidden in the mountains, stocked with food, with electricity and running water, with its own security, no squaddies, and where everyone is a Christian. These days, it sounds like Heaven on earth."

"It sounds too good to be true. But I admit—it's intriguing."

Andy stood. "You can put the horses in the garage tonight. They'll be safe there."

"Thanks. It's getting toward dusk. I'd better round them up." Caleb finished his beer and headed for the garage. But then his steps faltered.

He stopped, peered into the forest, and leaned against a tree.

A racing fire, ravenous wolves, and troublesome squaddies. He had a family to protect. He could move to the shore. But then what?

Dangers were closing in on all sides, and Caleb didn't know what to do next.

CHAPTER 3

THE INTREPID MOOSE GENERAL STORE AND SANDWICH SHOP

Tofte, Minnesota — August, Year 4

Caleb found his two mares, Betsy and Martha, munching the high grass beside the main highway, a road that hadn't seen a passing car in two years. After the quake, weeds and grass, now dried up, pushed everywhere through cracks in the asphalt. He whistled, the horses threw their heads in the air, and they trotted after him toward the garage. He'd had to work on that, but they were now obedient animals. After the gas ran out and the car became useless junk, he'd turned the cabin's one-car garage into a stable and fortified it against the wolves.

Andy's advice had led him to three frightened American quarter horses. Other than the two mares Andy had stabled in his garage, they were the last survivors of an abandoned horse farm twenty miles down the shore. The skeletal remains of their equine cousins lay scattered over the pasture, victims of the wolves. In the barn, he'd found saddles, bridles, combs, saddle blankets, and bags of oats. In the house, he'd found the farm's moldering occupants, murdered by lawless wayfarers of the kind that, in the first year, had plagued the coast.

He'd never been a "horsey" person, but the animals seemed grateful to accept his care. And with Andy's advice, he learned how.

No one was mowing the ditches, so, for the first two summers, there was no problem finding feed. It had been extra work gathering enough hay to keep the animals through the winters. They'd traveled far, seeking abandoned farm fields, gathering volunteer oats, wheat, and barley for the animals.

The horse manure was good for their growing expanse of garden.

And he smiled at the memory of Tanya and Brianna in shorts last summer, harvesting volunteer barley beside him. Tanya's long blonde hair fell over her chest while Brianna gathered the cut swatches and Nika panted in the shade, her tongue lolling out.

He now had a family, something he'd never dreamed of. Soon after they arrived, he'd suggested to Tanya that they were now man and wife. Then she hugged him, kissed him, and that was that. Though there wasn't a pastor around for miles, the two agreed they were now married.

Three months later, twelve-year-old Brianna wandered onto their place, frightened, thin, and starving. A black bear had killed her parents while she was out scrounging for berries, and for two months in the depths of winter, she'd been on her own. They took her in, and she was now part of the family. She was a great help with the garden and the horses.

Looking back on it now, he breathed in deep, his chest filling with warmth.

This morning, on the fifteen-mile canter from cabin to lakeshore, he rode one horse and led Martha as a packhorse. Ever since the wolves appeared, he made Nika stay behind.

But on each trip to the store, he carried fewer items to trade. Andy complained constantly that he had so few customers, it was a miracle he was still in business. Without internet and banking access, bartering had long ago replaced cash on the North Shore.

Yesterday, looking at the sky, Caleb had reservations about leaving home. But every summer, there had been smoke. Nothing unusual about that. And Tanya had insisted he go. They needed salt and anything else he could get. Wolf pelts, shelled corn, and homemade bread—from their own wheat—were all he could offer. But Andy would take anything from Caleb in trade.

He pulled down the garage door and locked in his three mounts. With Andy's, that made five animals. By the time he entered the Hart house, shadows darkened the lawn. Once he was inside, Mary barred the main door.

It was always a special occasion when Caleb arrived, and in his honor, she'd cooked a pot of chili with beans and jalapeno peppers saved from before V-Day. She also made cornbread with honey. And, of course, Andy provided copious mugs of his homemade beer.

They ate by the light of candles and pinewood logs burning in the fireplace. Everyone now lived with the smells of woodsmoke, candle wax, and unwashed bodies. But tonight, Mary added the aroma of cornbread and chili.

"That was delicious." Caleb pushed back from the table, his palate satisfied after the cabin's monotonous diet of wolf meat, bread, and corn.

Mary smiled and began collecting dishes. "You should bring Tanya and Brianna here sometime."

"We'll all be back here tomorrow afternoon. Today, I came alone for supplies. The wolves are so bold, I couldn't risk bringing them. But after hearing how bad the fire is"—he dropped his gaze to the tabletop—"we've no choice but to leave. If it's okay, we'll stay tomorrow night."

"I wouldn't hear of anything else." She laid a hand on his shoulder. "To have you folks here will be grand. Grand, indeed. Are you moving on?"

"I don't know." He scratched his beard. "Maybe."

She stood then whirled toward her husband. "He's considering it. Yet here we are—you and me—staying put. We should get out of here before the fire hits."

"We'll be safe." Andy waved a dismissing hand.

"Even if the fire burns up every green thing right down to the water?" A bit too loud, she landed one dirty plate on top of another.

"That's not going to happen."

"You don't know that." She gathered an armful of dishes and stalked off to the kitchen.

Alone again, Andy gave Caleb a shrug. "She wants us to move. But it ain't going to happen."

"I gathered that." He smiled and stood from the table. "Excuse me. I'll try calling my siblings now."

Andy nodded, and, taking a candle, Caleb ambled toward the spare bedroom. He put the brass candlestick on the low dresser then sank into the bed quilt. By flickering candlelight, he examined his bearded face in the mirror above the dresser. He still hadn't gotten used to the look. But a beard was warmer in winter, and it conserved water not to have to shave every day.

He pulled out the shiny phone and stared at the first piece of functioning electronics he'd held in three years. Memories of a bygone age flooded back. How was it possible that civilization had changed so much in so short amount of time? If he dialed the numbers he'd memorized for his brother and sister, would they answer? Would they even be alive? His heart raced, and he wondered if he really wanted to know.

He powered it on, the registration screen popped up, and he stared at it. They wanted his name, address, and social security number. All he had was the bogus ID info that the ex-spy, René LeClerc, had procured for him three years ago in Paris. His address would now be a rural route in Tofte. Maybe they wouldn't connect the dots to his old self, and he'd be safe? Swallowing hard, he gave it what they wanted. Then the home screen popped up.

His heart beating faster, he punched the first set of digits for Dylan's number. He put the device to his ear and heard the familiar sound of a ringing phone.

A voice came on the line, but it was automated, telling him the number was no longer in service. Of course, after all this time, who knew what might have happened to an old phone on an old service?

His fingers shaking, he dialed Chelsea's number and waited. But again, an automated voice reported that her number, too, was out of service.

He stared at the phone, trying not to let disappointment turn to despair. But there was one more option, one more number he could try. Bettino was now his only hope of reaching his brother and sister.

He'd last seen Bettino after Dylan and Margot had rescued him and Baruch from a Unitum Imperium prison. They'd driven all night to Bishop Emilio Gallo's villa where Bettino had arranged for them to stay. The Turner family's Tuscan villa, just over the hill from the bishop's, had been compromised.

His heart beating even faster, he entered the numbers. As the dial tone filled his ears, he prayed: *Please, God, let Bettino know where they are.*

Instead of an automated response, a familiar voice came on the line.

"Bettino? This is Caleb."

"Caleb Turner?" His voice rose, ending in a gasp. "Are you all right?"

"Yes, my old friend. For the first time in three years, we have internet and phone service here on the North Shore. For you Italians, that's in Minnesota. How is it with you?"

"Without you and your friends, lonely. Your father comes rarely, but he's changed. And not for the better. It's not like it used to be."

Caleb gripped the phone tighter. Did Father still head the Ministry of Truth? Did he even care about his sons and daughter? Caleb shuddered. Then he asked the question that had troubled him these last three years. "Can you tell me how to get in touch with Dylan and Chelsea?"

When Bettino explained that Dylan was all right, Caleb's heart surged with joy. But because Dylan was hiding at an undisclosed location in France, Bettino couldn't reach him directly. He could only relay a message the next time Dylan checked in.

But when Caleb asked about Chelsea, Bettino became evasive. "She is alive, Caleb, but that is all I will say about her. You should hear of her situation from her lips, not mine."

While Caleb was glad she was okay, Bettino's cryptic answer was worrying, and the old man would say no more. After they hung up, all that was left was to wait for Dylan and Chelsea to call him back.

Tomorrow, Caleb would return to the cabin, prepare for a long and dangerous journey, and bring Tanya, Brianna, Nika, and everything the horses could carry back to the shore. But they had to be off the road before the wolves came out.

By Andy's estimate, he had three days, minimum, before flames engulfed the cabin.

But what if the wind picked up and the fire accelerated? What if they took too long to pack?

He tossed under the quilt. Andy wanted them to take over the Johnson place, and Tanya might like that. But if the fire burned down to the waterline, what would be left to keep them here? They might be better off heading south along the coast toward what was left of civilization.

Into squaddie territory.

In the distance, the wolves howled, followed by muffled whinnying from the garage. Andy said he hadn't seen them at the shore recently, but with how fast the beasts were racing ahead of the fire, that could change overnight.

He left the bed, went to the window, and peered through cracks in the boards. Out on the road, two lupine shadows slunk toward the garage, followed by four more.

They were already here. But they wouldn't get past the garage doors. He left the window and went back to bed.

He had a plan for tomorrow, but after that? He had no idea.

CHAPTER 4

THE TEMPLE OF GAIA

Revelation 18:4–5 (NLT): "Come away from her, my people. Do not take part in her sins, or you will be punished with her. For her sins are piled as high as heaven, and God remembers her evil deeds."

New Babylon, Iraq – August, Year 4

Surrounded by thousands of worshipers, Chelsea turned her attention to the front of the Temple of Gaia. The Prophet's words still echoed through the vast hall, exhorting everyone that after the dancing, they should find someone with whom to join, flesh to flesh, body to body. Beside her, Grady kept nudging her and glancing toward the stairs leading to the flesh rooms above.

"Not today," she answered as forcefully as she could. Most of the time, those in attendance relied on the earth priests and priestesses upstairs for a partner. Today, the Prophet had made an exception.

"Then when?" he asked with a frown.

She shrugged and looked away.

His face bright with expectation, Grady then beckoned to a young woman ahead of him. She wore a see-through blouse, a sure indication of her willingness to participate. The woman nodded and sidled beside him. As they stared into each other's eyes with apparent lust, Chelsea ripped her gaze away. These last few weeks, he'd changed. She hardly knew him anymore.

How long could she, a member of Davato's personal staff, hold back from this part of group worship? Would anyone besides Grady notice her failure to engage?

She shrank from an advance by an older man, and then, happily, the dancers distracted him, beginning their performance up front. Handsome young men and beautiful young women, all naked, spread out on both sides of the central statue.

Twenty feet tall, the naked idol of polished green jade squatted, its breasts exposed, its head encircled by a halo of stars, an obscene jade phallus sprouting between crossed legs. In one hand, it held a shock of wheat. In the other, a lightning bolt.

Then began the wild throbbing music, the bass, the drums, the electric guitars, and the synthesizer. The dancers gyrated this way and that, throwing their hands in the air and encouraging the audience to join in. On all sides of her, people danced with abandon. They bumped against each other. She had no choice but to join in. Soon, the floor vibrated with the stomping of a thousand feet, the beating of drums, the pulsing of the bass.

The dancing went on and on. Fifty meters ahead on the stage, the naked dancers writhed and squirmed and gyrated in an obscene parody of dancing. Pretending to do her part, Chelsea danced until sweat dripped from her forehead. Despite her previous vow to resist, she couldn't stop the heat spreading to her loins. One by one, couples and individuals began leaving the floor, holding hands, heading for the stairs or the escalators that would take them to one of the flesh rooms above. If you didn't have a partner when you left, you could always join with an earth priest or priestess there. When she glanced aside, Grady and the young woman had already gone.

She had to get away from this madness. Was it now safe to leave? Looking around, she saw no one she knew, so she wended her way through the mass of twisting bodies. But she headed—not for the stairs leading to the private rooms above—but to the exit.

"Chelsea!"

She whirled toward her father's voice.

"Are you not participating in the Prophet's sharing time?" He'd been crossing the floor from the restrooms by the entrance, and now he stopped.

A shiver rippled down her back. That was what they called it—sharing time. And Father's enjoyment of it surprised her. He was part of Davato's inner circle, yes, but his insistence that she prostitute her body for the sake of this new, unwholesome ritual disgusted her. "I–I'm not feeling well. I'm going to my room."

Momentarily silent, he narrowed his eyes. "Have you joined with anyone recently? I haven't heard that you have."

She swallowed. How did he know that? No cameras or listening devices had been placed in the rooms of anyone in Davato's inner circle—too much chance of sensitive information leaking from the trusted few. But there *were* cameras in the hallways, and Grady had entered her room on many occasions. Wasn't that proof they might have had a liaison? Or had Grady mentioned to someone that she was avoiding him? Lifting her gaze to his, she took a deep breath and lied. "Yes, Father. It's none of anybody's business, but I have. Just not today."

The seconds ticked by as he stood there, saying nothing. Then he spoke. "I'm worried about you, Chelsea. You are my daughter, and I care about you. If you don't fit in here . . . well . . . bad things happen. People end up in the shooting galleries. Or the camp. Or the colosseum. So just . . . be careful." Then he continued toward the stairs leading to the flesh rooms.

He headed the Ministry of Truth, under which was the feared Central Security Agency. But now he had taken onto himself every immorality promoted by Davato and the Unitum Imperium. She hardly knew him anymore.

In this city, she hardly knew anyone anymore.

Shuddering, she hurried through the revolving doors, out into the sweltering heat of an Iraqi summer. Already drenched with sweat from the dancing, she slowed on the pedestrian walkway leading to the World Casino. Away from her father's accusations, apart from the dancers' wild gyrations and temptations, she breathed deeply.

But the air was scorching, and the row upon row of dead and dried-up trees only reminded her of the two witnesses sent by God who had inflicted a drought upon the entire world.

Had no one else noticed? Was she the only one who realized what that meant? That God disapproved of everything they were doing here? The evidence was before them all:

Two witnesses sent by God had inflicted a drought upon the entire world!

Her heart sped up again.

She hurried toward the World Casino and her air-conditioned room. At least, she'd escaped another worship ceremony without giving her body to some stranger. Or to Grady.

* * *

Later that afternoon, she stood from her cubicle, slid the opaque plastic door open, and headed for the break room. Still troubled by the worship service, she'd not been able to concentrate on anything, and she needed a cup of coffee, tea, maybe even a glass of wine—anything really. They served everything in the break room.

Davato appeared from an aisle between cubicles, nodded in her direction, and turned right, following the same path as she was. Was it a good sign he only nodded? If he suspected her of not participating this morning, wouldn't he have thrown her a dark look?

She followed, slowing her pace so as not to catch up with him.

Up ahead was the entrance to a room renovated only two weeks ago, a room about which everyone was whispering. After the workmen had finished, someone had fixed a sign on the door with the words *Admittance Strictly Forbidden*. Since the door was locked with a keypad, the sign seemed unnecessary. Yet, shortly after the workmen left, whenever she passed the door, she shuddered, and such a feeling of dread possessed her that she would hurry down the hall.

Davato stopped before the keypad. He bent and entered a four-key combination, and she heard the tone each number made. The door clicked open, and he entered.

She kept walking. But as she passed the open door, she threw a glance into the room. There waited the Prophet and something else—something intelligent, alive, and swirling with shadows. Something ancient and profoundly evil.

Within the room, darkness churned and gathered. A feeling of dread crept into the hall, circled her, and rippled down her back.

The door clicked shut, but her brief glimpse left her heart pounding in her stomach. Her feet bore her down the hall where she ran straight into Grady, nearly knocking him over.

"What's wrong?" Gripping her shoulders, he steadied her.

She breathed deeply and threw a glance toward the locked door. "Later. Right now, I'm going to my room."

He checked his watch. "But it's an hour before quitting time."

Feeling as though she might be ill, she didn't answer. Instead, she hurried for the elevator.

But as she stood before her apartment door, she stared at the keypad. The sounds Davato made when opening the door to the hidden room were still clear in her mind. She punched the numbers in sequence, listening to each until she had the combination: *3, 5, 8, 1*. Why she did this, she didn't know. She'd be a fool ever to enter that horrible room.

Shaking her head, she pushed through into her apartment and hurried for the refrigerator where she kept the wine.

CHAPTER 5
A MATTER OF WOLVES

Minnesota's North Shore – August, Year 4

Four horses' hooves clopped over the asphalt as the forest darkened, throwing deep shadows across the road. A tether led from Caleb's mount back to one of Andy's borrowed mares, loaded down with all they could salvage from the cabin. He'd even strapped extra bags behind his saddle. Still, they'd left too much behind.

In another mile, they'd reach Andy's place and safety.

Back at the cabin, Caleb had taken the M16 and mounted Sally while Tanya rode Betsy and carried the AR-15 semiautomatic rifle.

Brianna had strapped the Glock 17's holster around her slender hips and mounted Martha. "I'm the sheriff woman of Tofte," she said with a grin. "And I'll shoot every wolf that crosses my path."

"Not so cocky, young woman," Caleb had said. "No shooting unless I say so."

"Right, Caleb, sir." Still grinning, she had saluted, straightened in the saddle, then slapped her holster. She was spunky, that girl, but sometimes, at unexpected moments, as fragile as a broken teacup looking for glue.

Ever since their group left the cabin, the clouds had been smoke-black, the air thick with the smell of burning wood, leaves, and brush. And when the road topped a hill and he looked back, an angry red glow stretched from north to south. In the north, flames and showers of burning ash occasionally leaped into view over the treetops.

They'd left none too soon.

"We left too much behind," said Tanya.

"What choice did we have? The Northwoods is burning up."

She shrugged. "I guess you're right. And it might be good to live by the water."

"Is the Johnson place nice?" Brianna leaned toward him in the saddle.

"It needs some cleaning, but when I was there a few months ago, it looked okay."

Ahead and wagging her tail, Nika, their black-and-white miniature Australian shepherd, led. But the dog kept sending occasional worried glances behind and into the woods.

Caleb, too, gazed back at the road they'd left. Barely visible, a half dozen lupine shadows slunk over the asphalt.

"They've found us." He kicked his mount. "Faster!"

Tanya and Brianna spurred their horses, bringing them to a canter.

When they caught up to Nika, she also picked up the pace.

Behind them, the wolves now numbered a full dozen.

After the quake and with no one maintaining the roads, weeds and grass were poking through cracks in the asphalt, often making the way uneven. But the horses seemed to manage.

They turned a corner, and the highway appeared two hundred yards ahead. The lake, gray and white-capped, lay beyond. The Intrepid Moose General Store and Sandwich Stop was down the road, only fifty yards to the left. They hadn't far to go. But the horses were tired, and the wolves were gaining, only fifty yards back.

Again, Caleb kicked his mount. Andy's horse with the load balked and pulled on the lead before matching Sally's gallop. The two women kept pace in the rear. Tail wagging and showing no signs of slowing, Nika raced once in a circle then bounded ahead.

At highway 61, they veered left onto the broken asphalt.

But the wolves were thirty yards behind and closing.

Caleb slowed until the others caught up. As they approached, he held out the packhorse's reins for Tanya.

"Put the horses in the garage. I'll catch up."

The lupine forms loped faster.

"What are you going to do?" she asked.

"Slow them down. Go!"

She kicked her mount, and the three horses galloped on. Brianna was already far in the lead.

He swiveled in the saddle, aimed his M16, and fired off a few shots. One of the beasts fell, but the others came on, tongues hanging out, eyes shining a soulless yellow. They'd closed the gap to twenty yards. He aimed, his finger pressed against the trigger, and he fired everything left in his clip, all twenty rounds.

Five more beasts fell. The pack scattered left and right. He'd slowed their advance.

He whipped to the front, kicked his mount, and galloped the rest of the way to the garage.

Andy must have heard the shooting as he now stood in the middle of the road, waving his own AR-15. "Get your horse inside. I'll cover you."

Nodding, Caleb rode into the yard. Tanya and Brianna were just emerging from the garage. Mary was beside them, and they carried armloads of goods.

"Get into the house!" shouted Andy from the road. He aimed and fired a few more rounds at the wolves, who had recovered and were racing toward the men.

Caleb dismounted, hurried Sally into safety with the other four horses. He yanked off her saddle and bridle. Andy had filled the trough with water and laid up plenty of dried grass. After the long ride, the horses would need it. The cabin supplies lay on the floor, but he couldn't take them now.

He slammed the door shut, twisted the lock, and spun toward the road. As he walked, he rammed in a new clip.

Andy was backing away from a pack now numbering over twenty. He aimed and let loose a volley. Three more beasts fell. But when Andy next pulled the trigger, his magazine was empty.

Caleb waved his rifle. "Run! I'll cover you."

Andy bolted for the open door, and Caleb brought the weapon to his shoulder. After all that they'd killed, where had all these wolves come from? What remained of the entire wolf population of Northern Minnesota must be on their way to the shore. Why didn't they give up? He shot another four racing toward him.

He whirled. Sprinting as fast as his feet would take him, he made for the door. He could hear one of them panting close behind, closing fast.

"Faster!" shouted Brianna, standing in the doorway. "It's right behind you."

She took two steps outside, spread her feet, aimed her pistol, and fired.

Caleb entered first, then reached out a hand, and yanked her inside. A last glance back revealed that she had, indeed, brought down the wolf. He admired her spunk, but she should have stayed with the others. Andy slammed the door shut, and Mary bolted it.

Something rammed the outside door, and claws scraped the wood. Then came a fingernails-on-chalkboard howling that started Nika barking and growling at the door.

"That was close. But we beat them." Breathing hard, Andy stepped forward and hugged the newcomers, followed by Mary.

"You shouldn't have gone back out, child!" Mary scolded Brianna.

"Caleb needed some support. A sheriff woman worth her salt has gotta help her dad?"

"Thanks, Brianna. You saved me." Caleb smiled. Was that how she was thinking of him now? As her dad? He dropped his rifle by the door and headed for the table. Sweat drenched his shirt, and he wiped his brow.

"Could you use a beer?" Before receiving an answer, Andy pulled a bottle from the icebox in the kitchen. With no electricity, Caleb had followed Andy in creating an old-fashioned icebox with a drip pan out of their useless refrigerator. But it was August, and their store of ice was almost gone.

He accepted the homemade brew, not quite ice-cold, and thanked his host.

"There are a lot of wolves out there." Brianna unstrapped her holster and hung it on a hook by the door. "But I got one."

"There are." Tanya went to Brianna's side and smoothed her blonde hair. "But we're safe now."

While Tanya and the men took seats at the table, Brianna sat on the nearby couch and petted Nika.

"I don't remember seeing wolves act like that before," called Mary from the kitchen. She filled a pot with water from a faucet attached to a rainwater cistern Caleb and Andy had raised to the roof. She laid the kettle on the stove then threw another log into the firebox. They'd hauled in a wood cookstove from an abandoned cabin a few miles down the road.

"Nor do I." Andy clutched a beer of his own. "It's unnatural. They're usually afraid of people."

"It's the judgment of the fourth seal." Caleb had searched Revelation for answers to what was happening. "It's the rider on the pale green horse, the one who brings death by the sword, famine, plague, and wild animals."

Inside the cabin, silence fell. Outside, the wolves began another fingernails-on-chalkboard howl. From the garage next door, the horses whinnied. Nika growled, and Brianna hugged the dog close. "It's okay," she whispered. "The wolves won't get us."

"Sure, I get that the fire is driving them east." Andy cradled his mug. "But they shouldn't be massing like this, acting like they've got some kind of vendetta against us. I reckon you must be right."

"They're most active after dark." Caleb took a seat at the table. "Not so much in the day. If that holds true, we can move to the Johnson place in the morning, assuming the house is still fit to live in."

"It is." Andy saluted with his mug. "Mary and I went over today. I boarded up the windows, and Mary cleaned out the mice and cobwebs. We've been collecting coolers for water, and we took over some we didn't need and filled them. I'll help you make your own cistern when it's safe."

"You folks didn't need to do that," said Tanya.

"Of course we did." Mary returned to the kitchen and pulled the pot off the burner. She poured boiling water over mint leaves into three cups. "I also changed the sheets and blankets and brought theirs here to wash."

"Mary, you're too much." Tanya smiled.

"The place has a tin roof for the house and garage, something I wish we had—if we'd had the tin." Andy regarded his beer with a frown. "That'll be good protection from burning ash."

"When will the fire arrive?" Mary brought cups for Tanya, Brianna, and herself. Then she waved toward the west. "This morning, I saw flames on the horizon above the treetops."

"A day or two maybe." Andy laid a palm on his wife's arm. "But this fire is out of the ordinary. We've always had an occasional fire in the summer, but nothing like this. It's worse now because of the drought. Besides the wolves, that's another odd thing. Since February, we haven't seen a flake of snow or a drop of rain. The woods are a tinderbox, ready to flare up at the tiniest spark."

Caleb took another sip of beer. "After you gave me that phone, last night I found a website with news from Jerusalem. I know why there's a drought."

The others lifted their eyes to him.

"Last February, two prophets appeared in Temple Square. I saw the video, and I couldn't believe my eyes. Supernatural fire came from their mouths and consumed the six goons Davato sent against them. Then they declared a worldwide drought for six months. That's why our forest is burning up. But that time is almost up. The rains should return any day now."

"Glory be." Mary covered her mouth with her hands. "We surely are living in the time of the end."

"Yes, we are living through the prophecies in Revelation, and you know what?" He lowered his voice to a whisper. "The worst is yet to come."

CHAPTER 6

MINE NUMBER FIVE

Weisserwald Uranmine, Southern Germany – August, Year 4

Margot had been in the camp for a month, and today, as she often did, she looked back on that first morning after her arrival. . . .

* * *

Grosse Frau banged her truncheon, shouted orders, and ushered the ninety-six prisoners of barracks number 1,679 to a meager breakfast of thin potato soup. Barely had the last spoonful been consumed in the yard when she gathered her charges and shouted an announcement. "You new Christian scum who just arrived—listen! Out of all the arrivals yesterday, you were chosen by lot for this barracks. Our purpose here is to service mine number 5, and that's where you're going today and every day thereafter, as long as you have the strength to wield a shovel and pick. Bring out your quota of ore, and you live. Come up short two days in a row"—she grinned—"and you die."

A sigh of relief swept through the newbies, and Margot exchanged hopeful glances with the woman who occupied the bunk next to hers. Everyone had feared they'd be sent to the guillotines.

"My name is Eva," said her bunkmate. "Let's stick together today, all right?"

Margot nodded. She desperately needed a friend in this place.

Then Grosse Frau—for that's what the veterans called her—marched the group to the camp's main gate where a platoon of machine-gun-toting CSA guards met them. They proceeded to mine number 5, stopping at a rickety, clunking elevator leading into the deep.

Margot could distinguish the veterans by their thin faces and ragged uniforms. The night before, a stout prisoner named Klara told her that thirty years before, all eight mines of Weisserwald Uranmine had been decommissioned. But they still held a low grade of uranium ore that, by orders of the Unitum Imperium, was now being brought to the surface where it was the job of other barracks to break it into gravel and shovel it into rail cars for transport to a processing plant.

While Grosse Frau remained on the surface, half the group filled the elevator and rode it—chains clinking, pulleys squeaking—down into the bowels of the earth. At the bottom, as Margot's eyes adjusted to the dark, new guards took over. Each wore a pistol, a truncheon, a helmet with a light, and a full-face respirator mask with two protruding filter cartridges.

After seeing the men, Margot whispered. "Why are those guards wearing those face masks, and we aren't?"

"Don't you know?" Klara grinned. "There's a high concentration of cancer-causing radon down here. We're expendable. The guards aren't."

They formed a line, and the guards handed each prisoner a shovel or a pickax. A lucky few also received a mine helmet with a battery-charged light—head injuries were apparently common. The rest received only a strap-on light.

Margot and Eva were assigned to a team of eight that included Klara, two other veterans, and three more newbies. Their team also received two of the mine's wheeled handcarts. Then the guards herded them to one of a dozen small shafts slanting down into the earth.

"Your team," came a guard's muffled voice through his respirator, "will work this shaft today." He waved them on, and they started down.

She looked back. "Why aren't the guards following?"

Klara laughed. "They never go past the tunnel junction. They're afraid of cave-ins. And they don't like the cramped conditions we work in. But it leaves us free to talk."

At the end of the shaft, they stopped at a wall of black rock. Klara was apparently the team leader, and she faced the newcomers. "We have a system here that we use to make quota. Two women dig. Two shovel ore into a cart. When the cart is full, two women rest. Two women push a full cart up to the elevator, and two women work on filling the second cart. With two of us always resting, we conserve our strength and make quota. Failure to meet quota two days in a row, well . . ." She shook her head. "We have no illusions here. Eventually, everyone fails to meet quota."

"What's the longest anyone has lasted?" asked Eva.

"Five months."

The answer sent a shudder down Margot's back. "Then what happens?"

"They send you to a new barracks, and you go on a death watch. Word is that they can't keep up with the executions, and there's a big backlog. But when your turn comes, one morning, the guards take the entire barracks to the guillotines."

Margot grabbed a pick and started digging.

That day, they met quota. Then the guards marched the women, now covered with uranium rock dust, to the elevators, and back across the grounds to barracks number 1,679.

That evening, their potato soup contained a few pieces of some unnamed meat, something they would receive two or three times a week.

Klara lifted a spoon and examined the watery soup. "Because we work, they say we're privileged to receive better slop than the others in camp."

And that was Margot's first day in Weisserwald Uranmine.

* * *

MARGOT HAD BEEN IN THE camp for a month now, and two teams—sixteen women—had failed to meet quota and been replaced with new arrivals. Another team, including two guards, had perished in a cave-in.

But as the weeks passed, she noted with alarm how thin her arms and legs were becoming, how her strength was ebbing a bit more each day. It was the same with Eva and the others. Especially with Klara and the veterans.

Klara was right. One day, none of them would have the strength to meet quota.

And each night, as she laid on her wooden pallet and pulled the thin blanket over her head, Margot prayed that Jesus would give her team the strength to meet quota, and that, somehow, she would once again see Dylan and the others.

CHAPTER 7
ADAM'S CURSE

Ezekiel 39:9–16 (HCSB): "Now on that day I will give Gog a burial place there in Israel—the Valley of the Travelers east of the Sea. It will block those who travel through, for Gog and all his hordes will be buried there. So it will be called the Valley of Hamon-gog. The house of Israel will spend seven months burying them in order to cleanse the land. All the people of the land will bury them and their fame will spread on the day I display My glory." This is the declaration of the Lord God.

"They will appoint men on a full-time basis to pass through the land and bury the invaders who remain on the surface of the ground, in order to cleanse it. They will make their search at the end of the seven months. When they pass through the land and one of them sees a human bone, he will set up a marker next to it until the buriers have buried it in the Valley of Hamon-gog. There will even be a city named Hamonah there. So they will cleanse the land."

Hamonah, Israel – August, Year 4

Adam Turner woke, sweating and miserable, in his tent near the desert site where the dead slept. Crickets surrounded him with a chorus loud enough to wake the corpses rotting in the nearby battlefield. Rubbing sleep from his eyes, he sat on the edge of the contemptible cot they called a bed. He reached for his half-empty bottle of whiskey and poured a full glass.

As head of the Ministry of Truth and beneath that, the Central Security Agency, he was charged with burying the dead Iranians, Libyans, Sudanese, Russians, Turks, and the hill fighters from the former Soviet provinces. Indeed, the Imperator had insisted on Adam's personal involvement. In November, after the Battle of Gog and Magog, as the Israelis were fond of calling it, he'd appointed Ehud, an Israeli army major, to oversee the project. His hope was to wash his hands of the project as soon as possible.

Taking a jeep, Ehud had driven Adam through kilometer after kilometer of stinking, rotting, carrion-covered corpses and twisted, broken, endlessly charred metal. To assess the battle's aftermath fully, it had taken two days of driving from one end of the country to the next, all the while being covered with dust, bounced over rocks under a scorching sun.

Even his full-face respirator couldn't keep out the stench. And the endless kilometers of rotting human remains, the millions upon millions of vultures and crows dipping their beaks into all those corpses, filled him with such nausea and revulsion that upon returning to his squalid tent, he spent each evening with a hand wrapped around a whiskey bottle.

"I want this cleaned up as fast as possible," he ordered Major Ehud on the third day. "I don't want to spend one more minute than is necessary in this cesspit."

"As you wish, my lord minister, but"—Ehud had opened his hands— "the task is monumental. It will take nearly the entire army to do it."

"No. You can't have the army. We don't know how long it will take. You may have one company of engineers. For the rest, you must conscript workers from the Jewish populace."

Ehud had scowled. "It will make for ill will. There will be resistance."

"Do what you must. Anyone who refuses to work—take them into the desert and shoot them."

Stony-faced, the major had nodded. Then the press-gangs had gone out into the villages, towns, and cities, conscripting men and women at random. Anyone could be taken—walking down a lane, eating at home in a kitchen, or managing a shop behind a desk. The sight of a press-gang on a street, dragging their chain of prisoners behind them, was enough to turn a crowded village into a ghost town.

In the north, Ehud gathered the workers into a tent city far enough from Khan Alsheh, Syria, to avoid the stench, at a place they named Hamonah. Ehud established a similar camp in the Negev.

The major divided his laborers into teams of twelve, each with a leader. Units were given a daily quota of corpses to haul to the thousands of trucks driving endlessly back and forth to Jordan, east of the Dead Sea, to the Valley of Gog's Hordes, as the locals began calling it.

But each night, men and women defected from the ranks of workers and secretly returned to their homes. This slowed the task, forcing Ehud to send out press-gangs to replenish the workforce again.

Within months, Hamonah, the city of tents, morphed into row after row of corrugated metal bunkhouses. But the bunkhouses were noisy and unclean, and the best his incompetent staff could do when Adam arrived from New Babylon was to give him his own tent, away from the unruly riffraff, on the edge of the stinking desert.

He took another sip of whiskey, discovered he'd emptied the glass, and poured another. Outside, the crickets started a war with each other. Why were there crickets in the desert anyway?

Hamonah was a city divided, with half the populace frequenting the growing number of bars and whores of all sexes. The other half kept to themselves, abstaining from worldly pleasures. But the city harbored both, and though Adam wondered if the abstainers secretly worshiped the Enemy, how could he separate one from the other? And besides, he'd do nothing to slow the work.

He had tried to leave the project to Ehud and absent himself. But upon every visit back, he fumed and railed at the slow progress the major was making. By May, after seven long months, most of the dead had been removed. And yet, after another two-day tour of the battlefields, too many bones still stuck out of the sand. Too many vultures and crows still picked through the rocks and brush.

"Send out details to mark the spots where you find even a single bone," he ordered Ehud. "Cover the entire country, anywhere the enemy might have fallen. Afterward, send teams to bury the bones. Then we must start on the weapons. The number of wrecked and abandoned tanks, artillery, rifles, and small arms still lying about is staggering. We cannot leave that kind of weaponry spread across the entire Israeli desert. The Imperator wants the land returned to its prewar state. In years to come, he wants no reminder that such a force ever dared come against him."

Again, Ehud had bowed low and done Adam's bidding. He'd brought in workers with bulldozers, forklifts, and trucks to collect and gather the wreckage. Engineers constructed coal-fired furnaces at major battle sites and began the process of melting down vast quantities of twisted, useless metal.

Time and again, Adam returned to the battlefield sites and wondered when, if ever, he would lose this millstone from around his neck. From the first, the rotting, carrion-covered bodies haunted his days and nights. In his dreams, he saw them, field upon field of decomposing corpses, a stark reminder that life was fleeting, that beyond the here and now lay a dark unknown, an impenetrable mystery.

He drained his glass, wiped sweat from his forehead, and laid back on the cot.

What awaited the newly dead? A welcome oblivion? Or, as the Christians claimed, a conscious, living eternity?

Of only one thing was he certain—there was no God. But that thought brought him no comfort. What would it be like living in eternity? Was it a place of darkness? Or of light? Would his past deeds follow him there? Would there be human companionship? Or would he exist in a state of eternal loneliness, floating forever in space, apart from anyone else?

Such thoughts brought a shivering to his shoulders, a desire to leap to his feet and run to a place of safety. But where such a place might be, he didn't know.

This task, with its constant reminder of death, was a burden nailed to his soul, and he was drinking more, sleeping less, and dreading his frequent visits to Hamonah.

The sooner he was rid of Valley of Gog's Hordes and his dreams of the dead, the better.

He rolled onto his side. Perhaps, after having consumed enough whiskey, he could now get to sleep.

CHAPTER 8
THE JOHNSON PLACE

Minnesota's North Shore – September, Year 4

Inside the Johnson house, even with the boards Andy had nailed over the windows, the blaze roared in Caleb's ears. He peered through the cracks then turned to Tanya and Brianna on the couch. "The trees beside the house are on fire."

"Just as Mary feared," said Tanya.

At Brianna's feet, Nika lifted a paw and laid it on her knee. Brianna cuddled the pet closer. "It's even scaring the dog."

He bent his glance toward the lake. Plumes of flaming ash drifted far out over the waves. "Mary was right. It's consuming everything right down to the water."

Tanya went to his side and peered out. "Burning ash is coming down everywhere. What if the roof catches fire? Or the grass beside the house?"

"The roof's tin, but I should check the outside walls."

"I'll help." Brianna stood.

"No, girl. I'll do this." He strapped on a pistol, grabbed an ax and a rake, opened the door, and stepped out. The fire's roar, mixed with the sound of crackling, falling limbs, was primeval. Fiery rafts of burning leaves floated around him. He jumped aside as several fell across his path. The nearest trees were fifteen yards away, but the heat from their fiery crowns and the flaming bushes and grass at his feet nearly seared his skin. The air was heavy with smoke, and he coughed. He raised a hand to shield his face and whirled toward the house.

Yesterday afternoon after they'd moved in, he'd scraped most of the grass from the perimeter and even ripped out most of the shrubs. But sunset had cut short his work.

Now the heat was so intense it felt like his skin was burning. He edged around the house, looking for problems.

On the backside facing the lake, flames engulfed the single large bush he hadn't removed. From it leapt red and yellow tongues of fire that lashed the siding. If left unchecked, the house might catch fire.

Three yards beyond, two wolves huddled in the corner where the spare bedroom jutted into the lawn. He laid a hand on his pistol.

When they saw him, they emitted a low, rumbling growl, took a step toward him, but quickly retreated to their shelter.

A glance at the shore revealed another half dozen wolves standing in knee-deep water as waves lapped their underbellies.

"Sorry, guys," he said to his lupine companions. "But I've got to take care of this." He hefted the ax, brought it down on the bush. Sparks flew, and a burning limb fell off.

The wolves drew further into the corner.

He landed another blow, showering more sparks, some of which headed toward the wolves.

They burst from their corner, and he reached for the pistol. But they raced over the smoldering yard, between burning tree trunks, and splashed into the lake up to their knees.

Again and again, he brought the blade down on the stump until he cut through the main branch. Then, with a sideways wallop using the flat of the ax, he sent the whole ball of flaming brush rolling across the yard.

Caleb continued his perusal of the perimeter. When he found no other problems, he swerved between patches of fiery grass to the garage. There the situation was worse.

Inside, the horses whinnied in terror. Flames encircled the structure, threatening to set the wooden walls on fire. He should have worked harder on this, but dusk had prevented him from raking a clear path around the walls. Now he struggled to find a place to stand where his jeans wouldn't catch fire.

Sweat drenched his torso, dripped down his brow into his eyes. The tree beyond the garage was a flaming pyre. A fiery branch crashed down, sending sparks flying in all directions.

Frantically, he raked burning grass away from the walls. Inside, the horses kicked against the wood. His heart pumped harder. He was running on adrenaline.

By the time he'd circled the garage and raked away all the flammable material, his skin burned, and he coughed from the smoke. One last trip around the building convinced him he'd done all he could.

Shielding his face from the heat coming off the trees, he turned toward the house.

But twenty feet away, beneath the trunk of a large oak, his glance caught a young rabbit—shaking and screaming. All around it in the grass, fire raged. He'd never heard a rabbit scream, and its soul-gripping fright mirrored something he felt but was trying hard to repress.

He sprinted the distance, reached down, scooped the frightened creature to his breast, and raced to the house. He burst through the door, flung it shut behind him, and slammed his back against it, breathing fast.

"You're drenched, and your face is red." Tanya raised a hand to his cheeks.

"It's burned. The heat out there is intense."

"And you're holding a rabbit." Brianna cocked her head.

"It was screaming. The poor thing was going to burn up. Here." He passed it to her, and she cuddled the shivering creature to her bosom.

"We should put it in a box." Her eyes lit up as she petted the ball of fur.

"Yes, honey," said Tanya. "But when it's safe, we have to release it."

"Why?" Brianna lifted a puzzled glance.

"Because it's not right to imprison a living creature against its will."

"Right." Brianna couldn't take her eyes off it. "But for now, we're keeping it."

Caleb ran for one of the coolers Andy had left, filled a pitcher, and poured it over his head. He let the cool water drip down over his forehead, drenching his shirt. "Ah, that's good."

Tanya shot him a worried glance. "It seems pretty hot out there."

"It is." He lifted a bottle of beer from the stash in Andy's cooler and drank deeply. "I hope Andy and Mary will be okay. They've got more trees around their place."

"And us?" Brianna glanced up from the rabbit. "Will we be okay?"

"We'll be fine." But as he staggered to a seat at the kitchen table, he wasn't so sure.

As if sensing their peril, Nika trotted over, licked his hand, then raised a questioning glance to the rabbit Brianna was holding.

"It will be all right, Nika." Caleb smiled at the dog's concern and patted her head. "I think."

* * *

Caleb stayed awake all that night and the next morning. Occasionally, he checked the house and garage, putting out fires that came too close. By noon, all that surrounded them were smoldering ashes, the smoking limbs of fallen branches, and a pall of lung-choking woodsmoke. What was left of the wolf population huddled by the lakeshore, standing in a foot of water, afraid to venture onto the smoldering land.

The gentle lapping of waves against the rocks replaced the roaring of flames.

"The fire must have decimated the wolves," he said after returning from an inspection trip. "I only count seven, still standing in the lake."

"Let's hope so." Tanya rose from the couch and hugged him. "But now what are we going to do? Everything's burned up."

The air was still so hot, he wiped sweat from his brow. "The forest is gone. So is the grass in the ditches. If we stay here, how are we—"

The crack of a rifle shot ended his sentence. He whirled toward the door. "Andy?"

Volley after volley echoed after the first shot.

He grabbed the M16 and left the house. He sprinted around the back toward the lake.

Holding his horse's reins and an AR-15, Andy tottered on the bank. Below, red waves slapped the lifeless bodies of wolves against the rocks.

"Andy!" Caleb rushed to his friend. "Are you all right?"

The face that turned toward him was smoke-blackened and dirt-smeared. But it wasn't the face of the friend Caleb had known. Gone was the laughing, playful smile, the easygoing manner. In its place was a visage twisted by some deep, life-changing emotion. "She's gone, Caleb. We lost the house and the garage. We lost one of the horses. We tried to leave, but the smoke took her. She's gone, Caleb. And I killed her."

As the reins dropped from his hands, a fit of coughing overtook him.

Just then, Brianna appeared. While Tanya helped Andy to the house, Caleb asked Brianna to put Andy's horse in the garage.

When everyone, including Brianna, was back inside, tears streamed down his friend's cheeks. "I lost her, Caleb. She's gone, and I killed her."

"You didn't kill her."

"Mary's gone?" Brianna raised worried brows. "Mary's dead?"

Andy dropped his head into his hands and sobbed. "May the Lord forgive me. I didn't listen, we should have left, and now she's dead."

Brianna's whole body seemed to shudder, and she, too, sobbed. "No, no. Not Mary too."

Tanya pulled her close into a hug.

"Why, Caleb, why?" Brianna raised a moist glance over Tanya's shoulder. "Why did she have to die? Why did my parents have to die? Why does anybody have to die?"

"These things just happen." Trying to control his own grief, he took Brianna from Tanya's grasp and hugged her. "It's not Andy's fault. He didn't cause her death. It's the times we're living in."

"I know." Brianna caught her breath between sobs. "But why Mary? She's actually gone."

"Yes." Caleb sucked in breath. "She's gone."

"How can I ever forgive myself?" Andy raised hollow, red-rimmed eyes.

"You thought the place was safe, and so did I." Caleb spoke over Brianna's shoulder. "It wasn't your fault. But we have to go on. All of us. We have to go on."

* * *

The rest of that day, as the fires burned down outside, they mourned, each in their own way.

Mary's death brought the return of the fearful, withdrawn child they'd rescued after a bear had killed Brianna's parents. All Brianna's spunk and bravery seemed to vanish. It was as if she'd just arrived here after surviving on her own through two lonely winter months.

Caleb tried, again and again, to comfort Andy and convince him Mary's death wasn't his fault. And finally, after Tanya joined in, he seemed to accept that. Then all that was left was the loss itself, a loss that, for today at least, stole whatever mirth and joy the world had for any of them.

And Tanya? When she'd done what she could to comfort the others, she fell into Caleb's arms and shivered until he held her close. "Brianna is right, Caleb," she whispered in his ear. "This is hard to take."

Toward evening, after everyone had cried and sobbed and comforted each other, Tanya served a meal by candlelight. Then Caleb convinced an exhausted Andy to take a beer.

They'd just finished eating when the storm hit.

A flash of lightning, a peal of thunder shook the house. Then came a driving wind, smashing pellets of rain onto the windows and tin roof. Waves pounded the rocks and competed with the storm's booming thunder.

While Nika hid under the bed, Caleb, Tanya, and Brianna went to the window. Then he headed outside to rip away some boards so they could see. When he came back in, he was soaked.

A bolt of lightning struck close, rattling the walls, and everyone jumped.

The puddles grew, the droplets exploded onto the blackened ground, and electric fireworks lit up the heavens. Tongues of lightning flickered between lowering clouds.

"This is good." Peering out the window beside Caleb and Tanya, Brianna rubbed red-rimmed eyes. "The grass will grow again. Maybe the trees will come back."

"Yes, but not for a long time." Beer in hand, Andy rose from the couch and stood beside them, looking out. "What's here for us now?"

"Nothing." Caleb waved at the blackened landscape, now slick with rain. "It's all burned up. If we don't leave, we'll starve."

"You're right," said his friend. "We have to leave." And with those words, Caleb knew that his friend would be all right.

"Leave?" Brianna's voice was suddenly tense. "What about food? Where will we sleep? Where will we go?"

"We'll go to the Sanctuary." He faced his adopted daughter, and lightning lit the worry on her face. "That's our best hope now."

"But where . . . is it?" Her voice trembled. "You don't even know where it is."

"We'll find it." He went to her. She'd lived all her life on the North Shore, and now, still recovering from Mary's death and faced with leaving the only place she'd ever known, all her spunk and bravery had vanished. He gripped her shoulders with both hands. "We'll go to the Black Hills. We'll listen to what people are saying, and if it's not in South Dakota, we'll go wherever they think it is. No matter how long it takes, we'll find it."

"Yes, let's find it." Tanya's voice was strong.

"Yes." Andy faced him. "Let's get out of here. Let's find the Sanctuary."

"I'm scared, Caleb." Brianna closed her eyes and fell against his shoulder.

"It will be all right," he whispered. "You're family now, and nothing's going to happen to you."

"Really?" Even in the dim light, he could see the flicker of a smile breaking below puffy eyes. "I'm family?"

"Yes, really." Over her shoulder, he faced the others. "We'll leave as soon as the rain stops."

CHAPTER 9

FLIGHT

Matthew 24:9–10 (NLT): "Then you will be arrested, persecuted, and killed. You will be hated all over the world because you are my followers. And many will turn away from me and betray and hate each other."

Marseille, France – September, Year 4

Dylan lay on the couch in their hotel room while, outside, the seagulls cried and sailed in circles under a sun-drenched, cloudless sky. From the nearby harbor, an occasional tugboat blasted its horn. In the rail yards, black with soot, train wheels screeched, and metal banged against metal.

For the last month, ever since the CSA took Margot and raided the farm, Dylan and all who were left of the Nazarene Friends—Angelo, Danielle, Pasqual, René, and Victor—had lived in run-down hotels near the Marseille docks.

They'd moved once already, and René talked of moving again.

The docks, always less than safe, crawled with the refuse of men. "All the better," said René, "to keep the CSA off our backs."

René still had contacts in the city, former spies refusing to work for the Unitum Imperium. Like him, they lived on the edge of the law, shunning all governments. He claimed only they could provide what they sought and so spent most of his days with them.

"When are we going to search for the camp?" Dylan would ask.

"After we find a permanent refuge that's not constantly under suspicion." René would respond. When questioned about when that would happen, René's answer was always, "I'm close to finding a place. Only a little longer."

Searching for food gave Dylan something to do. They had euros—the Nazarene Friends had enough of those—but finding black-market shopkeepers willing to bypass the new digital global payments and credits system was risky and took time.

Besides the thieves, gangs, and occasional rioters on the streets, squaddies were everywhere. At René's suggestion, the men now wore dirty shirts with food stains, ragged jeans, and holsters with loaded guns displayed on hips—anything to blend in, confuse the squaddies, and not become a target from thieves. Or from the Truth Squads.

Day after day, Dylan passed the graffiti-covered buildings, the garbage piled in the yards and alleys, and the hucksters waving passersby toward stacks of secondhand, stolen merchandise.

When he wasn't on the street, he lounged on the couch and tried to read his pocket Bible or the novels the previous tenant had left behind. But too often, his mind wandered.

René's answers didn't satisfy, and Dylan wondered if they'd ever begin the search for Margot. Even if they found the camp, rescuing her was a goal that, with every passing day, seemed to slip further away.

Still, somehow, he felt she was alive. Against all logic, deep in his soul, he sensed—as through some extrasensory connection with her— that Margot was alive.

Then late in the day on the last week of August, everything changed.

Red-faced and out-of-breath, his eye sockets deeper, darker than ever, René burst into the apartment and scanned the room. "Where is Angelo?"

Dylan lay on the couch. Pasqual and Victor sat at the kitchen table, playing gin rummy. Danielle was in her room, reading.

"Still out." Pasqual looked up from his cards. "Why?"

"We can't wait for him." Breathing heavily, René leaned against the tabletop. "There are two black vans outside. They followed me here. We need to leave. Now!"

"CSA?" Pasqual rose from his chair.

"Oui! Everyone, get moving. *Now!*"

Dylan shot to his feet, and Victor pushed back from the table.

Over and over, René had grilled them on their escape plan. They were always packed, ready to leave on a moment's notice, and Dylan ran to the bedroom he shared with Angelo and Victor. He shoved more belongings into his backpack and did the same for Angelo. Victor gathered additional personal items and what little equipment he'd salvaged from the farm and his trips on the street. Danielle worked on the kitchen supplies.

In less than five minutes, they were back in the main room. But as the group headed out the door toward the stairs, two gunshots reverberated up from the street, followed by a third. Then came footfalls on the steps below. But they were hesitant, halting.

"They're . . . here!" cried Angelo up the stairwell. But his voice was ragged, weak. "The CSA—they're here!"

"Everyone, to the roof!" René waved up the stairs.

Angelo topped the steps to the landing, one hand holding his pistol. But blood streamed down his chest, and he collapsed against the railing.

"You've been hit." Pasqual started toward him, but Angelo waved him away.

"It's no use." He staggered forward, spun, and slumped back against the wall. His legs buckled, and he slid to the floor, painting a trail of red behind him. "I'm . . . finished."

Two shots had hit him—one in the left lung, the other in the gut. Dylan gasped and hurried to kneel beside him.

"The rest of you," said René, "up the stairs!"

Victor, Pasqual, and Danielle said hurried goodbyes and ran up the steps while René squatted beside Angelo. "Are you sure you can't—?"

"No." Angelo spat blood on the floor, and his eyes lost focus. "I can't go on. I'll keep them . . . busy."

His heart thumping hard, Dylan laid a hand on Angelo's right shoulder. "No, no. Come with us. We can—"

"Leave me. You'll only get yourselves captured." He coughed and spat more blood.

Footsteps pounded up from below.

Dylan wiped tears from his eyes and patted Angelo's good shoulder. "Then thank you. For everything."

Smiling, he waved his pistol. "Save yourselves. I'll give them something to remember me by."

René squeezed one hand. "You're a good person, my friend."

Then Dylan and René ran for the stairs, taking them two at a time.

On the roof, René slammed the door shut. Weeks before, he'd left a wooden bar, and now he dropped it into the slots he'd created, locking the door from the roof. As they fled across the tops of three adjacent buildings, muffled gunfire came from behind. By the time they reached a fire escape leading down to an alley, the shooting had stopped. With their pursuers banging on the barred door, they hurried down a fire escape onto empty streets and then to their van parked three blocks away.

As René drove them north on the A51, Dylan kept glancing back. No one followed.

But Angelo's death cast a shroud over them all.

"There's not much left of us," said Victor from the front seat, and Danielle laid a hand on his shoulder.

"I, too, mourn his loss," said René from behind the wheel. "It's true, we are now only five. But I do have some good news."

"What?" Beside Dylan, Pasqual's voice was drained of energy. "Another fleabag hotel?"

"No, my friends." René swiveled and caught each of their glances. "Today, I arranged for a permanent hideout. It's in the Appenzell Alps in rural Switzerland, and that's where we're going. We should be there by morning."

The news should have lifted Dylan's spirits. But they'd just lost one of their own, and he closed his eyes against tears fighting their way to his cheeks.

Under an ashen-gray sky, they drove in silence toward a new hideout.

But they'd barely started when the skies opened and unleashed a torrent of rain.

CHAPTER 10

SWITZERLAND

The Appenzell Alps, Switzerland — September, Year 4

As the rain drummed on the roof and windshield, Dylan and the Nazarene Friends entered Switzerland and passed through Geneva's last checkpoint. The downpour beat down so hard, René had to stop the van several times before they could drive on.

Months before, Victor had prepared identity cards and travel passes for an emergency departure. To explain why so many were traveling together, René created the fiction that the group was going to a conference on raising crickets to replace real meat, an agenda item of the climate change people that Davato had continued. They'd already passed through a dozen checkpoints without a problem. Still, each time the rain-drenched, mackintosh-bedecked guards approached the van with their submachine guns, Dylan gripped the seat and silently prayed there'd be no trouble.

But with the deluge, the guards made only cursory inspections. Perhaps they were eager to return to their dry booths, their card playing, and their hot coffee? Only the rich, the squaddies, and the government officials still had coffee.

Now, the storm was letting up. On his right, the waters of Lac Léman flashed briefly in the setting sunlight before clouds lowered and drizzle swallowed the view.

In another four hours, they'd be in Appenzell, and Dylan decided to check in with Bettino. It had been months since he'd spoken with the caretaker of his father's villa in Florence. Now that they were heading to a new location, he should let him know. He punched the numbers and waited. Victor's scrambling technology should keep anyone from tracking them.

The familiar voice of his old friend answered. "Dylan! I've been waiting to hear from you. Caleb called me!"

His heart thumped hard against his ribs. A rush of adrenaline seemed to lift him bodily from his seat, and he wanted to shout for joy. "Caleb is alive?"

"Yes, my friend. He's in northern Minnesota. I'll give you his number."

Dylan added it to his contacts and said goodbye. He told the others what he'd found, accepted their congratulations, then checked his watch. It was noon in Minnesota. Caleb would be awake. He made the call.

Caleb's voice came on the line. "Yes? Who is this?"

"It's Dylan. Bettino just gave me your number."

"Dylan!" The shout rang in his ear. "It's so good to hear from you. It's been almost three years. A lot has happened."

"We thought you were dead, Caleb. What made you leave Chicago?"

"After what you said, I had the same premonition as you did." Then Caleb related how he and Tanya had moved to the Northwoods, how they were now "married" with an adopted daughter named Brianna. He told them about the drought and the wildfire that destroyed the Superior National Forest and about their plans to leave with a friend and search for the Sanctuary when the rains quit.

"You and Tanya have a teenage daughter?" Dylan slapped his knee.

"We do, and she's the light of our lives. And smart. But, Dylan, what about Chelsea? Bettino wouldn't tell me anything about her."

Then he told Caleb how Chelsea had become Davato's personal secretary and about Dylan's meeting with her in Paris where she confessed that she felt trapped with no way out. But the minute he said it, he regretted it. What if someone were listening to their conversation? "I really shouldn't say any more. It's not safe."

Silence from the other end. "Of course. I didn't think of that."

"We should make this short and avoid details about locations. We can talk later."

"Yes, but once we leave here, there may not be many cell towers past Silver Bay. The center of the country is now the Wild West, Dylan. Civilization has pretty much collapsed out here. And cell coverage is spotty. Or nonexistent."

"Of course. But if you find another hot spot, call me. Take care, brother."

"You too."

After they hung up, Dylan sat back and wondered if his face was glowing. Caleb was alive, living with Tanya, and they had adopted a teenage daughter.

* * *

They arrived in the town of Appenzell after midnight, drove into the country, and parked on a little-used side road. "All I have for directions to this place are landmarks," said René. "I can't see them in the dark in this downpour."

With the rains again pattering on the roof and windshield, they slept in the van that night.

The next morning, under cloudy, rain-free skies, they drove twenty kilometers into the hills on a winding country road, meeting just one other vehicle. They turned onto a drive, perhaps half a kilometer long, and parked before a four-story, peak-roofed wooden structure.

They left the van and stretched.

Rolling brown pastureland stretched to the horizon, and Dylan breathed in the smell of wet fields. Overnight, a few green shoots had popped through the husks of dried-up grass.

A sign above the door read: *Das Ländliche Skihaus*. "The Country Ski House?" asked Dylan. "This is now ours?"

"Oui." René lit a cigarette. "The owners had started a cross-country ski retreat, but I'm told without much success. The Rapture took many of the locals in this region, including the owners. The house has been empty for three years."

They left the gravel drive and climbed the porch steps. Like many others in the region, the farmhouse was attached to a barn with space for maybe a dozen milk cows, empty now. Stacked in three stories, eight bedrooms faced south.

Inside, the kitchen held a wood-fired cookstove. Both the large sitting room and dining room boasted potbellied woodstoves. After the promise of wind and solar energy too often failed to deliver in winter, many places had returned to reliable, if more primitive, heating.

"It needs cleaning." Danielle scrunched her face at the cobwebs, the dirty windows, and the mouse nest in the corner. "But it has charm."

Crisscrossed skis from another era, pictures of early 1900s skiers, and wooden cross-country poles hung on the pinewood log walls.

They tromped up creaking wooden stairs, still oozing the smell of pine, to the second floor and the first of the bedrooms. "We can each have our own room," said Victor.

"And there are sheets and pillows in the closet." Danielle whirled to René. "They need washing, but this is nice, René. Far better than those rat-infested hovels in Marseille."

René nodded and followed the others as each found a bedroom.

Dylan chose his room on the third floor, sank into a chair, and breathed out. The place was perfect. But as he let the tension leak out of his body, he winced from a twinge of guilt. What was Margot doing now? He stood, went to the window, and looked out over the dried-up fields, slick now with rainwater. How were they ever going to find her? Were they going to hide out here in comfort while she rotted away in a death camp?

In the distance, a car drove along the main road. It was only the second vehicle they'd seen all morning. He followed its progress until it reached the drive leading to the farmhouse.

Then it turned. Someone was coming.

He whirled, pounded down the stairs, found René in the sitting room, and warned him.

René's face slumped. "It was too good to be true, wasn't it? That we'd have a safe, isolated place and not be bothered? Well, let's see who it is."

He strapped his pistol to his waist, as did Dylan. With Pasqual, Victor, and Danielle, they exited to the front porch as a white Audi parked beside their van.

On one side, a man and a woman with the look of farmers got out. They wore jeans, boots, and sweatshirts. He was tall with a black beard and a rugged weatherworn face. She wore shoulder-length blonde hair.

Another man, definitely not a farmer, exited on the other side. He wore tan slacks and a white shirt. As they approached, Dylan sucked in air. On his hip, the man carried a pistol.

René scowled, and his hand dropped to his weapon. But when the three came closer and stopped at the foot of the porch stairs, the ex-spy smiled. "So, Klaus Martin, have you given up your evil ways to become a Swiss farmer?"

"Only long enough to get away from the squaddie-infested city." The blond-haired man addressed as Klaus grinned, leaped up the stairs, and hugged René. "It has been a while, mein Herr. I am glad to see you made it. How was the drive?"

"No problems. Our forgeries are perfect."

"Only what I would expect from a man of your expertise."

Dylan and the others gazed with wonder at the reunion of two old friends as René introduced everyone.

Then Klaus introduced Jakob and Emma Huber, a farm couple living a few kilometers over the hill. "We saw your van on the road," said Klaus, "and knew it must be you."

René turned to his companions. "Klaus found this place for us. He and I occasionally worked together in the old days. On the same side."

With his wife behind him, Jakob stepped forward with an outstretched hand. "Welcome, all of you, to the Appenzell Alps. We are so glad to have you as neighbors. And Klaus tells me you are Christians?"

"That's right," answered Dylan.

"Come inside and let's talk." René waved everyone through the door.

When they found seats in the sitting room, Klaus grinned. "I, too, welcome my new companions in rebellion against the Empire."

"How is the squaddie situation here?" asked René.

"Not as bad as Marseille. The nearest village of Appenzell, twenty kilometers away, does harbor a small nest."

"We passed through it last night," said René. "Is there any place on earth that's free of them?"

Dylan couldn't keep quiet any longer. "Now that we've found a hideout, what about searching for the camp and Margot?"

René raised a hand. "Patience, my friend. We are indeed closer to southern Germany where we think the camp is. But even if we find it, we don't yet have the equipment we need to break in or to break anybody out."

"Like what?" Narrowing his eyes, Dylan sat back.

"Like dynamite, wire cutters, and more weapons. Some rocket-propelled grenades and launchers would be nice."

"Don't forget about me," added Victor. "I need to replace the equipment I lost."

"I can help you with all of that." Klaus grinned. "There's a lightly guarded squaddie headquarters about seventy kilometers from here. I've been eyeing the site. I'm guessing they've got everything you need. A few of us sneaking up in the dead of night could overwhelm the two guards and clean them out."

"Great!" René slapped his thigh. "Victor and Klaus—are you up for it? Shall we go tomorrow?"

"Count me in." Klaus sat back with a satisfied grin. "We can take my Audi."

"Me too," added Victor.

"What about searching for the camp?" Dylan gripped his knees. René was too cautious, always concerned about the base, his equipment, and lining things up. When would they search for Margot?

"I haven't forgotten, my friend." René scratched his chin and reached for his pack of cigarettes. "Now that we're closer, you won't have to pass through so many checkpoints. It's only a shot in the dark, but oui. What if we send you and Pasqual on an exploratory mission to southern Germany. When do you want to leave?"

"How about tomorrow?" ventured Pasqual.

"Yes!" Dylan sent him an appreciative smile. "Let's go tomorrow."

"While you men are out on your missions," said Danielle, "I'll make this place livable."

"I can help with that," added Emma. "It will be good to talk with another woman."

"Please, Fraulein Danielle, talk with her as long as you want." Jakob waved toward Emma and rolled his eyes to the ceiling. "All she wants to do, all day long, is talk, talk, talk."

Dylan joined in as everyone laughed. But his happiness stemmed not only from the company but also from the knowledge that, finally, at long last, they would do something about finding the camp where he hoped Margot was still alive.

CHAPTER 11

THE VILLAGE

Redwood Falls, Minnesota — September, Year 4

For sixteen days, Caleb, Andy, Tanya, and Brianna listened to the clop-ping of horses' hooves and the creak of wagon wheels as they traveled a distance of 370 miles. At first, they rode horses loaded with saddlebags with Nika prancing beside them, stopping often to rest. Their goal—to get as far west as possible before winter.

South of Two Harbors, they left the burned lands and, in an abandoned barn, found old hay and oats, not too moldy, for the horses.

In Duluth, they raided an empty museum and picked up a nineteenth-century horse-drawn wagon with harnesses for two mounts. After that, they traveled faster and in greater comfort. Then two of them rode while the other two occupied a wagon seat with Nika sometimes sitting between them. In the wagon bed, they accumulated food, sleeping bags, tents, tools, and a barrel of beer Andy purloined from an abandoned Duluth brewpub. "We don't know what we'll find later on," he'd said. "Better to be safe than starving."

"And of course," said a grinning Brianna, "without beer, you'd starve."

"Of course." Andy returned her grin, and that small response warmed Caleb's heart. His friend was recovering from the loss of his wife.

Outside Cloquet, two men tried to rob them at gunpoint. For tense seconds, the four had stood with three rifles and Brianna's Glock 17 pistol pointed at two shotguns. The firepower of Caleb's group won out, and the amateur thieves, their faces white, their weapons trembling, backed away before breaking into a run.

"After this," said Andy, "we need to carry at all times. People are desperate for supplies, and we aren't parting with a thing."

Afterward, they vowed to avoid big cities and towns. They headed cross-country toward Brainerd, after which they planned to follow state highways through Little Falls, Sauk Centre, and Willmar toward Redwood Falls. Along the way, they encountered abandoned cars, houses, and stores. It was a country decimated by the Rapture, gripped by anarchy, and fallen back to the year 1900.

After the first heavy downpour, the rains came every few days. As if eager to make up for lost time, the fields sprouted green shoots, buds sprang from tree limbs, and the birds, which had fled the Northwoods before the fires, again sang in the treetops.

"It's good to see green again, to hear birds singing." Gradually, Brianna's old self was returning.

"Yes, but it's already fall," answered Caleb. "We have to land somewhere before winter."

Northwest of St. Cloud, Caleb picked up a cell signal and discovered that the Bubonic Plague had spread everywhere across the country except, apparently, in isolated pockets like their corner of the North Shore. With that knowledge, they raided an abandoned drug store in Willmar and stocked up on antibiotics and medical supplies.

They approached Redwood Falls in late afternoon, wagon wheels rumbling over broken asphalt, parting the newly sprouting weeds. As the highway crossed the Minnesota River and headed into town, water thundered over the falls.

"Time we showed our firepower." Andy pulled out his AR-15, and the others followed, displaying weapons they'd laid aside while traveling empty highways.

Tanya drew Nika up onto the seat beside her and Brianna.

Now the horses trotted, and the wagon rolled over broken concrete. On all sides lay abandoned cars and stores, empty houses, and in the street, tumbleweeds.

"To be safe," said Caleb, "we'll camp outside of town tonight."

The road was wide, the houses sparsely situated. On rare occasions, a woman or man peered through darkened windows, only to draw the blinds. Before losing cell coverage, Caleb had learned that the place once had a population of barely over five thousand. Now, it was nearly a ghost town. They turned west toward Minnesota 19, crossed a bridge over Lake Redwood, traveled a few hundred feet, and passed fewer houses on their right.

Then they came upon a woman with curly blonde hair trudging the road ahead. She wore a gray smock and pulled a cart loaded with ears of corn in the husk. As they passed, she waved and smiled. "Howdy, folks." She was freckle-faced, in her twenties, and she stopped to catch her breath. "Where you headed?"

"Out of town before nightfall," answered Caleb.

"My name's Heather." She cocked her head and laid a hand on the pistol holstered at her hip. "Are you good people, not out to rob and pillage?"

Caleb laughed. "Yes, miss. We're just looking for a place to bed down tonight."

"You don't look like bad folks. Why don't you come with me? We're fixing to have a barbeque this evening with a hog old Farmer Davis left us. It's cookin' right now. Old Davis was taken on V-Day, and now we use his greenhouses to grow this here corn I've got. Most folks in town, what's left of them, aren't that friendly, but we at the Village appreciate newcomers. That's what we call ourselves—the Village. Good folks got to stick together in these troubled times against the ones that ain't so good. Don't you agree?"

"We do." Tanya turned to the others with raised eyebrows. "What do you think?"

"A barbeque sounds great to me," said Brianna.

"Me too," said Andy, his face lighting up.

Caleb sent a glance to the highway ahead then back to the woman. "I suppose we can stay for supper. But then we're leaving."

"Wonderful!" said Heather. "Put away your weapons and follow me. I'll introduce you to Damon. He's been a true savior."

She led them to a side street at the entrance of which stood two men with shotguns.

"These folks are with me," she called, and, after a moment's hesitation, they let the group pass.

"We got to defend ourselves from gangs and thieves," she explained.

"Yeah," answered Caleb. "We saw our share of that on the road."

Heather brought them to a cluster of twelve houses built fifty or more years ago. In the center of the cul-de-sac lay a pile of branches, covered with a teepee of logs. A half dozen men and women milled about, throwing more wood on the growing pile. Three of them, including a short man with a handsome face and a sweeping mane of blond hair, wore the same gray smock as Heather.

As the newcomers dismounted, Heather spoke with the blond-haired man. Smiling broadly, he approached the newcomers. "Welcome to the Village. I am Damon, leader of our little refugee fellowship, and Heather says she vouches for you folks—so welcome!"

"Thanks." Caleb introduced everyone then said, "You've started quite a community here."

Damon's wave encompassed every house on the block. "After V-Day, I brought folks together and moved them here. We all worship the Lord here, and with essentials being so scarce, we share what we have according to Acts 2:44 and 4:32. As a community, we got to stick together to survive. Don't you agree?"

"Of course." Familiar with both passages, Caleb smiled.

"Are . . . you?" Damon cocked his head. "Do you folks worship the Lord?"

"We do."

"Good!" He slapped Caleb's shoulder. "Then I welcome you most heartily. Tonight is a special night, and we'd love for you to join us. We are celebrating The Night of Damon's Vision. Exactly two years ago, God visited me and told me to gather whoever would listen. I scoured Redwood Falls, found willing souls, and brought them here. Now we share whatever we have, exactly as they did in the early church. We're hunkering down, waiting for the day I can lead them again to the Lord."

Caleb shifted from one foot to the other. That's the second time Damon had mentioned "sharing" and the first time he talked about being their "savior". Caleb wondered: Had God actually talked to this man?

Yet Caleb had seen how the spiritual worlds were leaking through to this one, both for good and for ill. And hadn't God sent messages through Margot's paintings? And hadn't an angel in biker garb visited Caleb in Spearfish, South Dakota? Saying someone was a "savior" could just be a figure of speech. Yet something about the man warned him to be careful. Sometimes, folks weren't what they seemed.

"I hope you folks can stay for the feast." Damon smiled again. "We've plenty of food. Tonight, we're roasting a pig, and we make our own beer. We also have sweet corn, buttered potatoes, and honey bread baked from wheat we grew in Farmer Davis's greenhouses."

"Sounds good to me." Andy stepped forward, his face brighter than Caleb had seen it since the fire.

"Honey bread?" came Brianna's voice from behind. "Let's stay, Caleb."

Scowling, he whirled toward Tanya. "Maybe we should move on. There's plenty of daylight left."

"What can one night of feasting hurt?" Coming up beside him, she cocked her head. "Let's stay for supper."

"All right." He swallowed. "But then we're leaving."

"Wonderful!" Again, Damon slapped a hand on Caleb's shoulder.

* * *

As the Villagers prepared for the celebration, Damon led the newcomers to a pole barn across the highway where they could stable their horses. "You can give your animals some of the hay we feed to our half dozen cows," he said. "Farmer Davis left us some livestock. He must have had horses at one point, as there are six empty horse stalls."

Caleb thanked him, and they carried bales and water to the stalls separating the equines from the bovines.

An hour before sunset, the Villagers emerged from their houses—eight men, nine women, and four youths, two boys and two girls near Brianna's age. Half wore the gray smock Heather and Damon sported. Everyone seemed friendly enough, but the identical smocks made Caleb uneasy.

The men set up chairs and tables in the street, and after Damon prayed to God, thanking him for their food, and after everyone was so friendly, Caleb relaxed. They made small talk and passed plates heaping with boiled corn, roasted pig, buttered potatoes, and homemade honey bread, and he ate his fill.

As the sun set, a September chill settled over the evening.

The women cleaned the tables, and the men placed torches in stands to dispel the shadows. Heather brought a guitar from one of the houses, and everyone who wasn't cleaning up gathered in a circle. Then she led the group in some popular and a few Christian songs.

Caleb had never seen Brianna so happy as when she was singing and talking with the other youths.

As he sang, he relaxed even more. To be part of a group again, a Christian group, filled a hole that V-Day had left in him. For the last three years, and even before that, the world and people everywhere had thrust at him one obstacle after another. But here, everyone was friendly and seemed to enjoy each other's company.

When the singing ended, Damon made an announcement. "It's dark enough to start the bonfire. But first, we must officially welcome our four newcomers and their beautiful child to the Village. Everyone, let's form a line and shake hands with them and make them feel right at home."

He lined them up, and then, one by one, the Villagers passed by, gave them hugs, and said how glad they were that the four newcomers had come tonight.

When they'd finished, they left a warm glow in Caleb's chest. Their welcome had been sincere, so different from his interactions with nearly every other person they'd met on the way.

The group then headed for the woodpile. Damon lit the bonfire, a massive pyre that rose, crackling and hissing, fifty feet into the sky. Smoke and sparks climbed even higher.

"Beer for everyone!" came the shout from a man with a stomach as big as the barrel on the table beside him. Caleb and Andy stood in line, grabbed mugs, and filled them from the cask.

Sipping the foam, Caleb returned to the bonfire.

The party went on. Heather led them in more songs. Folks came up to Caleb, engaging him in small talk: What was the North Shore like? How was your journey here? Did you encounter many gangs and thieves? And what did you do before V-Day?

As people milled about and the fire burned lower, Damon appeared beside him. "You folks can sleep tonight in the empty MacPherson place. In fact, if you decide to stay a while, the house is yours if you want it."

"Thank you, Damon. That's very generous."

"Think nothing of it. Maybe you would consider joining our little community? Your horses and wagon could help us out. Next spring, we'll plant wheat, barley, and more corn and potatoes, and the horses would be a great help with the plowing. With food so scarce, we can offer you full bellies besides great companionship."

"Thanks for the offer. You folks have been nice, but we're headed for the Sanctuary. We plan to be further west before winter."

"The Sanctuary . . ." Damon frowned. "I've heard so many rumors about that place. What if it's just a myth? Only a collective dream? Everyone's wish for the life we once had? Consider this: The journey will be long and dangerous. Here, we've already built a nice little community with everything these Sanctuary rumors promise the gullible. I'd love it if you folks would join us."

"Thanks, again, but we should move on in the morning." It was now too late to continue this evening.

"I understand. But do consider my offer. I'll ask you again tomorrow." Smiling, he patted Caleb on the shoulder. "I can tell you are a leader, Caleb, a man of integrity, and if you stay, there'll be a place of importance for you here." Then he wandered off to talk with some of the men.

As soon as Damon left, Andy, Tanya, and Brianna approached. "We heard what Damon said." Tanya gripped both his hands. "We want to take him up on his offer." She squeezed his hands. "This is the first time in months I've felt like I belong somewhere, that we aren't alone in the world. These people are nice."

"But do we really know enough about them? Didn't we want to get farther west before winter?"

"Why look further?" asked Andy. "Here we've got safety, companionship, and a Christian community. Like Damon said, the Sanctuary could be nothing but a myth."

"What about you?" Caleb caught Brianna's glance.

"I want to stay. There's a boy here who says I'm pretty." She blushed. "I like him."

Maybe it was the good food and beer, all the eager smiling faces, or the grand welcome they'd received, but his wife's and his daughter's entreaties melted his reservations. "Okay. I'm convinced. We'll stay."

Andy raised his mug, Tanya clapped, and Brianna laid a kiss on his cheek.

The party went on until the moon was high, the stars bright, and the fire dim.

Then Damon gathered everyone together and stood before them. "Folks, before everyone turns in, I will close our celebration of The Night of Damon's Vision."

Heads nodded around the firelit circle.

"It's been two years since the vision came upon me, two years since the Lord God above told me how I should gather you here and how we must share everything we have. Someday soon, God will come in person to our little community. Then he will lead us out of this vale of tears to live with him in paradise. Thank you all for your part in making the Village a place where we can live in peace, harmony, and with the expectation of God's eternal home. I bid you now good night."

Loud choruses of "thank you" came from the circle of smiling faces. Then they formed a line, and, one by one, they passed by Damon. When they reached him, each planted a kiss on his cheek. He held out his right hand, and they planted a kiss there too.

As Caleb watched this ritual, he shifted his feet and tried to keep from gaping. What kind of church kept talking about sharing, celebrated a vision someone had two years ago, and lined everyone up to kiss their leader's cheek and hand? Maybe he'd made a mistake? Maybe they should move on in the morning?

After the Villagers left, only the newcomers and Damon remained.

"Don't feel you have to participate," called Damon beside the dying embers. "They're only showing their appreciation for what I've done for them. I'll see you in the morning." Then he left for one of the houses.

Andy came up beside him. "I know what you're thinking—that was weird."

"You got that right."

"But I want to stay anyways. These people are nice. They've got a place here as good as what I imagined the Sanctuary to be. So what if they like their guy so much they want to kiss his hand and cheek. I say let's stay."

"I agree, it was weird," said Tanya. "But I want to stay."

"Me too," added Brianna.

"Okay." Caleb swallowed and released the breath he was holding. "If that's what you want, we'll stay."

CHAPTER 12
QUOTA ISSUES

Weisserwald Uranmine, Southern Germany – September, Year 4

Each morning, as Grosse Frau beat her truncheon on a bedpost, Margot noticed how everyone in her barracks seemed a bit thinner, weaker, and paler than the day before. No longer able to keep up, one team after another failed to meet quota—all except Margot's. Then, for two days in a row, her team, too, didn't deliver the required tonnage of ore. They were allowed to keep working, but now, with every sunrise, she wondered: Would this morning be her last?

Rumors spread like lice through the camp. So many prisoners were arriving by bus, truck, and train that the executioners couldn't keep up. And so, even after the entire barracks failed to meet quota every day for a week, the bullet-shaped matron nicknamed Grosse Frau, continued to lead her prisoners to mine number 5.

This morning seemed to be no different, and Grosse Frau repeated her routine. After Margot finished her bowl, the stout German matron banged her truncheon on the outside table and shouted—for shouting was the only tone she ever used. "Line up and follow me!"

But as she walked, Margot's heart was beating fast, and she grabbed the table to steady herself. Fuzz clouded the edges of her vision. Beside her, other women also staggered.

Had they all been drugged?

"*Schnell*, schnell!" came Grosse Frau's cry.

They all moved as one, for they had learned long ago that anyone disobeying orders could earn a bullet to the head or a fatal beating. Instead of the usual platoon, a new company of guards wearing green-and-white uniforms met them with truncheons and pistols. And then—oh no!—the guards bound the women's hands behind their backs.

Then they were marched through camp, but away from the entrance leading to the mine. They passed the men's barracks, heading toward the smokestack.

This, then, was the day everyone feared.

Beside her, the women's eyes were glazed, and their feet struggled to keep the path. Several fell, and the guards prodded them with truncheons until they regained their feet.

Everything was out-of-focus, otherworldly. Margot knew where they were headed, but the fear she should have felt—indeed all emotions—refused to come.

She struggled to concentrate, to shake off the drug's effects. She prayed to herself: *Lord Jesus, save me from this. I know you once had plans for me. Am I now to die in this concentration camp? Can I not be of use to you? Can I not help further your plans? Dear God, give me a clear head. Dear Jesus, please save me.*

She marched through a fog as the smokestack appeared around a corner. The crematorium was one building away. At the door to a long low building, Grosse Frau lined them up in single file. A poster of the Dragon, flanked by Davato and the Prophet, hung beside the door.

Down the way, more entrances opened before which hundreds of women from other barracks lined up. As Margot approached the door, a scarecrow of a prisoner wrapped a blindfold over her eyes and shoved her inside.

The smell of blood and death accosted her nostrils. Sounds attacked her ears—men and women praying out loud, feet shuffling over concrete, blades crunching down onto bone and flesh before motors drew chains and gears clanked.

"Move along now," came a man's voice. "Keep in line. Follow the woman ahead. Don't slow down."

She'd drawn the painting, and she could picture where she was, what was happening. She was in a long queue, being ushered between wooden gates toward one of the guillotines. When she slowed, a truncheon poked her back to keep her moving. At the end of a row, a guard would turn her around and head her back the other way. They wound back and forth through the gates, and the more turns she made, the louder came the sounds of the crashing blade and the clanking chains.

Her toes rammed wooden steps. Someone ordered her to climb. Her heart beating faster, she stepped up. From her painting, she knew there was only one person ahead of her. The chain clattered against gears and came to a stop. The clank of a lever. The screech of the blade down through metal grooves. The spattering of flesh, the crunching of bone, then the grinding of a conveyer belt. A motor started, and chains returned the blade to the top. Death was only moments away.

Margot was next.

"Step forward," came an order. "Don't stop."

She balked, and rough hands yanked her forward, forced her to kneel, slammed her head onto a metal block slick with blood. The metallic smell of blood filled her head. Something sticky and wet soaked through the knees of her uniform.

Her heart raced out of control. She was breathing fast, and even the drug couldn't hold back the fear now clawing at her chest, trying to escape.

Something soft thudded onto the floor ahead of her. But the sound came from no machine.

"What's the matter with her?" came a man's nearby voice. Footsteps led around her, and he shouted at someone a few meters away. "Get up, do your job, or you'll be next."

Margot struggled to move her head, but the block held it. What was happening? Who were they talking to?

"She's dead," came the man's astonished voice. "She up and died!"

A click of metal, and the block holding her head released. Rough hands jerked her to her feet and ripped off the blindfold. "You will take her place."

The man freed her hands and led her to the opposite side of the guillotine.

"Help me get the body to the conveyer belt." At the man's feet lay a woman so thin and pale, Margot was amazed she hadn't died earlier.

She now saw that when she had knelt, her knees rested on a conveyer belt slick with blood. It sloped off the platform and led to a dumpster.

"Stop gawking and grab her!" came the command.

Margot knelt, grabbed the dead woman's hands, and helped the guard drag the corpse off a metal grid, around the guillotine, and onto the belt.

The guard removed the woman's rubber raincoat, splattered with blood, and passed it to Margot. He flicked a switch, and the conveyer ran the body to the dumpster. Then he pulled Margot around to the back of the guillotine, slapped her face, and ordered her to pay attention.

Her heart beating hard, she tried to concentrate.

"After the blade comes down, it's your job to grab the head and hurl it into the dumpster. Don't miss."

The dumpster, filled almost to the brim with corpses, was about three meters away at the end of the conveyer belt.

"Whenever they remove the dumpster, you will take that hose over there and clean the blood from the equipment and the ramp. This is your lucky day, woman. Do that, and you might live."

The rest of that day, she lived in a nightmare. Shortly after Margot began her task, a freckle-faced woman arrived at the top, and the breath squeezed out of Margot's lungs.

It was Eva.

She stared, unmoving, her heart in her throat, as the man clamped Eva's head and flicked the switch and the blade dropped down. When the head rolled toward her, she stood frozen, unable to take her eyes off it, unable to touch it.

"Pick it up!" shouted the guard as the conveyer took Eva's body down the ramp.

Margot picked it up. She threw it toward the dumpster. Then she leaned over and retched.

But the drug was still working, and, for a time, it dulled the horror of what she was doing. Were it not for that, she might never have been able to do it at all. By the time it wore off, she moved in a zombielike haze, watching women die, grabbing their severed heads, heaving them toward the dumpster. By the end of the day, she was numb.

But when dusk fell, she was alive. The termination chamber emptied of victims. Then they led her and the other workers to cold showers where she washed the raincoat and her clothing. A woman guard gave her a clean uniform and led her to building number 67, a smaller barracks devoted to a handful of women spared from execution, women assigned to maintaining the camp and the machinery of death.

That evening, she received another bowl of soup, but it had more vegetables. Once, she found a piece of meat, but of what kind, she couldn't say.

That night, she lay under a thin blanket on another hard wooden bunk, and she prayed. "Thank you, Jesus, for saving me. But now I dare to ask for more. Please let me see Dylan one more time before I die. Please let my life mean something. Please don't let me waste it here in this death camp. Amen."

CHAPTER 13

THE SOLAR PHONE

New Babylon, Iraq – October, Year 4

The meeting with the Iraqi president, her second that day with Davato, was over. While the Imperator perused his notes, Chelsea stood from her laptop, arched her back, and glanced out the window at the expanse of the Temple, glinting bright in the harsh Iraqi sun.

In the Battle of Gog and Magog, every mosque, prayer tower, and imam in the country, every vestige of Islam, had been destroyed. Only some of its followers remained. Combined with the powerful and growing presence of Davato's armies, the country of Iraq had been reduced to a Unitum Imperium satellite state. In the meeting she'd just recorded, Iraqi President Zaafir Aboud had come with petitions and demands that fell, unanswered, like coins dropped down a wishing well.

Slow the heavy traffic through the villages to Israel, he pleaded.

Give us the payment you promised for the New Babylon land.

Return our rightful share from the oil fields your troops occupied.

But none of it was going to happen. By the time Zaafir Aboud left, he'd been reduced to an obsequious beggar, ready to serve the Imperator, calling him lord, happy to escape with his life.

The group for the next meeting was arriving, and she resumed her place before her laptop. At the table now were her father, two German techies, Gerhard and Gunter, and, of course, Davato. The Imperator began, and her fingers typed.

"How many phones are we manufacturing now?" Sitting at the table's head, Davato faced his tech people and waved a solar phone.

"Six thousand a day, my lord," answered Gunter, the phone's inventor, now technology advisor for the manufacturing plants.

"Not enough." Davato turned the shiny metal over. "We need to quadruple that number. We're manufacturing phones for the entire world."

"If we had more tellurium," said Gerhard, Gunter's assistant, "we could make more. Tellurium is the holdup."

"And where does that come from?"

"My lord, the demand for solar panels reduced the supply to just two mines in the entire world. One is in southwestern China, but the area is in such a state of chaos, hardly anything is getting in or out."

"And the other?"

"The Skellefte VMS district in Sweden. We control it, and they're already producing at capacity. But it's still not enough."

"I see. Well, do what you can to increase production. We will just have to ration what we deliver. Eventually, I want one of these in the hands of every citizen. Don't you agree, Turner?"

Adam nodded. "Yes, my lord. We will be able to track whoever has one of these, no matter where they are. With the old phones, a few rebels have found a way around our tracking. But with these, once we change the tower signals, all the old phones will cease to function."

"Good." A smiling Davato sat back. "Very good, indeed."

"Are we finished, my lord?" asked Father.

"Yes, the meeting is over. But, Chelsea, I want you to stay."

She finished her notes and closed her notebook. Then she was alone with the Imperator.

Davato moved to a seat beside her and grasped her hands. "How are you doing, Chelsea?"

Her heart thumping hard, she looked into his eyes, so mesmerizing and bright. Why today, of all days, did he choose to be alone with her?

"I–I'm doing just fine, my lord."

"That's not what I'm hearing." He squeezed her hands, and she gasped. "People tell me you've been avoiding the sharing ceremony in the Temple services. According to our records, no one has ever been with you, Chelsea, and that has me greatly concerned. What's the problem?"

"I–I would rather not be with anyone right now." A drop of sweat trickled down her forehead into her right eye, but he held her hands fast. "I'm not comfortable with it."

"Even if it reflects badly on me? As one of my inner staff, you have a responsibility to be a role model for others. That includes participating in all the pleasures New Babylon has to offer. When I first offered you this position, you seemed taken with what awaited you in our fair city. Your friend Grady has availed himself fully. But I suspect you have not. Why don't you and he get together?"

"Maybe I will. Soon. Yes, soon."

"Very well. See that you do."

She squirmed in her seat, and he released her.

"You are dismissed. But get me a paper copy of today's meetings. Lately, reading the electronic version has been hard on my eyes."

"Yes, my lord." She stood, bowed, and hurried out the door toward the copy room. But her heart was beating hard, and her brow was covered with sweat. What was she going to do? She didn't want to sleep with Grady or anyone else. And now she knew: They were keeping tabs on her every movement. She needed a way out.

In the copy room, she found a desk, cleaned up her notes, then sent them to one of the printers. But the machine only printed five pages before running out of paper. She took what came out, rose from her chair, and went into the supply closet, of course taking the laptop that was never to leave her side.

But the moment she knelt to a box of paper, two voices entered the room she'd just left. She recognized them as Gerhard and Gunter.

"Are we alone?" Gunter spoke softly.

"Ja," answered Gerhard. "Do you have the circuit board schematics?"

"I do." A rustling of paper followed, and for a time, both men were quiet.

"And these, here, are the five dip switches?" asked Gerhard.

"Ja, and this copy"—more rustling of paper—"shows that if you set them in the sequence shown here, and if you flip the highlighted switch in the far corner to zero, then the server disables all tracking for that phone. Normally, these switches control some error corrections for power levels and nonstandard frequencies. Country tech support will receive only the official settings. This particular setting is not in the manual. Once set, the phone sends a signal to the server that starts a clock. For the next three hours, no server will acknowledge the phone on the network. Whoever changed the settings might think they'd broken the phone. But after three hours, the server will broadcast a unique signal to all phones in the region. But the only one to act on that special signal will be our particular phone. The server will then do two things: It will reenable communications, and forever after, it will erase all knowledge of that phone's location. No servers anywhere will then be able to track it. The support coding is embedded in every server, worldwide. Anyone looking at the code will think it's part of a diagnostic program."

"Brilliant, Gunter, simply brilliant. But what if someone accidentally stumbles on your backdoor setting and complains their phone isn't working?"

"Tell them it's a feature to prevent only approved settings. And if they immediately set the switches to an approved setting, the servers will reenable the phone through a broadcast and a series of handshakes that will reenable tracking."

"Brilliant. Absolutely brilliant."

"Yes. I've always had a backdoor to protect myself. If things go south one day, this could be quite useful. I'm bringing you in on the secret in case someone stumbles on the setting and complains. Only you and I know about this."

"Thank you, Gunter! I'll need a printed copy, of course."

"That's why we're meeting here. I want no electronic copies, but I don't trust my memory, so I'm keeping the original printed schematics in a safe place. I'll print one copy for you, but after you memorize the setting, you must destroy it. I've put a misleading label on the paper, so even if someone finds it, few will have any idea what they're looking at. But, Gerhard, no one must ever discover what I've done."

"Of course. Of course."

What followed was the whirring of the copy machine as it sucked in and spit out paper. After a time, they left.

With a box of paper in hand, Chelsea peered around the corner into the main room. Empty.

She ran to the one copy machine with the lights still on. It had a buffer, didn't it? And she knew how to recall the last thing copied. She knew because after printing or copying anything for the Imperator, she had the codes and ability to recall and delete the buffer. After she pressed the buttons she needed, the printer started up and spat out the last two printed pages—hand-drawn figures of a circuit board marked with the magic dip-switch settings.

She had yet no plans to escape, but if she did, this might be useful. With it, she'd be able to call Dylan without being tracked. She stuffed the copies in her purse. Breathing slower, she returned to printing the notes Davato had requested.

Upstairs, she slipped the notes through the mail slot leading to Davato's study. The slot led to a metal box hardened against explosives and equipped with bomb and poison detection.

Back in her apartment, she kept going over what the Imperator had said to her in private. It was clear to her: More than ever before, she needed a way out. And soon.

CHAPTER 14
LAZZARO

New Babylon, Iraq – October, Year 4

The sun had gone down, and Chelsea approached New Babylon's central park to the click, click, clicking of sprinklers. A walk before turning in, and before the rock bands started up for the night, was what she needed right now. It had been a week since Davato's warning, and being in his presence all day increasingly left her tense and on edge.

She strolled, letting the cold air wash her skin. How quickly the hot desert days had turned to cool nights! Recessed lights, hidden on both sides of the walkway, illuminated the concrete path. Even in the dark, the smell of living foliage lifted her spirits. She passed couples of all sexes, holding hands, also out for an evening stroll.

Footsteps approached from behind. "Can I talk with you?" came a voice barely above a whisper.

Whirling, she found Lazzaro, Davato's food taster. As usual, he wouldn't hold her glance. She hadn't spoken with him since he and Ernesto, Davato's chauffeur, had shared their plans to assassinate the Imperator. Wanting nothing to do with the man, she placed hands on hips. "What do you want?"

"Just to talk. And to ask a question."

She narrowed her eyes. "About what?"

"First, have you read the Bible I gave you?"

Before answering, she glanced in all directions. No one was within earshot, but it was safer if they were off the path. She pointed to a bench under a leafless tree some thirty meters away. "Over there."

She led him away from the walkway lights to the dark bench where they sat by moonlight.

"What about my question?" He raised his long, thin face to her, but again, he averted his eyes.

"I've read what you gave me. All the way through. Why do you ask?"

Apparently startled, he jerked his head back. "And Revelation? Did you read that too?"

"Yes."

"Do you know who Davato is?"

"Yes." She swallowed. "I've known for some time."

"Then you agree he must be stopped?"

She turned her gaze toward the lights in the tall buildings across the park. She'd stop Davato if she could, but fighting against such power as he possessed was hopeless. It would be like trying to stop a hurricane. Anyone foolish enough to try would be swept away in an instant. "He is a danger, I admit."

"But?"

"But there's nothing anyone can do about it."

"Maybe there is. You don't have to be involved in what I'm planning. All I want is for you to answer a simple question."

"What are you planning?" She gripped the sides of the bench.

"To assassinate both Davato and the Prophet. I have dynamite from a construction site."

Her heart sped up, and she gasped. This was why she didn't want to be seen with him. He was beyond reckless. He was insane. "What is your question?"

"Whenever those two are together, it's always in a public place, surrounded by guards and people." His voice, still barely above a whisper, hardened. "I want them alone—just the two of them. Better than most, you know their movements and habits. What I need to know is when and where they will be together—just the two of them. Something I can count on."

She snapped her head away, then stood, and walked a few paces from the bench. Could he actually do it? Could Lazzaro, filled with what appeared to be righteous fervor, kill them both? The evil they controlled was growing each day.

A chill shivered up her legs. Was it from the desert? Or from the danger Lazzaro had just brought into her life? She wrapped her arms about her chest and tried to think.

Lazzaro was right about one thing—the Imperator was rarely alone with the Prophet. She could think of only one place where they often met together. But no! Anywhere but there!

She whirled and returned to the bench. "I know of a place where you can find them together and alone. But it's far too dangerous." She shook her head. "No, it's impossible. I shouldn't have mentioned it."

He gripped her hands and stared into her eyes. This was Lazzaro, and for once, he was holding her gaze. "Tell me! Wherever it is, if that's where they meet—that's where I'll do it."

She took a deep breath and nodded. Then she told him about the secret room with the keypad lock where they often met in the afternoon. Then she added, "But there's something in that room, something living and powerful—a dark spirit, an evil demon, I don't know what. You don't want to go into that room. Ever!"

He released her hands and sat back against the bench. In the distance, the beat of drums and the pulse of a bass guitar thumped in the night. One of New Babylon's many nightclubs had started its evening revelry. Sometimes they played until dawn.

"How do I open the door?"

She gave him the combination she'd memorized and told him when, in the afternoon, they usually met. "But you'd be a fool to enter that room. Whatever's in there, you don't want to meet it."

"Let me worry about that." He stood. "Thank you, Chelsea. You've done your part. Now it's up to me."

"Don't!" She shook her head again. "It's suicide."

Lazzaro smiled, strolled across the grass, joined the walkers on the path, and headed back toward the city center.

CHAPTER 15

THE COMMANDANT

Weisserwald Uranmine, Southern Germany — October, Year 4

It was the last day of October, the carts creaked endlessly toward the chimney stack, and Margot had worked in the termination chamber for a month.

She dreaded the mornings. From the moment she left barracks number 67, crossed the gravel yard, and arrived at guillotine number 30, she prayed. She marveled at how many Christians the termination chambers "processed". For that's what they called it—"processing". The numbers arriving by train, truck, and bus each day were beyond counting.

Some women in her barracks worked on expanding the camp. Some were raising new barracks. Others were building a second termination chamber and crematorium.

The odor of ash, smoke, and death hung ever in the air. Now that fall was upon them, the nights turned colder. One morning, there was even frost on the ground. Her single blanket wasn't going to keep her warm this winter.

But yesterday, something unusual occurred. After supper, a new guard, a man, stopped each woman before entering her barracks. The line snaked around the corner as he interviewed everyone before allowing them back inside.

"Do you know how to paint?" he asked each woman. "Have you ever painted a portrait or a landscape?" And then: "Describe to me what one does with a palette and tubes of oil paint?"

To each of his questions, Margot gave the answers, and his eyes had lit up. When he had finished questioning, he took her aside, put a brush in her hands, pointed to a canvas and a palette holding fresh yellow, red, and green oil paint. Then he asked her to paint a flower beside the other amateurish attempts at artistry. She did, and when she'd finished, he seemed pleased.

But nothing came of it. He dismissed her, asked for the next woman, and she went to her bunk as usual. This morning was the same. As the condemned women approached guillotine number 30, fear fought its way through their drugged minds. It twisted their faces, brought futile resistance to their limbs, and prayers to their lips. And just like the day before and the day before that, she moved in a zombielike daze, reaching down, grabbing the severed heads, and throwing them toward the dumpster.

Then everything changed.

A CSA guard in a green-and-white uniform climbed the steps behind her guillotine. He led a young woman, an obvious newbie as her features registered shock and horror when she saw the scene before her. They mounted the platform, and Margot's guard halted the work of her guillotine. Her guard conversed with the new CSA man then faced Margot. "Give that woman your raincoat. You're with him now."

She pulled off the bloody coat and followed the CSA man down the back steps. He led her to the showers, gave her soap and a different uniform, gray and new and without holes. With the soap—something new, indeed—she washed off the blood. When she reemerged, feeling cleaner than she had in months, he spoke. "If you want to live, you will be on your best behavior. We're going to the commandant's office."

They marched past the women's barracks and the men's barracks to an edge of camp she'd never seen. Just before the outer fence stood a three-story house, painted blue, with a yard surrounded by razor wire and guards. The lawn boasted trees, green grass, and a hedge. On a far corner of the lot stood a tiny, one-room shed, also blue, with white-trimmed windows, flagstones leading to the entrance, and a leafless oak beside it.

At a gate through the razor wire, the CSA guard passed her off to another man. He opened the gate with a key card and led her down a flagstone walkway to the main house. They mounted porch steps, and he knocked on the door.

A woman of about thirty, wearing a yellow flowered dress and black leather shoes, answered. "Yes?" When she saw Margot, she frowned.

"Here is the artist they've selected for you." The guard bowed and took a step back.

The woman's gaze swept Margot from head to foot. "*Sehr gut.* I hope she can paint. The last woman didn't work out."

She led Margot inside, but when the guard tried to follow, she raised her hand. "No guards inside. I will take it from here."

She shut the door on his face. Then she faced Margot with hands on hips. "My name is Frau Keller, and you are here to paint portraits of me, my husband, and our son. We also want one of the entire family. If your work is satisfactory, you will sleep in the servant's hut in the yard outside, receive decent meals, and, for a time, be spared the fate you deserve."

Joy lifted Margot from the floor, and she feared she'd hit the ceiling. She bowed, smiled, nodded, and bowed again. "Yes, Frau Keller. I will do my best."

"Max is at work and will be home this evening. You can start to-day with Ernst. He's our son. Ernst!" Several times, she called his name down the hall. Finally, a blond-haired youth of about fourteen sauntered around the corner holding a tablet.

"She's prettier than the last one." Ernst grinned. "But I bet she can't paint."

"You will sit for her, do what she says. Or we'll take away your video-game privileges."

Scowling, he nodded.

Frau Keller led them to a sitting room outfitted as a studio. On one wall hung a framed picture of the Dragon with Davato and the Prophet on either side. A drop cloth covered the floor beneath an easel, a clean palette, tubes of oil paint, and brushes of all sizes. The easel faced a stool behind which was a floor-to-ceiling window opening onto the garden.

"We want our portraits taken with the garden in the background. The grass and trees aren't as green as I'd like—the drought, you know. But since the rains, I've had the prisoners watering, and everything's coming back to life. I'm sure you can make it a lot greener."

"Yes, Frau Keller, I can do that." She bowed.

"See that you do. I'll leave you with Ernst and check back with you in an hour or so to see how you're doing. If I don't like your work, well, it's back to where they found you." Then she faced Ernst. "You will be good. You will sit for her and do what she asks. Hear?"

Still frowning, the boy nodded.

Again, Margot bowed and smiled as the woman left her alone with the boy.

"I don't want to sit for an hour. Even for half an hour." Ernst's first words were not encouraging.

"What game were you playing?" She grabbed the palette and a medium-sized brush.

He cocked his head. "*Shooter*. It's this game where you get in a helicopter and fire a machine gun down at fleeing Christians. But the helicopter can land, fold its rotors, and turn into a car. And if the Christians escape in a boat, it can transform itself into a speedboat. Or even a submarine."

She swallowed. Was this what the Unitum Imperium was now teaching its children? "Why do you want to shoot Christians?"

"Because they are—well, because they're Christians. And the Imperator says we should."

"Well, I'm a Christian. Do you want to shoot me?"

A grin split his face. "Not really. You seem nice. But I was in the middle of my game. On level ten. Tell you what."

"What?"

"You have to paint the background, don't you?"

"Of course."

"Well, why don't you work on that while I sit over there in the corner and get to a point where the resistance isn't trying to kill me?"

"Sounds like a deal. But can you pose for me long enough so I can outline where I'm going to put you?"

Smiling again, he nodded.

She positioned him on the stool then quickly, using a pencil, drew the shape where she'd paint him in. While he sat in the corner, killing Christians with the noise of whirring helicopter blades, machine gun fire, and screams, she began painting the window and garden area surrounding the outline.

An hour later, when Frau Keller returned, Margot had part of the window showing the green grass and a tree in full leaf beyond.

The woman stared at it for so long, Margot worried it was not to her liking. Then she turned to Margot with wide eyes. "You've decided to do the background first?"

"Ernst and I had a deal. He wanted to end his game at a good point while I did the garden."

"Well, it's fine work—it's Margot, isn't it?"

"Yes, Frau Keller."

"Call me Sophie." She smiled then turned to Ernst. "Can you put that thing away and sit for her now?"

Ernst looked up. "Yes, I can stop now. I'm at level twelve."

Sophie Keller left. Ernst sat still on the pedestal. And Margot painted.

At noon, she ate her first real meal in months: Beef stew with potatoes, onions, and carrots. Fresh-baked bread with butter and strawberry jam and a glass of milk. The food invigorated her, filled her with energy, and she couldn't believe her good fortune.

That evening, Maximillian Keller, the camp commandant, appeared. He dismissed his family and met with her alone in the studio. A brusque man, short and balding with a black mustache, he looked her up and down with apparent disdain. But when he saw the beginning of Ernst's portrait, his demeanor softened. After examining her painting for some time, he nodded. "Your work is satisfactory, Fraulein Margot. But tomorrow, you will set aside Ernst's portrait and work on mine. I need something to hang in my office before the regional CSA head visits next week."

He shifted his feet and moved closer to her. One hand lifted a lock of her hair. "You are far prettier and younger than the last artist pretender. If your work continues to be as satisfactory as what I'm seeing, perhaps you can also fulfill another need I have. You understand how privileged you are to be here, to have your own quarters, to receive special meals, and to sleep in a soft bed?"

She nodded.

"Well, then, perhaps you can return the favor? To me, personally that is. With the utmost discretion, of course. By that I mean you will serve me at night, in your quarters, after the family has gone to bed."

A shudder rippled down her back. Fearing to do anything right now that would send her back to the barracks or the guillotine, she nodded.

"Sehr gut!" Taking her nod for acquiescence, he led her to the small house and locked her in. Not much more than a dollhouse for rich people's children, it held only a bed, a table, and a chair. But on the table waited a supper of cold spaghetti and meatballs, a glass of red wine, and a small loaf of bread with butter. She devoured it all. Satisfied and feeling stronger than she had in weeks, she laid down on the single feather bed under a heavy quilt. Before falling into the deepest sleep she'd experienced in months, she thanked the Lord for her deliverance.

But after the commandant's lecherous suggestion, she feared her reprieve was only temporary.

CHAPTER 16

THE SECRET ROOM

New Babylon – November, Year 4

Sweat poured down Lazzaro's forehead, and his hands gripped his bag so tightly, his knuckles ached. "Jesus, forgive me for what I am about to do," he whispered. The room was just ahead, on his right, and—good!—the hallway was empty. Just a few more steps, and then—

"What are you doing here, Lazzaro?"

He whirled to find Adam Turner, head of the Ministry of Truth, close on his heels. Why hadn't he heard the man's footsteps? "I–I was told to report to the Imperator this morning."

"Well, he's not here. Try the fourteenth floor."

"Thank you." Lazzaro wiped his brow. "Could you point me to a restroom?"

"Back down the hall the way you came. Turn left. Two doors down."

"Thanks." He spun and began retracing his steps, but slowly. When he reached the turn, he glanced back. Turner had gone on.

Breathing deeply, his heart racing, Lazzaro hurried back to the hidden room. He checked the hallway—both directions this time. Empty. He bent to the keypad and entered the numbers Chelsea had given him: *3, 5, 8, 1.*

The mechanism clicked. He pushed into the room and pulled the door shut behind him.

He felt only a vague unease, not the gut-wrenching fear Chelsea had described. Maybe whatever presence she'd felt was not here today. What incredible good fortune.

Why Ernesto wanted no part of this, Lazzaro didn't understand. "I have other plans," was all Ernesto had said. "And if your plan fails, I'll implement mine."

Ernesto was a fool not to join him. Today, everything was falling in place. Lazzaro had made it inside the room, and there was no evil presence.

The room was square, twenty meters on a side. Swirls of gray, white, and black, intermixed with red and yellow flame, decorated the walls. Five meters from the far end, a statue, vaguely phallic, like a thumb without a nail, stuck out of the floor at an angle. Recessed ceiling lights illuminated the statue's surface shining like gold. Was it pure gold? Surely, when the Imperator and the Prophet entered, they would come before this statue. What did they do here? Some kind of satanic rite?

Kneeling, he opened his bag. He pulled out four sticks of dynamite, already wrapped with duct tape. The dynamite he'd purloined from a construction site on the city's edge. He stuck in the detonators and attached the wires from a cell phone.

One call to a special number and—*boom*! No more Imperator. No more Prophet.

He laid the package behind the statue and stood. If three o'clock was when they met, that's when he'd make the call from a safe distance.

But he hadn't taken two steps toward the door when everything changed.

His vision filled with black mist. His feet turned to anvils. And fear, unlike anything he'd ever experienced, reached an icy hand deep inside his chest, gripped his heart, and squeezed.

He gasped.

He crumpled to the floor. He shook uncontrollably, his legs jerking, arms shivering, eyes rolling back inside his head.

How long he lay like that, he didn't know.

The next thing he remembered was the Prophet standing over him, green eyes staring down. Beside him stood Davato, his eyes black and cold and boring deep into Lazzaro's own.

Rough hands grabbed his arms and dragged his paralyzed body across the floor, out into the hallway—

Into the waiting arms of CSA guards.

"What should we do with him?" asked the Prophet.

"Keep him for special treatment," answered Davato, his voice as cold as ice. He faced the guards. "Give him something to remember his visit. But don't kill him."

Truncheons lashed down, landing on his legs, arms, shoulders, chest, fingers, and toes. With each blow, pain jolted through him and raced along his nerves until he gritted and ground his teeth. He tried rolling into a ball, but the blows fell on his back, his spine, his calves.

One struck his skull. And that's the last thing he remembered.

CHAPTER 17
THE SIGN

Revelation 12:1–2 (HCSB): A great sign appeared in heaven: a woman clothed with the sun, with the moon under her feet and a crown of 12 stars on her head. She was pregnant and cried out in labor and agony as she was about to give birth.

Jerusalem, Israel – November, Year 4

The weather had turned colder, and when Chelsea left her apartment in the Clal Center wearing only a sweater and heading for the Old City, she shivered and could see her breath. Hawkers called out from their stands, selling pita bread and falafel for a dear price. Shopkeepers begged passersby to buy their miniature plastic statues of the Imperator and the Prophet. But she ignored them all.

Her feet echoed over the cobbles as she entered the old Christian quarter. She passed the Church of the Holy Sepulcher, now empty and abandoned. Nowadays, no one wanted to be seen inside a church.

She'd been in Jerusalem for a week, and tomorrow, they were returning to New Babylon. But all day, even as she took the Imperator's notes in meeting after meeting, last night's dream haunted her.

In the dream, it was dusk, and she was walking down a familiar lane in the Old City. But something made her look up. Hanging above a door on hinges of gold was a sign. Though its wood was cracked and ancient, its paint was new. The sign bore the figure of a pregnant woman, and the garment wrapping her torso was as bright as the sun. Indeed, it shone so bright, Chelsea had to shield her eyes. At the woman's feet was the moon, and on her head lay a crown of twelve stars. In the dream, the woman turned her glance toward Chelsea, and then she knew the woman wasn't a painted figure, but an angel. The angel beckoned toward the open doorway beneath. Chelsea entered.

And then she woke.

That was last night, and now, she questioned if it had been a dream at all. Was it instead a vision? All morning, the desire to return to that street grew and built within her, for she'd passed that way only yesterday.

Her feet led her around the corner, and she stopped. Before her, unplanned, was the very street with the sign and the angel.

It was dusk, shadows crowded the walkways, and few people were about. Ever since the plague, much of the population spent their evenings indoors, avoiding public spaces.

Up ahead, the sign stuck out into the street, and she approached. It was the pregnant woman clothed with the sun, standing on the moon, with a crown of twelve stars. Yesterday, that sign was *not* there.

Her heart sped up, but her feet slowed down. At the entrance and its open doorway, she looked up.

Today, it was just a sign, and the woman above her was just a painted woman. She examined the posters behind the glass. Pictures of Paris, London, New York. Intrepid travelers smiling and holding hands as they stepped off their planes. Athens, Rome, and Barcelona. Happy people, eager for an adventure, feasting their eyes on new sights. Visions of a bygone era before the vanishing, travel permits, and the CSA. Back when people traveled freely, and the world wasn't ending.

Inside, a light was on in back. She knocked on the door, and it squeaked inward. She pushed it open all the way and stepped inside. "Hello," she called. "Is anyone here?"

"Come in, come in," came a kindly voice.

She walked past dark chairs and desks to the back where a middle-aged man with curly black hair, thick eyebrows, and a wide nose rose from a desk. He met her with a smile and an extended hand. "I'm glad you came, Chelsea Turner," he said in English. "I've been expecting you. My name is Baruch Abramovich."

Stunned, she took the offered hand. "How do you know my name, Mr. Abramovich?"

"I know a great deal about you and your family." He set down a glass mug of espresso. "We've never met, but three years ago, you, Chelsea, were instrumental in freeing me from a Unitum Imperium prison. I was imprisoned with your brother Caleb."

"Y–you were the man chained with him that night?" A hand went to her mouth.

"I was. After Paris, we went our separate ways, and I've seen neither Dylan nor Margot nor Caleb. But many times, I have seen you on television."

"Yes. The public announcements." Had her brothers seen her also? If so, what would they think of her association with Davato? "Last I knew, Dylan and Margot were fine. But no one's heard from Caleb since he landed in Chicago. We fear the worst."

"Yes. The war. The harvest of the second seal."

Silence descended between them. What more could one say about the millions presumed dead? "But I saw this place in a dream. That's what led me here. How is that possible?"

He smiled and offered her a cup of the strong coffee with sugar that the locals drank from glass mugs. She declined.

"The dream wasn't my doing, but I'm glad you came. It's vitally important you hear what I have to say. Won't you sit down?"

She took the offered chair across from him.

"In about two months, I'm leaving Jerusalem and taking with me all the new Christians, many of them former Jews. I'm leading them far from Davato, who is the Antichrist, the man of lawlessness, also called the beast. Soon, he will begin a purge of all who do not worship him. I will offer sanctuary to all who believe in Christ. I will lead them to a place of refuge that the Lord is preparing for us."

"I am not a Christian. In fact, I work for Davato. And still, you are offering this to me?"

"Yes, Chelsea." He reached across and laid a hand on one of hers. "Because I believe you do not belong where you are. But there is one, nonnegotiable condition."

"What's that?"

"That you turn your heart to Jesus, the Son of the living God, the one who died on the cross for your sins so that you could have eternal life in the presence of a loving, all-powerful, omniscient God."

Her head swirled with the magnitude of what was happening, and she drew her hand back—

A dream with an angel had led her here.

Three years ago, she had unknowingly freed Baruch, a man who knew her brothers, who was here in the place where the dream had led her.

Now, he was offering her sanctuary, a way out.

Their fates seemed inextricably linked.

Like Dylan, Baruch also called Davato the Antichrist, and she knew it was true. Lately, Davato was calling her to fewer meetings where sensitive issues were being discussed, and she was coming under increasing suspicion.

Finally, there was this: She'd heard the Christian message from Dylan and even back in her liberal New York church, but it had never really sunk in. Even now, something inside her resisted. Why did Baruch have to put a condition on his offer?

"So, what do you say?" He sipped his espresso. "Will you accept Jesus as your savior?"

"When are you leaving?"

"As I said, in about two months. The timing is not up to me. My offer is only for Jews and Christians. But I'm asking you to leave your Davato and come with me now. We'll find a place for you until it's time."

She covered her mouth with her hands and squeezed her eyes shut. She could almost believe, almost accept his offer. But something held her back. Opening her eyes, she looked into the shadows across the room. "I . . . need . . . more time."

"You must decide, Chelsea." His voice slowed with sadness. "If you don't leave the Unitum Imperium and become a Christian—you may never find the Refuge in the desert where I am going."

"Where in the desert?"

"Even if I told you, unless you accept Christ, it will be difficult to find."

"If I decide later, can I still go there?"

"It's possible, yes. But dangerous."

"But still possible?"

"Yes."

She stood, paced into the shadows, whirled, and returned. "I . . . can't. Not yet. Not now. I want to, but . . ."

"But what?"

"I need more time."

Silence filled the room until Baruch stood and approached. "Then may the Lord go with you, Chelsea Turner, and guide you on your way. May he offer you comfort, peace, and safety on your journey to faith, and—if God wills it—to the Refuge."

His words were so kind, loving, and unexpected that tears filled her eyes. "Th–thank you."

"You're welcome."

Then—and she didn't know why she did this—she stood, wrapped her arms around him, and hugged him.

When they parted, he squeezed her hands. "Know that this building will remain a place to meet for as long as we can keep it going. If you change your mind, if you have turned your heart to the Christ and want to join us later, look for a brick with the sign of the pregnant woman with stars on her head." He pointed to the wall beside him. "It's not there yet, but when I leave, I will paint the symbol. Behind the brick, I will place directions to the Refuge, as I'm calling it. But only if you have given your heart to the Savior can you follow them."

Puzzled by his last statement, she thanked him, nonetheless. Then she hurried through the door into the darkened street. The criminals would soon be out, if they weren't already, looking for victims to rob, beat, or rape. She was a fool to be out this late.

She fled past shadows in the doorways, her feet echoing too loud down the empty lane. But no, that wasn't what bothered her.

It was as if she'd swallowed some caustic poison, as if something were gnawing, eating at her insides. She wondered—

Had she just made the worst decision of her life?

CHAPTER 18
THE PORTRAIT

Weisserwald Uranmine, Southern Germany – November, Year 4

On her third day in the commandant's house, as the pigeons cooed outside the garden window, Margot worked on the portrait of Maximillian Keller, commandant of Weisserwald Uranmine Internment Camp. He was short and round-bellied, and he had given her instructions to make him look thinner. Indeed, before he posed, he would always remove his cell phone and wallet from his jacket pockets, and his holster and pistol from around his waist, then place them on a table in the corner. "Makes me look fatter," he would say.

And whenever he did this, her glance would fall on the cell phone, and possibilities raced through her mind. But no way could she ever get to it with Keller in the room.

Now, he sat on the stool with his head held high, one arm on a hip, the other straight at his side, his mustache black and trimmed, long strands of black hair combed to either side to cover his bald pate. She could paint faster but feared that, when she finished, they would return her to the barracks. If she took two days per portrait, she could stretch this out to eight, maybe nine, days.

"I am impressed by your workmanship, Fraulein Margot," he said without moving his head. "I presume you will finish this afternoon?"

"Yes, Herr Keller. In about an hour." She dipped her thinnest brush in the black paint and added another strand of hair.

"Sehr gut. Tonight, expect to receive me around ten o'clock after my wife has gone to bed."

Her brush froze before the canvas, and she swallowed. How was she going to get out of this?

"Before you return to your quarters this evening, you will shower in the main house."

She nodded and resumed painting. But now her heart beat faster, her hand was unsteady, and she stepped back to take a breath. In the garden beyond the commandant, the rains began again, dimming the light.

"Is something wrong, Fraulein?"

"No." She batted a stray lock from her forehead. "My hand is getting tired. That's all."

"I hope I will please you as much as I know you will please me."

"Yes, Herr Keller. I'm sure you—"

A knock on the door, and a woman in the green-and-white uniform of the CSA stuck her head inside. "I'm sorry to disturb you, Herr Keller, but—"

"I gave explicit instructions I was not to be disturbed." He shot her a withering glare.

The woman averted her glance and lowered her voice. "Ja, but this requires your immediate attention. I was told you must see to this personally. Your head of security is in the hall."

"Oh, all right." He stood from the stool and faced Margot. "I'll be back shortly."

He left the room and closed the door.

Margot's glance shot to the table where he'd placed his cell phone. He was talking on the other side of the door with another man. How she'd waited for this moment! She hurried to the table, picked up the phone, and punched the special number Victor had created for emergency use.

The phone rang. Once, twice, three times. But no one answered.

Outside in the hall, the conversation was wrapping up. The voice was getting closer to the door.

She brought up the text dialogue box and began typing: "This is Margot. The camp is called Weisserwald Uranmine in southern Germany. I am painting a portrait of the commandant and sleeping in his servant's quarters on the edge of the camp. Come quickly!" She sent the text and saw the confirmation.

Someone had their hand on the doorknob to the studio, and it clicked. Her heart pounded wildly. Then the conversation resumed.

She deleted the history. She backed out to the outgoing call screen, intending to delete that history as well.

But the door squeaked and began to open.

She dropped the phone on the stool and hurried toward her easel. Halfway there, she stopped and peered toward the garden and the rain. Sweat dripped off her brow.

"Sorry about that, Fraulein. There's always another crisis, isn't there?" Herr Keller glanced at the garden. "Ja, it's pouring. Good for the grass."

Back with her easel, she tried to slow her racing heart.

Within the hour, she finished the portrait. Afterward, he led her to a ground-floor bathroom where she showered. Then he returned her to her quarters and locked her in.

She ate a supper of veal schnitzel, buttered potatoes, and bread and butter.

Then she laid down to wait for the evening when Maximillian Keller would come with lechery in his heart.

* * *

Long before ten o'clock, the outside lock clicked. Still fully clothed, she shot upright in bed and turned toward the door, her heart pounding. What could she do to stop this?

But instead of Herr Keller, two CSA guards wearing raincoats burst into the room and pulled her out into the rain. "You will come with us."

"I don't understand." But when her glance fell on Maximillian Keller, rain dripping off his bald head, his glare burning into her, she suspected what he would say next.

"I trusted you, Fraulein. I gave you special privileges and opened my home to you so you could do our portraits." He took two steps toward her. A hand reached out and slapped her, hard, across one cheek. "You made an unauthorized call from my phone, and now you're going back to the barracks. Such a pity."

He faced the two guards. "Get her out of my sight!"

They dragged her through the gate, over the mud, and to barracks number—oh no!—to barracks number 1,679 where Grosse Frau waited at the entrance.

The CSA guards released her, and the stout matron looked her up and down, a grin spreading across her face. "What have we here? Somehow, you made it back here alive. How lucky for you!"

By now, the rain had slicked Margot's hair and soaked her new dress to the skin. She shivered from the chill.

Slapping her truncheon against a palm, Grosse Frau circled her victim.

A blow landed on Margot's calf, and her legs buckled. Another strike hit her shoulder, and she winced.

"Lucky, lucky you," said the matron. "This barracks is scheduled for termination two days from now."

More blows fell, one after another, on her arms, chest, back, and legs. She cradled her head with her arms to protect it, but Grosse Frau beat her mercilessly.

When Margot lay crumpled in the mud, crying, pleading for mercy, and shaking with pain, the woman stopped. Then the guards dragged her inside and threw her on the floor beside an empty bunk.

As she crawled up onto the bare wood, soaked and shivering, she pulled the single blanket over her head and prayed: *Lord Jesus, hear my plea. Save me from his camp. Reunite me with Dylan and my friends. Or else take my life and spare me this suffering.*

CHAPTER 19
A SCOUTING EXPEDITION

Weisserwald Village, Southern Germany – November, Year 4

When Margot's call came in, the emergency-use phone rang unanswered in Victor's room on the fourth floor of the ski house.

No one answered because Danielle was downstairs in the kitchen and Dylan and Pasqual were driving back from their twelfth fruitless search through southern Germany's villages and towns. René and Victor were also heading home from their ninth unsuccessful mission to scour parts of the country the other two hadn't covered.

Both groups arrived back at the Skihaus within an hour of each other. Sunset came in midafternoon in November, and it was already dark.

After showering, Dylan took a candle downstairs and slumped into a chair in the sitting room while Danielle prepared supper in the kitchen. Footfalls creaked down the wooden staircase, and Pasqual sauntered to a seat beside Dylan.

"We've been looking for two months, and we haven't a clue where the camp is." Dylan leaned forward, gripped both knees, and stared at the pinewood floor. "What if it's not in southern Germany? Everywhere we've looked—no one knows of any camp."

"We must hold on to hope. We must have faith and pray that she's all right."

More footsteps descended the staircase, and René entered the room. "We barely escaped from two overeager squaddies on that last trip. There was a gun battle, and we had to shoot them both."

"Oh no." Pasqual jerked his head toward René. "Ever since the raids to restock our equipment, they've been searching for us. This will only rile things up."

"We just have to be more careful." René drew a hand through his hair. "Maybe we should lay low for a few weeks."

"Lay low?" Dylan jerked his gaze up from the floor, feeling as if he might explode. "Margot's been in that camp for five months now. Who knows how long someone can survive in a place like that? We can't give up on her."

"Let's face it, Dylan." René's voice was soft, low. "We don't even know if—"

Feet pounded down the stairs, and the three men turned as Victor hurried across the room, his face flushed, his eyes alight. "She's alive! Yesterday, she sent a message from the commandant's phone. She's painting his portrait and staying near his house. She told us where the camp is!"

Dylan shot out of his seat, spun in a circle, raised his hands to the ceiling, and shouted for joy. "She's alive!"

The others rushed to his side and slapped him on the back. Danielle hurried in from the kitchen to see what the commotion was, and when she found out, she kissed Dylan on the cheek.

"Then tomorrow," said René, "we'll all go on a rescue mission."

"Good," said Danielle. "There's no way I'm staying behind on this one."

Victor read her entire text, and then a smiling René hushed the group. "At first light, we'll head to Weisserwald Uranmine."

"Weisserwald?" said Pasqual. "We searched there. It's only two hours away. No one there said anything about a camp."

"I remember it," said Dylan. "It's so close, we could be there tonight."

René checked his watch, scratched his chin, and examined the floor. When he looked up, even his dark, fathomless eyes seemed brighter. "Oui. Let's eat Danielle's supper, pack the van, and go tonight! It would be best if we stay the night in the village and scout the camp tonight. Once we know what we're up against, we can make plans to get her out— either tomorrow night or the night after."

As he gathered a few things, Dylan's grin felt like it might split his face.

* * *

IN AN ONLINE SEARCH, VICTOR found an inn called Gästehaus und Pension. While René ensured they had everything they needed, Dylan called the place to check if they had rooms but didn't make a reservation. Within minutes, they piled into the van and started north into Germany.

On the village's outskirts, they passed modern buildings, but the village center was ancient. René parked the van on the main Strasse in front of the hotel.

Dylan followed René into the two-story pension. They approached the desk behind which sat a wizened old man with a full gray beard clenching a pipe between his teeth. "Can I help you?"

"I called earlier to see if you had rooms," said Dylan in German. He laid both hands on the counter. "But I didn't make a reservation."

"Ja, ja." The man waved a pipe. "Plenty of rooms. No one here right now. No one travels these days. Not since the vanishing. Not since the mine closed. Not since the new regime." He knocked his pipe in an ashtray. "Nothing's the same anymore, and tobacco is dear, too dear, indeed. My name is Jacques."

"I'm Dylan."

"And I'm René," said the ex-spy standing beside Dylan.

"You can have my three best rooms, no extra charge." Jacques examined them and squinted. "You don't look like government folks. Are you?"

"No," answered René. "We're not. Will you take cash?"

The old man nodded. "Not many do, nowadays. But I do. Cards can be traced. The government wants a piece of everything, don't they? Cash still buys nearly anything. If you know the right people, of course. I don't need last names. And don't sign the register. Only causes trouble."

"Thank you . . . Jacques. And oui, we'd rather not be traced. Can we park on the street?"

Jacques glanced toward the van. "Best in the alley behind. Best not to give the Truth Squads your license, ja?"

He winked, and Dylan felt his shoulders relax. Was this man a fellow conspirator against the Unitum Imperium madness?

"Do you need supper?" Shaking his head and frowning, Jacques stuffed his pipe with fresh tobacco. "All I can offer is a few hunks of stale bread, and the price is dear. Everything's dear. But of wine, I have plenty. You can dip the bread in the wine."

"Thank you, we've eaten. But breakfast tomorrow would be nice."

"Same thing. Stale bread, but I can give you a slice of cheese for a dear price."

"That will do." René shifted his feet. "But can you answer a question, Jacques?"

"If I can." He lit his pipe and puffed.

"Is there a camp nearby?"

A frown distorted his face, and he looked away. "A camp, you say?"

"Oui. A very large camp."

"And if such a camp existed, what business would you have with it?"

René held the man's gaze. "Personal business. Private business. Not government business."

"That, I'll accept. Go north about seven kilometers. An abomination against God, it is. We here in Weisserwald do not speak of it to strangers. But I see no government men standing here. And I sense you and I believe alike, ja?"

René nodded.

"Ja, I cannot abide the Unitum Imperium and the man running it. You won't repeat that to anyone, of course?"

"No, Jacques, we won't." René grinned, and they shook hands.

Having secured lodging and a likely coconspirator, they brought their bags to their rooms then met in René's and Pasqual's quarters.

"While it's dark is the best time to check out the camp." René dropped his bag on the floor. "We need to find out what we're up against. Let's go!"

They returned to the van and drove north from the village on dark country roads. Once, they stopped for a train heading their way and crossing the highway. It hauled boxcar after boxcar. Were they full of prisoners? Then they followed two moving vans and a line of buses, also heading their way. More prisoners?

Three kilometers from the village, they came upon old weatherworn signs directing them to the mine. Ahead, over the next hill, lights lit up the clouds.

When the road topped the rise, René pulled over. While they exited the van, the trucks and buses ahead of them descended to the plain below. In the valley, searchlights illuminated row after row of corrugated metal barracks. The camp filled the vista nearly to the horizon, and Dylan gasped. Black smoke billowed from the crematorium's chimney, and even here, the scent of burnt flesh and bone drifted around him.

"It's massive," he said. "How are we ever going to find her in all that?"

"She said she was on the edge of camp in the commandant's servant's house," answered Victor. "Maybe we should circle the place?"

"Oui. We'll park and search the perimeter," added René.

Back in the van, René followed signs for the main entrance until they came to a dirt track veering left. This they drove to a grassy path descending into the trees. The van bounced over ruts and tall grass until they were out of sight of the dirt road. There, he parked.

"Now we go on foot." René hung a set of binoculars around his neck. "But the camp's so big, this could take a while."

For half an hour, the ex-spy led Dylan and the others into the forest, across streambeds, and through underbrush until they reached a swath of cleared ground, about fifty meters wide bordering the camp. Hidden in the shadows under the trees, they followed the perimeter. A kilometer later, they spied a three-story house, painted blue, surrounded by green grass, a garden, and trees. "That's got to be the commandant's house," said Dylan.

When a searchlight swept the clear-cut area and the edge of the tree line, they dropped to the ground.

Lying on his stomach, Dylan begged the binoculars off René and peered toward the house. Razor wire isolated it from the rest of the camp. In one corner of the lot stood a tiny servant's or guesthouse. "That's where she is. We've found her!" His heart raced. She was only seventy meters from where he lay.

René took back the binoculars and examined the area. "This is worse than I feared. Fifty meters to the right, there's a guard tower with machine guns. Seventy meters to the left, there's another one. The whole area is swept by searchlights. And do you see the attack dogs racing in the space between the border fencing? They'll rip your throat out. And just beyond the commandant's house, that looks like the barracks holding the guards for the entire camp."

He dropped the binoculars and flipped onto his back. "I'm sorry, but I don't know how to do this."

"What do you mean?" asked Dylan. "We've been waiting for months, searching for weeks, and now that we're here, you don't know what to do?"

"It's too dangerous. How are we going to get close enough to cut through the fences without being seen? There are two fences, and even if we cut through the first one, the dogs will rip us apart, alerting the tower guards. They'll cut us down with machine guns in an instant. They'll also alert the guard barracks. Then we'll wake up the whole camp. No, my friends. I don't know how to do this."

"What if we blew up the guard towers?" asked Pasqual. "Then we could plant explosives under the fences. Wouldn't that frighten the dogs away? Wouldn't that be enough to get us into the camp?"

"Oui, it might. But with those searchlights, how could we even get close enough to topple the towers? Even then, we wouldn't have much time before the guards poured out of their barracks. It would be suicide."

Silence descended on the group, and Dylan stared across the gap to where Margot must be right now. She was so close. After finally finding the camp, were they just going to give up?

René checked his watch. "It's nearly midnight. We'd better get back."

As they headed back into the undergrowth, Dylan noted two tall oaks standing just back from where they'd found the house.

On the trek through the forest and brush, he dragged his feet and fell behind. If René, of all people, said the mission was hopeless, what was left? Would they just abandon Margot to her fate?

"We'll find a way." Danielle came up beside him. "René must be wrong."

"But without René, what can we do?"

By the time he found his bed at the pension, a deep and sinking loneliness had taken possession of his soul. Victor was already snoring in his bed, but for Dylan, sleep wouldn't come. He slipped out of bed, knelt, and cupped his hands together.

"Dear Lord, I know you can help us. I know you have a plan for Margot and me. Do not let her wallow in that place. Send us a way to get her out. I ask you this in Jesus's name. Amen."

Only much later did he fall into a fitful, restless slumber.

CHAPTER 20
THE SIXTH SEAL

Revelation 6:12–14 (NLT): I watched as the Lamb broke the sixth seal, and there was a great earthquake. The sun became as dark as black cloth, and the moon became as red as blood. Then the stars of the sky fell to the earth like green figs falling from a tree shaken by a strong wind. The sky was rolled up like a scroll, and all of the mountains and islands were moved from their places.

Weisserwald Uranmine, Southern Germany – November, Year 4

Dylan woke to the sound of a ringing phone. Rubbing sleep from his eyes, he groped on the nightstand then put the device to his ear. It was five forty-five in the morning. Who could be calling him at this hour? "Hello?"

"Dylan! It's Caleb. You won't believe what I'm about to tell you."

"Caleb?" He sat up in bed. "Where are you?"

"Redwood Falls. We've been here for two months, staying with some folks, but I don't think it's going to work out. But I've got to be quick. We haven't had a cell signal here since we arrived, but tonight, for some reason, we do. I don't know how long it will last."

"What do you want to tell me?" He gripped the phone tighter.

"I had just fallen asleep when I had a dream—no, it was a vision. And it was powerful. This biker dude came to me. He's an angel, and he gave me a message to give to you. It's really important."

"A biker dude who's an angel? You're not making sense."

"Yeah, listen. I didn't tell you about this earlier, but it was the same angel who came to me after the vanishing. He warned me then, and I didn't pay attention. And, because I didn't, the demon attacked me. But never mind about that. I know this sounds crazy, but he was insistent. And he was an angel, so I believe him."

"Caleb, this is crazy. Really crazy. Are you okay?"

"Yes, no, now just listen. I don't know what this is about, but I'm supposed to tell you something important, so just listen: 'Go to the fence before dawn,' he said, 'and take only the wire cutters. Don't take the explosives.' He emphasized that. 'Don't worry about the dogs,' he said. 'You'll be okay. Cut away a section between fence posts. Do this for both fences and do it right before dawn. You can't be late. Right before dawn,' he said. Then, after that, this is what he said: 'Trust in the Lord with all your heart . . . and he will guide you on the right paths.' That's it. That's the message. I don't know what you're involved with, Dylan, but this came straight from an angel's mouth! And this time, he didn't wear biker garb—he glowed!"

Dylan gasped. Without doubt, an angel of God had spoken through his brother. "Caleb, I believe you. Thank you. This was the answer to my prayer."

"Breaking up . . . signal . . . going . . ." Then the phone went dead.

Victor was up and had apparently heard part of the conversation. "What's going on?"

"Get dressed." Fully awake now, Dylan leaped out of bed. "We're going back to the camp."

When he told René, Pasqual, and Danielle what Caleb said, they didn't need further convincing. No way could Caleb have known about the camp or the fence or the dogs they'd seen earlier, unless he'd had a vision from God.

"This is crazy," whispered Danielle. "But I believe it."

René checked his watch. "Sunrise is in an hour. But how are we to avoid being seen by the searchlights?"

"It's a matter of faith, René." Pasqual laid a hand on René's shoulder. "'Trust in the Lord . . .' The angel was quoting one of the proverbs."

René shrugged. "I don't like this, but if we're going to do it, we should assume we're not coming back here."

They lugged their bags to the van and left the pension at six twenty. Outside, a light mist was falling.

The drive to the camp took longer in the poor visibility, and when they topped the hill that should have overlooked the camp, fog obscured the view.

"Fog!" cried Dylan from the back seat. "We'll be hidden."

Squeezed in front, a smiling Danielle swiveled to face René. "See, René? Faith."

They drove the dirt road and stopped in the tall grass where they'd hidden the van the evening before. Carrying only wire cutters and heavy gloves, they wended their way through the underbrush. When they found the two tall oaks marking the spot, fog obscured their view of the camp.

Dylan checked his watch. "We've only got twenty minutes before sunrise."

"Then let's go!" René hurried across the clear-cut area to the fence. The others followed. He began cutting wire.

Wires snapped and coiled and fell all around René as he worked. Dylan glanced again at his watch. "Ten minutes left."

As René snipped through the last wires of the leftmost post, Dylan looked up from his watch. "Only five minutes!" Would they be too late?

"But the sun's not up yet." Pasqual waved at the sky. "Must be the fog."

Indeed, it was still dark. René began cutting beside the rightmost fence post.

In the distance, dogs barked.

René's clippers snipped, wire twanged, and the barking moved closer, louder.

"Time's up!" said Dylan.

As he said this, Pasqual and Victor pulled the last of the downed wire into the gap between the two fences. Barely had they done so when three Dobermans appeared, growling and snapping, unable to advance beyond the tangled mess of wire blocking their way.

But there was now a clear path into the camp.

"Shouldn't we go to the house and get her?" asked Dylan.

"No," said Danielle. "We're supposed to trust in the Lord and wait."

"What does that mean?" Victor sent a questioning glance to the others.

"Look!" René pointed along the clear-cut area. "The fog is lifting."

Not only was it lifting, a strong wind arose that gained such strength and power, it flapped and tore at Dylan's pants and sweatshirt. In seconds, it stripped away the mist, leaving them completely exposed.

Shouts came from the guard tower on their right, followed by machine gun fire. Bullets ripped a swath of ground, heading toward them.

The sun burst over the eastern horizon, and the ground shook. The earth rose, throwing Dylan into the air. Supports for the guard tower cracked. The structure groaned, leaned, and toppled across the fence into the compound.

The earth moaned and rumbled. It heaved and tossed.

For what seemed an eternity, the land fought with those on the surface, shaking the foundations of what man had wrought, wreaking havoc on his works, splitting, crumbling, and knocking his buildings to the ground.

Off to their right, between them and the toppled tower, the ground ripped apart. A crevasse opened under the fence and raced toward the blue-painted house. The roof caved in, the walls collapsed, and then the chasm swallowed the structure whole. The house, the lawn, the garden, and the servant's quarters where Margot was supposed to be—it disappeared into the earth.

"No!" cried Dylan, but the quake gave him no time to mourn. Again, it launched him into the air.

He tried to gain his feet, but there wasn't enough solid ground to remain upright. He landed on all fours on top of dirt so soft and broken, it was as if someone had tilled it.

Beside him, the others also fought for balance as the quake tossed them to and fro.

When the shaking stopped, it left him prone, face down in the dirt, breathing fast, wondering why he was still alive.

He stood and brushed himself off. The others also stood.

As far as he could see along the clear-cut area, every guard tower had fallen. Everywhere, fencing had collapsed. Inside the camp, most of the barracks' walls had split open, some of the roofs had fallen in, and prisoners were surging into the yards.

Where the guards' barracks had been was a yawning hole. The earth, it seemed, had a special affinity for the managers of death. In the distance, the crematorium chimney no longer rose into the sky, and the termination building was only a pile of twisted metal and broken timbers.

The camp's interior now filled with a mass of escaping prisoners. A few pistol shots broke the shouts of joy, and from where he stood, Dylan saw men grappling a guard to the ground and taking his weapon. Gaunt men, women, and youths in ragged dress poured into the alleys between the ruined barracks, heading for newly opened gaps in the fencing. A steady stream skirted the crevasse around the commandant's house and headed toward the opening the Nazarene Friends had created.

But how could she be among them when she said she was staying in a place the earth had swallowed? Was she really gone? He gripped his head with both hands and moaned.

"It took her, didn't it?" René pointed at the place where the house had been.

"This cannot be." Dylan shook his head from side to side.

"Maybe . . . she wasn't there?" But Pasqual's voice lacked confidence, as if he were trying too hard to give comfort.

Escaped prisoners rushed past them into the clear-cut area then broke left or right. Only a few entered the underbrush.

"What should we do?" asked Victor. "Is she gone?"

"'Trust in the Lord,' the message said." Pasqual's voice was stronger now. "We should wait."

"Wait for what?" asked René. "It seems clear she's gone."

"Wait for the Lord to direct our path." Pasqual laid a hand on Dylan's shoulder. "Let us wait a bit longer."

Dylan sucked in breath and nodded.

Have faith. Trust in the Lord. And he will direct you on right paths. Wasn't that what an angel had said? Why was it so hard to believe that?

"Look!" Victor pointed up, and everyone's gaze lifted to the sky.

The clouds that had brought the rain and mist were rolling away with a violent churning. As if driven by some supernatural wind, they swirled and seethed and fought each other in their escape to the horizon. In their wake, they left a sun burning bright and yellow.

But no sooner had sunlight burned hot upon Dylan's face than the light dimmed, the sun darkened, and something black and mottled, as of a giant cloth, was pulled over the orb that gave warmth and light to the planet.

He grabbed the top of his head again and stared.

In the space of seconds, a giant porous cloth had appeared, blocking the sunlight. Now, only weak rays—dimming, brightening, then dimming again—escaped through the holes.

The day had been stolen, replaced by flickering twilight.

"What . . . the . . . heck?" René stood open-mouthed, looking up.

Some of the fleeing prisoners also stopped, looked up, and cried out in fear. Others kept running. Still others knelt and prayed.

A flash of something came from the right, and Dylan jerked his glance toward the darkened sky. Hundreds of meteors streaked across the heavens, leaving glowing trails. Soon, the entire horizon filled with the flaming contrails of falling meteors.

"Dylan?"

It was weak, and he hadn't heard that voice for five months. But he would know it anywhere. He spun, saw her, then shouted for joy.

Before him, her hair short and unkempt, her face thin and covered with welts, stood Margot.

CHAPTER 21
ESCAPE TO SWITZERLAND

Joel 2:30–31 (NLT): And I will cause wonders in the heavens and on the earth—blood and fire and columns of smoke. The sun will become dark, and the moon will turn blood red before that great and terrible day of the LORD arrives.

Weisserwald Uranmine, Southern Germany – November, Year 4

As the mass of prisoners flooded through the gap, Dylan raced into Margot's open arms and hugged her. He planted kisses on her cheeks, her forehead, her nose, her lips. He held her at arm's length then pulled her close and hugged her again. "You're alive! You weren't in the house!" He pointed to the crevasse that had swallowed the commandant's house.

"He discovered my call to you. Then they took me back to the barracks and beat me. I was to be executed this morning." She squeezed him tight and laid her head on his shoulder. "I knew you'd come. And when the walls fell, I hoped you'd be here by the house."

His heart so lifted with joy, he again squeezed her to his chest and kissed her forehead, her nose, her lips. Could a person explode with happiness?

"If you two can break apart from this very touching reunion"—René stood, hands on hips, a wide grin splitting his face—"we should probably get the heck out of here."

Dylan released her, giving Pasqual, Victor, and Danielle an opportunity to hug her, followed by René.

Around them, hundreds of prisoners streamed through the gap and broke left or right. Some paused to look with terror at the sky.

"Let's go!" René ran across the clearing, and the others followed. When they entered the forest, fallen trees now crisscrossed the path, and the dry streambed they'd passed earlier now gushed with water.

Overhead, tiny meteors streaked the sky in a never-ending light display.

At the van, René backed out of the tall grass. But the earth had been shaken, and the tires sometimes spun in the loose dirt. He drove slowly, bouncing over fallen saplings, once steering into a field to escape a tree blocking the way. On the main highway, hundreds of prisoners flooded the road, but with every seat in the van taken, René drove on.

Occasionally, they came to newly opened crevasses blocking the road where they had to detour far into bumpy fields to find a way forward. With the dim light, Danielle and Pasqual sat up front and helped René watch for dangers on the road ahead.

The moon came out. And it was a deep shade of red—blood red.

Something about it made Dylan shudder. The color was unnatural. No, more than that, it was bone-chilling. God was showing the world who he was, and now only fools would deny him.

Too often, a crevasse appeared out of the dark, and René was forced to backtrack onto secondary roads before they could again join the main highway. Twice on the route, aftershocks stopped them as the earth rocked the vehicle from side to side before they could drive on.

As they passed through picturesque Memmingen, half the houses were now rubble. Bricks were laying in the street, and cobbles were up-ended, making for a bumpy ride. Most of the townsfolk were in the streets, looking heavenward with terror-stricken faces, probably wondering if the world would end today, terrified of what had happened to the earth and sky, and afraid of more aftershocks.

They took 96 south, but the drive was so treacherous and slow, they hadn't made it halfway home before René pulled off the road. "It's too dark. We can't go on. We'll have to sleep here."

"Before we sleep, we've forgotten something important," said Pasqual. "Let's all get out for a minute."

Dylan and the others followed him, looking to him with questioning glances.

"We've forgotten to thank God for this rescue, for getting Margot out safely." Pasqual knelt, as did the others, and everyone bowed their heads.

"Dear Lord," he began, "today, you have shown your great power and majesty to all who would see and believe. We stand in awe at how your prophecies are being fulfilled. We thank you for rescuing Margot from that camp, that place of death where evil itself had made a home. Please forgive us our sins, hear our praise, and accept our gratitude for what you have done. In Jesus's name, amen."

A contented silence filled Dylan's soul as he reentered the car and snuggled into the back seat. Margot planted a kiss on his cheek and laid her head on his shoulder.

Out the windows, occasional meteors streaked the sky. The moon shone a bloody crimson. Sporadic aftershocks rocked the van.

But for the first time in months, he was content, and sleep came quickly.

* * *

When the sun rose again, its light, filtered as through holes in a black veil, allowed René to drive on. Several times, he screeched to a stop before yawning cracks in the road.

For half the day, they traveled like this—peering ahead, alert for danger, creeping along under a dim sky illuminated by falling meteors.

Then the worst happened.

The road sloped down, and though René was only traveling at twenty-five kilometers an hour, a dark abyss opened in the road ahead, coming up fast.

He hit the brakes, but the front wheels slid, failed to grip, and slipped over the edge. Danielle struck her head on the windshield and slumped down.

"Danielle!" shouted Victor. "Are you all right?"

She didn't answer. He grabbed her and began fumbling with her seat belt.

The van rocked back and forth as though on a fulcrum between the front and back seats. When the vehicle rocked forward, a dark abyss yawned through the windshield.

"No one move!" cried René. "Those in front need to get out first."

Dylan had rarely heard such fear in René's voice. "Or the weight will take us over the edge."

René opened the driver's side door, but below him was only empty space. He shut the door. "We'll have to climb out the back. Ready, Victor?"

"No. She's out cold, and I can't get her belt."

"Do what you can. We have to shift the weight to the back." René crawled over the seat into Pasqual's and Margot's lap. Both Pasqual and Dylan opened their doors.

The van shifted back and seemed to settle.

"Don't anyone get out yet," said René. "Okay, Victor, now you."

"No! I got the belt, but she's unconscious."

"Pass her over to me. We'll pull her back."

Victor raised her limp arms over his head, trying to get them to Pasqual's and René's open hands.

Beneath them, metal ground over a lip of concrete, and the van slid. It teetered toward the chasm. The black, ragged walls of the abyss loomed below.

Dylan scrambled over his seat to the back row. He shifted his weight enough so the van tipped away from the edge.

Pasqual and René grabbed Danielle's arms and pulled her into the back seat. The van settled back further.

"Margot, get out first," said René. "Then go to the back, open the hatch, and sit on the tailgate. Then, Dylan, take her place."

She stepped out, ran to the back, and opened the hatch.

"Pasqual, get out and join her."

He, too, left the van and went to the rear.

"Now you, Dylan."

Dylan followed. With three sitting on the tailgate, the van seemed to stabilize.

But when Victor and René pulled Danielle onto the pavement, the earth shook, and the vehicle again began to slide. Metal ground over concrete.

"It's going!" cried Pasqual. "Get out!"

Dylan reached behind him, grabbed two backpacks, and leaped off the tailgate. The van tipped forward. The back wheels hit the lip of the crevasse. Then the vehicle plummeted into the abyss, bounced once off the walls, and crashed at the bottom.

It took another day and a night to walk to Lustenau, Switzerland, where they commandeered an abandoned Opal van. From there, it was a short ride back to the Appenzell Alps.

But as they reentered the ski house, nothing seemed the same. Margot was back, but the world they'd known was gone.

Cracks had appeared in the walls. The sun burned dimly through black cloth. The moon shed a crimson light on the mountain slopes. And meteors flashed across the sky.

CHAPTER 22

THE RIOT

Jerusalem, Israel – December, Year 4

The crowd was a storm, and the angry murmurs rising from its midst were gusts before a gale.

With David Benjamin beside him, Baruch Abramovich hurried through the Old City. Ahead and behind poured Jews of all kinds—Ashkenazi Jews, Sephardi Jews, Mizrahi Jews, Beta Israel Jews, Cochin Jews, Bene Israel Jews, and Karaite Jews. "Temple Mount" and "blasphemy" were the words on their lips.

Above, the sun filtered through a black gauze, casting dim light on the cobbled streets. An occasional meteor streaked across the sky, briefly banishing the shadows.

Baruch knew the Bible and the events it prophesied. Still, whenever he glanced toward the heavens, he shuddered. Nothing was the same anymore, not even the sky. And now, the Jews of the city were in an uproar, and he didn't know why.

They passed one of the collection centers for cell phones that were cropping up all over the city. Soon, everyone would have to turn in their old phones for the new, trackable solar phones. The Unitum Imperium's grip on the populace was tightening. He hurried on.

They turned a corner and passed an old man in rags selling pita bread. The scars of the bubonic plague marred his face—one of those who'd recovered. "Laffa for sale," he cried. "Baked only this morning. Baked in a taboon. Laffa for sale." But his price was so dear, how did he expect anyone to buy it? Flour had so risen in price, the man had probably put everything he owned into his enterprise. Baruch doubted that he owned a taboon oven. And he probably paid someone to use it.

"Wait a second." He laid a hand on David's arm and doubled back. "How much for one pita?"

"Eighty shekels." When the man grinned, he was missing a front tooth.

Baruch fished out a hundred-shekel note, dropped it into the man's wicker basket, and took a slice of bread.

As he and David resumed their way, David told him he'd paid too much.

Baruch munched on the pita, passed some to David, and nodded. "Yes, I did."

When they climbed the steps to Temple Mount, the square was packed. From the crowd came raised fists and angry shouts of "blasphemy" and "traitor". Filling the front, where the Imperator often erected his dais and made announcements, were over a hundred green-and-white uniformed soldiers of the CSA. Each held a submachine gun.

"Whatever Davato's done," said David, "he's poked a stick in a hornet's nest."

Baruch touched the shoulder of a Hasidic Jew wearing a long black coat, black hat, and gartel belt with tassels swaying. "Shalom, my friend. What is this trouble about?"

"Don't you know?" He waved a fist toward the front. "They've taken over the Temple and won't allow anyone inside. For reconstruction purposes, they say. We don't believe him."

Nodding, Baruch let the man join other Hasidic Jews as they shouted their protests.

"This isn't good," said David. "What are they up to?"

"I don't know, but Davato has created a firestorm. Look there." Baruch pointed to a CSA officer holding a bullhorn, moving in front of the other guards.

"You must disperse and leave the square at once!" came his amplified voice. "Or we will be forced to clear the area."

In response, the crowd began chanting. "Open the doors! Open the Temple! Open the doors! Open the Temple!"

Twice more, the CSA officer repeated his warning, but the crowd wouldn't move and continued their chant.

The mass of Jews surged, and a handful climbed the steps with a banner that read, "Blasphemy!" Down the way, two more climbed with a banner reading, "Open the Temple!"

Shots rang out, people screamed, and movement, like a wind driving a troubled sea, swept the horde. The CSA army stepped to the edge of the stairs, aimed, and fired at the banner carriers.

Baruch grabbed David's elbow, and they spun away from the crowd, away from the square. As they raced down the staircase leading back to the Old City, the rat-a-tat-tat of machine guns filled the air, fighting with the screams and shouts of Jews trying to escape.

Only when they had found seats in their favorite café, one of the few establishments still open, did Baruch slow his breathing.

David drew a hand through hair wet with sweat. "That was insane. Closing the Temple? What did Davato think was going to happen?"

"I don't know, but something like this wasn't supposed to happen until next month. He's up to something, and it doesn't bode well for Israel."

"What's going to happen?"

Baruch brushed off the question and leaned forward. "We must prepare for the flight to the Refuge."

"We're leaving?"

"Yes, David. You and I and everyone who believes in Jesus our Lord."

CHAPTER 23

SHARING

Matthew 24:23–24, 27 (NLT): "Then if anyone tells you, 'Look, here is the Messiah,' or 'There he is,' don't believe it. For false messiahs and false prophets will rise up and perform great signs and wonders so as to deceive, if possible, even God's chosen ones. . . . For as the lightning flashes in the east and shines to the west, so it will be when the Son of Man comes."

Redwood Falls, Minnesota – December, Year 4

As Damon preached his Sunday service, he paced back and forth, and his feet echoed in the barn's open space.

Caleb shifted in his chair. As usual, Damon's sermon dwelt on sharing, and too often, a glance of accusation fell on the newcomers from the North Shore. Each Sunday, the Villagers met in an equipment barn across the highway. It was the same corrugated metal hut where they kept the community stores under twenty-four-hour guard in a room Farmer Davis once used for an office. They'd cleared the main floor, brought in folding chairs, a wood-burning stove, and turned it into a church. Four candelabra on waist-high stands provided a weak, flickering light.

"What's mine is yours, and what's yours is mine—Is that not what the Bible says?" Damon stopped pacing and faced his flock. "Is that not why we founded this place? On V-Day, you were all left behind. You were lost, going your own way in dreadful sin. You weren't part of a godly community. You were headed for oblivion. But didn't I save you and bring you here? Didn't I lead you out of the darkness into the light, to await the day of the second Rapture?"

"What's he saying?" whispered Tanya in Caleb's ear. "What's this about another Rapture?"

Caleb put a finger to his lips.

"Didn't I prophesy the quake that hit us last month?" Damon continued pacing. "The dark sun, the blood-red moon, and the meteors?"

Heads nodded, and a few amens came from a man in back.

"Yes, and that is only a harbinger of worse to come. And only those who follow me, who give their loyalty and obedience to me, will enter heaven when Christ comes again. Without me, you will perish." He splayed his fingers and stretched out his hand. "You will perish like this—"

Flames appeared out of thin air, burning from an invisible wick only six inches from his open hand.

The Villagers gasped. The women slapped hands over mouths. Wide-eyed, the men gawked.

Brianna sat open-mouthed. Then she leaned toward Caleb and whispered, "Is he a holy man?"

Beside Caleb, Andy sat rigid.

"Yes, my friends." Damon clapped his hands, and the fire ended in a puff of smoke. "You need me. We need each other. And all of us need to share our earthly possessions with each other, which is the Village, in order to survive the trials ahead."

It went on like that. And when they were dismissed and the group walked across the empty, snow-covered highway into the cul-de-sac claimed by the Village, Tanya whispered in Caleb's ear. "That was scary."

"Yes. And have you noticed, none of these people ever carry a Bible? Has Damon ever once preached from it? And how many times have you heard him mention the name of Jesus?"

Ahead of them walked Damon, burly Frank, and thin-faced Bradley—the Village "elders". As the elders veered off to Damon's house, Caleb, Andy, Tanya, and Brianna entered the MacPherson place that had been their home these last two months.

Above, the sun struggled through a patchwork web of dark cloth while random meteors streaked the sky. Now every time Caleb looked up, he shuddered.

As they mounted the steps, Andy turned to him. "We need to talk."

Caleb shot a glance down the street to Damon's house. "Yes, we need to talk."

* * *

In the living room, Tanya sat in the rocking chair, Andy took the threadbare couch, and Brianna settled on the floor beside Nika. Caleb stood before the others. "Damon is a false prophet. He's dangerous. And these people aren't what they first appeared to be."

"I agree." Andy slapped his knee. "That parlor trick had them all fooled, but for me, that was the last straw."

Brianna gave him a surprised look. "How did he make that fire if he wasn't a man of God?"

"Don't believe it. And there's more you need to hear about that man." Tanya's brows furrowed. "Twice in the last week, he's caught me alone. Both times his eyes were . . . full of lust. I was . . . uncomfortable."

"But he seems like such a nice man." The disappointment in Brianna's voice made Caleb want to hug and comfort her, and if not for his anger at the Village's betrayal, he would have crossed the room and done just that.

"He's the worst kind of charlatan, child. Today proved that." Andy shook his head and softened his voice. "Don't fall for his tricks."

She only raised a puzzled glance.

"When we first got here," said Tanya, "everyone seemed so nice, so caring. But that's all changed."

"I need to tell you what happened last night." Andy dropped his gaze to the floor's worn-out linoleum. "Did you know Frank and Bradley have been living in the barn, guarding the storehouse, and they always carry rifles? Anyway, yesterday evening, I went to look in on the horses, and Frank stopped me. He said the horses now belonged to the community, and he wouldn't let me see them."

"He wouldn't?" Caleb crossed his arms.

"I would have mentioned it last night, but you'd all gone to bed."

"What are we going to do?" Tanya rubbed her temples.

He slammed a fist into a palm. "We're leaving."

"And go where?" whispered Brianna. "There's six inches of snow on the ground."

"I found a map." Caleb waved toward the window. "Only fifty miles south of here, there's a town with a big lake and a state park. That's one or two days away with the horses. The park has a group cabin. According to some literature I unearthed in the closet, it's away from everyone. Might be perfect for us. Then we can hunker down until spring."

"But first," said Andy, "we need to get our stuff back."

"I agree. So we'll confront the elders." Caleb grinned. "Now!"

"Right. I'll get my rifle." Andy climbed the stairs to the bedrooms.

Caleb went to the downstairs closet where he kept the AR-15 and M16. Since the quake, he had to yank on the door to open it, but when he did—no rifles. He reached to the shelf above and groped for his two Glock pistols in their holsters—nothing. Even his ammunition boxes were gone. He whirled, looked to Tanya, and opened his hands in a question.

"Don't look at me," she said. "I don't know where they went."

Andy's feet pounded down the stairs. "It's gone!" He paused and faced the others. "My rifle and all its ammo—gone."

"Mine too."

"They took them!" Andy smacked a palm with a fist. "When we were in church this morning, someone—it was Frank!—came in here and took them. He came in late, didn't he?"

"Okay, this isn't good," said Brianna.

"It isn't, and we should've seen it coming." Caleb paced the floor.

"On second thought, it's probably better we don't show up at Damon's meeting with guns. But we need to confront him—now!" He headed for the front closet and his coat. "Even if they're in their so-called elders meeting."

* * *

It must have been noon as Caleb's and Andy's feet crunched over the snow-covered walk under a sky dimmed by perpetual twilight. At Damon's house, Caleb marched up the steps onto the porch.

Bundled in a heavy parka and stocking cap, freckle-faced Heather rose from a chair. "They're having a meeting. You can't disturb them."

He paused, held her gaze, then walked around her, and entered the house.

"You can't go in there!" she called from the porch.

Damon held his meetings in the dining room behind double glass doors. Caleb strode down the hall and pushed through. Inside, Damon, Frank, and Bradley sat at a long oak table.

"Caleb, this is a private meeting." Damon frowned at the interruption.

"We are leaving, and we want our stuff back—all our weapons, supplies, horses, and the wagon we brought."

Dead silence fell around them as Frank's and Bradley's startled glances met Damon's.

"That will not be possible." Damon sat back and laced his fingers on the tabletop. "The items you mentioned now belong to the Village. That was part of the arrangement when you joined us."

"We never agreed to that!" Arms crossed, Andy stepped from behind.

"Whether you agreed or not, those are our rules," said Bradley, his voice high.

"Everyone in the Village shares everything." Damon stood, pushed in the chair, and gripped the back of the seat where he'd just sat, his long blond hair falling around his shoulders. "That's what makes us strong. We follow Acts 2:44, which says: 'And all the believers met together in one place and shared everything they had.' "

Caleb sucked in air. "You have misinterpreted that passage. It's not talking about Communism. Those early Christians shared what they had out of their own free will, not because they were forced to. They did it out of love for what Christ had done for them. And later on, folks still had possessions to give to the church."

"Damon is our leader." His back to them, Frank turned his considerable bulk toward the intruders. "And he, not you, interprets the Bible. Whatever Damon says, goes."

"No one ever leaves the Village, Caleb." Smiling, Damon lowered his voice. "I thought you understood that."

"We understood none of that." Caleb narrowed his eyes. "We're leaving, and we want our stuff back."

"What are you going to do? Leave with the clothes on your backs?" His smile fading, Damon leaned forward. "Without weapons or supplies, you wouldn't last a day. Not only will you stay, but you will begin sharing what, to date, you have failed to share with the rest of us."

"And what might that be?" asked Andy.

"Tanya and Brianna." Bradley grinned.

Caleb gasped. To that, he was speechless. He shot a glance to Andy standing beside him with mouth open. Tanya's remark now made sense. The Village was into free sex and wife swapping, and Damon was using the Bible to justify it.

"This was actually one of today's agenda items." Damon pulled out the chair and sat. "Thank you for helping us resolve it. You may now leave."

Andy grabbed Caleb's shoulder and whispered. "Come with me."

Back in the MacPherson house, the men told the women what the "elders" had said.

"Not going to happen." Tanya leaped off her chair. "If they try to 'share' me—well, I wish we had our guns back."

"Share me?" Brianna's jaw hardened. "I'd put a bullet in the first man who tries it. If I had a gun, that is."

"Everyone, wait here." Andy ran up the staircase to the second floor. Moments later, a smiling Andy reappeared with a Ruger GP100 revolver in each hand, guns he'd taken from a Scheels they'd raided on the trek south. "I stuffed these under my mattress."

"You sneaky dog." Caleb took one pistol as Andy pulled boxes of ammunition from his pockets. From his belt, Andy also pulled out a one-foot Bowie knife with a serrated edge.

"All right." Caleb hefted the pistol. "Now we can take back our stuff. But tonight. When everyone is asleep."

CHAPTER 24

DEPARTURE

Redwood Falls, Minnesota – December, Year 4

Under a crimson moon and a dark starless sky, the travelers from the north, bundled in winter coats, stocking caps, and boots, crept out of the MacPherson house. The temperature had dropped, and the snow crunched loud, too loud, under their feet as the group followed Caleb down the walk. Each carried a backpack filled with clothing, food, and supplies. Brianna led Nika by her leash. Though it was only an hour or two after dusk, the candles and oil lamps in the windows along the cul-de-sac were out. Dim as the days had become, folks now lived by what passed for sunrise and sunset.

Tiny balls of light sped occasionally across the sky, illuminating the snow with their glowing, sparkling trails.

Where the sidewalk ended at the highway, Caleb faced the women. "Wait out of sight behind that billboard. When we signal, come help us load the wagon. But it could be a while."

"What if you don't overpower them?" asked Brianna. "Frank is a big guy."

"I served in the marines." Andy grinned, patted the knife at his belt, and waved his Ruger. "We'll take them."

The men followed the trampled snow across the highway. A single set of footprints led around the side of the building, and they followed. They passed their wagon, now laden with six inches of snow in the bed. When they reached the back door, Caleb tried the knob. But as he suspected, it was locked. Tracks led to an outhouse thirty feet away.

"They were drinking beer when I was here last night," said Andy. "Sooner or later someone will need to use the latrine."

Since neither had a functioning watch—the batteries had run out long ago—they waited behind the door, stomping their feet to keep warm.

Then the door opened, and Bradley—the least imposing of the two—headed toward the privy. But he hadn't taken two steps when, with bowie knife in hand, Andy leaped from behind, gripped a hand across Bradley's forehead, and laid a serrated blade against Bradley's throat. "One loud word and you'll be bleeding out your jugular, unconscious in five minutes, dead in ten. I was a marine, and if you don't think I can do it, think again."

"W–what—?"

Caleb waved his Ruger in Bradley's face before holstering it. "So don't try anything." He checked Bradley for weapons and found none.

"Now listen carefully," said Andy. "We're going back inside. Where will Frank be?"

"By the easy chair near the storeroom." Bradley's eyes were wild.

"Which way is he facing?"

"Toward the street."

Caleb caught Andy's worried glance. To get to that location, they'd have to cross thirty yards of concrete. Their footsteps would echo all the way.

"We will all walk toward him," said Andy. "You will act as if nothing is out of the ordinary. Right?"

Bradley nodded.

"Then let's go."

"B–but I have to use the outhouse. I really do."

Andy gave Caleb a look of frustration.

"Will you be a good boy," asked Caleb, "and not try any funny business?"

"Yes."

Caleb shrugged. "Let him go."

They walked him to the outhouse, let him do his business with the door open, then marched him back. Bradley opened the door, all three entered, and they began to cross. Now both Andy and Caleb held their Rugers.

Frank's back was to them. Raising a mug, he shouted without turning. "Do we have any more of this hooch?"

Andy nudged his prisoner with an elbow and whispered. "Answer him."

"I'll get it for you," said Bradley.

"Great!" But that was when Frank turned around. "What the—?" He leaped from his chair and raced toward a rifle leaning by the street door.

"Don't!" shouted Andy. "We've got two Ruger .357 magnum revolvers pointed at you."

But Frank kept going.

Andy gripped the weapon with both hands, aimed, and fired. The shot boomed and echoed through the building. It missed Frank but punched a jagged hole in the corrugated metal wall. Frank slowed then stopped.

"It's not worth it, my friend." Andy raced toward Frank as Caleb pushed the barrel of his weapon hard into the small of Bradley's back.

Andy reached Frank. "Down on your knees."

Frank obeyed, and Andy pulled out a zip tie. He tied Frank's hands behind his back, and they did the same for Bradley. Then they gagged their prisoners and zip-tied their calves to chair legs.

"There." Andy stood back, grinning. "You should both be right comfy now, fixed to your easy chairs. If you try to get out, you'll fall flat on your faces. Sorry we have nothing for you to watch on that dead TV over there. But you should be just peachy till morning."

Bradley made muffled sounds through his gag, his eyes wild, but Frank only glared.

Caleb unlocked the front door and called out to the women. They hurried across the highway into the barn.

"It's cold out there." Brianna stamped her feet and hugged her chest.

"I'll bring the wagon inside and start loading it," said Andy. "But we'll have to clear off the snow first." Tanya joined Andy and headed for the front exit.

"We'll get the horses." With Brianna and Nika following, Caleb went to a door on the building's north side. Opening it led to a second, smaller shed holding the Village's six cows. Caleb opened the stall doors where the Village had stabled the four horses.

They whinnied and shook their heads under Brianna's touch. "Glad to see me, aren't you, girls?"

Back in the main room, they opened the big double doors Farmer Davis used for access to his tractor, cultivator, and combine. Cold air washed in until they had the wagon inside and closed the doors.

They brought out everything from the storeroom that belonged to them, including food to replace what the Village had consumed.

When the wagon was loaded and covered with a tarp, they hooked two horses to the neck yokes, saddled the other two, and again opened the big doors. Tanya lashed the reins and drove the rig outside. Beside her, Brianna snuggled under a blanket with Nika. Andy followed on his mount.

Before leaving, Caleb threw more wood into the stove then removed the gags from Frank's and Bradley's mouths. "Shout all you want now," he said. "They can't hear you with the doors shut, and we'll be long gone before anyone's awake."

Back outside, he mounted, and the group started out.

The axles creaked. The wheels ground over the frozen snow. In a cacophonous symphony, the horses' hooves broke through the white crust, and the wagon headed south.

The road was a ridge of white, a raised bump in an endless snowfield, broken with fewer weed stalks than the surrounding fields. A meteor, brighter than the ones before it, raced above, showering light on the way ahead.

They would travel until they were well away from the Village. Then they would find an abandoned house to sleep in until what passed for a sun brought the dim light of day.

It would take two or three days to get to Shetek State Park.

CHAPTER 25
THE GIANT

Revelation 13:15 (HCSB): He was permitted to give a spirit to the image of the beast, so that the image of the beast could both speak and cause whoever would not worship the image of the beast to be killed.

New Babylon, Iraq – December, Year 4

All day, the offices on the top floors of the World Casino were abuzz with rumors about the approaching event. A glance at the calendar told Chelsea it was Christmas Eve, but no one had mentioned it to her. Indeed, the very word *Christmas* had been purged from the Unitum Imperium lexicon.

When the time came, she accompanied her father, Davato, the Prophet, the ambassadors, Grady, and the rest of the core staff. They entered buses that dropped them off at the central park.

Davato then led them past acres of newly greening grass and recently empty fountains where water now poured from the mouths of naked statue women. All around them, people were converging on the center, and the air throbbed with conversation.

Floodlights on the perimeter overshadowed the blood-red moon above. An occasional meteor burned a trail across the heavens.

She followed Davato's close personal staff to a platform beneath a central structure now covered with a mammoth shroud of opaque plastic. Workmen had been building it for months, and recently, no one had been allowed near the park. They waited in the square as folks arrived by foot, bicycle, and bus. Chelsea looked back and up. The thing towered ten stories above her.

A half hour later, when people had crowded every empty space, Davato gave the word to proceed, and the Prophet walked to the mike. "We are gathered here today to unveil the Giant." He waved to the massive structure behind them. "It is the world's tallest moving statue. Back in 2021, the Giant Company began constructing these statues in twenty-one cities. For years, they used it commercially, for advertising and to promote green energy. But two years ago, the Unitum Imperium bought the company, and I"—he chuckled—"I made some modifications. Since then, we have erected statues in every major city and province of the world. People of New Babylon, you are the first to see it in action. I give you the Giant."

He lifted a control device and pushed a button, and the plastic shroud floated down. It revealed a mammoth statue of a man whose features bore a striking resemblance to Davato himself.

Oohs and aahs, gasps and claps, arose from the crowd, and Chelsea's breath stopped in her throat. Tens of thousands of tiny silver plates covered its surface. As workmen gathered up the plastic and hauled it away, Davato stepped off the podium and entered a door at the base.

"It's magnificent, isn't it?" The Prophet stared up and beamed. "But now watch."

He pressed a button, and the whole thing lit up. As if by magic, black dress pants, a white shirt and tie, and a suit jacket clad the body—the same clothes Davato was wearing today. Far above, the Imperator's face appeared on the head. The head turned, strands of silver hair fell over one eye, and the Giant peered down on the gathering.

"Yes, my friends, it is I." The voice that boomed and echoed over the crowd like thunder was Davato's. A shuddering began in Chelsea's shoulders and crept down her back. "This is how I will now address the world."

Around her came gasps of—shock? surprise? admiration?

It moved its arms, and the Giant pointed directly down at those on the podium.

"Welcome, Sebastien Rey, Adam and Chelsea Turner, and my other guests." It pointed toward the huge crowd gathered on the grass beyond. Its voice thundered, shaking even the podium. "Welcome, everyone, to this first unveiling. With the flip of a switch, the Prophet can connect any one statue with every other, simultaneously, wherever they are in the world. Thanks to his ministrations, I now have a medium worthy of broadcasting my words to the world."

A clapping began near the podium. It spread until the vast assembly of New Babylonians—filling the park and spilling out into the streets a half kilometer away—clapped and shouted its approval. It went on and on until Davato spoke again. "But the best is yet to come. When we return to Israel, we will make our premier to the world from Temple Mount. At that time, I will announce that the old religion is passing away and a new one is coming, one that everyone will embrace. Then you must choose whom you will follow: your Imperator. Or the enemy."

The statue bowed and leaned out from the waist, and Chelsea was stunned. How could it move like that? How could it look and speak just like Davato? It *was* Davato—but he had become a giant. The shivering began again, and she wrapped her arms about her chest until it stopped. Was he erecting a similar statue in Temple Square? That would surely send the Jews into full revolt. She'd heard about a riot happening back in Jerusalem. Was that what caused it?

The statue bid them good night. Then it went dark, its arms returned to its side, and its head returned to its resting position. Moments later, Davato appeared from the base.

They were ushered back to the buses, but Chelsea declined and walked instead. She hadn't gone far when Grady appeared beside her.

"That was surreal," he whispered.

"Beyond surreal," she whispered back.

"I saw a news clip about the Giant a few years ago. But now the Prophet has improved the technology. The effect Davato will have by delivering messages from that machine will be overwhelming. They'll think he's a god."

"Yes." She shivered again. "A god."

But a new thought crept from the back of her mind, and she shivered again. What had Davato meant when he said, "You must choose whom you will follow?" Was he talking about the mark of the beast?

With every fiber of her being, she feared to make that choice!

If she rejected it, she would starve.

But if she accepted it . . . she'd be damned for all eternity.

CHAPTER 26

THE GROUP CAMP

Shetek State Park, Minnesota – December, Year 4

During the trek from Redwood Falls, their constant companions were the grinding of wagon wheels and the clopping of horses' hooves breaking through the frozen crust. By day, a dark sun shed a weak illumination through holes in a black screen. By night, a crimson moon and a starless sky gave barely enough light to see by.

On the first night, they ventured into one of the dark houses beside the road where no tracks led from any door and no light shone from inside. The vanishing took more folks from this part of the country than any other, and everywhere, houses stood empty. They broke in through a back door window, explored the dusty, abandoned interior, and found beds and couches to sleep in. They put the horses in the garage.

The next morning, their route led them west on Route 19 over an unbroken ridge of snow before bending south. When they passed through the village of Vesta, a handful of snow tracks testified to a few residents, but no one emerged to greet them. To avoid Walnut Grove, they headed south on County Road 11 and passed through the town of Tracy, where it was the same—tracks in the snow, but no greeters.

On the evening of the second day, Christmas Eve, they followed signs pointing to the park. They rode several miles over old tracks until they entered the park, following signs leading to the Zuya group camp. There Caleb was pleasantly surprised to find the dining hall fitted with a stone fireplace on one end and a cast-iron, wood-burning stove at the other. With the frequent, intermittent electricity outages after the state converted its electrical grid to green energy, someone had installed a reliable heat source. It had served as the dining hall, and ten tables for eight occupied the interior. But they only needed one. They could move the rest outside and bring in four beds and mattresses from one of the nearby cabins.

And if they removed the bunk beds from a group cabin, that one could become a stable.

No one had been here for years, and mice scurried across a dusty floor into a corner hole. Cobwebs hung over the windowpanes, in the corners, and from the ceiling.

"We can make it livable," said Tanya, stamping her feet to shake off the snow. "And it's Christmas Eve. I'll make some soup with the rabbits Andy shot today and fry some flatbread with sugar for dessert."

"But it's so cold." Brianna shivered.

Beside her, Nika shook her fur and sniffed the mouse tracks.

"I'll start a fire." Caleb went back outside to gather kindling and logs from what remained beside the cabin.

By sunset, the women had cleaned the place, the men had moved tables outside, brought in beds, and emptied the cabin next door, turning it into a stable. They'd also cooked their first hot meal since Redwood Falls. With the stove and the fireplace both burning, they'd warmed the interior enough to remove jackets and stocking caps. Now they sat huddled around a red-hot stove.

"We can't go further this winter." Caleb raised open palms toward the heat. "This will have to do until spring. Here, we've got a decent house, fuel, water, and possibly game. Except for some tracks, we didn't see anyone else using the park. It's as good a place as any."

"I'm guessing"—Andy raised a mug of beer he'd filled from one of the Village's barrels—"that with the little sun we've got, it's going to get a lot colder."

"I thought of that." Caleb scratched his beard. "We'll have to cut more wood—a lot more—to keep this place warm. It seems well insulated. We'll also need feed for the horses. But we can do this."

"But what are we going to do for fun?" Brianna raised an impish grin.

"We'll make some games, and I brought a deck of cards." Tanya laid a hand on Brianna's arm. "We'll make do."

"At least we escaped the Village people." Andy sat back, and the bench creaked. "We got most of our stuff back. And we—"

A knock on the door stopped him, and everyone whipped their heads toward the front.

"Who's there?" Caleb shot to his feet and reached for the rifle he'd laid against the wall.

"We saw your tracks," came a deep, muffled voice. "And the smoke. Can we come in?"

Andy grabbed a Ruger and nodded. Caleb opened the door and stepped back.

A man in a deerskin hide jacket with a fox-fur hat held a shotgun, and Caleb tensed. The woman behind him held a revolver.

Dressed the same as the man, the red-haired woman smiled. "We mean no trouble here," she said. "We're just comin' to welcome you folks to Currie."

"You don't look like the kind of thieves and ruffians we had a while back," added the man. "We'll set our shooters aside if you will."

Caleb examined the two then pointed his rifle at the ground. He nodded to Andy who shoved the Ruger into his belt.

The man set his shotgun against the outside wall, and the woman holstered her revolver.

Caleb released the breath he was holding. "Then welcome and come in." He waved the two inside.

They entered, breathing frosty plumes and stamping their feet by the entrance to free their boots of snow.

"My name's Jack Manson, and this here's Linda May." His glance swept the four, and a smile broke a bushy brown beard. "Linda May used to live in Georgia. Nowadays, that's a mighty fur piece from here."

Caleb introduced everyone and invited the visitors to warm themselves by the fire.

Andy asked if anyone wanted a beer, and Jack's face lit up. He agreed, and so did Linda May.

After everyone had mugs in hand, Linda May, her eyes bright, settled into one of the empty chairs. "Where have you folks come from in such bitter weather?"

"We left the North Shore after fires destroyed the forest. Then we stayed the last months in Redwood Falls, but—"

Jack and Linda May exchanged looks.

"But it didn't work out. The people there are—"

"Yeah, we know about the Village." Jack narrowed his eyes. "So they weren't your cup of tea, hey?"

"You could say that." Andy's voice was low. "We barely escaped."

"All of us here in Currie have come late to Christ," said Linda May. "We got some who had weekend houses on the lake and were living here when V-Day hit. And we got a few old-time Currie residents. But we aren't some kind of cult, makin' folks do things that ain't in the Bible like up in Redwood Falls. Have no worries 'bout that."

"Thank you for saying that." Tanya shuddered. "Their men wanted to 'share' me and Brianna among themselves."

"Yeah." Jack leaned toward the stove. "That's what we heard. But we aren't like that. We got a sort of church goin' down the road. 'Least, that's what we're callin' it. And if you folks are Christians—you are Christians, aren't you? With what's been happenin', most around here now believe we're livin' through Bible prophecy."

"Yes!" Brianna gave a fist pump, surprising Caleb with the force of her interjection.

Her answer warming his heart, Caleb clapped a hand on her shoulder. "Yes, we are."

"Good!" Linda May's smile was broad. "Then y'all are invited to our potluck next Sunday after church. If you don't have much to bring, bein' as y'all just arrived, that's okay."

"Since you're our new neighbors and Christians," added Jack, "we'd sure like you folks to come. Currie's just down the road. We meet at the old American Legion post on Mill Street. Come to church, too, if you can. 'Bout an hour or more earlier."

"Thanks for the offer," said Caleb. "We'll think about it."

"If y'all come," added Linda May, "we'll give you some barley from our greenhouse. We've got plenty."

They exchanged more pleasantries. The visitors thanked their hosts for the hospitality then left.

"What do you think?" asked Andy when they were alone again. "We could replenish our supplies."

"Let's give them a chance," added Tanya.

"Yeah," said Brianna. "Give them a chance."

"Okay," said Caleb. "Maybe this Sunday or next."

THE FORTY-THIRD THROUGH THE FORTY-EIGHTH MONTHS

—

THE MIDPOINT AND BEYOND

CHAPTER 27

CHELSEA

Jerusalem, Israel — New Year's Eve, Year 4

I am lost and alone in a world gone mad, and I don't know what to do.

I stand here at my window in the Clal Center, listening to the hum of the air conditioning, the whine of the electric guitars, the throb of the bass and drums from the nearby clubs. It's New Year's Eve, a time of wild revelry, but all for what? Two hours before midnight, and the music has been going since seven. It vibrates the windows, and tonight, they'll play until dawn—from vast halls filled with obscene dancing and drunk people desperate to forget, even for a few moments, that the world is ending. They keep grasping and reaching, but never get what they really want.

Lately, there've been rumors of muggings, robberies, and random murders after dark. Lawlessness breeds lawlessness, and chaos breeds chaos.

Jerusalem never used to be like this. Davato must be proud of his work.

The world is ending. I can feel it in the air, the sky, the people around me. Everyone knows it, deep in their hearts, that it's ending, but they resist, they refuse to acknowledge what's coming. They're lost, falling into themselves like stones dropped into a dark well. They want it all, and they want it now—pleasure, power, influence, sex—anything to distract them from the destiny that awaits. But the distraction is a lie. I know because that's what I chose.

All but the sex. That I cannot do. Not right now.

Every decision I've ever made has been the wrong one, and I'm out of options. I was lured by false promises, wrapped in sugar and chocolate. They don't bring happiness. Not when they suck you into the place where I am now. They were seductive bait for a trap with iron teeth— sharp metal, jagged incisors—digging into my soul and never letting go. And now, it's too late.

Iron teeth dig deep, and one must endure a lot of pain to get out.

I guess I'm not as strong a person as I thought.

But soon, I fear, I will have to get out, forced to do something rash and dangerous. That's the only recourse left to me now. Yet . . . no one ever gets out, do they? They track you down and bring you back. Then they send you to the shooting galleries or the colosseum or the death camp they're rebuilding at a furious pace, even bigger than before.

I am nursing a glass of white wine, thinking I'll switch to brandy, and I look out over the ancient city where Christ once walked, this man whom Dylan and Margot and Caleb—if Caleb is still alive—believe is the Son of God. But something has kept me from knowing and believing deep in my heart, the same as they.

What's wrong with me? Why do I not see what they do? Am I doomed?

Baruch almost had me convinced. Now I regret not going with him. Why didn't I accept his offer to escape this madness? Because I can't be-lieve—that's why.

A better person would be thinking about her brothers, about Margot and Baruch, but here I am, thinking only about me, lost in myself. Am I no better than the lost souls in the nightclubs?

We arrived late this evening from New Babylon, and everyone on the plane said something big is going to happen tomorrow. I sat next to Father and asked him what it was. But all he would say was that, at tomorrow noon, we will be ushered to the Temple where Davato and the Prophet will make an earthshaking announcement.

An earthshaking announcement.

In times such as these, for people such as me, that's bad news. Nowa-days, change is always for the worse.

Then Father's brows furrowed, he gripped my hands hard, too hard, and he told me I needed to get serious. He told me he loved me and cared what happened to me—and that, alone, shook me. He hardly ever says anything like that. He is, after all, the head of Davato's Ministry of Truth. Inside, he's always been a hard man.

One way or another, he told me I needed to make a decision. The CSA has a list, he said, and I was on it. That shook me even more. Tomorrow, he said, I either give myself—heart, mind, and soul—to Davato. Or face the consequences.

I'm ten feet under, too long underwater, and if I take a breath, my lungs will fill with water. I have barely the strength to kick to the surface.

Tomorrow, he said—that's a night and a morning away.

Sometimes, I think drowning is the easy way out. Just give in and let it happen. Become like the rest. Stop resisting the inevitable.

When I left the plane, shaking and nauseous, I wanted to run, far, far away. But where to?

With the CSA on my tail, what chance would I have? Where would I go? And with whom? I fear to go it alone. They have their ways, you know? Ways beyond their trackable phones. Every transport ticket has the passenger's name, identity number, and destination. The CSA is relentless in their pursuit. It becomes their life's goal—to find their targets, arrest them, torture them, kill them. It doesn't matter in what order. And they enjoy it. They're witless ciphers, steeped in the mindless righteousness of their cause, doing the bidding of their Imperator. I guess that's what happens when totalitarianism takes over your soul.

Dylan says that Davato is the Antichrist.

I know him as the monster he is, and now, I'm thinking Dylan was right. And there—I've said it. And because that's how I think, I'm doomed. I might as well pin a sign to my chest.

If I ran, Davato would never rest until he saw me captured, chained, beaten, and publicly executed.

The end is coming. It's in the mottled sun shining dimly above, in the random meteors streaking across the sky, and in every tortured soul groping through empty space for something solid to hang onto.

I am lost and alone in a world gone mad, and I don't know what to do.

CHAPTER 28

THE ABOMINATION OF DESOLATION

Daniel 9:27 (HCSB): "The ruler will make a treaty with the people for a period of one set of seven, but after half this time, he will put an end to the sacrifices and offerings. And as a climax to all his terrible deeds, he will set up a sacrilegious object that causes desecration. . . ."

Revelation 13:11a, 12a, 15–17 (HCSB): Then I saw another beast coming up out of the earth . . . He exercises all the authority of the first beast on his behalf. . . . He was permitted to give a spirit to the image of the beast, so that the image of the beast could both speak and cause whoever would not worship the image of the beast to be killed. And he requires everyone—small and great, rich and poor, free and slave—to be given a mark on his right hand or on his forehead, so that no one can buy or sell unless he has the mark: the beast's name or the number of his name.

Jerusalem, Israel – January 1, Year 4

The Clal Center buses braked with a hiss and emptied below the Iron Gate. Then everyone who worked for Davato, plus the upper echelon of the Unitum Imperium, those who happened to be in the city, were ushered up the steps leading to Temple Mount. It was New Year's Day, and the winds of change were ripping through the streets.

Davato and the Prophet had already gone up, and Chelsea walked beside Grady, who kept glancing her way with a questioning look. For weeks, she'd been avoiding him.

"Don't you like me, Chelsea?" he asked.

"Of course, I like you." She stared straight ahead. "You were my best friend in New Babylon."

"*Were*? But no longer?"

They'd climbed half the steps, and now they could hear the roar of the crowd up on the square. She'd heard there'd been some kind of riot, but it had been months since she'd been back to Jerusalem. Now the Jews were again gathering in protest. "No, it's not like that. It's just that I . . . I don't want to sleep with anyone right now. It's personal."

"You're playing with fire, girl." His voice deepened. "They're keeping track of who participates in the sharing time and who doesn't."

She came to a stop and pulled him aside. "What's happened to you, Grady? You've changed. You never used to talk like some die-hard member of the CSA. What happened to personal freedom? Can't a girl decide for herself whether share her body with someone or not?"

He narrowed his eyes. "You have to change with the times. You don't have a choice. And besides"—he smiled, leaned forward, and planted a kiss on her cheek—"I like you."

Touched by his gesture, she blushed. "Maybe, Grady. Maybe someday. But not right now."

"Come on. We're falling behind." He started back up the steps, and she followed.

At the top, torches lined the square's perimeter, shedding an eerie light on a day only dimly lit by a sun shrouded with black cloth. An occasional meteor lit the heavens.

The square was packed, and the crowd on the perimeter was in an uproar, shouting, gesturing, raising angry fists. Many of the men wore yarmulkes. A solid line of CSA guards with machine guns separated the Jews on the fringes from the non-Jews in the center. Whatever Davato was doing, even the previous deaths in the last riot couldn't quell the Jews' anger.

Through the center crowd, CSA soldiers forged a path so Davato and the Clal employees could pass. Large screens—blank and silent now— loomed above the Temple steps.

Davato sent a scowl at the protestors and motioned to Adam Turner, head of the Ministry of Truth, who bent an ear to what the Imperator had to say. Then Chelsea's father spoke with a CSA officer bearing epaulets on his shoulder. The officer hurried away to do his bidding.

Chelsea followed her coworkers through the milling throng, up the stairs, and—what was this?—into the Temple itself.

She gasped. No wonder the Jews were so upset. No Gentile was ever allowed inside the Temple, and now, today, Davato's entire entourage was going inside.

They climbed the steps through the Beautiful Gate and entered the Court of Women. More dark screens were mounted high on the far wall. The CSA led the privileged few through the East Gate into the Court of Israel, where, in the past, the Jewish men were supposed to gather. They continued past the animal-holding and skinning pens into the Court of Priests. Ahead should have been the Holy Place and the great Veil, behind which should have been the Holy of Holies.

But the walls were gone. So was the Veil. And the Holy Place was no more. Neither was the ceiling.

In its place stood a one-hundred-foot-tall structure shrouded in opaque plastic.

Chelsea slapped a hand over her mouth. "Oh no!"

"Are you thinking what I'm thinking?" Grady bent closer.

"No wonder the Jews are in an uproar."

"I hear they've been rioting off and on for the last month."

The CSA positioned her, the other Clal employees, and the high officials of the Unitum Imperium at the structure's base. Everyone waited as the space filled with new arrivals. The screens on both sides of the Holy Place now came to life, and cameras focused on the plastic shroud.

Minutes passed. Then the Prophet mounted a dais beneath the mammoth edifice and stepped to the microphone. "Welcome, one and all, to this most auspicious moment in world history. You have seen the awesome ability and power of our Imperator. How he single-handedly united the countries of Europe into the Unitum Imperium, making it the most powerful nation on earth. You have heard his oratory, his wisdom, and his magnificent vision. Well, today, you are privileged to witness how he has passed from the commonplace into unimaginable greatness. Yes, even into immortality and divinity itself. Ladies and gentlemen, I give you Davato, our divine Imperator."

Sebastien pressed some buttons. The plastic sheath fell away. And the giant statue of Davato beneath came alive, moved its head, smiled, and looked down on the dwarfed people below.

"Yes, my people, it is I." The voice boomed and echoed through the Temple, and Chelsea shuddered. "For this is how I will give future addresses to the world."

Just as in New Babylon, the crowd oohed and aahed. Others stood stunned, mouths agape.

From behind rose more shouts and complaints from the Jews in the square.

"From this day forward, I claim the Temple of Jerusalem as my own. I declare, here and now, that the treaty with the Jews is over, that the Jewish people stand in the way of greatness and have outlived their usefulness." He waved both arms, and Chelsea felt the breeze, even where she stood, ten stories below. "The Jews serve me no longer."

From the Jews in the square outside came a collective groan of agony and cries of "Traitor" and "Blasphemy".

"From now on, there will be no further sacrificing of bulls, goats, and chickens to the Enemy. It stops today. Neither will anyone worship Gaia, the goddess of the earth. She, too, has served her purpose. Instead, you will worship the deity most deserving of praise, honor, and glory—your Imperator!"

His last words shot like thunder through the crowd, nearly bursting Chelsea's ears. Then the statue did something no statue should ever have been able to do. It stepped away from its pedestal, reached down, and grabbed a block of stone weighing perhaps a ton. Bending to the side, it let the stone fall. It smashed onto the Temple floor behind and shattered.

Again, the statue faced the crowd.

"You've all seen the symbol of the Unitum Imperium, the six-sided hexagram with the letters of my name on the outside." The giant stepped back onto its pedestal, and as its feet slammed down, the ground shook. "From this day forward, everyone must accept that mark in the form of a tattoo on the right hand, or failing that, on the forehead. Henceforth, only those with the mark will be allowed to engage in any type of commerce. That includes the purchase or sale of food, housing, and transportation. Here in Jerusalem, my people are right now erecting tents in the square with tattoo artists at the ready. Yes, my friends. From this moment forward, you must worship and show allegiance only to your Imperator."

Still standing at the podium far below the giant, the Prophet spoke into the microphone. "Now, people, to whom will you bow down and worship?"

All around Chelsea, men and women fell to their knees, bowed their heads, or prostrated themselves on the stone. Fearful she'd stand out, but feeling as if she might be sick, she, too, bowed.

As the noise from the Jews outside grew to a crescendo, the people inside murmured, then shouted, praises to their Imperator.

"Now rise!" came the voice of the giant. "Rise and follow me to Temple Square to see a demonstration of the power I have bestowed on my Prophet. Afterward, the tattoo booths will be open. Then you must decide. Will you take the mark and live? Or will you refuse the mark and die?"

The pixels covering the giant darkened, and the life went out of it. Then the screens showed Davato in person beside the Prophet at the statue's base. A phalanx of CSA guards led the way, pushing a hole through the throng's center toward the East Gate.

But when Davato was even with Chelsea and Grady, he stopped, turned aside, and approached her. "One way or another, Chelsea Turner, you must decide. My people are watching."

His words stopped her heart, and she felt as though she might faint. Before she could muster a reply, he resumed his course toward the exit. CSA soldiers led the inner circle behind Davato through the Court of Women to the top of the Temple steps. With Chelsea behind, the Imperator stopped and waved to the people below.

A cheer sprang from the crowd. But from the protesting Jews came only silence. Rising onto her toes, Chelsea searched the square for the reason.

The center of the square was now filled with a dozen of the rioting Jews—perhaps their leaders? Their hands were tied, their mouths gagged.

Surrounding them were hundreds of machine-gun-toting CSA guards. As she scanned further, she saw other Jews at the far edges of the crowd. Something had pressed them into silence.

But standing on a center pedestal, also bound and gagged, was a vaguely familiar figure. Bruises covered his arms, and his face was puffy, bloodied, and discolored.

Then recognition dawned, and she drew a deep, rattling breath.

It was Lazzaro.

CHAPTER 29
SIGNS AND WONDERS

Revelation 13:11–12a, 13 (HCSB): Then I saw another beast coming up out of the earth; he had two horns like a lamb, but he sounded like a dragon. He exercises all the authority of the first beast on his behalf . . . He also performs great signs, even causing fire to come down from heaven to earth in front of people.

Jerusalem, Israel – January 1, Year 4

Like a sea before a storm, a thousand whispers rippled through the crowd below. Flickering torches lined the square's perimeter, shedding an eerie glow, while above, the sun burned dimly through black cloth.

Below Chelsea in the square's center, the prisoners were roped and muzzled. Beside her, Davato and the Clal Center employees spread across the top of the Temple steps.

The Prophet approached a microphone. "Those you see in center are the rioting Jews, the ones who rejected the divinity and authority of their Imperator. The one on the pedestal has committed an act against your Imperator so heinous, I cannot repeat it. He, above all others, belongs with the traitors. Now watch and observe! Davato the Divine has bestowed on me such powers as only a god may grant."

Then Sebastien Rey, dressed in a full-length white robe with a black sash around his waist, stood to his full height. He raised his arms, his hair stood on end, and tongues of electricity flicked away from his body. In the heavens above, dark clouds gathered. Tumbling and roiling, the clouds grew and churned until they covered the sky. Lightning sparked within, followed by peals of thunder.

The Prophet pointed his hand at the Jews and at Lazzaro. A finger of cloud twisted down, swirling and darkening.

The CSA guards and the crowds trembled and drew back from the prisoners. Chelsea gasped and slapped both hands over her mouth.

"Here, then, is my judgment on the traitors and rebels working against our divine Imperator!"

Like a magician casting a spell, Sebastien slowly turned and dropped his hand. A bolt of lightning shot from above and rocked the square. It crashed onto the platform and engulfed Lazzaro. Streams of electric fire flashed over the Jews bound in the center. They swept the center cobbles. And when they stopped, echoing and thundering through the crowd, all that was left of the prisoners and Lazzaro were charred and smoking corpses.

"Yes, my friends, that is the judgment awaiting all who rebel and plot against your Imperator. Now let the booths be opened. Now let your hearts decide whether you will take the mark of your divine Imperator— and live. Or reject it—and die!"

As if they were a single organism, the crowd rushed the booths.

Beside Chelsea, Grady tugged at her arm. "Let's get our marks now. You heard him. We must choose."

A shivering started in her shoulders and rippled down her back. She shook her head. "Look how long the lines are already. Maybe we should wait till later?"

Grady paused, watched the booths for a time, then faced her. "You're right. It will take hours to get through those lines today."

They started for the exits behind the Clal party, many of whom must have also decided to wait. They followed Davato and his CSA escort.

But before they'd taken ten steps, machine gun fire erupted from the square's perimeter, followed by screams. The rat-a-tat-tat of more guns echoed from the opposite side. The CSA was mowing down the leader-less Jews who hadn't fled. By their yarmulkes and singular Jewish dress, the Jews were easy to spot.

When Chelsea had entered the Temple, Davato had spoken to Adam Turner who had given the word to his subordinate officers. Now the men under her father's command were murdering the remaining Jews.

Everyone stopped moving. The rush for the tattoo booths ceased. Thousands of Davato's well-wishers, knowing they were safe, gathered in the center, watched, and waited for the massacre to end.

Chelsea covered her open mouth with a hand as the victims tried to flee—mostly men, but also some youths and women. Dozens, no hundreds, of bleeding bodies lay on the stone floor and steps leading down and away from the square. The gunfire went on and on. Trembling, she slapped hands over her ears and prayed for it to end.

Ten minutes later, it was over. Then the CSA walked through hundreds of fallen bodies and, raising their handguns, put bullets through the heads of any still alive.

When the shooting had ceased, the crowd, seemingly oblivious to the massacre, resumed its rush to the tattoo booths.

Chelsea followed Davato and the Clal employees across the floor toward the stairs.

Then Davato's entourage neared the Two Witnesses.

Earlier, the rioting and the day's commotion had drowned out the prophets' voices. Now, the two men stood, staffs in hand, looking as if they'd been ripped out of a biblical play. As usual, the crowd had cleared a circle around them.

As the Imperator approached, their voices rose suddenly in timbre and volume.

"Reject the mark of the beast!" cried the white-bearded prophet as he struck his staff upon the cobbles, "and turn to the Lord before it's too late."

"If you take the mark," echoed the old man with a mottled gray beard, "you will perish in the fires of Hell, forever and ever."

Davato stopped and whirled toward them. "Rail and shout all you want, old men." His jaw was rigid, his eyes dark with hate, his hands balling into fists at his side. "But nothing you do or say will ever change my plans. I do not believe what is written in the Enemy's book. Tell the old fool that no one can set the course of history. Tell him I am working night and day to prove him wrong."

Then the eyes of the white-bearded prophet widened, brightened, and speared Davato. The old man rose to his full height. He spoke, and his voice rose to such a volume, it thundered louder than the milling throngs and the murmur of thousands, and it vibrated in Chelsea's chest. "Man of lawlessness, know this—you have defiled the Temple with your abomination. Thus, I decree that, for a month and a day, everyone working for the abominations you call the Truth Squads and the Central Security Agency shall be plagued with boils. Let it be so!" He struck his staff, hard, onto the cobbles, and the sound echoed like thunder across the square.

The gray-bearded old man standing beside the other also raised himself to his full height. And when he spoke, his voice, too, sounded as though it had been amplified a thousandfold, echoing across the square with earthshaking power. "Because of your arrogant tongue and your atrocities, I add this to the first decree. For a month and a day, every soldier in your army, navy, and air force, and every Unitum Imperium official working at every checkpoint shall also be plagued with boils. Let it be so!" His staff struck the cobbles so hard, the earth shook.

Immediately came cries from CSA guards on the perimeter, and when Chelsea turned to look, their faces were covered with ugly pink blobs. Their hands ran over their clothing, possibly feeling places where their skin had suddenly broken out. Even her father, walking ahead beside Davato, was now moaning in pain, gingerly running hands over his arms, legs, and chest.

Still standing before the two prophets, Davato was red-faced and shaking. "Someday, you old fools, I will have your heads." Then he whirled and stalked away.

The Clal Center entourage followed.

"Come on," called Grady, "or we'll miss the bus."

But as she boarded the bus, it hit her—for the next month, the boils would hinder and distract the CSA and the Truth Squads and everyone manning the checkpoints.

CHAPTER 30

EXODUS

*Matthew 24:15–16 (HCSB): "So when you see **the abomination that causes desolation**, spoken of by the prophet Daniel, standing in the holy place" (let the reader understand), "then those in Judea must flee to the mountains!"*

Daniel 11:40–41 (HCSB): At the time of the end, the king of the South will engage him in battle, but the king of the North will storm against him . . . He will invade countries and sweep through them like a flood. He will also invade the beautiful land, and many will fall. But these will escape from his power: Edom, Moab, and the prominent people of the Ammonites.

Sela, Jordan – January 1, Year 4

Behind Baruch, thousands of cars, trucks, and buses filled with Jewish converts and new Christians rumbled and bounced over the desert. They stretched in a caravan for kilometers.

For months, he'd been preparing for this day. Every house church leader had instructions on where and how to evacuate. Everyone should already have procured tents and camping gear. At one thirty in the afternoon, after the Two Witnesses declared a plague of boils on the CSA and the Truth Squads, he'd sent out the word and put their plans into motion. The plague would nearly incapacitate the enforcement arm of the Unitum Imperium, giving people the opportunity they needed. It was almost as if it was divinely appointed. He smiled. Indeed, when they approached the checkpoints along the highways, the guards were absent. No doubt, some were also nursing hangovers from their New Year's Eve revelry.

As if to expedite their passage, the dark cloth over the sun began melting away. And by the end of the day, the shining orb in the sky burned as bright as it always had.

As the convoy passed through the West Bank, more vehicles joined them. When they entered the country of Jordan, they followed the Jordan Valley Highway east of the Dead Sea. They traversed a desert landscape between monoliths of sculpted red rock, over oceans of red sand dotted with wormwood, saltbush, and sea squill. Occasionally, they paused to let nomads cross the highway with their herds of floppy-eared goats.

They passed the burned-out, tumbled-down ruins of a mosque, the recipient of fire and brimstone from the Lord of Heaven and Earth during the battle of Gog and Magog. As the other vehicles continued, the buses stopped at At-Tafilah, one of their prearranged meeting places, to take on passengers from the south of Israel.

By the time they reached As Salá, it was dusk, and the moon was a sliver of white as it was always supposed to be. Passengers left their vehicles, and the Bedouin police force, still riding camels, greeted them. Baruch was surprised how much God had created a welcome for the Christian exodus in Bedouin hearts.

As uncounted thousands left their cars, buses, and motorbikes, each carrying a bag or two, select drivers turned around and headed back to prearranged collection points in the cities, towns, and villages where more Christians waited to be picked up. Others drove abandoned vehicles out into the desert to be camouflaged.

Ahead lay the east-facing entrance to the ancient mountain stronghold of Sela. The greeters he'd assigned earlier reminded everyone to take no food or beverage onto the mountain. With much grumbling, the travelers abandoned whatever provisions remained from the journey, and the Bedouins were happy to accept what they had. From here on, according to Baruch's instructions, they must rely only on God.

Baruch received a torch from the greeters and walked at the caravan's head. As they passed the stone guard tower, he turned to David. "This land was once part of ancient Edom, founded by Esau, the brother of Jacob."

"Esau," said David, "the one who sold his birthright for a bowl of spicy red pottage."

Nodding, Baruch led the ascent up the narrow rock staircase, the only passage leading to the mountain fortress. David Benjamin was two steps behind.

Baruch's torch swept the towers of sandstone rising on all sides. Above, the narrow rock walls twisted around the bend and vanished in shadow. He was already sweating from the climb.

David fell into step with his friend. "Won't the Unitum Imperium be able to find us here? We must have given directions to a tenth of all Israel?"

Baruch smiled and continued walking. "Have faith, David. The site is remote. God will hide us."

David scrunched his face toward the leader of the exodus, and Baruch laid a hand on his shoulder. "Nothing is impossible for the one who created Heaven and earth."

They continued climbing the one hundred meters to the summit. Thousands, many also carrying torches, now followed the two leaders, eager to hear every word said. At the top, they arrived at a rocky plain dotted with the remains of ancient houses, their stones scattered over the flat. A few workers were already there, and their torches lit the scene.

Baruch waved his free hand over the plateau. "In 597 BC, Amaziah, King of Judah, took this place in battle from the Edomites and called it Joktheel. Now, in the last days, it will serve as our Refuge from the forces of evil."

David followed Baruch's wave. "It's certainly a mountain stronghold. It will be difficult for any army to conquer." Then David jammed his hands on hips. "But tens of thousands will soon be arriving after us. Where will we find water for all those people? How will we feed them? We left all our provisions below."

Baruch pointed to a cliff on their right and led him toward it. At three different locations, huge basins had been scraped from the rock next to the cliff walls. Baruch stopped at the first basin. His torch flickered over clear water filling it to the brim. One meter above, a water stain led from a hole in the cliff wall, painting a trail of wet rock into the basin.

With a wave at the cliff, David raised a questioning glance. "Water from the rock? But everything's so dry. How . . . ?"

"I was here a month ago and instructed workers to dig these basins.

When we went to bed that night, people asked me how we were going to fill them. To haul water from outside for tens of thousands would take a continuous stream of vehicles, and the desert heat would soon evaporate whatever we carried. But the next morning, when we returned, these holes had appeared in the cliff face, and all the basins were full. Take that bucket and fill it."

With a questioning glance, David knelt and grabbed the bucket. He dipped it in the water and lifted it out. Instantly, a clear stream jetted from the rock face, replacing what he'd taken. He nearly spilled the bucket in his astonishment.

"Now drink some of it."

David set down the bucket, cupped his hands, and brought some to his lips. "Why . . . it's fresh and cold!"

Baruch grinned. "God provides, does he not?"

Some of those who'd followed them also drank from the water and marveled among themselves.

"All right, I admit. This is amazing." David cocked his head. "Now I suppose you also have an answer for how to feed the thousands of people who will soon arrive?"

Baruch gripped his friend's arm. "How were the Israelites fed when they wandered forty years in the desert?"

"With manna at first, then with quail." David's eyes widened, and he took a step back. "No, you aren't going to tell me . . ."

"Yes, and tomorrow morning, when people wonder why we told them to leave their provisions, their wine, and their beer outside, when they wonder what they will eat, sweet manna will appear everywhere on the ground. Then they will collect what they need for the day. Quail will also drop from the sky, but only enough to satisfy the people's taste for meat for one day. That is what God has promised."

David shook his head and grinned. "We are truly a modern-day exodus. And you are our modern-day Moses."

A chorus of ayes came from the crowd behind them.

"No, no." Baruch frowned. "I am just a poor servant who's following what my Savior whispered to me in my sleep. This is all God's doing. He pledged to protect those who refuse to take the mark of the beast and who follow us here. He has given us this Refuge, a place of safety apart from the abominations and atrocities of the Antichrist."

Then he knelt and began to pray. As he did, David and the dozens who'd followed also knelt.

"Thank you, Lord Jesus, for rescuing us from the fate ordained for the man of lawlessness and his followers. We praise you for our salvation, for the food and water you will provide. We thank you for how you will supernaturally hide us from the forces of the Unitum Imperium. Now we ask you humbly to help those who are still on their way. Help them to reach this Refuge safely. In Jesus's name, amen."

When he again rose to his feet, hundreds were pouring into the desert valley and setting up tents among the rocks.

The great exodus was underway.

CHAPTER 31

THE MARK OF THE BEAST

Jerusalem, Israel — January 1, Year 4

After Davato had made his stunning declaration of divinity and announced that everyone must either take the mark or starve, Chelsea was gripped with indecision. That afternoon, she'd sat in her apartment by the window, watched the sun return to normal, listened to the hum of the air conditioning, and stared at the sandwich she'd made but couldn't eat. Then she'd paced the floor into the kitchen, returned to her seat by the window, and sat down again.

And all the while, she pondered what to do.

It was now evening, and she left the apartment. But as the elevator door opened, as luck would have it, the car's only other occupant was her father. She cringed, but nonetheless, she stepped inside. The smell of whiskey permeated the space.

Ugly boils, oozing pus, marred his cheeks, his forehead, and his bare arms. His face twisted into a permanent grimace, and he shifted from one foot to the other. "I can't sit, can't lie down, can't even stand. I've even got them on the soles of my feet. I'm going to need a lot of whiskey to get through this. There's a clinic down the street where they supposedly have a salve that might help, but . . ." He threw an angry glance at his left arm, reached for it, scratched, then withdrew.

Then his stare fixed on Chelsea, and he lifted his right hand to her face. His wrist bore the six-sided tattoo with the letters of Davato's name. "Daughter, here is my mark. Where is yours?"

She faced away from him, and her eyes found the door. "I—I'm going out now to see how long the lines are. Th—they were too long earlier."

"From anyone else, I would accept that excuse. But from you, Chelsea, I cannot. Not any longer. As a member of Davato's inner circle, you need to show unquestioning, immediate allegiance, no matter how long the lines were. You've already been avoiding the sharing time. Now this!"

He gripped her hands, and she squirmed. Hadn't those fingers just scratched a boil? He jerked her around to face him.

"Davato warned you at noon. Now I'm warning you this evening. You are my daughter, yes, but this issue goes way beyond family. If I don't see a mark on your hand by tomorrow morning . . ."

"Then what?" Her voice rose, and she ripped her hands from his grasp. "Then you'll turn me in? You'll send your own daughter to the shooting galleries? Will you watch them cover me with burning pitch in the colosseum and light me on fire? Or feed me to the lions? Is that what we've come to? What's happened to you, Father?"

His face reddened, and his jaw tensed. Without warning, he slapped her—hard—across the cheek.

She reeled. One hand went to her cheek, burning now. Tears welled up in her eyes, and her back slammed against the opposite wall. He'd never hit her before.

"By daybreak, if I don't see a mark on your hand . . ." His eyes bulging, he shook his head side to side. "Then . . . then you are no longer my daughter."

The elevator stopped at the bottom, and she rushed out, tears streaming down her face. She bumped into a woman, spilling wine from the glass in her hand. She ran, her feet echoing across the vestibule's marble. She pushed through the revolving doors onto the walk beside Jaffa Road. Turning left, she headed for the Old City under a star-bedecked sky and a half-moon. At least, something was normal.

She had to decide. Tonight. With the CSA and the Truth Squads nearly incapacitated with boils, now was the time to leave. But where would she go? And how?

Wiping moisture from her cheeks, she let her feet lead her. Maybe three-quarters of the city's streetlights were out because of the quakes, but she didn't care. Meandering through street after dark street, she breathed deeply, tried to slow her rapid heartbeat. Without plan or intent, she staggered as in a dream, her head down, her gaze on the cobbles, traversing the buckled pavement rent by earthquakes, her mind grasping for a plan, any plan, to rescue her from this madness.

Her toes rammed a curb, and she looked up.

She was at the head of a familiar street. Yes, just as before, her wandering had led her—unplanned—to the lane with the travel agency. A few doors down would be the sign of the woman with the sun at her head and the moon at her feet.

A plan formed in her mind. She would go to Baruch's Refuge. Hadn't he said it was still possible, even after she'd rejected his earlier invitation? She hurried past closed shops, dark windows, and too many buildings the quakes had reduced to rubble. She came to the familiar sign above the door, and she breathed out. The travel agency was mostly intact. The quakes hadn't destroyed it. She entered through the open door, now hanging on broken hinges.

She switched on her phone's flashlight to dispel the dark. Part of the roof had collapsed, scattering stones across the floor. What had Baruch said? There were directions to the Refuge beneath a painted brick? Her light played along the wall until it came to a crudely painted figure—a sun above a woman with the moon beneath.

Her heart sped up. She gripped the brick, slid it back and forth to loosen it. She pulled it from the wall. Behind lay a leather parchment. She laid the brick on the floor and held the scrap of leather to her light.

Then she read: "If you have given your heart and soul to the Son of the Living God, then heed what is written below. . . ."

But beneath the message was only blurry scribbling that kept going in and out of focus.

She rubbed her eyes and looked again. It was indecipherable. Something was keeping her from reading it.

Lowering the scrap of leather, she closed her eyes. Then she remembered what else Baruch had said. Even if she knew where the Refuge was, she couldn't find it unless she was a Christian. Now, through some unknown magic, she couldn't even read how to get there. Again that day, tears filled her vision.

What was wrong with her? Why couldn't she believe? Was she destined to take the mark of the beast and be doomed for all eternity?

No. Never. She would never take the mark.

What then? Would she starve?

But maybe there was a third choice. Maybe she could reject the mark and leave Israel, find someplace safe, far from Davato and his Truth Squads.

Yes, she would join Dylan and Margot wherever they were. Last she'd heard, they were in France. She'd get out of this city where Davato's presence was everywhere. When she was in a safe place, she'd call Dylan and arrange to join him.

Breathing fast, adrenaline giving her new energy, she replaced the parchment and brick then hurried back to the street, heading toward her apartment. She'd leave this very night, but first, she needed to meet with Grady.

She'd give him one last chance. Maybe he hadn't taken the mark yet. Maybe she could convince him to go with her. To go on such a journey alone, facing who knew what dangers, was more than frightening. It sent shivers down her back.

* * *

It was past eight when the revolving door whooshed her onto the sidewalk outside the Clal Center. She carried a single backpack filled with two changes of clothes, a half dozen sandwiches, a bottle of water, a sharp knife, the Bible Lazzaro had given her, and a wad of bills—real cash she'd been hoarding. Feeling self-conscious carrying a full pack, she hoped no one would question what she was doing or where she was going. Though people with backpacks were a common sight, hers was full.

When she'd regained the street, she sent Grady a text then hurried to their favorite restaurant only a kilometer away. The front of the building had collapsed, but miraculously, the interior was open, and the owner had cleared a path through the rubble to a few tables. She sat, ordered a glass of white wine, barely sipped from it, fidgeted with her phone, then glanced toward the street.

And she waited.

When Grady finally arrived, he took a chair opposite hers, glanced at her right hand, and scowled. "What in the world are you doing, Chelsea? Don't you know that Davato is making a list of everyone who won't take the mark?"

"I can't do it. Do you know what it means to take the mark? Do you know what the Bible says about it?"

"*The Bible.*" His voice rose, and he crossed his arms. "Possessing a Bible is a sure way to get sent to the camp they're rebuilding. Why are you talking about the Bible?"

"Because it says if you take the mark, you'll be damned for all eternity. You'll burn in the fires of Hell, forever and ever. Once you take the mark, there's no turning back, no changing your mind—ever!"

He pushed back from the table and narrowed his eyes. "What's happened to you? Why are you talking like some Bible-believing Christian? Did you destroy the book Lazzaro gave you like I asked you to?"

"N–no."

"Well, you know where his Bible led him, don't you? No, Chelsea. I don't believe the drivel in Lazzaro's Bible, and I'm shocked you still have it. And I don't believe there's such a thing as a Hell or a God who would send people there. What I do believe is that those who don't take the mark are going to starve to death." Then he pulled back the sleeve covering his right hand, and he held it out. It bore the tattoo, the sign of the man of lawlessness, the mark of the beast.

Chelsea gasped and drew back. "I–I'm sorry, Grady. I guess this means we part ways. Because I can't ever do what you've done."

"Are you one of *them* now? One of the Christians?"

"N–no."

"Then what are you doing? How will you survive?"

"I'm leaving, going someplace, anyplace—away from *this*!" She waved her hands at the street.

"Then good luck to you, Chelsea Turner, because from here on, you and I are on opposite sides."

Again that day, moisture clouded her vision, and she wiped away tears. "I guess that's what it means. I like you, Grady. But now I'm sorry for you, and sorry you can't come with me."

"Don't be sorry for me. Without this"—he waved his tattooed hand—"you're the one who'll soon be sorry. This, then, is goodbye."

But as he stood from the table, she reached across and grabbed his left hand. "You won't tell on me, will you? Even though we're of different minds about this?"

His visage softened, and he gripped her hand with both of his. Then he lowered his lips and kissed her wrist. "Go and do wherever you want. I won't tell anyone what we talked about. Your secret is safe with me."

She stood, crossed to his side of the table, and kissed him on the cheek. "Thank you, Grady. I wish things could have been different."

For a moment, his fingers lingered on the place where her lips had grazed, and he was silent. A look—was it pain, regret, sorrow?—stormed across his face. Then he hurried out the door.

She paid and headed back to the street.

But now what? How was she going to make the journey to France alone? Who knew how long such a trip would take? She didn't have enough to pay for airfare out of the country. She could use her travel pass one last time, but then what? When they found out what she'd done, they'd revoke it, use it to find her. After tonight, it would be useless for travel. Yet she had to get where she was going before the CSA recovered from the boils.

Breathing fast, she turned left and headed for the bus station.

CHAPTER 32

ON THE RUN

Jerusalem, Israel – January 1, Year 4

As her feet echoed down the dark lane, a sliver of a moon lit her way. No one besides Grady knew Chelsea was leaving. The CSA wouldn't find out till morning. Even then, they'd all be in agony, unable to do much of anything. That should slow them up. She searched her bag and found the travel pass she'd used on the plane from New Babylon. It would be good for one more trip, enough to get her to Tel Aviv.

But what about her phone? They could track her with that. Not far down the street was one of the collection centers for old phones, and she started for it. Davato had decreed that all old cell phones be turned in and replaced with a new solar phone. Someday soon, the cell signals would change, and the older models would stop working. New Babylon had only begun setting up collection centers, and with all that had happened, she hadn't yet gotten a chance to exchange hers here.

At the center, still open at eight thirty in the evening, she handed over her old phone. Manning the shop, the bright-eyed youth spouted a lot of technical jargon as he asked if he could transfer her contacts. Frowning at his display of technical superiority, she agreed. Without her contacts, she would be utterly lost. Then, as he attached a USB cable and did the transfer, he expounded at length on the wondrous technical advances she was about to receive. The phone could charge either in sunlight or with a USB cable. After the transfer was complete, he handed her the shiny new device.

"Can you erase everything on my old phone?" she asked.

"Of course."

She watched as he started the procedure to erase its memory. Satisfied it was progressing, she left the shop, headed down the street, and ducked into a restaurant where the electricity still worked. She locked herself in the WC and fished out the printed sheet from her backpack—the instructions on how to disable solar phone tracking. But the dip switches were so tiny, she had to use tweezers to set them. Convinced she'd done it correctly, she left for the street.

Except for the travel pass and her UI credit card, no one could track her now. Once in Tel Aviv, she would find a way, somehow, to get as far away from Davato and everything related to the Unitum Imperium as she could get.

The bus station was only four blocks away.

* * *

It was ten o'clock when the bus brakes hissed, the door clanked open, and she stepped into the Tel Aviv central bus station. This was as far as the CSA would be able to track her. And this was the last place she could use her UI credit card.

But without a credit card, how would she eat? Where would she sleep? How would she pay for transportation? She had only so much hard cash, and that was only good with a proprietor willing to take real money. Such businesses were becoming scarcer each day. With the new digital currency, they could track you and approve or deny everything you bought.

The station was enormous, and she wandered through an endless variety of shops, filling her bag with as much food as possible. She went to an ATM and tried to withdraw more cash. But they'd already installed the digital payments system. Already, here in Tel Aviv, they were no longer dispensing cash. What she had with her was all she was ever going to get.

As everywhere else, posters showing the Dragon flanked by Davato and the Prophet were cropping up on every wall.

Entering an Italian restaurant on the strip, she ate a good, but pricey, meal of spaghetti, meatballs, bread, and wine. When she'd finished, she pulled out her new solar phone and tried to bring up her contact list.

But—oh no—it was empty! Every number and every person she needed to reach—gone! Frantically, she searched around for another icon, a different way to find the numbers, but all her contacts were gone.

The bright-faced young techie, so full of himself at the cell phone collection booth, had screwed up. Whatever he'd done hadn't worked. He hadn't transferred her numbers, and she hadn't memorized any of them. Now she couldn't reach anyone.

She dropped her head in her hands. Now what? How would she ever get in touch with Dylan now?

Then she thought of the family villa in Tuscany. If she could get there, Bettino would know how to reach Dylan and Margot. Forget France. She'd go to Italy.

But how? Planes were out. They checked everyone thoroughly before boarding a plane. Overland routes were also out. Too many countries, too many checkpoints.

What about a boat? Something commercial that wouldn't draw much attention? That might be her best bet. The Namal, Tel Aviv's upscale dock complex, wasn't far. Maybe there she'd find someone willing to take her by boat to Italy.

She paid her bill with her UI card, stood, and threw her rucksack over her shoulder. With a scissors from her pack, she cut the now-useless credit card and travel pass into pieces. "Goodbye, tracking."

She dropped the plastic into a trash bin, left the station, and headed for the Namal.

CHAPTER 33

NEW FRIENDS, NEW DANGERS

Mark 16:17 (NLT): "These miraculous signs will accompany those who believe: They will cast out demons in my name . . ."

Currie, Minnesota – January, Year 4

It was Sunday, and much to everyone's relief, the sun had returned to normal, bouncing brightly off the snow ahead. The horses' hooves and the wagon wheels broke through the frozen crust with a peculiar, percussive, clopping, crunching melody.

While Caleb and Andy rode horses, the women sat in the wagon. They breathed plumes of air so icy it hurt the lungs, and Caleb was glad of the scarf covering his mouth. Even the long underwear beneath his winter coat wasn't enough to keep out the chill. On the wagon seat, Brianna and Tanya had wrapped themselves in blankets. When they left the cabin, it was ten below. He hoped that with the sun's return, it would soon warm up. But it was, after all, Minnesota.

The trip was only two and a half miles, and they arrived at the American Legion post on Mill Street to the sounds of a piano, a guitar, and singing. They were late.

"What's this going to be like?" asked Brianna. "I've never been to a real church before. Only what they had in the Village."

"We'll see." Caleb dismounted, hobbled his horse, and threw a blanket over its back. "If these folks are the least bit weird, we're out of here."

The others also hobbled their horses, gathered at the entrance, and sent him questioning glances.

"Well, let's not just stand here." Tanya stamped her feet on the sidewalk. "It's got to be warmer inside."

"Right." He pushed through the doors into a hall where twenty-five folks sat on folding chairs.

The singing stopped, and smiling faces turned their way. Sitting two rows from the front and wearing the same clothes they had on the day they'd visited, Jack and Linda May Manson rose, walked down the aisle, and extended their hands in greeting.

Then Jack spoke to the assembly. "These, here, are the folks I was tellin' you about. They're at the group camp in the park."

Most of the congregation rose from their seats, filled the aisle, and approached. They shook the newcomers' hands, welcomed them, and said how glad they were to see new faces.

"We were just gettin' started." Linda May bid them to take seats beside them, and Caleb sat beside Jack near the front.

The music resumed—a middle-aged guitar player, a gray-haired woman on piano, and a young, red-haired woman singing. Printed sheets on the chairs held the words, and they sang a mix of traditional hymns and newer Christian songs.

As he sang, Caleb felt his heart swelling with joy. Beside him, Brianna smiled as she joined in. Two seats beyond, Tanya's face beamed. Worshiping the Lord with others was something they desperately needed.

When the music stopped, a man in blue jeans, a plaid shirt, and boots took the front. "For our new friends out at Shetek, my name is Henry Adams, and these folks here in Currie elected me preacher. Like everyone else, before V-Day I was a hard-hearted idiot, not believing in the Bible, Jesus, or God. But since then, we've all studied and seen how what's been happening was prophesied thousands of years ago, and now we're living through the end times. All of us here have given our hearts to Jesus."

He stared at the floor, drew a hand through a mop of black hair, then looked up.

"I'm preaching today's message on love, 'cause that's what's missing most in what we see around us."

He preached from Matthew 22:36–40, from the Great Commandment, and the text boiled his message down to two, simple commands:

First, and most importantly, love the Lord God with all your heart, mind, and soul. And don't forget that loving God means following and obeying the commands and teachings of Jesus.

Secondly, love your neighboras yourself but not to the exclusion of the first commandment.

When he'd finished, everyone moved to the far end of the hall. All through the message, two cast-iron, wood-burning cookstoves tried to warm the place while wafting the smells of beef stew with vegetables, beans, and fresh-baked bread, all mixed with woodsmoke.

As Caleb took a heaping portion of food to a seat at one of the long tables, Henry Adams brought his plate and sat across from him while Jack Manson sat beside him. "We're so glad you could join us," said Henry. "I understand you left the Village?"

"Yeah, we had no idea what we were getting into there. We barely escaped."

"We've heard the same from others who've passed through. How was your trip from the North Shore?"

Caleb told him about some of the close calls they'd had with gangs and with Truth Squads. Then he turned to Henry. "Have you had any trouble with squaddies here?"

"Squaddies?" A grin split Henry's face. "By that you mean Truth Squads? What a great name!"

But then a worried look crossed both their faces, and Henry spoke. "Squaddies is a great name for those weasels. And yes, there's a half dozen stationed over in Pipestone. Two weeks ago, they came here for the second time, but in daylight. It was just men this time, and they showed up with rifles pointed, telling us we could no longer worship Jesus. 'You're going to have to turn in all your weapons and follow the Imperator,' they said. 'He's the real god, and if you don't start worshiping him and stop being Christians, you're going to a camp. And there's a new law. Firearms are no longer allowed in the hands of citizens.' "

"A camp?" Caleb's spoonful of beef stew stopped halfway to his lips. "What kind of camp? Where is it?"

"Rumor says it's south of Sioux Falls," said Henry. "That's the regional headquarters for what you call squaddies."

"Rumor also has it," added Jack, "that they're killin' people there. I'm agin' killin' others, but if they come here with rifles, tryin' to take any of us to one o' them camps or take our guns from us, well . . ."

"I know what you mean." Caleb set down his spoon. "They want total obedience to Davato." Then he looked up. "He's the Antichrist, you know."

"Yeah, we figured that out," added Jack. "But we haven't told you the worst."

A cloud passed over Henry's face, and he exchanged a dark look with Jack.

"About the squaddies?" asked Caleb.

"Yeah. That was the second time the Pipestone Truth Squad was here. Last summer, they came at night, and someone—no, it was a *thing*!— came with them." Henry cleared his throat and again exchanged glances with Jack, and then, his voice low, he focused on Caleb. "That night, believe it or not, they came with what most of us are calling a–a demon."

"*A demon?*" A chill started in Caleb's shoulders and ran down his arms, only stopping when his hands began to shake. "Did it give you its name?"

Both of his new friends looked up with startled expressions. "Why, yes. So you believe us?"

"I do. I may have encountered one before. What did it call itself?"

"Morgoth!"

Caleb's mouth opened, and he stared at the men. He looked at his hands, now shaking uncontrollably, and the men saw it too. Then he took a deep breath and meshed his fingers together until the shaking stopped. "Right after V-Day, I realized that what we were hearing about UFOs—that they had taken the Christians—wasn't true. My brother had been telling me the Rapture was coming, and I didn't believe him until it actually happened. That's when I started a blog called the *Real Truth*."

"No kidding!" Henry's eyes lit up, he slapped the table, and then he reached over and pumped Caleb's hands. "That was the blog that helped me realize aliens had nothing to do with what happened. So that was yours! That blog really helped me understand the Rapture and got me to studying the Bible and the end times. That's when I figured out that this Davato wasn't who everybody thought he was."

Caleb grinned. "I had no idea it was affecting people like that. I am truly heartened."

Jack looked at him with admiring eyes. "Well, I'll be. If that doesn't beat all!"

Henry nodded, and his expression became serious again. "But I interrupted. You were telling us a story—something to do with a demon?"

"Right. Well, I began receiving messages online from someone called Morgoth, and—"

"Morgoth sent you *messages*? *Online*?" Now Jack's mouth was open.

"It did, and they were ominous warnings to stop doing what I was doing. I had an apartment in Chicago at the time, and I ignored them all and kept blogging. Someone else had advised me earlier—but I won't get into that right now—and he gave me a warning to beware of dark places under the trees at night. Well, I didn't listen. I went out at night and strolled under dark trees, and there Morgoth attacked me. An invisible force paralyzed me. Invisible hands began beating on me. And it wasn't until I spoke the name of Jesus that it stopped and Morgoth vanished. It took weeks for me to recover. By then, the Antichrist's men had inactivated my blog. Then Unitum Imperium goons broke into my apartment, kidnapped me, and took me to Rome, Italy. Later, my brother and sister helped free me from an underground prison. And somehow"—he waved his hands and smiled—"I ended up here."

Both men now stared at him in silence so long, Caleb wondered if they believed him.

Then Henry spoke so low Caleb could hardly hear him. "The night the demon came here it was like this: We met the Pipestone Truth Squad on Mill Street in the dark and listened to their commands. They wanted us to stop meeting and worshiping Jesus. We said we wouldn't. Then they stepped aside, and this Morgoth, this evil dark shadow, came forward from behind them. And then, Caleb, we all *felt* it. I can't describe how we knew what it was, but we did. And we were scared. I mean I was shaking, like I saw your hands shaking a moment ago. And it asked me, of all people, a question. It said, 'Is there a man among you with blond hair from Chicago, who speaks the falsehood that aliens weren't what took the Christians?' Of course, I answered no. And then we all felt such a powerful sense of evil, we all fled. We never invoked the name of Jesus like you did. What fools we were! Where was our faith? Instead, we ran, and fortunately, the squaddies, as you call them, left with their demon. But we didn't stop meeting."

"Since then," added Jack, "we've lived in fear that the thing would return. Some of the men have wondered if, because of what we saw, if we should stop these services. But we are agin' it."

For the second time that morning, Caleb's hands began to shake. It was as if they belonged to someone else, and he couldn't stop them. Morgoth was after *him*! For some reason, the thing was in Pipestone with one of the Truth Squads, but even here, when it confronted these Christians, the first thing it asked was: *Where is Caleb?* He shuddered and gripped his hands together to calm them. Then he caught both Jack's and Henry's glances. "Don't let it win. I drove it away with the power of Jesus's name, and you can too. I don't know how it got here or why it wants me, but we can't let it win."

"You're right, friend." Henry reached over and laid a hand on Caleb's shoulder. "And you've shown us how we can stand up to it next time."

"But if the squaddies come with guns . . ." added Jack.

"Yeah." Caleb frowned. "That's a different issue. Fighting with real-world weapons. I don't know which is worse."

"We're fighting both a physical and a spiritual battle, aren't we?" Henry stared at something across the room. "The world has turned upside down, and no one has ever experienced what we're facing today."

"Right." Jack stood and motioned for Caleb to follow him. "This is all important stuff, but now Caleb needs to meet some of the folks. We're scaring ourselves half to death with this kind of talk."

They laughed, and afterward, Caleb spent the rest of the afternoon visiting with new friends.

Before they left for the state park, Linda May led them to a barn at the edge of town where they picked up sacks of oats and barley. "You can give it to your animals," she said, "or eat the grain yourselves."

They thanked her, and as they rode home, the sun reflected so bright off the ice, Dylan had to shield his eyes much of the way.

Back in the cabin, after they'd all warmed up, Andy and Brianna went outside again to cut more firewood, leaving Caleb and Tanya alone.

"This was a good day." He threw a few more logs into the wood-stove. He'd tell the story of the Pipestone squaddies and their demon later, when everyone was present. Right now, he had more pleasant things on his mind. "Going to that church and meeting those folks was what we all needed."

"It was." Sitting in a chair by the stove, Tanya smiled. "And I liked the message. It wasn't about 'sharing'."

"It was about love, and you know what?" He grabbed her hands and pulled her out of her seat.

"No?" A silly smile crossed her face.

"I don't say this often enough, but—"

"But what?" She cocked her head.

"But"—his lips pressed against hers, and energy shot through him—"but I love you."

CHAPTER 34

ARIEL GELLER

Tel Aviv, Israel – February 1, Year 4

Ariel Geller sat at the wheel of one of his many trucks outside an upscale restaurant frequented by UI thugs. The vehicle was running, its engine purring.

Today, as on most days of the last month, Ariel couldn't stop grinning at his good fortune. The CSA and the Truth Squads had been sidelined, confined to their barracks, drinking themselves senseless to escape the agony of the boils wracking their bodies. The moment he'd heard what the Two Witnesses had decreed in Temple Square, he called his network of runners and thieves into action. Then he'd thrown caution aside and left the shadows.

But today was the last day. And he must make the most of it.

He glanced in the side mirror and waved to Eli, one of a dozen youths in his employ, now wheeling another hand truck loaded with boxes from the back of the restaurant.

For a month, his people had been looting CSA storehouses, haunts, and the houses of Tel Aviv UI government agents and lackeys. Whatever his secret warehouses needed most, he was now procuring, and they couldn't stop him. He had two dozen men, women, and youths out on the streets, watching targets, recording occupants' schedules, so that, when the time came, his cadre of thieves could sweep in, back up a truck, and take back what the brutes had stolen from others. Sometimes, when they entered a house whose occupants weren't afflicted with boils, his people just tied up whoever was there and went to work. Any phone call made to the authorities after they were gone would go unanswered.

He also employed a group of young women. The Unitum Imperium thought they had hired them. But undercover, they worked for him. Their jobs were to visit the homes of suspected plague or famine victims and remove the bodies, then clean the houses of official credit, travel, and identity cards. Back at government headquarters, they were supposed to invalidate all such cards and passes.

But nowadays, there were so many thieves, weren't there? And who was to say if someone hadn't gotten there first and already taken what the UI was looking for? And who was to say there were even bodies to be found in such houses? Maybe the folks were still alive, and they'd just fled somewhere else, leaving an empty house? It was a great source of commerce—marketing those cards. He kept quite a few, and often, he gave some to special folks in need.

And the bodies? Once a week, garbage trucks left for the country, hauling away corpses. Some from the death houses. And some from unfortunate encounters with the UI scum that led to a shooting and yet another dead body. All of his runners had weapons, of course, and no one was going to turn them in like the new law required. Such was the darker side of his business.

Davato had given him his life's mission. With his every breath, Ariel now fought back against the man who'd taken Shoshanna, his sister, and her family. After the Great Catastrophe, Shoshanna had abandoned her Jewish faith for Christianity, something Ariel wasn't yet prepared to do. Then, one night, CSA hoodlums burst into her home and took her, her husband, and Shoshanna's fifteen-year-old daughter, Tiki, whom Ariel loved dearly. Yes, Davato's minions had taken everyone he loved, and no amount of revenge would ever salve the wound.

Ariel's people had shot and captured one of the thugs who'd taken his family, and before the man was killed—he didn't ask about details—they'd learned that Shoshanna's family had been flown to New Babylon. There they would become target practice in the shooting galleries for the rich, the well connected, and the fools mesmerized by Davato's honeyed words and false promises. Ariel gripped the wheel tighter until his knuckles hurt.

The Christians called Davato the man of lawlessness. Ariel grinned again, for he'd become adept at turning the spirit of Davato's lawless age against the one who'd created it. Lawlessness worked both ways, didn't it?

The Christians also called Davato the Antichrist.

But Ariel called him the enemy, and he'd do whatever it took to fight back. And besides, working against the Unitum Imperium had its benefits. Every day, as people feared to take the mark, they realized they had no other option but to buy on the black market. It was making his organization rich.

Above, a meteor briefly lit the alley where his vehicle was parked. Of all the evidence the Christians in his employ used to try to convince him their faith was real, the earthquake and what had happened to the sun and moon and what happened in the Battle of Gog and Magog was the most powerful. In a single day, the Islamic nations that had attacked Israel had ceased to exist. His workers even showed him how these events matched what their Bible said.

He could never take the mark of his enemy, the mark of the beast. But was he ready to declare himself a Christian?

No. Not yet.

His walkie-talkie squawked, and he picked it up. Not being able to use cell phones was a problem. Too easy to track. To work around it, he'd created a network of walkie-talkies. A runner with a message would call up another runner, someone within a five-mile range. That runner would call another, and so on until they reached their destination. Every other day, they changed frequencies. But he feared the system wasn't foolproof. He feared that sometimes, they were listening in. He needed another method to communicate, and soon.

"Big Matza here. What's up?" Ariel derived great pleasure from coming up with code names based on Jewish food. The Antichrist's people hated Jews and their food.

"Kishke here." Kishke was beef intestine skin stuffed with matzah meal, spices, and boiled, like sausage. Kishke was one of his best runners on the Namal, charged with finding strays needing food, transportation, or refuge from the UI thugs. "I've got a woman here who's starving and in bad shape. She's been asking a lot of indiscreet questions on the dock, trying to get a ride to Italy, but I doubt she'll find it on the Namal. She's out of cash, of course, and can't pay for anything. She's been sleeping in the park. If it weren't for the boils on the thugs, they would have picked her up long ago. Tomorrow, if the CSA starts to recover, she'll be in big trouble."

"So why call me? Send her to our food kitchen. We can't take in every stray."

"Because there's something else you need to know. At first, I didn't recognize her, but . . . I've seen her before. On TV. Standing on the dais in Jerusalem next to Davato."

The news rocked Ariel into silence. One of Davato's bigwigs had escaped and ended up in his lap? The possibilities swirled in his head.

"Big Matza, are you there?"

"Say no more. Keep her there. Where are you?"

"At the Kichel." Kichel was a cookie made with eggs and sugar, but in Ariel's world, it was a code identifying a certain bench in Namal's main park, one of their meeting points.

"Right. Be there in"—he checked his watch—"ten."

* * *

ANOTHER OF ARIEL'S RUNNERS DROPPED him near the park. He exited the car and set out on foot.

So she was looking for a boat to Italy? But Namal Tel Aviv was no longer the port it once was. After the renovation, it was more of an upscale playground, filled with expensive restaurants, hotels, and beaches. Much of the commercial shipping had moved north to Haifa. Like everywhere else, the Great Catastrophe, the famine, the plague, and the worldwide depression had done their work. Half the hotels had closed. The rest were far below capacity. Only the CSA thugs could afford the upscale restaurants, and now too many bodies washed up on the beaches or lay rotting in the alleys.

As he passed a metal statue of the Dragon, Davato, and the Prophet, he lobbed a wad of spit onto the Imperator's face. A hundred meters later, he approached the rendezvous point. Ahead, Kishke sat on a bench beside a dirty-faced woman wearing clothes in need of washing, her reddish-blonde hair in snags. But underneath, Ariel recognized the person who once stood at the center of power beside Davato.

Kishke stood. "Big Matza, this is Chelsea Turner."

"Big Matza?" A hint of a grin crossed her face as she stood and received Ariel's extended hand. "Some kind of joke?"

"Yeah. On the UI thugs. I've seen you on television next to the man whose brutes took my sister and her family." He crossed his arms and regarded her. Despite looking like one of the many homeless they encountered way too often, she carried an air of authority.

"Caught me. I'm running from Davato because I worked for him. But he's a monster. Everyone around him lives in fear they'll do or say something wrong and end up a target in the shooting galleries. Or they'll be sent into the New Babylon colosseum, running from the lions. Or they'll disappear into the German death camp they're reconstructing even bigger than before. A month ago, I escaped. But I admit, I'm not very good at this." She waved a hand over her dirty clothes. "I need to get to Italy."

"What did you do for him?"

"I was his personal assistant. I recorded many of his meetings, escorted his visitors, and traveled with him. But I never"—her forehead scrunched into a grimace—"I never slept with him."

Ariel scratched his chin. With her job, she would possess valuable—and helpful—information. "Why do you want to get to Italy?"

"When I changed phones, I lost all my contacts, and I need to get to my family's estate. A servant there can connect me with my brother."

"What can you tell me about the Imperator, as he calls himself?"

"Not much you don't know already."

Ariel frowned. Not the answer he wanted. "Kishke told me you were asking questions about a boat?"

"It's the only way I could think of to leave Israel without being stopped. Without a valid travel pass, I can't go by plane or overland."

"I agree. A boat, a fishing trawler maybe, would be better. I could get you a travel pass. But your face is too familiar for planes, and if I were you, I would avoid all checkpoints. I know a man in Haifa with a ship. But he's expensive. What can you pay me?"

"I've spent everything I had on food. I couldn't find a place to sleep except in the park. And there are so few proprietors willing to take cash." She waved her hands. Were those tears forming at the corners of her eyes? "They overcharged me."

It was the same old story, wasn't it? Always a pushover for a woman in tears—and this woman was obviously not scamming him—he laid a hand on her shoulder and squeezed.

He had a man in mind. But he didn't completely trust him, and he charged too much. Regardless of the tears, Ariel needed something in return. "Surely, as an employee of the great Imperator, seeing his deepest secrets every day, you can share something with me that will make it worth my while to pay the cost to get you to Italy?"

"You can get me there safely?" She wiped moisture from her cheeks, and her voice rose. "By boat?"

He snorted. "I'd hardly call it safe. And it's expensive. What can you do for me?"

She reached for the garbage bag at her feet. They always ended up with a garbage bag, didn't they? For this woman, privy to the highest echelons of power, this kind of life must be a huge letdown. She pushed aside a blanket then pulled out a backpack, from which she fished a piece of paper.

"What's that?" He peered down at the copy. It contained technical schematics.

"One day in Davato's headquarters, I was out of sight in the copy room. There, I overheard a conversation between two men who had designed and then worked on the manufacture of the solar phones. The inventor told his companion he had built in a back door, an ingenious way to permanently override the tracking mechanism."

Ariel's mouth opened, and his heart raced. "Does anyone else know about this? Other than you and these two tech guys?"

"I don't think so."

"Yes, Chelsea Turner, that piece of information will do nicely. If you explain to me how to disable solar phone tracking, here is what I will do for you: I will put you up in a hotel, give you new clothes, a wad of cash, and new UI identity and credit cards—they should be good for several months yet. I'll give you a travel pass as a backup, and I will personally drive you to Haifa. I know a man there who operates a fishing trawler. He's due to arrive in port in a few days. He told me his next run will be to Venice, Italy. Is that close enough to your destination?"

Her somber, defeated expression changed to one of joy, and she nodded.

"But I must warn you. I don't completely trust the man. Like so many others these days, he charges more than he should, and he won't negotiate. And there are other clues, subtle, that I've picked up. I don't like the man."

"But his destination is Venice?"

"So he says."

"Then I'll do it. I've got to get out of here, and soon. With what you'll be giving me, even if he doesn't work out, I can find another way to get there." She crossed the distance to him and laid a kiss on his cheek.

He stepped back. One hand went to his cheek, and he smiled. Kiss or no, she needed a bath.

"Good. Let's shake on it." They did.

Then he led her to the runner's car and to a trusted hotel that he paid for. He handed her a wad of cash, and this afternoon, he'd have one of the women bring her fresh clothes. With the cash, she could eat at the restaurants on his list who hated what the UI was doing, hated what was happening to their world, and were secretly working against the man the Christians called the Antichrist. One-fourth of the world now depended on the black market.

But this was Ariel's day for grinning. With what Chelsea Turner would provide him, he would soon have a network of untraceable cell phones.

CHAPTER 35
SQUADDIE TROUBLE

The Appenzell Alps, Switzerland – February 2, Year 4

With skis in hand, Dylan shot a last glance out the window at the black Audi turning down the drive. It belonged to the squaddies, and this was their first visit to the Skihaus since the epidemic of boils. Moments before, Victor's roadside camera had beeped its warning that the car was on its way. It had to be squaddies, as the vast majority of vehicles traveling their remote country lane were old, beat-up cars, trucks, or tractors. Victor had rigged his camera to sound an alarm for anything crossing a strip a kilometer down the highway.

"Get out!" Danielle waved Dylan away from the window. "They'll be here any minute."

"Yeah, I'm going." On his feet were ski boots, and he wore a ski jacket. On his back was a knapsack. He also carried poles, and he clutched them to his chest as he hurried through the chalet's back door.

The sun glinted off the frozen snow, and the cold air filled his lungs. Slapping his skis down onto the icy hardpack, he stepped into the bindings until they clicked. Then he drove both poles, crunching them into the hard crust. He followed the tracks made by René, Pasqual, Victor, and Margot. If the squaddies stayed inside for only a few minutes, he'd have enough time to cross the field and enter the next valley to the warming hut.

He gained the hilltop and glided in the others' tracks down the hill. He snowplowed to a stop, removed skis and poles, and entered the one-room hut. They were already listening to the exchange Danielle was having with one of the Truth Squad people—an exchange that one of Victor's microphones was picking up. Inside the hut, someone had lit the wicks of two candles.

"Ven vas dis establishment open for business, Fraulein?" came the voice of a man, probably middle-aged, probably stout, probably with short hair. "We were unaware of it."

"Not long, mein Herr," answered Danielle. "We have only a few customers."

"May I see the ledger?"

"Ja, of course, it's over here."

Then came the sounds of feet crossing the wooden floor and of rustling paper.

"You have drei guests, ja?"

"Three guests today, ja."

"And these are their ID card numbers with travel passes?"

"Ja, mein Herr."

Dylan held his breath. Victor had created fake IDs based on his ability to hack into the digital payments and credit system. But whether the squaddies would check and find some discrepancy—who knew?

After some time, another man, probably younger, spoke. "You live here alone, Fraulein?"

"I take care of the place, ja. My husband bought it, but he died in the plague. I'm close with a farm family down the way. They help me out, look out for me."

"A pretty young thing like you, living here all by yourself?"

Dylan didn't like the man's tone.

"Are you not worried someone will take advantage?"

"N—nein. I can take care of myself." But her voice registered wariness. Or was it distress?

Then Victor spoke to the others. "If he tries something, what should we do?"

"Nothing." René lit a cigarette. "We can't blow our cover. Then we'd have to search for a new place."

Scowling, Victor nodded.

"Enough, Reinhold," came the older man's voice. "We're not here for *that*. Now we must check the premises upstairs, Fraulein, if that is acceptable to you?"

"Ja, of course, check all you like."

Feet tromped up the creaking stairs, and Danielle whispered into the mike before following them. "The young one's making eyes at me. I was afraid for a moment the older man would have to step in. But he backed off."

Since there was no speaker on her end, those in the warming hut couldn't answer. So for a time they waited.

The shack held six chairs, a brick fireplace—but no fire today—and a narrow wooden table.

"Did you have time to make your bed, Margot?" Pasqual pulled up a chair and sat.

"It was close, but I did." Still standing, she slapped her arms about her chest. "And I hid everything in the wardrobe. Unless they break the lock, the room will look unoccupied."

Dylan also sat, removed his jacket, but decided it was too cold, and pulled it back on.

Puffing on his cigarette, René sat beside them. "Your warning system worked, Victor. Congratulations!"

"Thank you. But we barely had time to get out. What if the squaddies don't leave? What if they wait until we return?"

"They won't. If they do, we can stay here all night. But they'll want to be on the road long before dark. It's a long drive back to Appenzell."

The sound of footsteps came over the speaker, and everyone in the hut stopped talking.

"Everything seems in order, Fraulein, so we'll leave you. But you haven't filed a business permit. We'll give you a pass on that today, but you must do that before we return. The requirement is relatively new. And"—laughing from the other man—"after the plague of boils, everything is in much disarray."

"Fools, all of them," came the younger man's voice.

"Thank you, meine Herren," came Danielle's voice. "I will look into getting a permit."

"See that you do," said the younger one.

Then came the sounds of the men leaving. Moments later, Danielle spoke into the mike. "They're gone. You can return."

They left the hut, stepped into their skis, and climbed the hill back to the house.

* * *

"That went relatively well, I thought," said Danielle when everyone was lounging before the iron stove back in the Skihaus.

"Oui, but now we need to apply for one of those permits." René had lit another cigarette, and he flicked ash into a tray. Everyone had given up trying to get him to smoke outside in such bitter weather. "Victor, can you give them what they want?"

"I'll look into it. But I might have to hack into a different system."

"Do what you can," said Pasqual. "It's almost time for the broadcast. We should hear what they're saying."

Victor turned on the flat-screen TV and tuned it to the Worldnet satellite channel. But they must have caught the end of the broadcast.

The picture focused on a gigantic statue of Davato—so eerie and unreal Dylan squirmed—as it faced the audience inside the Temple. The figure dwarfed those at its feet, and the camera zeroed in on the dignitaries and high-level functionaries comprising the Imperator's inner circle. They included his father, the Prophet, and a man who might be the Grady that Chelsea had talked about. There were others he didn't know. But where was Chelsea? No matter where the camera panned he didn't see her.

He gritted his teeth and crossed his arms. At every such broadcast in the past, Chelsea had been present. Something was wrong.

"Yes, my friends," came Davato's thunderous words from the giant's mouth, "the world reeled at the curse the Enemy placed upon the earth. For a time, he dimmed the sun, blackened the stars out of existence, and poisoned the moon." The giant's head glanced down, and it raised both hands in a question. "But what else can we expect from a fiend, from one who threw the earth into chaos with his earthquakes and who let the aliens take our children?"

As Dylan shuddered at the effect this giant, speaking such abomination, was having on him, shouts of agreement and praise rose from the Temple crowd. The camera panned over the thousands packed into the area.

His command over the people was frightening. They were mesmerized, sucked into everything coming out of his mouth. And the image of this monster, towering over everyone like a god—a god he declared himself to be—made even Dylan feel small and insignificant.

He shook himself to ward off the effect. It was all a fraud.

"Unlike the Enemy who cursed our planet, I stand before you as the deity, supreme in power, majesty, and grace, promising you prosperity, peace, and freedom, and today, a free gift. At the end of this broadcast, I'm giving everyone the opportunity to sign up for a lottery to win a two-week trip to the world's premier playground—New Babylon. It's a kindness I have ordered for you, and all who win will be blessed. Alas, though tens of thousands will win, it is not possible for everyone to come, though I wish it were so. In consolation, we will issue a hundred thousand cash prizes to those who don't win the trip. "

Then the giant smiled and opened its arms as though encompassing its audience. "So whom will you worship, my people? Who is most worthy? An Enemy who curses your world, shakes it apart, and dims its light? Or one who brings you peace, prosperity, and gifts?"

The picture then focused on the Prophet standing below the Giant at the dais. "Bow down, people of earth. Bow to the one god to whom you owe allegiance and thanks. Bow to the one who hasn't cursed you with plagues, famine, and earthquakes."

The camera drew back, showing thousands of men, women, and youths dropping to their knees, prostrating themselves before the Imperator. More images appeared of squares and parks in Paris, London, Miami, Tokyo, and other cities. Hundreds of thousands of people from all over the world were bowing and praising the giant, giving him their fealty, their hearts, their souls.

When Dylan saw his father's prostrate form near the dais, he sucked in breath. How far had he fallen! All his life, Adam Turner had given his soul to power and wealth, and now he worked for the Antichrist, a man in league with Satan himself. This was the man who'd been part of Dylan's life as a baby, a young child, a youth. Sometimes, though not often, they'd done things as a family. Though his father had his faults, Dylan believed that, deep down, Adam Turner still held some kind of love for his children.

But he'd changed. His association with Davato had brought out the worst in him. Chelsea had said it before, and now, seeing Father on the headquarters platform, Dylan knew that Adam Turner was beyond hope.

Everyone in Davato's orbit would have taken the mark of the beast, the mark dooming them for all eternity.

He brushed a tear from his cheek. The man was truly lost, wasn't he? And now nothing could ever change it.

It was happening not only to his father but also to hundreds of millions across the world.

The broadcast ended with more pleas from a giant Davato to take the mark, and Victor switched off the program.

"That was disturbing." René stubbed out his cigarette. "More than disturbing, it was . . . bone-chilling. He's got the entire world worshiping and bowing to him."

"It was all prophesied," said Pasqual. "Now it's come to pass."

"I didn't see Chelsea up there." Dylan stood and headed for a quiet spot by the front door. "And it has me worried. I'm going to call her."

As the others waved an acknowledgment, he pulled out one of the GPS-encrypted phones Victor had created and punched the numbers. But instead of getting through, he received a message telling him her phone was out of service.

It was true. Chelsea was in trouble.

CHAPTER 36

STARTING OVER

On the road to Haifa, Israel – February 3, Year 4

The sun was already setting as Chelsea sat in the passenger seat of an Alfa Romeo Stelvio, its tires humming over the asphalt. Big Matza himself drove. They'd started late in the day on purpose. The checkpoints were returning, and Big Matza wanted to pass them in the dark. And for some reason, the Jewish sea captain they were meeting only did business at night.

She smoothed her new flowered dress and stared out the window at the dimly lit, rock-filled fields now touched with green after the rains revived them. The hotel showers, the food, the new clothes, the clean bed—though they lifted her spirits, they had not erased what she'd been through.

Four weeks living as a homeless beggar on Tel Aviv's fashionable Na-mal had dragged a knife across her soul, made her wary of what life might throw her way next. She'd always had everything—a good car, an upscale apartment, expensive restaurants, and stylish clothes. But after a month of living like the scum of the earth, she'd been shaken.

Huddling her arms about her chest, she told herself she must over-come this new, unwelcome sense of fear. Fear was the mind killer. It curled you in a ball and backed you away from every encounter, hiding you from strangers, many of whom, of course, were out to take advan-tage. Fear made you indecisive, weak.

How would she ever get to the villa with that attitude? No, she must try to be the person she was before, the fearless Chelsea ready to strike back against the world's injustices in the face of all opposition.

She sat up straighter in the seat, breathed deeply, and turned to her benefactor. "You've never told me your name."

"I haven't, have I?" He grinned. "Well, now I trust you. My name is Ariel Geller."

"Pleased to meet you, Ariel Geller, aka Big Matza." Smiling, she extended a hand.

"Likewise, Chelsea Turner." Still grinning, he reached over and squeezed her fingers before returning to the wheel. What secret joke kept this man grinning all the time?

"I gather your black-market operation is quite large. I've met so many people who work for you. And you have a soup kitchen. And you put up refugees in hotels, give them new identities, and help people running from the Truth Squads. I'm impressed."

Ariel grinned. Half the time when she turned his way, he was grinning.

"I do what I can. I am no friend of the man the Christians call the Antichrist. But you worked for him. Tell me truthfully: Do you think he's the Antichrist?"

She scowled. "The man is evil beyond imagining. There were times when I was in the building with him when a creepy feeling came over me. It's hard to describe, but it was like I had acquired a sixth sense warning me I was in the presence of someone—or some *thing*—possessing an overwhelming, evil power not of this world. It was deep, soul bending, and at such times, I wanted to run—far, far away. But I couldn't. Sometimes, it happened in the elevator or in the hallway or passing a certain door. But it was real. And sometimes, it brought on such a fit of shivering, I had to flee to the restroom until it passed."

"So you think he is truly the Antichrist?" As he turned to her, his grin disappeared.

"Yes. He's a man in league with the Devil. When you first meet him, he seems kind, gentle, charismatic. But as you get to know him and see his atrocities, the death and destruction that follow in his wake, when you peer into the icy center of his soul, you see through to the man behind the mask. And pure evil overwhelms you."

She wrapped her arms about her chest and shuddered. "I was such a fool." She shook her head. "I had other options, and I rejected them all. And now I'm separated from my brother and his friends. And if I don't get to Italy and find them . . ."

She wiped a tear from her cheek and faced out the window. Why, lately, had she become so emotional?

Ariel reached across and laid a hand on her shoulder. "Don't berate yourself for the past. Don't look back. We'll get you to Italy. You've got your whole life ahead of you. I've met too many like you whose lives that bastard has destroyed. Don't let yours be one of them."

She faced him again and smiled. "Thank you, Big Matza—I mean, Ariel. You have done a lot of good for a lot of people, I think. And I'm not going to look back. I'm going to put this behind me and look ahead."

"Good."

"I have to overcome what happened to me, yes. But now, can I say something to you, Ariel? Something personal?"

His grin faded, and he briefly took his focus off the road. Slowly, he nodded.

"I like you, but you seem fixed—no, consumed—with revenge. I know we must all fight against Davato, this Antichrist. He is truly evil. But we mustn't let it take over our lives. And after hearing you, I fear your devotion to the fight is consuming you. I know whereof I speak, because I've been fighting for causes all my life, and I'm beginning to think I need to refocus—but on what . . . I don't know. But I do know one thing. There is no end to revenge."

He shot her a sideways glance in which there was no mirth, only a visage twisted in agony. "You may be right, Chelsea Turner. Nonetheless, it is my destiny. It's what I must do."

"Then may God go with you. May he heal your soul as I hope he will heal mine." But the minute she'd said that, she surprised herself. Was she now believing in God? Or in the Son he sent? Yet . . . it seemed like the right thing to say. And strangely, she believed it.

For some time, they drove on in silence until buildings and streets surrounded them.

"We're coming into Haifa," he said, his voice subdued.

Moments later, he parked and led her from the parking lot down to the pier.

She carried her new backpack with all her earthly possessions. Everything was newly purchased except her solar phone and the Bible Lazzaro had given her.

They hadn't gone ten meters when Ariel stopped her and thrust a hunk of gray metal and plastic into her hands. "Take this. It's a Ruger LCP Max. It has a short 2.8-inch barrel, easily concealed, and here—" He handed her a magazine and a pack of bullets. "The magazine holds twelve rounds. It's full."

She stared at it. "Why do I want this?"

"Insurance for your trip. In case things go south."

After hesitating, she took the gun, the magazine, and the box of bullets and stuffed them in an interior pocket of her knapsack.

"And, Chelsea?"

"Yes?"

"I think it wise if you do not give them your last name."

"Of course. Thank you."

CHAPTER 37

FABIO CARUSO

Haifa Harbor, Israel – February 3, Year 4

Chelsea followed Ariel down a creaking ramp to a skiff at the bottom where a gentle breeze bumped the craft against the dock.

He turned from her and called someone on his phone. After a brief conversation, he scanned the boats in the harbor. Hundreds were anchored inside Israel's largest port. About a hundred meters out, someone flashed three bursts from a flashlight. "That's our man," he said. "Let's go."

He rowed the skiff between ships rocking at anchor. As he rowed, she feasted her eyes on the moon and stars, so familiar and comforting. Having the sun back was a great relief. Funny how such small things—stars and moon in the sky—reminded her of how things used to be. Always surrounded by electric lights, always inside before a television, she hardly ever noticed the moon and stars before.

An occasional meteor still fell, lighting up the water, the masts, the hulls. The creaking of oars, the wash of the sea against the hull, and the loud music from a few boats accompanied their passage.

Ariel maneuvered them across the bow of a freezer trawler with a name in Arabic. The ship was maybe twenty by seventy feet with a superstructure amidships. After Ariel's examination, he explained it had radar, VHF, and GMDSS walkie-talkie antennae sprouting from the top. "That's good," he added. "It's probably no more than fifteen years old. In case you get in trouble at sea, it has good communications."

But Chelsea wondered if, nowadays, there existed anyone to rescue troubled ships at sea.

It was night, and the ship's portside blinked a red light. From atop the superstructure, a white light flashed upon the nearby waters.

When Ariel had positioned his skiff aft, a tall, skinny man with dark hair extended a ladder. Ariel tied up his craft, and they stepped aboard.

"Hello, friends. I am Fabio Caruso, owner of this poor vessel." He bowed, and when he raised his head, jet-black eyes peered out from dark, weathered skin. "Welcome to the *Am Albahr*. I apologize for the Arab name. It means Mother of the Sea. I haven't had time to change the registration, yes?"

Behind him, another, shorter man peered at the newcomers and lounged against one of the ship's four winches. He was lighter skinned, with short blond hair, of Northern European stock.

Fabio waved to him. "My crewman there is Altin Tolan. Unfortunately, he's Albanian." Fabio chuckled, but Altin did not. "Never trust an Albanian, yes?"

Apparently puzzled by the remark, Ariel cocked his head. Then he introduced Chelsea.

Though the night was warm, Fabio wore a long-sleeved shirt. He waved a hand across the deck. "As you can see, we are short-staffed. And now, before we proceed, I must ask you, signorina: Will you be able to help with the catch on our way? It is necessary. A condition of passage I must insist upon. My other passenger has already agreed to this."

Ariel frowned. "This was not what we agreed upon. And you have a second passenger? This, too, was not in the deal."

"Ah, but I make so little, I require both. And if we encounter fish, I must have help. Either she works, or the deal is off."

Ariel opened his hands to her in a question.

"I can help," she said.

"Good!" Fabio clapped. "Then come aboard, and, Big Matza, I will now take the payment you promised." He rubbed his fingers together.

No longer grinning, Ariel pulled out a thick envelope and passed it over. Fabio left them, took it to the wheelhouse, turned on a light, and counted. When he returned, he was all smiles. "Well and good. Now, Big Matza, our business is complete, and you may leave. We must make sail within the hour. The harbor patrol will pass by in forty minutes, and we must be gone before they arrive, yes?"

Ariel caught Chelsea's glance and crossed his arms. "You will take good care of her, Fabio Caruso, and let nothing happen to her? I have become fond of her."

Nodding and smiling, Fabio said, again and again, that she was in good hands and that he would get her to her destination.

"Then this is goodbye, Chelsea." Ariel extended a hand, and they shook. But then she gave him a kiss on the cheek, and he paused, smiled, and only then left for his skiff.

As dark waters swallowed the craft from view, another man appeared on deck, light-skinned, about Chelsea's age, with a prominent nose. He stepped forward, glanced at Fabio and Chelsea.

"This is my other passenger," said Fabio. "Enzo Rivera is also bound for Venice." He introduced Chelsea, but then frowned. "You never told me your last name, Chelsea."

"You don't need to know that," she said.

"Ah, yes, of course. We all have secrets, don't we?"

Enzo smiled and offered a hand, and she took it. "I am a Christian, Chelsea without a last name, and I freely confess I am fleeing Israel and the Unitum Imperium for my hometown of Bergamo. I have been living in Haifa, working for a computer company, but"—he scowled at the deck—"everything is different now. I cannot take the mark."

"I understand," she added. "Neither can I."

"Now, come, and I will show you the vessel." Fabio pointed to four winches used for hauling up the trawls, or nets. "Those stairs lead below to the engine room and a Mercedes-Benz 484 kilowatt diesel engine with a maximum cruising speed of nine knots. My quarters are behind the wheelhouse above the main deck. Amidships on the main deck are four crew cabins and a compressor room, and in the bow area, a cold room, galley, and our crew mess area."

The entire ship smelled of fish, and in the floor between crew cabins, hatches led down to the fish freezer area. "We can stay at sea for twenty days," he added. "My hold is larger than most."

"But we have paid for passage to Venice," said Enzo. "What will you do with only two crew once we depart?"

"Let me worry about that. I will take on new passengers, who must also work."

Chelsea frowned. Four people to work a ship designed for five crew, including the captain? She didn't like the sound of this.

"But now, signorina, here is your cabin." Fabio pointed to a door, but she stopped and stared. "Why is there a deadbolt lock on the outside? And why the permanent screws?" The screwheads could only turn in one direction. She'd need a drill to take them off.

"Again, I apologize. Recently, we had a mission to carry two prisoners, and I haven't had time to remove the locks. The screws do make it more difficult, yes?" He waved to Enzo's room next to hers. It, too, had a lock. But the two rooms across the passage had none.

"That one is Altin's." Fabio waved. "Again, I apologize for not removing the locks. So many things to do. So little time."

She stared at the doors, at the deadbolts, and remembered Ariel's warning about this man. But she was here, and in order to get to Italy, what other choice did she have?

Fabio led her into her room, perhaps two meters by four. It held a single bunk, a chair, a desk with a reading light, a washbasin, a toilet standing out in the open, and a rack for clothes. A tiny porthole in the outside wall, covered with a curtain, led to one of the open passageways on either side of the ship. At least she could get some air once in a while.

"Conditions are cramped, yes?" He waved his hands again. "But 'tis a small craft."

She dropped her bag on the floor, sat on the bed, and nodded. She was exhausted, and the bed was soft enough. "It will do."

"Good, then make yourself comfortable while we get underway." He closed the door on her, and the others left.

But when she tried to lock the door, the only inside lock was a flimsy hook-and-eye latch. She dropped the hook into the eye, scowled at it, then shook her head.

As the engine throbbed from below, she hung up her clothes then examined the gun Ariel had given her.

The trip was not starting well.

She hid the gun, magazine, and bullets under the mattress.

CHAPTER 38
ONE WORLD RULE

Daniel 7:19–20, 23–24 (HCSB): "Then I wanted to know the true meaning of the fourth beast, the one different from all the others, extremely terrifying, with iron teeth and bronze claws, devouring, crushing, and trampling with its feet whatever was left. I also wanted to know about the 10 horns on its head and about the other horn that came up, before which three fell—the horn that had eyes, and a mouth that spoke arrogantly, and that was more visible than the others.

"This is what he said: 'The fourth beast will be a fourth kingdom on the earth, different from all the other kingdoms. It will devour the whole earth, trample it down, and crush it. The 10 horns are 10 kings who will rise from this kingdom."

New Babylon, Iraq – February 3, Year 4

The mood was nervous, expectant, and subservient as leaders from all over the world shuffled over the plush carpet and poured into Davato's new conference room two stories down from the top floor of New Babylon's World Casino. On the perimeter, League of Abaddon translators sat in plexiglass booths with earphones, mikes, and anxious glances.

The Imperator himself possessed the head of a long ebony table and peered down the row of seats now being occupied by his chosen ten. Molded in the shape of a horn, the room was meant to awe, cower, and impress upon visitors a sense of power and helplessness. At the wide end behind him, a wall mural forty meters high swirled with red and yellow flames and towering spires of black rock.

On the wall above and to either side hung three symbols of the Imperium:

On his left shoulder—a ten-meter-in-diameter white skull crossed with a lightning bolt, the logo of the feared Central Security Agency.

On his right shoulder—a similar-sized emblem bearing a dragon in the center, an image of Davato on the right, and the Prophet on the left.

And in the middle—the familiar six-sided symbol, fifteen meters wide, with the letters of Davato's name on the outside and lines pointing to a center globe displaying Europe and Northern Africa.

Anyone seated at the room's far end and glancing down the twenty-meter-long, shiny, black ebony, past the water glasses clinking with ice, beyond the leather notepads and gold pens, all the way to the massive throne at the end, its seatback covered with black felt and embroidered with red flames—surely, anyone looking his way must cower to insignificance before the power, authority, and—dare he suggest?—majesty displayed there.

Off to his left and a meter lower, sat Adam Turner, the Minister of Truth; General Eric Hofmann, the Minister of Peace; Sebastien Rey, the Minister of Virtue; and Gaston Soucy, the Minister of Charity. Every important head of government must witness what occurred here today.

The final stage of his assumption of world power was minutes away.

Adam Turner had outdone himself with the research, ensuring that each man and woman now seated was qualified and, most importantly, would bend to his direction. Even before coming to Worldnet, Turner had refined an unparalleled ability at finding the smallest crime sufficient to bow any will to the Imperator's.

Naturally, every person of any importance in the room had received the mark and pledged fealty to him.

Carlo Scutari was in charge of security. But today, no aides were being admitted. Each leader was on his own.

On his right, sitting lower in one of the common chairs, François Desroches nodded. Everyone was in place. It was time to begin.

Seated a meter higher than the others, Davato opened the meeting in English, French, Italian, and German. Translators filled in for the rest. "Welcome, governors, to the first meeting of Unitum Imperium world rule! Today marks the conclusion of a long series of preparations of which you have all taken part." Then his voice filled with the power of command. "From this moment forward, there is only one country, one nation, and one ruler upon the earth—the Unitum Imperium and its Imperator!"

His gaze swept down the table to his chosen governors. Positioned before him were the future provincial leaders of Northern Europe, Southern Europe, Eastern Europe, Africa, the Mideast, India, Asia, Australasia, South America, and North America.

"The world is now divided into ten great provinces, under ten great leaders—you who sit before me, you who will rule in my stead, under my direction. You were chosen not only because of your skills, abilities, and political prowess, but because of your expected loyalty and obedience to the one who reigns above you."

Then Davato's voice rose in power and strength and echoed down the table to the room's far end. "When you leave here today, you will carry only the power and authority I grant you. Let no one here forget from whence that power comes. FOR IT IS NOT A MERE MORTAL YOU SEE BEFORE YOU, BUT A DIVINE BEING, ORDAINED AND APPOINTED BY HISTORY TO RULE THE WORLD!"

Silence swept the room as startled glances caught his then quickly dropped. For how could such insignificant creatures hold the glance of a being like him?

"You are mine, and the one thing I cannot, will not, abide is disobedience, going one's own way, and not following the will of one's Imperator. As the hurricane washes away a child's sandcastle, so will the power bestowed upon me obliterate and sweep out to sea any hint of rebellion, cowardice, or personal fortress erected against my rule." Then his glance, dark and penetrating and filled with malice, pierced each member seated until everybody shifted and every glance averted.

A woman coughed. A gilded pen clattered to the table. A water glass full of ice touched the ebony and echoed.

Then Davato's features relaxed. He laid both hands on the table before him and smiled. "Yes, you are mine. And I have just told you the consequences of not being mine. Long ago, you agreed to join this venture by signing a treaty of intent, and, for the most part, you have kept it. Those who didn't are no longer with us, are they?"

Again, he smiled, thinking back on the unfortunate automobile accident that removed the president of Brazil and the unexplained stroke that snuffed out the life of the Indian president.

"And because you are mine, I now announce the rewards that come with your positions. Before you leave today, each of you will receive a digital key to a Unitum Imperium account worth one-point-five billion Euros. In addition, my vice imperator, François Desroches, will hand each of you the deed to a luxurious villa, mansion, or estate in your lands. From this point forward, you will lack for nothing. We are also arranging for personal slaves to accompany you back to your home provinces, slaves willing to do your every bidding in whatever manner you desire. You are my leaders, and we must not neglect the inner man or woman or whatever sex you have claimed. My goal is to satisfy your deepest desires—your every need, whether it be political, financial, sensual, or carnal."

The faces at the table nodded and broke into smiles. Good. He had chosen well.

"This afternoon, we meet here in secret conclave. Tonight and tomorrow, avail yourselves of all the pleasures New Babylon has to offer. I wanted you to see for yourselves what we have done here. But three days from now, we will fly to Jerusalem, and everyone will stand with me before the cameras inside the Temple. There I will announce the second treaty you signed long ago, the one giving up your nations' sovereignty. Then we will have entered the final stage. From then on, the planet will have a single ruler, higher and greater than any that went before, without opposition, as decreed by history itself.

"Yes, my governors, from that historic moment, your Imperator will reign supreme. From then until the end of time, the planet will exist UNDER ONE IMPERATOR, UNDER ONE WORLD RULE!"

On cue, those seated off the side, those among the highest echelon of the Unitum Imperium, rose in applause. Milliseconds later, the governors seated at the shiny ebony table rushed to stand and join them.

Hands clapped until they were raw. Nodding heads turned to him, jaws tight, eyes wide, in postures of subjugation.

Pride and arrogance and ego swelled his inner being nearly to bursting. He was the Imperator, appointed by the Dragon himself, raised by the League of Abaddon for this exact moment. And now, he ruled the earth and all that existed upon it.

He was God himself.

CHAPTER 39

THE RECEPTION

Somewhere Over Iraq — February 6, Year 4

After the Learjet Bombardier roared away from New Babylon's International Airport, one of the flight attendants tapped Grady Wilson on the shoulder with a message that the Imperator wished to speak with him forward. Already startled that he'd been one of the select few onboard the eight-passenger luxury craft, Grady swallowed and followed the lithe beauty to a seat opposite the most powerful man in the world. This morning, Davato exuded all the charm, charisma, and ease of manner that had wowed the world. The Imperator was in a good mood.

"I am so glad you are here with us, Grady Wilson." The Imperator reached across, laid a hand on Grady's knee, and squeezed. "I have been watching you for some time, and I like what I see."

Surprised by the compliment, Grady offered a weak smile.

"Yes, and with the departure of the traitor Chelsea Turner"—a cloud flitted across his brows before the smile returned—"I have a position to fill."

His heart racing, Grady sank back against the soft leather as the attendant brought him a glass of whiskey with ice, his usual drink, pulled out the gold-plated tray, and set it before him. He thanked her, grabbed the crystal glass, and sipped.

Davato lifted his own tumbler of brandy. "So today, Grady Wilson, I offer you the position of personal secretary to the Imperator, replacing the traitor. You will take notes at private meetings, escort visitors, and attend me on my trips. I have already contacted President Cole and informed him of the change. He is sending someone to replace you. Your importance to me far exceeds any possible loyalty you may have had to Camp David. So what do you say, Grady? Do you accept?"

Stunned by the suddenness of the request, but knowing that to reject it would be fatal, he nodded. Then he realized he should speak. "Yes, my lord, I accept. Most assuredly, with all my heart, I accept."

Davato rubbed the chair's soft leather and smiled. "I knew you would. So congratulations!" He reached a hand across, and they shook. "I will announce it at the grand reception before the announcement."

Grady's chest swelled with pride and joy. To be appointed to such a position was the greatest honor he'd ever receive in his lifetime. He beamed and thanked the Imperator a second time.

"But now I have some good news for you. As I said, your replacement is on his way, a man whom I'm told knew your family well. Alex Reed is his name, and two days ago, President Cole appointed him as the North American Ambassador to the Unitum Imperium. He was not in Boston when the bombs hit and escaped the carnage. You will have plenty of time to get reacquainted as you'll be working together."

Grady's mouth opened, and he sucked in air. A friend of the Wilson family who knew the real Grady? Was he now to be undone by the very deception that had brought him this new, exalted position?

"Yes, it's quite a shock to find out someone survived the attack when you thought them dead." Davato patted Grady's knee. "But now, if you will excuse me, I need to polish my speech."

Nodding, Grady took his drink and returned to his seat. Or was it Cam Weinberg whose body now rested against the plush leather?—a Jew named Chaim, who'd exchanged dog tags and uniforms with a corpse floating in the waters of the Taiwan Strait after the Chinese sank their destroyer?

Davato had just declared a vendetta against all Jews. Anyone suspected of belonging to that race would now be a special target of the Truth Squads and the CSA. Was he now to be one of them?

He shuddered.

Who was this Alex Reed? What if Grady didn't recognize him when they met? How close had he been to the Wilson family? He pulled out the computer screen on the seat tray and searched on the name. Yes, here was his picture. At least, he knew what the man looked like. The bio was brief, but it gave a few details on the man's background.

His fingers dug into his palms. How could the heights of joy raise him one moment, only to drop him seconds later into a deep, gnawing anxiety? What would Davato do if he discovered Grady was really Chaim Weinberg, a Jew? He glanced at the mark on his wrist, and for one second, it appeared like a spider's web.

Was he, as Chelsea had warned when he took the mark, indeed cursed?

* * *

After the Learjet emptied its passengers at Ben Gurion Airport, limousines drove them the forty-five kilometers to their rooms at the Clal Center where Grady acquainted himself with the more sumptuous room Chelsea previously occupied. Aides had already disposed of her things and moved in his belongings. He changed and, with heart pounding, went straight to the reception hall on the twelfth floor. Newly remodeled, the vast hall teemed with dignitaries, heads of corporations, famous glitterati, authors, actors, and actresses. Every important personage from the Unitum Imperium government was present.

He grabbed a glass of champagne from a tuxedoed waiter and tried to find a corner where no one would notice him. If he made himself invisible, perhaps he could escape a fatal meeting with Alex Reed? But for how long?

No sooner had he found a quiet corner than President William Cole appeared. "Ah, there you are, Grady." He extended a hand. "I was hoping we could talk alone."

Grady took the offered hand. "We haven't met in person since you sent me overseas to work with the Imperator."

"Unfortunately, yes." Cole frowned. "It's been a difficult assignment, I dare say. You and I have had conversations as frank as could be allowed under the circumstances. I thank you for your service to me and to your country. And now I should congratulate you on your promotion."

"Thank you."

"But I was hoping that in your new position you could still be of service to your country—or at least what has now become of it." He shook his head. "We're now the Province of North America, and I will be its governor. But, of course, you know that."

"Yes." Grady feared what Cole would say next. Any private arrangement between them would *not* be to Davato's liking.

Cole lowered his voice. "So here is my request: If you come across any shred of information, any hint that Davato is slighting what used to be the United States and is favoring the other provinces, I would appreciate it if you would inform me through our new ambassador. You will now be privy to the inner seat of Imperium power, and if I have a heads-up, perhaps I can work behind the scenes to improve my country's—your country's—position. I suspect this kind of favoritism is already happening, and I fear it will get worse. So what do you say, Grady?"

He swallowed. To do what Cole asked would put him in great danger. He remembered his conversation with Davato on his first day and the explicit threat of what would happen to anyone caught spying on him. "I–I'm afraid I can't do that, Mr. President—or should I say, Governor? The Imperator has warned me and others, repeatedly, what would happen if I or anyone were ever to attempt such a thing."

Cole stepped back and regarded Grady. "Oh . . . all right. I should have known. We never had this conversation. Forget I ever mentioned it."

"Of course."

"But here is someone I think you know." Cole stepped back as the man whose picture Grady had looked up on the plane approached. "I will leave you two to get reacquainted. You will be working closely with him in the future."

Cole departed as the new North American ambassador took his place.

Manufacturing his best smile, Grady reached out and took Alex Reed's hand. "It's been some time, hasn't it?"

"Yes." Alex was older than his internet picture, and after shaking hands, he pulled Grady into a hug. "It's good to see someone from the old days, back before the world got crazy. I am so, so sorry about your family."

"Thank you. But what about yours?"

"Mine? Well, I assume you mean my mother. I've been single all my life. We lost her in the attack on the city." He dropped his gaze. "Like so many others."

"Yes, yes, of course. I meant your mother." Already Grady was getting himself in trouble.

"I'm trying to remember the last time I was at your father's estate on Martha's Vineyard. Was it five years ago at Thanksgiving? Yes, I think it was. You had just graduated from midshipman's school. You rose fast through the ranks after that." Alex gripped Grady's shoulder. "Do you remember that game of touch football we played on the lawn and how your father sprained his ankle?"

"I do. He shouldn't have joined us."

"No, we were too rough. And I fondly remember your mother's cream pies. And that turkey stuffing." Alex smacked his lips then frowned. "But that was another age, wasn't it? How the world has changed!"

"Too much so. Nothing is as it was." Grady finished the last of his champagne, and as a waiter bearing a tray passed by, he exchanged his empty glass for a full one.

"What's this?" Alex's eyes widened. "You've always been a southpaw. Have you now joined the rest of us right-handed folks?"

Startled by the man's discovery, Grady shrugged. "Since our ship sank, my left arm was injured, and I've been using my right more often. I'm becoming quite ambidextrous."

"Oh, of course. Cole told me about the sinking." Alex frowned. "I'm going to look up the episode with your boat. We've resurrected many of the old files from backups. We lost so many that day. But in the end, we gave as good as we got—for all the good it did. China has Taiwan, but oh, the price it paid!"

Desperate to leave family remembrances behind, but wondering what Alex would find, Grady raised his glass and took a sip. "How is it at home after the war? I haven't been back since I arrived."

"Not good, Grady. The country has been set back, and much of it is beyond the government's purview. We have a bit of control on the east and west coasts, some in the south, but other than a civilized pocket here and there, the interior is pretty much on its own. The stories I'm hearing from the heartland are of widespread chaos. V-Day, the famine, the plague, and the war took a great toll on us, far more than in Europe. There are Unitum Imperium outposts, of course, but they're isolated, badly connected, and cell service is spotty, mostly nonexistent. It may be years, even decades, before we resurrect what we once had. We are not the country we once were." Alex shook his head. "And I fear we never will be again. You are lucky to be here, in the center of things, where civilization doesn't hang by a thread."

At the far end of the hall, Davato's voice boomed through a microphone. "May I have your attention, please. I welcome everyone who is attending this reception in honor of their Imperator and our grand announcement tomorrow. But before I toast the occasion, I would like to acknowledge the appointment of my new personal secretary, Grady Wilson. Where are you, Grady? Come forward."

Breathing relief for any excuse to get away, Grady raised his hand, left Alex Reed, and wove through the milling crowd toward the front.

There Davato laid a hand on his shoulder, said his name, and congratulated him, after which the Imperator raised a glass and toasted the Unitum Imperium and its Imperator.

At Davato's side, Grady raised his glass and joined in. But after the accolades, the praise, and the clapping died down, he melted into the crowd, slunk toward the exit, and slipped out the door and back to his room where he collapsed into a chair with a can of beer.

He was living a lie, wasn't he? Tonight, he'd barely kept his façade intact. Everything about his life here with Davato was a house of sticks stuck in the sand, and the first high tide would take it away.

CHAPTER 40
THE THREE ANGELS

In the Eastern Mediterranean – February 7, Year 4

As she had the previous three nights, Chelsea slept to the throbbing of the engine, the washing of waves against the hull, and the rocking of the boat. On their fourth morning at sea, an early knock brought Fabio Caruso to her door.

"We are nearing an island, and as before, you must wear what I have for you in the closet." He pointed to a pair of jeans, a sweatshirt, and some hanging tee shirts. "If a patrol boat stops us, you must appear to be part of the crew, yes?"

She ran her fingers over the garments, rough and a bit big, but they fit. Beside them hung a rubber coat, pants, gloves, and a rain hat.

"Dress and come to the galley."

When she'd donned her fisherman's outfit, she met Enzo Rivera and Fabio Caruso at the galley table for their usual breakfast of fried sardines, toast, and coffee.

Altin Tolan wasn't present. Either he or Fabio was always steering the ship.

"Every morning, I marvel that you have coffee." A smiling Enzo lifted his mug and sipped.

"We trade for many goods. But business is poor." Fabio waved a hand. "And this morning, I'm concerned about a noise in the engine. Regardless, we are nearing a shoal, and if we sight a school, this morning we will fish. Then you must learn, yes?"

"We will learn," answered Enzo.

Fabio finished first and left Chelsea and Enzo alone.

"What do you think of our captain and the Albanian?" asked Enzo.

"Altin hasn't said three words to me since we left. And I'm still uneasy about the locks on our doors."

"Yes." Enzo lowered his mug. "But I must return to my homeland.

I will never take the mark, and to continue working where I was, they insisted on it. What other choice was there?"

"It was the same with me—none." She lifted a forkful of sardines.

"You've said you do not have the mark, Chelsea, but you haven't said whether or not you are a Christian."

"Not yet. Maybe someday. But I've been thinking about it."

"That's a good start." He cradled the mug in his hands. "Seek and you shall find. That's what Jesus said."

"Then I guess I'm seeking. We'll see what I find."

Fabio Caruso burst in. "We're following a school. Breakfast is over. Get your rubber gear on and meet me at the stern."

Taking a last bite and swilling her coffee, she returned to her cabin and donned the rubber suit and gloves from the closet. Then she met Fabio and Altin on the aft deck beside the winches. Above, clouds obscured the sun over a gray-blue sea. Weeks ago, that orb had burned dimly through black cloth, casting an eerie deep purple over the water. How nice to have the return of at least some normality.

Altin glanced at the newcomers, scowled, and rested his hand on the winch motor. They'd already laid out the trawl on the aft deck, ready to be pushed overboard to scoop up fish.

"When we haul in a catch"—Fabio stood with hands on hips—"your jobs will be to send the fish through the cutting and filleting machines. While the nets are out, I will show you what to do."

He began walking back into the passage when Altin slapped a hand on his shoulder and cried out. "What's that?" His neck craning to the sky, he pulled Fabio out from under the superstructure.

Chelsea and Enzo followed.

A halo of blinding light moved slowly above them, and she squinted.

"W–what the hey?" Fabio shielded his eyes with his hands. "What is *that*?"

"An angel." Enzo's voice was low, somber, and reverent. "An angel of God."

Far above, Chelsea could make out the form of a heavenly being peering down at them, illuminating the sky, the sea, and the ship with blazing white and yellow light. Though far away, it appeared so close, she could see every fold of a robe that might have been woven from pure light. Shimmering with all the colors of the rainbow, the angel bore wings of gold.

Eyes filled with pure white light bored into her, and she felt its gaze was meant only for her.

"Fear God!" he shouted. "Give glory to him. For the time has come when he will sit as judge. Worship him who made the heavens, the earth, the sea, and all the springs of water."

Shaking, Altin cowered back against the rail. Beside him, Fabio's mouth hung open.

Chelsea, too, reached for the railing to support herself. Was this really happening?

"W–what was that?" Altin's hands gripped the top of his head.

No sooner had the first angel passed, than a second followed close behind, just as bright, just as ethereal. It, too, stopped and hovered in the same spot far, far above. Or was it only a few meters away?

"Babylon is fallen—that great city is fallen," he said, "because she made all the nations of the world drink the wine of her passionate immorality."

Chelsea sucked in air. Was this happening *now* to New Babylon? Or was this a declaration of what was to come? Inwardly, she rejoiced. These beings were proof—weren't they?—that God existed. And now, he was declaring the end of that city of hedonism, debauchery, and murder.

And yet, the appearance of these angels, these impossible heavenly creatures, shook her to the center of her being, for they bore judgment and warning. She clutched her arms about her chest and shivered.

The second angel departed, and a third appeared.

This one was larger, brighter, more fearsome than the previous two, and he hovered in the same spot as the others. Eyes of dark fire bored deep into her. What this angel said to her and to the others she had read before. And his words were like bolts of electricity jangling through every nerve of her body:

> Anyone who worships the beast and his statue or who accepts
> his mark on the forehead or on the hand must drink the wine

of God's anger. It has been poured full strength into God's cup of wrath. And they will be tormented with fire and burning sulfur in the presence of the holy angels and the Lamb. The smoke of their torment will rise forever and ever, and they will have no relief day or night, for they have worshiped the beast and his statue and have accepted the mark of his name.

The creature hovered, staring with glowing, fearsome eyes, and no one on board dared move. Then, mercifully, he flew over the horizon and was gone.

The blinding light that had surrounded the ship was gone. The gray clouds and the gray-green sea returned. The world was again as it had been.

But its departure left Altin Tolan shivering, clutching his arms around his chest. He looked at the mark on his wrist that Chelsea was only just now able to see.

"What kind of demon was that?" he asked. "By what right does it pronounce my doom? If I didn't take the mark, they would have taken me. I would starve. What choice did I have?"

He slumped to the deck, shaking his head, over and over, until he wrapped his arms about his legs. "Am I doomed?"

Then the captain backed against the railing, and shaking hands covered his eyes. As he did, the long-sleeved shirt he always wore slipped down his right arm. He had *not* taken the mark.

When she glanced at Enzo, he smiled. "Those messages were for those who are deciding whether to take the mark or not. But for those who have, they were messages of judgment."

Altin looked up from the floor and shook his head. "I'm doomed!" he cried. "The demons have doomed me."

Fabio stared at Enzo. "It was speaking directly to me. I felt it. I knew it."

"Me too." Chelsea looked to Enzo. "What about you?"

"I am already a Christian. I did not experience what you three did."

Fabio held Enzo's gaze then staggered toward the farthest aft portion of the ship and stared across the water.

While the captain stared and Altin cowered, Chelsea and Enzo exchanged glances.

"It was real, wasn't it?" she asked.

"It was, Chelsea, and if that doesn't convince you, I don't know what will."

She swallowed. "I'm ready, I think, to believe."

A wider smile broke Enzo's face, and he laid a hand on her shoulder. "When you get back to your cabin, get down on your knees, ask Jesus to forgive your sins, and tell him you believe in him and will follow him."

She nodded. After all this time, she couldn't deny what she'd just seen. She would do it.

Sudden joy, as if a great weight had been removed, lifted her from the deck, and she felt she might now fly away. A smile split her face. "Yes, Enzo, I will."

But Fabio stalked down the deck to Enzo. "Are you now saying this is what I must do, Christian man? Is that what these messengers from God—if that's where they came from—are telling me?"

"Do what's in your heart, Fabio." Enzo crossed his arms. "Chelsea heard and believed, and now she wants to become a Christian. What about you? Unlike Altin here, you haven't taken the mark. What are you waiting for?"

"I haven't taken the mark because I will not let any government place their tattoos upon me. That's why I only do business in the dark—so I can hide my wrist. But becoming one of these Christians?" He shook his head, and his eyes sought the deck. "It will ruin my business, my life. Always, I run from the government, yes? If my customers know me as a Christian, my business is dead. My life is dead."

"If you focus only on this life," answered Enzo, "you are doomed. You may not have the mark, but unless you believe in the Christ, the one who came to earth to save us, you will still face a fiery eternal future when you die."

Enzo's words seemed to strike Fabio as much as the angels' appearance had affected Altin. The captain stood motionless, his mouth open, staring at the Italian. "And you believe this with all your heart?"

"I do. And the proof of it was in the heavens just now. The angels spoke to you directly, did they not? The God who sent his Son just sent us three messengers to declare the truth, and now it's up to you to decide. You have free will. So make your choice."

Fabio gripped the top of his head. His eyes closed, and his brows twisted. "But if Davato is a god, there is another choice, isn't there? If I reject the mark, how will I ever be able to buy supplies? How can I sell my catch? How will anyone ever trust me again? Already, I have trouble landing this ship without the mark. So far, I've escaped detection by only doing business in the dark. But it's a dangerous game I play, no? Someday, the Truth Squads or the CSA or the harbor patrols will find out. Then they'll send me to the new camp they're building or to the colosseum where they burn Christians alive or feed them to wild beasts. I'm not ready to be a martyr."

He turned away and faced out to sea. "If Davato is a god, then we have two competing gods, do we not? Then, perhaps taking the mark is the right thing to do. That, at least, ensures survival in this world—if there exists anything more after this."

No one spoke, and the only sound was the throbbing of the engine. Then Fabio spun back to them.

"I am no longer in the mood for catching fish. If we fill the hold, to sell the catch, we'll have to dock and allow inspectors on board. The CSA might come with them. We've also been harboring two Christians, and I don't have the mark."

Alarmed, Altin shot to his feet. "Don't be stupid, Fabio. You promised a good catch and a good profit this trip. We must fish."

"We have the payment for their passage." He jerked his thumb toward the passengers. "For now, that's enough."

"So we're going to sail for another two weeks, not stop, and not fish?"

"I told you. Our destination is Venice. That's eight days away, not fourteen. It's my boat, and that's what we're going to do. From now on, we're going to avoid the government, including all inspectors, at all costs."

"Fabio, you are a fool." Shaking his head, Altin walked woodenly toward the bow.

The captain turned to his passengers. "You may return to your cabins."

Enzo raised an eyebrow toward the captain. "Why did Altin say two weeks? Is there some question about our destination?"

"No!" Fabio's eyes opened wide, and he waved his arms. "Enough! Return to your cabins!"

But as Chelsea followed Enzo amidships and he placed a hand on the door to his room, he turned to her and whispered. "I don't trust the Albanian. Not the captain."

Back inside, she removed the rubber suit, sat at the desk, and began reading Matthew 14:15 in Lazzaro's Bible.

When evening came, the disciples approached Him and said, "This place is a wilderness, and it is already late. Send the crowds away so they can go into the villages and buy food for themselves."

"They don't need to go away," Jesus told them. "You give them something to eat."

"But we only have five loaves and two fish here," they said to Him.

"Bring them here to Me," He said. Then He commanded the crowds to sit down on the grass. He took the five loaves and the two fish, and looking up to heaven, He blessed them. He broke the loaves and gave them to the disciples, and the disciples gave them to the crowds. Everyone ate and was filled. Then they picked up 12 baskets full of leftover pieces! Now those who ate were about 5,000 men, besides women and children.

It was all true, wasn't it? Jesus is God and the only way to salvation. She laid the Bible down, knelt on the floor, placed her hands together, and prayed.

"Dear Jesus, I have been such a fool. Forgive me my sins. I *do* believe in you now. I want to be a Christian and follow you, so now I give myself wholly to your embrace."

Such a feeling of joy entered her that she wept with happiness.

She was saved. Her eternal future was secure. She wept and wept and didn't want to stop, because now, at this moment, she felt God's pleasure filling her, lifting her, soaring her to heights she never imagined.

And nothing on this earth could ever change that.

Possessed with the Holy Spirit, her feet carried her out of her cabin, out onto the deck where she looked up at the sky. As if waiting for her to emerge, the clouds parted. Rays of sun burst down in all their brilliant, multicolored glory and shone a cornucopia of rainbow colors over iridescent, blue-green waters.

God's glory filled her. Even here, at the end of time, though she knew that many dark and terrible days lay ahead, that the world was about to end, and that all about her roiled with chaos and evil, God had sent her a precious, indelible glimpse of eternity.

She was now a child of God!

Had she ever felt so good? Had there ever been a time when life held more promise, when what lay before her seemed impossibly good and right and true, when all her troubles seemed to vanish like mists in a sunbeam?

Kneeling on deck, she prayed to the Son of the God of Heaven and Earth, thanking him for the gift of eternal life she had just received.

And when she rose, satisfied and at peace with all around her, Fabio stared down from the pilothouse, a look of utter incomprehension etched on his face.

CHAPTER 41
THE ANNOUNCEMENT

Jerusalem, Israel – February 7, Year 4

At eleven thirty, buses escorted by Unitum Imperium armored cars topped with machine guns took Davato's staff, including Grady, across town to Temple Mount. Among the passengers were important dignitaries, high government officials, and the new provincial governors with their staffs. At Temple Square, armed CSA troops broke a path through the milling thousands. Fortunately for Grady, the ambassadors were in a second group, following well behind Davato's bus. He wanted nothing to do with Alex Reed, the Wilson family friend from Boston.

The crowd had pushed the Two Witnesses and their continuous cries of judgment to a far corner.

This morning, the buzz and murmur of conversation focused on the angels that had just shaken the city to its core. Grady was still reeling from their appearance overhead. He was inside when they came, and, like everyone else in the building, some irresistible force had pulled him outside. As he looked up, his hand shielding his eyes from the blinding light, their messages left him rattled and doubting.

Was he and everyone else who followed Davato now doomed? He'd hitched his fate to the Imperator, and if Davato wasn't the god he claimed to be, Grady was lost.

With a troubled heart, he followed ten paces behind the Imperator as the group mounted the steps to the Temple. They entered through the Beautiful Gate into the inner courtyards. At the foot of the Giant, Davato disappeared into the structure's base while the Prophet took the podium five meters above the crowd.

Adam Turner beamed and bent his head to Grady's ear. "Today is the culmination of everything we have worked so hard for, and you, Grady Wilson, now stand at the center of it all. Congratulations!" He extended a hand, and Grady took it. Had Turner not been affected by the angels at all?

"I am overwhelmed and honored to take your daughter's place." But the minute he'd said it, Turner frowned, and Grady knew it was the wrong thing to say.

"Do not ever mention her again." Turner faced away. "She is no longer my daughter."

"Of course, I'm sorry."

"Apology accepted." Smiling again, he squeezed Grady's shoulder. "Look! It's about to start."

The Prophet raised both hands for silence, and the big screens high and on both sides of what used to be the Holy of Holies showed the green-eyed man as a solemn religious figure wrapped in a white robe, a black sash around his waist. "Friends and citizens of the world, this is the day for which we have all been waiting. For not only has our great Imperator risen to divine status, today he takes the scepter that empowers him to reign over every inch of this planet we call earth. Without further ado, I bring you Davato, the Imperator, our divine ruler."

As the Prophet bowed and stepped back, the Giant behind him came alive, glowing with Davato's visage. Towering one hundred feet over everyone, huge eyes aglow with light speared the people below. Enormous hands planted themselves on hips, and the head swept its glance over the crowds. "Welcome, citizens of the planet, to this broadcast. Today, we announce that all the nations of earth have merged into one. As of this moment, we abolish all national borders, rivalries, and allegiances. Going forward, you will no longer consider yourselves as belonging to this country or that. Instead, you are citizens of the world. It's a goal that every leader since the dawn of time has desired, and now, it is a reality.

"Today, I have divided the world into ten great provinces, and the governors I have appointed for each will now step to the platform below. Governors, please step forward!"

The ten heads of Davato's world government left the crowd and climbed onto the platform beside the Prophet. The cameras panned over each man, displaying each name and province on the screens.

The Giant crossed its arms and smiled. "Yes, my people, these will govern our lands, but now you're asking who is worthy to lead them? What exalted creature can carry a united earth into the future? Who, among all men, has the ability to guide you, help you, and send you on your way to peace, prosperity, and endless progress?"

It lowered its arms, dropped its head in a stance of ridiculous humility, and closed its eyes.

Cries of "Davato! Davato! Davato!" echoed out from the crowd.

"Yes, of course." It raised its glance. "It can be no other, can it?" Then it raised both arms and took a step away from its pedestal, and when its foot landed on the concrete, not five meters from the governors and ten from where Grady stood, the Temple shook.

"Yes, it is I, your Imperator, he who has crossed from mortality to immortality, from humanity to deity, from mere man to godhead." One leg lifted and thundered down onto the marble tiles, sending a shock wave through the crowd.

With frightened faces, the governors turned to look back and up then hurriedly exited the platform to rejoin the crowd.

As if on cue, the crowd again chanted, "Davato! Davato! Davato!" Thousands of arms waved in supplication. Thousands of bodies knelt on the tiles, bowing to the one who'd declared himself a god. The praise and accolades went on and on, and the Giant crossed its arms, looked from side to side, and smiled down on the people far below.

Finally, the applause, the praise, the supplications wore themselves out.

The light went out of the Giant's pixels, and moments later, Davato himself, appearing as the mere man he always was, joined the Prophet on the podium. He waved, and the applause began again.

Then he led the chosen few out through the Court of Priests, past the animal pens and the skinning pens, now clean and empty, into the Court of Israel, through the East Gate, and into the Court of Women, and then out through the Beautiful Gate. At the top of the steps overlooking the thousands gathered in Temple Square, Davato, now appearing as a mere man, paused and raised both hands.

And there was Grady, standing five paces away from the greatest man in history. He breathed in deeply, marveling at how he had gained such an honored position.

The square erupted in clapping, and people shouted his name, again and again. The huge screens above showed his image being broadcast to cities across the planet. The entire world was praising, honoring this man. He truly was a god, wasn't he?

And that knowledge swept away all the doubts that the angels' appearance had brought Grady earlier.

Movement caught his eye, and he glanced down the steps. Was that a man with a white beard climbing up? Yes, it was Ernesto, Davato's chauffeur, and he held something in his right hand. Grady tried to focus as CSA guards on both sides began moving fast toward him.

The crack of a pistol echoed.

The smell of smoke and sulfur washed the platform.

The right side of Davato's skull split open.

And the man who was god, who had united the world into one, collapsed.

CSA agents descended in a swarm and grabbed the assassin. Truncheons beat down on Ernesto's arms, legs, and head until the Prophet raised a hand for them to stop. "Don't kill him. For now, take him away!"

A physician ran to Davato's side and knelt. Those on the top steps clustered about their fallen leader, pushing Grady aside. He couldn't see or hear what was going on.

"Is he . . . alive?" came Adam Turner's weakened voice from the center. "Tell me he's alive."

"Dead," came a whisper from somewhere, followed by an ashen face rising from those huddled around the man who was to rule the world.

Then came the unmistakable voice of Dino Castiglione, louder, more insistent. "The Imperator is dead!"

Then someone, Grady didn't know who, shouted it, louder, to the crowd. "The Imperator is dead!"

The screens above the square had shown everything, and now the people below heard the impossible words. As a storm rushes across a calm harbor, the news swept through them with a deep, soul-numbing cry of grief.

The Imperator was dead. The man who would lead them into the future, the man who, a moment ago, was a god, had been killed.

And everywhere across the world, such a cry of mourning arose that it seemed to Grady that the people's love for this man had known no bounds.

But it didn't strike home until the Prophet, weeping uncontrollably, lifted the inert, lifeless body of Davato from the marble and carried him through the crowds toward the wailing of an ambulance beyond the square.

Grady had one good glance at exposed gray matter and a hunk of white skull hanging down, and he realized that no doctor or hospital, no matter how skilled, would ever be able to save Davato now.

And if Davato had been killed, he wasn't a god, was he? And if he wasn't a god, then what the angels had said was true.

And Grady was doomed.

The Imperator was dead, and the world had just flipped upside down.

CHAPTER 42
THE ABYSS

Revelation 17:8 (NLT): The beast you saw was once alive but isn't now. And yet he will soon come up out of the bottomless pit and go to eternal destruction. And the people who belong to this world, whose names were not written in the Book of Life before the world was made, will be amazed at the reappearance of this beast who had died.

In Hades – February 7, Year 4

After the bullet struck, Davato's world went black. Then he woke, stunned and disoriented, but feeling more alive than he'd ever been. A high-pitched whistling filled his ears, and he opened his eyes.

He was traveling fast down a long, dark shaft. The tunnel's sides flashed by, swirling with shades of black and gray and occasional yellow flame as he picked up speed and headed down. He knew it was down because when he looked back, the light of earth's sun fast receded to a pinprick.

He slowed and came to a stop, his feet landing on a vast rock plateau surrounded by rivers of molten lava. Leaping flames and sulfur vents opened at random across the flat, and from the distance came a prolonged scream.

Standing before him was the most beautiful man—or was he an angel?—Davato could have imagined. With his face so pure, his chin so perfectly molded, and his blond hair swept back in a flawless, manly coiffure. Clothed in robes that at first appeared like sparkling multicolored linen. When the man raised a hand in greeting, his whole body glittered, and the shimmering beams released by that gesture appeared to shine with a thousand shades of flickering gray.

But the beams morphed. They became black piercing shafts of endless, wandering shadows, so dark and unsettling, Davato shuddered. It wasn't light, was it? It was . . . *unlight*. And into itself, it sucked all the illumination for meters around.

"Step forward, Davato," came a voice so pleasant and ingratiating, he could do nothing but obey. "Come and receive that to which you are entitled."

He took a step toward the shadowy figure standing half again as tall as he, and he knew he was in the presence of the Dragon, the Master himself, once called Lucifer.

"Yes, Davato"—the Master raised a hand above his head—"it is I, and here you will remain with me for three days and nights, while above, the world mourns and believes you dead."

Was that what happened? Yes, now he recalled the figure of Ernesto climbing the steps, a pistol in hand, pointed at him. Davato ran fingers over his arms, and they were solid flesh. He put a hand to his head, where moments ago, something—was it Ernesto's bullet?—had smashed into him so hard, he'd lost consciousness. But his skull was intact. Down here, wherever this was, he was alive. He lifted his gaze to the Master towering above him. "I was killed?"

"That's right, but after three days and nights with me, you will return, alive and more powerful than ever before." The Master's hand hovered above Davato's head. Then the dark power that had fueled Davato all his life, that had come upon him before he made the covenant with Israel, came again as a rush of incredible energy—greater and stronger than before.

"You are mine, Davato, and when you return, together we will prove that the Enemy cannot decree the future, that the world above is ours to rule—yours and mine—and always has been. And nothing he or his people can do will ever change that. Sebastien Rey is also mine, and even now, I am consoling him, giving him instructions for your return."

The Master's words steeled him, strengthened him, energized him in ways he could only have imagined. His chest exploded with pride, arrogance, and ego. And in that moment, Davato knew the Master was right.

The world above belonged to him, and with the Dragon's power behind him, he would surely reign over it.

How true were the names the world had bestowed upon him, names which he would soon prove right, names in which he now reveled—
The man of lawlessness.
The son of destruction.
The man of sin.
The Antichrist.
And the beast.

CHAPTER 43
THE AFTERMATH

In the Eastern Mediterranean – February 7, Year 4

Chelsea waited in her cabin before supper as the ship crashed through heavy chop. All day the seas, like the day's events, had been wild, tumultuous, and finally, exhilarating. It had started shortly after noon. . . .

* * *

OUTSIDE, THE WIND THREW OCCASIONAL spray against the pilothouse windows, while inside Fabio Caruso gathered Chelsea, Enzo, and Altin Tolan to watch the proceedings via satellite. "They've billed it as the most important proclamation from the Unitum Imperium since they announced Davato was a god," Fabio said to Enzo. "And I want you, Christian man, to watch. I want you to tell me if the Imperator is a god or not."

Only Fabio and Altin occupied the pilot seats, swiveled now to face high on the starboard wall where hung the ship's flat-screen Samsung. Chelsea and Enzo stood and leaned against the port equipment console.

"Be careful not to touch anything," Fabio warned.

But as Chelsea looked behind her for a safe place against which to lean, her gaze settled on a yellow sticky upon which were written the words *Engine Start* and the letters *G, H, T, X, 7, 5, 3.* When Fabio discovered where her glance had roamed, he snatched the paper and shoved it in his pocket. She memorized the sequence and would write it down later.

But then, as events in Temple Square unfolded before the cameras, everyone in the pilothouse watched the broadcast in stunned silence.

Her father bowed obsequiously beside the Imperator. Several paces to the side, Grady had taken her place.

She should be disgusted, maybe even a bit jealous. Instead, an overwhelming sadness filled her. How far both her father and Grady had fallen!

Both men had been part of her life. In different ways, she had loved or at least cared for them both. But now for them, there was no turning back, no second chances. They'd made their decisions, and by their own free will, they had doomed themselves. She wiped a tear from her cheek.

But the cameras showed everything. And when Ernesto climbed the steps with his gun, she caught her breath. This was the same Ernesto who, with Lazzaro, had approached her and Grady in New Babylon's central park asking them to join in a plot against the Imperator.

And now, he'd actually done it. Ernesto had shot and apparently killed Davato.

Shock changed to joy, and she couldn't contain her happiness. She clapped and nearly jumped in the air.

Ernesto had finally done it. He'd killed the Antichrist!

Enzo, too, smiled and turned to Chelsea, and they hugged. She returned the affection, and they parted.

But the captain and his crewmate had different reactions.

Fabio stood open-mouthed, swaying on his feet, looking from Chelsea to Enzo to Altin with unbelieving eyes. "If the man was a god, how is this possible?" he asked. "What does this mean?"

"Earlier, you asked if he was a god," answered Enzo. "There is your answer."

The statement sent a storm of worry across Fabio's brows, and he looked away.

Meanwhile, Altin's hands gripped the top of his head, and he, too, whirled away from the television. He pounded a fist on the wheelhouse window. "I'll tell you what this means. I'm doomed. I believed he was who he said he was, and I took his mark. I needed the mark to eat, to live, to survive. And now what do I see?" His face twisted in pain, he waved toward the grief and chaos unfolding in Temple Square. "It was all a lie."

"I'm not so sure, Altin." Fabio spun back and rubbed his chin. "The government is still intact, is it not? The Unitum Imperium is still there. Perhaps someone else will take his place, yes? There's no way they will change what they said about the mark."

"But look at it." Altin raised his wrist and waved the six-sided tattoo before the others. "See what's written on the outside—the letters of his name. Without him, it all falls apart. If he isn't a god, I'm doomed."

On the television, a great mourning arose from the throngs in the square. The cameras followed the weeping Prophet as he carried the lifeless body through the crowd. The Worldnet channel's two news anchors revisited in breathless, mournful tones the events the world had just witnessed. One by one, the newsmen listed all who were present at the top of the Temple steps. When they got to Grady Wilson, they flashed a picture of the woman he'd replaced.

"Look!" Altin pointed an accusing finger at the television, and Fabio's gaze followed.

Fabio's mouth opened, and he stammered. "Th–that was *you*!"

The three men in the wheelhouse turned toward her with startled eyes.

"*You* were the traitor!" Altin now pointed at her. "They're looking everywhere for you, and *you* are Chelsea Turner. No wonder you wouldn't give us your last name. And there's a big reward for your capture."

Fabio crossed his arms. "This changes everything."

She placed hands on her hips. "Why should it? You agreed to take me to Venice for a great sum of hard cash. You made a promise to Big Matza and to me. Are you not going to honor our arrangement?"

Fabio stared at her then at Altin who was shaking his head.

"We must talk, Fabio." Altin waved him outside. "Now."

"Yes. We must talk." Fabio faced his passengers. "You two will return to your cabins while I confer with my shipmate."

"You must honor what you agreed to," said Chelsea. "Big Matza warned you."

"That he did, but neither of you were honest with me. I like to honor my deals. But now you have put me in great danger, and circumstances have changed. Go to your cabins. I'll come for you later."

Chelsea and Enzo left the wheelhouse, descended to the main deck, and entered the passageway leading to their quarters.

"Come inside, Chelsea, and let's talk." Enzo waved her through his open door, and she followed.

Inside, she sat on the bed while he took the lone chair.

"I thought you looked familiar," he said. "But I couldn't place where we might have met."

"I was hoping to remain incognito."

"It worked for a while." He sat back against the desk. "So you worked for the Antichrist himself and then left him? It must have been a terrible ordeal."

"You can't imagine." She closed her eyes, leaned forward, and dropped her head into her hands. "I have been such a fool. I made so many mistakes. I followed a monster, a man who is evil personified, and I let his charisma, his promises of prestige, wealth, and position overrule what my heart was telling me all along."

"And what was that? What did you decide?"

She raised her glance, her earlier joy returning, lifting her as if she might fly away. "After the angels flew over this morning, I gave myself to Christ. I told him I wanted to follow him. Enzo, what you saw on the screen—that part of my life is behind me. I'm now a Christian."

He clapped then stood. He opened his arms, and they hugged. "Then congratulations, Chelsea! And welcome to the family of God. You and I came too late, didn't we? But we have finally made the right choice. The past is past, and it's behind us. And what lies ahead is a great eternity— for both of us."

* * *

That was noon, and now the captain knocked on the door, announcing supper. The porthole was open to let in some fresh air, but spray from the crashing waves was wetting the floor. She closed it.

Because of the rough seas, they'd also closed the hatches to seal off the crew passage and mess area where she and Enzo now followed Fabio. As they sat, a frowning Fabio said he would make an announcement later in the wheelhouse, as he must include Altin, who was steering the ship. Then he said nothing, and they ate in a strained silence.

Afterward, he ushered them to the wind-tossed deck, up the wet ladder, and into the pilothouse where Altin steered.

"I have two pieces of news tonight, and both are bad." Fabio crossed his arms and frowned. "The first concerns the engine. It's making worrisome noises, and we cannot go on. We've changed course, heading for the island of Crete where we'll have to put into port for repairs."

"Repairs?" Chelsea cocked her head. "How long?"

"Not sure. Getting the parts we need may take days. Maybe weeks. We'll be docking at Chania on the island's north side."

"What's the other news?" asked Enzo.

"Yes, well, it concerns the Imperator, and . . . it's pretty bad." He glanced at Altin who took his focus off the controls. "A few hours ago while you were in your cabins, they confirmed that he's dead. The Prophet has placed his body in a stone tomb in the center of Temple Square. Thousands of mourners are now streaming past, laying wreaths and flowers."

"What did they say about the government?" asked Altin.

"Only that the vice imperator, François Desroches, has been appointed Imperator, and that the Unitum Imperium will go on as before. Just as I predicted, yes?"

"Unlikely." Altin shook his head. "Davato *was* the Unitum Imperium."

"But there's a slim ray of hope. After placing the body in the tomb, the Prophet made a prediction, and it's startling. He said that in three days' time, the Imperator would rise from the dead."

"Rise from the dead?" Altin laughed and returned to steering the ship. "Is this a joke?"

"No, Altin, it's not. I think we should wait for things to settle down. Meanwhile, we'll dock in Chania and repair the engine."

"Then where are we going?" asked Enzo.

"Venice."

"So you *are* going to honor our arrangement?" asked Chelsea.

Fabio shifted his feet and looked away. "We will wait to see if this Davato really is a god, if he really does rise from the dead. Meanwhile, we are heading for Venice."

"You know what I want to do with her." Altin's hands left the wheel and shot out in an angry wave.

"Hold your tongue, fool! This is my decision, not yours." Scowling, Fabio waved Altin toward the cabin passageway. "I'll take the watch, now. I wanted to tell everyone the latest news, and I've done so. Now you are dismissed—all of you!"

Fabio waved them toward the door and the ladder, grabbed the wheel, and stared out at the rollicking seas.

But after closing the hatch on the crew passageway and entering her cabin, Chelsea feared that Fabio's mind was as fickle as the weather.

CHAPTER 44

THE TOMB

Revelation 13:1, 3–4 (NLT): Then I saw a beast rising up out of the sea. . . . I saw that one of the heads of the beast seemed wounded beyond recovery—but the fatal wound was healed! The whole world marveled at this miracle and gave allegiance to the beast. They worshiped the dragon for giving the beast such power, and they also worshiped the beast. "Who is as great as the beast?" they exclaimed. "Who is able to fight against him?"

Jerusalem, Israel – February 10, Year 4

It was noon, and Grady was in the middle of Temple Square. But he stood, not beside those at the center of power, but surrounded by the hoi polloi, the unwashed masses. Since the assassination, no one had assured him that his exalted position was still intact. A moment ago, when he tried to follow the Prophet up the Temple steps, a CSA man had even blocked his way.

Everywhere around him, women were crying, and men wore somber faces. The city was in mourning, dressed in black.

For the last three days, he and everyone around him had been drinking a lot, haunting the bars into the wee hours, and sleeping late.

After Davato's grand announcement, Grady had been ready to believe the Imperator was a god. Now, his murder cast a shroud of gloom over the city, even the entire world. All the promises the Imperator had made and the great future he'd envisioned—Ernesto's bullet had shattered them all.

With Davato's death, the memory of the three angels and their dire messages had risen in Grady's mind like lava from a dormant volcano. For if Davato wasn't a god, Grady and all who'd taken the mark were doomed.

Then came a whisper of hope.

On the evening after they laid Davato's body inside the great slabs of stone in the center of Temple Square, the Prophet again took the microphone. With red eyes but a firm voice, he announced to the world he'd received a vision: In three days' time, the Imperator would rise again and walk from his tomb.

But Grady didn't know what to believe. He'd seen the Prophet do amazing things—miracles, even. But raising a man from the dead? It was a claim the Christians made about their Jesus, and no one he knew had ever believed that.

It was now noon, and the square was filled to overflowing with those who'd taken the mark. Anyone without would never dare attend.

A hush swept the assembled as cameras followed CSA troops making a path through the throng. With them came Sebastien Rey, gowned in white, a black sash wrapped around his waist. Huge overhead screens followed his progress.

The Prophet stopped at the tomb, constructed of massive stones four meters on a side, brought in by crane. He raised the microphone to his lips, lifted his gaze to the cameras, and spoke.

"People of earth, three days ago you witnessed the traitorous act that caused the death of our leader, Davato, our Imperator, the one to whom we pledged our lives, our fates, and our futures. Many of you thought him dead, and so he was. On the night he was killed, I returned to this square to place his body in this tomb. I carried with me a message delivered by the Master, also called the Dragon, whose power lived and breathed in Davato. What was that message? That three days and nights after Davato's death, I would stand here before his tomb and call him out."

He paused as whispers and murmurs swept the Square.

"I know what you've been thinking!" The Prophet's voice rose. "You've been whispering that if Davato can die, then he's not a god, then everything he and I have said is a lie. Yes, that is what those of you with little faith have said!"

His eyes seemed to bulge as they focused on the cameras.

"Well, here now is my answer to those who doubt." Then he spoke to four men off to the side. They pushed and shoved at the huge stone covering the tomb's entrance and moved it, revealing a dark hole within.

As the Prophet's right hand held the mike, his left hand pointed at the tomb. When he spoke next, his voice rose tenfold so that the power of it shook the square. "Davato, come forth!"

Grady held his breath and waited. He was close enough to see the tomb without needing the screen's image.

A figure stepped out. Still wearing the suit he'd been buried in, the Imperator walked out of the tomb—alive!

And when he stepped closer to the camera, his skull was intact, he was smiling, and when he raised both hands in a signal of victory, pandemonium exploded.

The crowd cheered, clapped, and sang his praises. They roared their approval, and Grady joined in. The Imperator was alive! He'd risen from the dead. And if that was true, then Davato truly was a god!

As Davato and the Prophet followed the CSA troops through the crowd, the rejoicing went on and on. At the top of the Temple steps, Davato stopped and waved, but that only reinvigorated the celebration.

Screens on the perimeter showed cities all over the world joining in.

Perhaps this went on for half an hour, maybe longer. Then Davato took the microphone and raised his hands for silence. When the people finally calmed down, he spoke. "Yes, my people, I am alive. I am back. And now you know who is your true god, who is worthy of true worship. For only a god can rise from the dead. And you have seen it with your own eyes."

That only started the rejoicing again, and he waited for the commotion to die down.

"But it was the Master, also called the Dragon, who gave me the power of divinity. He, too, is worthy of your worship. And like me, the Prophet is the Master's servant, and he, too, has received divine powers. So now I give you Sebastien Rey."

As Davato stepped aside, the Prophet took his place at the top of the steps. "Let there be no further doubt. You have seen a man rise from the dead. But no, he is not a man, is he? The Imperator is your *god*!"

Again, the applause thundered over the square. When it quit, the Prophet continued. "And now, to show you what happens to those who rebel, who plot and scheme against their Imperator and the Unitum Imperium, watch as the traitor is brought forward."

The cameras focused on CSA guards dragging a man barely able to walk, his face a pulpy mass of beaten flesh. And as Grady focused on the man, he recognized Ernesto.

A ladder had been placed against the tombstones, and men climbed with Ernesto, hauling him up top where iron rings were fixed to the stone. The guards chained their prisoner to the rings and departed.

Then the Prophet spoke, and his voice thundered and echoed across the square. "This, then, is what awaits all who plot against their Imperator."

Pointing with his right hand at Ernesto, he raised his left hand to the heavens. Out of a clear, blue sky, dark clouds appeared, gathered, boiled, churned. A tongue of fire, swirling and roaring, dropped down, engulfed the top of the tomb, and covered its victim.

Ernesto screamed, and his body burned. White-hot flames blazed and engulfed him, burning away his clothes, bubbling, boiling, sizzling, consuming skin, hair, flesh, and bone.

The fire receded. The clouds drew back. And all that was left of Ernesto was a pile of smoldering black ash atop the tombstone.

"Now, people of earth." The Prophet's words echoed across the square. "Whom will you worship? The Enemy who curses the earth and the sky? Or the one standing beside me? And the Dragon who gave us both our divine powers?"

As one organism, the throngs in the square bowed. The screens above showed others in far-flung cities across the globe also prostrating themselves. Praise was on everyone's lips—

For the Imperator who had risen from the dead.

For the Prophet beside him who performed miracles.

And for the one called the Dragon who had given them both their power.

Grady knelt and joined in.

Davato was a god, and because of it, Grady was no longer doomed.

CHAPTER 45
A CHANGE OF PLANS

Chania, Crete — February 10, Year 4

It was late afternoon after they'd watched Davato's resurrection, and Chelsea peered out her porthole at the rock jetty protecting Chania's harbor from the northern sea.

For the last three days, the *Am Albahr* had been anchored twenty meters from the dock. For some reason, the captain wouldn't allow any of them—Altin, Chelsea, or Enzo—to go ashore. When they first arrived at the marina, the harbormaster had tried to convince Fabio it wasn't necessary to moor so far from the other ships, yet the captain insisted he would anchor where he was.

Now seagulls cried and circled onto their nests in the rocks in the seawall as she tried to make sense of the day's affairs. . . .

At noon, she and the others had gathered in the pilothouse, and, in a stunned silence, they'd watched the events in Temple Square. When the Prophet had called fire down from the sky to kill Ernesto, Chelsea recalled what she'd read in Revelation. All of it had been prophesied, even the miracles of the false prophet. All of it was coming to pass.

When Altin saw the risen Davato, he became a different man. Shaking off the aura of gloom that had surrounded him since the assassination, he beamed. "You see, Fabio?" he said to the captain. "He is a god after all. For who can rise from the dead but a god? And the Prophet! Did you see what he did to Davato's assassin? Only someone with godlike powers could do such a thing. You need to choose which side you're on. You should take the mark."

"What about the angels who flew overhead?" A storm of worry crossed Fabio's forehead. Then he glanced side to side as if the answer lay somewhere in the wheelhouse. "Who is right?"

"They were demons!" Altin nearly spat out the words.

"They were angels, Altin," said Enzo, his voice soft. Then he turned to the captain. "Deep in your heart, Fabio, you know they came from God."

"I know no such thing! Maybe I should have taken the mark." Then the captain shut off the television and stormed from the wheelhouse.

"He'll come to my side," whispered Altin, apparently to himself. Then he faced Chelsea and Enzo. "If I was you two, I'd go to your cabins now and stay out of our way."

They did as he suggested for the rest of that afternoon.

* * *

At five o'clock, her door burst open, easily ripping the hook-and-eye latch from its roots. Fabio and Altin stormed in. As usual, both wore pistols at their belts.

The captain waved to a grinning Altin, and the Albanian went straight for her clothes. He began riffling through the pockets then through her backpack on the floor.

"Now, Chelsea Turner," said Fabio, "I regret to inform you of a change of plans."

She dropped her Bible and shot from the bed with hands on hips. "What do you mean?"

"Our destination is no longer Venice, but a palace in Tangier, Morocco. I am now convinced that Davato is who he says he is, and at the next opportunity, I will take the mark. This decision has weighed heavily on my soul, and with the mark, my life becomes so much simpler."

"I am sorry for you, Fabio." She was breathing fast, not understanding why he was doing this. "But what does your taking the mark have to do with our destination?"

"Ah, yes. We go now to Tangier because I have just talked with a very rich man there who will pay twice the reward the Unitum Imperium is offering for you. His name is Marzuq. Before the vanishing, he was an atheist who eschewed his Islamic roots. Now he returns to the ways of his distant ancestors—but without the religion." He chuckled.

"After the world descended into chaos, Marzuq became an emir in Morocco and a powerful man. He gathered a small army and now rules the port city of Tangier. Some might call him a warlord. He stands in opposition to Davato, and he vows never to take the mark. Chelsea Turner, I am selling you into slavery to this man, and you will join the harem he is gathering. He also needs eunuchs to watch over his many wives, and that is where Enzo Rivera comes in." He chuckled again, and Altin, fishing in her backpack in the corner, shot her a wicked smile.

"He offered me this deal before, but until we learned who you really were, his offer was insufficient. Oh, but now!" Fabio opened both hands and spread them wide. "Marzuq has seen you on television, and he so desires to possess the woman who once stood at his enemy's side. This afternoon, after I told him who you were, he quadrupled his previous offer. Now, it is more than worth my while to accept it."

The news rocked her, stole the words from her mouth, and she felt as if she might faint.

Sold into slavery to an Arab as his sex slave?

A prisoner for life, never to see Dylan or Margot or the others again?

Breathing fast, she slumped back onto the bed.

"I've got her phone." Altin rose with it in hand. "Nothing else here to worry about."

Fabio stared at her. "While we are in port, you will remain in your cabin and not shout from your porthole. If you do that, I will weld it shut, forever depriving you of fresh air."

She glared at him.

"Good. Now let us inform the good Christian of his fate."

They left. The deadbolt clicked from the outside. And she stared at the door, barely able to breathe.

Then she remembered the pistol Ariel had given her. Maybe there was a chance to get out of this yet.

CHAPTER 46
A RESCUE MISSION

Appenzell, Switzerland – February 28, Year 4

As Dylan sat in the van on an Appenzell side street with René, Pasqual, and Victor, he recalled every word of Klaus Martin's last call to René. At the time, Klaus had been with the Huber farm couple in the farmhouse a kilometer or so down the road, and the Nazarene Friends were in the Skihaus. The ex-spy had put the call on speaker for everyone to hear. . . .

"They've got the house surrounded," came Klaus's tense voice. "Jakob and Emma want to surrender. But there's no way I'm giving up."

"What are you going to do?" René had asked.

"Fight to the end."

"What about the Hubers?"

"Either way, we're dead, aren't we? They'll send us to the new camp or the colosseum or use us for target practice in the shooting galleries. Got to go. They're coming."

Instead of hanging up, he'd set the phone down.

Shots were fired. Afterward had come the sounds of the door crashing in, of scuffling, and of two more shots. Then Emma Huber cried out, "You killed him."

"Down on the floor with your hands out," came the response.

"Where are you taking us?" came Jakob's muffled voice.

"To Appenzell regional headquarters to await transport." In the background, men were laughing. "The lions in the colosseum are hungry."

Then came the sounds of feet leaving, followed by silence. . . .

It was now evening, a bit more than twenty-four hours after the Hubers' abduction, and a half-moon lit the alley where René was parked with the engine running. In the rearview mirror, a plume of exhaust rose into the frigid air.

René checked his watch then swiveled to face the others. "It's past midnight. We've staked out this headquarters before, so we know the layout. I'll repeat the plan again as I want no mistakes. I'll go in first, a drunk who has a beef with his neighbor. That would be Dylan, here." He waved a hand over a ragged parka Jakob must have used for his dirtiest jobs then pointed to Victor and Pasqual.

"Dylan will enter with me, but you two will wait below the front door, out of sight. Tonight, there should be three squaddies on duty, and all of them should be at the front. If you hear shots, enter with guns drawn, ready to back us up. But these are not professionals. They may just surrender without a fight. In that case, we'll call you."

"What if the others are with them?" asked Victor.

"The station has maybe eight, total. The other five will have commandeered cozy rooms in the village, and they'll be either asleep or drunk. Once we overcome those manning the front office, we'll get the keys and make our way to the back and the jail. Everyone ready?"

Everybody nodded, and they left the van, their footsteps crunching over hard-packed snow. They followed René to the end of the alley, made a left turn, and approached the CSA headquarters for the Appenzell region. On one side above the door hung the familiar six-sided sign with Davato's name and a map of Europe and Africa. The other held the emblem of a skull crossed with a lightning bolt.

On the street, snow began falling.

He swallowed. Would he have to shoot someone tonight? One hand held the Heckler and Koch pistol in his coat pocket to keep it from bouncing.

At the squaddie building, Pasqual and Victor hunkered down below the windows on either side of the door.

Dylan glanced inside to find only two squaddies behind the desk playing cards. Where was the third man?

René shot him a questioning glance. "Are you ready to do this, my friend?"

Dylan nodded.

At the Skihaus, he and the others had watched as the events of the last month had closely followed the Revelation prophecies. Now here he was, about to invade the headquarters of the CSA in a remote region of

Switzerland. In his own small way, he was striking back against the Antichrist's tyranny. But the Nazarene Friends weren't in the Bible, were they? And there was no guarantee tonight's efforts would be successful.

Staggering about for effect, René gave his coconspirator a nod, and they started the drama they'd rehearsed.

"You've no right to push me around, little man!" shouted René, loud enough so they could hear inside.

"And you've no right to break into my house and steal my food!" Dylan shouted back.

René stumbled through the front door, pretended to slip and fall to his knees, then stood and backed toward the desk.

Dylan entered behind him. "I want this man arrested! He's drunk, and he broke into my house tonight. And it's not the first time."

The two men behind the desk dropped their cards and rose from their chairs. "He's drunk?"

"Yes, I'm drunk," answered René. As he said this, he spun, pistol in hand.

Those words were Dylan's cue. Simultaneously, he pulled his Heckler and Koch from his coat pocket.

"Hands up, and come from around the desk," commanded René. "One false move, and you'll be bleeding out your life on the floor."

Their faces pale with fright, they did as ordered.

Dylan tried to calm his racing heart as he took their guns, cuffed them with their own handcuffs, locked them to their chairs, and gagged them.

After René called Pasqual and Victor inside, he threw Dylan a set of keys, motioned for silence, and pushed into the back hallway.

The crack of a gunshot met him. Glass at the building's front exploded.

"There's only one!" René ducked to the side. "I'll take care of him."

As René's pistol returned the shot, Dylan and the others dropped to the floor and crawled to the side.

What followed was a long exchange of gunfire. Each round sent toward René either smashed more glass, exploded on the bricks between the windows, or crossed into the street beyond. But would this attract the attention of the town's other squaddies?

Finally, the gun battle ended, and René stood. "He's down. Let's get the Hubers and get out of here."

Dylan followed him into the hall, now choked with smoke and the smell of sulfur. He stepped around the third squaddie, lying motionless and bloodied. At the end of the hallway, he unlocked a metal door with its single barred window. It crashed into the wall, and Jakob and Emma Huber rushed to greet him.

They hugged and gushed their thanks, and René hurried them down the hall.

Jakob stopped them and pointed to a locked door. "This is their supply room," he said. "It has our parkas."

René shot off the lock. Upon entering, he broke into a wide smile then called the others to join him. Metal racks held a small arsenal, and René told everyone to grab a second pistol, a submachine gun, and as much ammunition as they could carry.

Thus resupplied, they left the station for the street where two men, probably curious locals alarmed by the shots, were heading toward squaddie headquarters. But one look at the armament coming their way sent them scurrying back from whence they came.

"Come on!" René began running. "The others will be here soon."

They sprinted through falling snow to the van, René started the vehicle, and the tires spun as they left the alley. Minutes later, they were racing down the snow-packed highway with the lights off. But the snow wasn't falling fast enough to cover their tracks.

Dylan kept glancing back but saw no headlights.

"The locals will alert the other squaddies," said Pasqual. "And they'll see our tracks."

"Oui," said René. "Then they'll search every house up and down this road. I'm afraid we'll have to abandon the Skihaus. And you two"—he shot a glance to the Hubers—"you can't return to your place. We'll have to search for a new hideout."

"How about the warming station at the end of the ski loop," offered Jakob from the back seat. "It has a woodstove, bunks for a dozen skiers, and an outhouse in back. There's a similar station further on, halfway up the mountain. There's no cell coverage there, but these days, I doubt anyone is using those shelters. We have two sleds we can use to haul equipment."

"Ah, oui. I almost forgot. On our ski outing two weeks ago, we warmed ourselves there. It's halfway around the fifty-kilometer loop, isn't it?" René glanced back to the others, beside and behind him. "What do you say? It's rough living, but shall we make our home in the mountains beyond squaddie reach?"

"Yes," said Dylan. "Let's do it!"

The others agreed.

Their plan was to stop at the Hubers' place for supplies, then pick up Margot and Danielle at the Skihaus. "We'll park the van in the barn," added René. "I'll rip out the starter wires, take the plates and the keys, and hide the works in the wheel well. Then we'll load up the sleds with as much food and equipment as we can and head out tonight."

"Nothing like a midnight ski into the Appenzell Alps," added Pasqual. "And with fresh snow, I can't wait."

But as they drove on into the night, Dylan wondered again about Chelsea. Was she still alive? Even if she was, if they were living far from the nearest cell tower, how would he ever connect with her again?

CHAPTER 47

THE SEVENTH SEAL

In the Great Throne Room – May 1, Year 4

The archangel Michael bowed low before the Lord of Hosts seated on his throne high above. Light brighter than a thousand suns shone from the top, where sat God the Father, Creator of Heaven and Earth. Off to the side, Michael caught the glimmering of thousands of multicolored gems embedded in the throne itself. Beside him knelt his brother Gabriel. Surrounding them in the vast hall and extending for miles in all directions were lesser angels beyond counting. Mixed with these were millions of the redeemed from every age. All were kneeling and bowing, filling the air with the murmur of praises for the Creator of all that was, that is, and that will ever be.

They'd gathered to witness the opening of the seventh seal and the beginning of the Great Tribulation.

The four cherubim hovered before the throne, shooting fire and lightning between them. One pair of wings pointed to their feet—the hooves of calves, burnished like gold. A second pair covered each of their four faces—a man's, a lion's, an ox's, and an eagle's—and each face looked in a different direction. A third pair of wings hovered. Beneath each creature spun a giant wheel containing an inner wheel, and the outer rim gleamed like polished turquoise. All-seeing eyes circled the rims. And though the cherubim moved from side to side, the wheels beneath them didn't turn.

"Holy, holy, holy is the Lord God of Hosts," they cried in unison.

The millions of angels and the redeemed massed into the vast hall echoed the refrain, *Holy, holy, holy is the Lord God of Hosts.*

From behind the throne, thunder rumbled, and smoke rose in a billowing column, spiraled up to the brilliant crystals covering the ceiling, and spread out to the hall's distant corners.

A man stepped past Michael, and one glance revealed the spear wound in his side, the nail holes in his wrists, and the thorn marks on his forehead.

He was the Christ, appearing for one moment as he had on the day he was crucified.

The archangel bowed lower, the cherubim withdrew, and the lightning and fire between the creatures ceased. They nodded their heads toward the Lamb, the Son who was God become man, who died on the cross so that those who believed in him might live—the only one worthy enough to open the scroll and break the seals.

The Father reached down and pass him the little scroll, written at the beginning of time, the scroll decreeing the events at the end of time.

The Son took the parchment, and he unrolled it.

Six seals were missing. Six judgments had already been given.

The Son's fingers closed about the seventh seal. Then he snapped it open, and the sound echoed like a crack of thunder through the vast hall.

Everyone knew the enormity of this moment, what was about to transpire, and for half an hour, the peals of thunder, the flashes of lightning ceased. The endless prayers, the continuous praises ended. For half an hour, not an angel moved. Not a whisper was spoken.

The seventh seal announcing the final judgments of the trumpets and bowls had been broken. And Michael gaped in awe, realizing the import of what was about to happen.

Then the Son beckoned to the seven chosen angels. One by one, they passed Michael and approached the Son of God, who delivered a trumpet into each of their hands.

Now came Michael's turn. He lifted the heavy gold incense burner at his feet and approached the altar beyond. His brother Gabriel followed, bearing the urn containing the incense. Michael mixed the incense and the prayers of God's people into the incense burner then set it on fire.

Contained within the black column now spiraling up along the throne's height was the sweet aroma from the supplications of billions of saints over the last two millennia, desperate and earnest prayers pleading for the defeat of Satan, the end of evil, and the beginning of the reign of the Son of Man on earth.

The incense burned, and the smoke rose to the Lord of all Creation, the One who was, who is, and who is to come.

The Lord bent down, and he spoke. And the sound of his voice was like the roaring of many waterfalls, thundering through and shaking the vast hall. Michael, Archangel of the Host, take the incense to the earth and throw it down upon the land. Then let the chosen angel blow the first trumpet. Thus do we begin the final judgments.

Michael nodded, lifted the gold incense burner, and headed for the exit and the tunnel leading to earth. Beside him flew the first angel, clutching to his breast the first of the seven trumpet judgments.

Then Michael shuddered.

Oh, how terrible for those upon the earth when the trumpets were blown!

Oh, how terrible to behold were the judgments to come!

CHAPTER 48

THE VOLCANOLOGIST

Salt Lake City, Utah – May 3, Year 4

Randy Foster shoved his glasses back up his nose, stared at his computer screen, and sat back with a rare cup of coffee, a gift from his department head. On the tables down the row, seismometers scratched over graph paper. For the last thirty years, Randy had been with the University of Utah's Department of Geology and Geophysics, working closely with the Yellowstone Volcano Observatory, and he was concerned.

No, not concerned—frightened to death.

He studied the map on his computer screen again and shook his head. Never in his lifetime had he seen the number of M5 and M6 events increase at such a rate and in so many places. For the last two days, minor quakes were occurring in the San Andreas Fault in California, Mt. Rainier in Washington, Mt. Hood in Oregon, and Mt. Shasta in California.

Reports from Hawaii indicated four M5.5 events had occurred beneath the sea near Kilauea and five M5 events at Mauna Loa. All in the last two days.

Besides the volcanic activity, quakes had been reported yesterday from Charleston, South Carolina, and all along the Alaskan coast. Unlike the usual suspects, those sites weren't given the generators, the fuel, and the ability to measure such events. After the EMP disaster, they'd had to rebuild their seismic detection ability from scratch. Only a few research facilities were up and running, powered twenty-four seven by small, noisy generators.

News from overseas mirrored the North American situation. M5 and M6 events were occurring at Mt. Etna in Sicily, Mt. Vesuvius in Italy, Mt. Yasur on Tanna Island in the Vanuatu archipelago near Fiji, Mt. Sinabung in Indonesia, Mt. Merapi on the border between Java and Indonesia, Mt. Nyiragongo in the Congo, and at Mt. Pacaya in Guatemala. And the Chaîne des Puys cinder cones and lava domes in France's Massif

Central had also become active. It was the same story from Japan, Chile, and New Zealand.

Another worry—in the St. Francis Mountains of Missouri, the ancient Taum Sauk, Butler Hill, and Hawn Peak calderas reported quakes yesterday, and again, they hadn't the equipment to measure them. All three sites contained ring intrusions and ancient magma. In the distant geologic past, they had experienced extensive volcanic activity. Now, apparently, after millions of years, they were again active.

In the last two days, seismic and volcanic events were occurring everywhere, and the numbers were increasing.

Most concerning of all was what was happening under the Yellowstone supervolcano, under the Long Valley supervolcano east of Yosemite, under the Valles Caldera of New Mexico, and under Mt. St. Helens in Washington. Because of their importance, the Unitum Imperium had ensured that each site had whatever replacement equipment they needed.

Beneath the Long Valley caldera alone, it was estimated there were 240 cubic miles of magma, one-third of which was molten. If only a fraction of that exploded . . .

Randy closed his eyes and shuddered. Was it an asteroid that had killed the dinosaurs? Or an explosion of a supervolcano?

He grabbed his coffee and sipped. He mustn't let such a treat go to waste. In this life, one must take all one could, and then some.

Setting the cup back down, he stared at the mark on his wrist and shook his head. It was just like the vaccine mandates, wasn't it? Take the vaccine or be fired. But now it was take the mark or starve.

He had to admit—the overflights of the angels, if that's what they were, troubled him. But after seeing Davato's resurrection on TV, he could almost believe the man was a god. But so what? God or not, angels or not, after death, there was nothing. Zip. Zilch. Zero.

Randy was an atheist and always would be. And he would hold onto this life until the very end. Which was why what he was seeing on his screens was more than troubling.

He pulled up the Yellowstone chart on his monitor and leaned closer. Normally, the area experienced up to twenty-five hundred low-level quakes a year. But in the last two days, they'd recorded seven hundred and fifty events between Hebgen Lake and the Norris Geyser Basin. The screen that showed each quake as a red or blue dot was almost completely covered.

"Hey, Martin." He leaned back in his chair and called down the row of seismographs and monitors. "Come here and look at this."

Martin removed his headphones and shoved off. His chair rolled fifteen feet over the tiles past the electronics. Martin spent all day listening to rock music from the sixties, seventies, and eighties, and, much to Randy's relief, only stern, repeated warnings from his supervisor kept the music trapped inside Martin's headphones.

"Yeah, what is it now?" Martin gave him a lopsided smile as if to say, "Really, again?"

"It's getting worse every day. Something big—really big—is brewing."

"You've been saying that all week." He squinted at the chart, at the explosion of blue and red dots around Yellowstone. "You need to reduce the resolution on these. You can't even read what's underneath anymore."

"Shouldn't that tell you something?" Randy's face was burning. It was always this way, wasn't it? Every time he tried to bring up an anomaly, somebody—either Martin or Bryan Smith, their supervisor—would object, saying that yes, this was concerning, but what could anyone do about it?

A silly grin split Martin's face. "It's Credence Clearwater's 'Bad Moon Rising', isn't it? Earthquakes and lightning. Don't go out tonight, or you'll die. John Fogerty was a prophet."

"Maybe he was. Maybe he had a premonition of what was coming when he wrote that song. But seriously, what does this tell you?" Randy pointed to the screen, obliterated by red and blue.

"It tells me we'll just get in trouble if we rock the boat, and I need to go to lunch." Martin checked his watch. "I'm hungry."

"Shouldn't we tell someone? What are we here for if not to alert the public?"

"What public?" Martin waved and frowned. "We're lucky anybody's left alive out here in this pocket of civilization in the middle of nowhere. We're barely existing here at the U with our generators and armed guards. The whole thing we've got here could collapse any minute. When I go home, I have to carry a Glock to fend off the gangs. Here at work, soldiers patrol the entrances. This is Mormon City, Randy, where hardly anyone was taken on V-Day. The plague and the famine took a third of the population, and we only have electricity and food here because the government favors our work."

"All right, all right. We're privileged. I know that. But we're privileged *because* we're supposed to report what we see. I'm going to send something in, and you should put your name to it. Somebody, somewhere, needs to know what's going on."

Martin opened his mouth, closed it, then nodded. "All right. Maybe it is important. Put my name on it." Then he rolled his chair back to his station and stood. "You work on it while I'm at lunch."

Randy watched him leave. Then he opened an email directed to the head of the Department of Science and typed, "Dear Director Wong . . ."

Something big—really big—was about to hit the world. And somebody needed to know what was going on.

* * *

Moments later, an email detailing an imminent, catastrophic eruption of seismic and volcanic activity all across the world showed up in the inbox for Hugh Wong, the director of the Department of Science in the Ministry of Peace. But when the director's personal secretary opened the email and read it, she paused and cocked her head.

Who, exactly, was Randy Foster, and by what authority was he making such a disturbing claim? A brief search revealed he was a mere underling, reporting to Bryan Smith who reported to Amanda Sullivan, who reported to three other heads before reaching the top of the bureaucratic hierarchy. Or what was left of it after the war.

Her finger hovered over the delete button. She'd felt the quakes that had rocked the world. Who hadn't? But to make such outlandish claims as this man had? He should have gone through channels. She wasn't going to rock the boat.

She hit the button. The email vanished. Then she stood and went to lunch.

CHAPTER 49
THE ASTROPHYSICIST

Mt. Locke, West Texas – May 3, Year 4

It was a ten-minute walk from the Astronomer's Lodge at the McDonald Observatory to the Harlan J. Smith telescope, and tonight, Ben Smiley was scheduled for two precious hours to continue his search for planets in the Messier 82 galaxy. Only twelve million light-years away, M82's proximity to the Milky Way made it ideal for a planetary search, and the government wanted to know where the UFOs had come from. As he passed the bank of generators powering the site, their roar disturbed a crystal-clear, star-filled night, and he pressed hands over his ears.

Yesterday evening, clouds and rain had interfered, and tonight was promising. This remote site in West Texas had the darkest sky of any observatory in the US, and after the EMP attack, the Harlan J. Smith scope was the one they chose to keep working. They'd had to cannibalize parts from all four of Mt. Locke's scopes to get one that worked, and it was one of the only two giant telescopes in the US still functioning. With portable generators from Mexico and a generous supply of government fuel, they were able to keep going.

Because of his loyalty, expertise, and familiarity with the Harlan J. Smith, he, above hundreds of others, was chosen to use the one-hundred-sixty-ton, one-hundred-and-seven-inch mirror.

He checked his watch and smiled. It was two a.m., and tonight, Sally Stewart would again be assisting. Encouraged by the government's continuous pleas, he and Sally had a "sharing" thing going. After their time with the scope, they often took a blanket and strolled down the mountain for a quiet spot to do just that.

Crossing the floor, he glanced up at the thirty-two-foot-long telescope aimed through the open slit at the sky. He zipped up his sweatshirt. It was fifty degrees outside, and to keep delicate instruments from getting misaligned, they maintained the temperature the same, inside as out.

In the control room, he waved to Sally; to Mike, the technician; and to Harry, the IT guy. With the famine, the plague, and with only one working scope, they'd been pared to a handful of staff. Then when the University of Texas required everyone to take the mark or be fired, three more folks got in their vehicles and never came back, leaving only the four of them.

"Hi." Sally pushed back from the bank of five monitors. "It's a good night for it."

"Maybe we can finally zero in on that promising area we saw last week?"

"Let's hope so." She glanced both ways. Mike and Harry sat around the corner, and she lowered her voice. "Maybe later, we two can take a private tour of the mountain?"

He smiled. "A bit chilly, but I'm game."

She grinned. "Can't wait."

He sat at the controls, tried to focus on the work instead of his lithe coworker, and brought up his program. He entered, "RA=9h 5.58m, Declination=69° 41' ". That would zero the telescope on the Ursa Major spiral galaxy. This began the whir of motors in the vast space behind the control room, moving the scope into position.

More clicks should bring him a close-up visual of M82. A few more adjustments, and he tried to fine-tune the section he would investigate tonight.

But something blocked his view. Two dark smudges interfered with his target. He rechecked what he'd inputted, but he'd entered everything correctly. "Hey, Mike," he called around the corner, "can you do a diagnostic? Something's not right on my screen."

Moments later, Mike assured him everything was working properly.

Sally rolled her chair beside him. For a time, she studied the monitor. "Can you change the focal point? Those might be nearby objects."

He gave her a sideways glance, entered the adjustments, and began dialing back the focal point. As the motors whirred behind him, the blurriness lessened, and the dark blots increased in size. He made some final modifications, and the picture sharpened.

"They're asteroids!" He sat back and stared. "And they're in line with my target. Day before yesterday, they weren't there! Where did they come from?"

"I don't know, but we need to find out where they're headed. Maybe they'll pass from view?"

For another hour, Ben recorded pictures of the two objects and compared the changes between them. Then he sat and did some calculations.

"The first one is about thirteen million five hundred thirty thousand miles from earth, traveling at 11.185 miles per second."

"Where are they headed?" As Sally leaned over his shoulder, he could smell the perfume she'd put on in anticipation of another nighttime tryst.

"Just a minute." He took another reading. It had now been an hour and a half since he'd started. He redid his calculations, stared at them, and shook his head. "This can't be."

"What?" She raised a worried glance.

"I don't trust myself. Hold on." He picked up the phone and called Jeffrey McPherson at the Mauna Kea Observatory on the Big Island of Hawaii. He and Jeff had been college roommates, and Hawaii had been spared the destruction from the EMP nukes. "Hey, Jeff, Ben here in West Texas. I have a favor to ask, and it's important."

After some small talk, Jeff agreed to schedule a look in a half hour after the current observation concluded. Ben waited impatiently, grabbed a cup of coffee—one of the perks of working for the University—and paced. In the interim, the next shift arrived. He gave up his seat at the control panel and moved to a work terminal down the row. It was now four thirty in the morning.

Another hour came and went, and Ben called his colleague back. "What did you find?"

"There are two large bodies, both asteroids, and they're headed our way. I'm cross-checking my calculations now, but—"

Silence filled the earpiece. Even though both were privileged to use Elon Musk's Starlink satellite network that the government had confiscated, sometimes there were glitches. "Jeff, are you there?"

"Y–yes, and—oh no! This is not good."

"What? What did you find?"

"They're headed straight for earth. Both of them. The first one is three days ahead of the second and is about a kilometer wide. The second is three times as big. That's the one to worry about."

"That agrees with what I found." Ben ran a hand across a sweaty forehead. "We have to report this."

"We have no choice. These are big. Not planet killers, but big. Really big."

"Yeah. I'll send it up the chain to the department head. Email me your observations and figures."

"I will. Good luck."

Ben hung up, waited for Jeff's email, then, for backup, printed both his and Jeff's calculations and supporting pictures.

By now, the sky was lightening, and Sally had gone to her room, giving up on the two of them getting together.

He began an email to the head of the Department of Science in the Ministry of Peace. "Dear Director Wong," he typed. He finished his warning, hit send, then sat back.

Something big—really big—was about to hit the world. And somebody needed to know what was going on.

It was six o'clock. He would return to the Astronomer's Lodge, grab some breakfast, then sleep until two or three in the afternoon. Researchers were on a different schedule from the rest of the world.

* * *

WHEN TWO MEN IN GREEN-AND-WHITE CSA uniforms shook Ben awake, it was eleven o'clock in the morning, and he was dreaming about him and Sally alone in the desert.

"Pack a bag," came the order from the taller man. "You're flying to New Babylon for a meeting with the Imperator and his staff."

"Huh?" Rubbing sleep from his eyes, only then did he notice Sally standing behind them, holding a bag, her brows arched with worry. He sat up in bed.

The second man crossed his arms and peered down at him. "Gather everything you need to explain to the Imperator what you found last night."

Ben nodded, dressed, gathered up all his printed observations, calculations, and supporting evidence. But his heart was thumping hard. He would see the Imperator himself?

The CSA men walked him and Sally down the mountain to a helicopter waiting on the flat. The copter then flew them to Fort Bliss where they boarded a Boeing 747 someone had obtained from Brazil. They were headed for the Big Island of Hawaii, where they would pick up a startled Jeff McPherson.

Then they would head west toward Iraq and New Babylon.

CHAPTER 50

PREPARATIONS

New Babylon, Iraq – May 5, Year 4

As Ben Smiley settled into a leather seat in the conference room of New Babylon's World Casino, someone was clicking a fountain pen, and Ben couldn't slow his thumping heart. Sitting on his right, Jeff McPherson whispered to him. "What have we gotten ourselves into?"

On his left, Sally Stewart kept glancing his way with a look bordering on panic.

At the end of a long ebony table sat Davato, the Imperator himself, and by his expression, his mood wasn't good. Above him on the wall hung three giant circular emblems: the CSA's lightning-and-skull logo, a dragon with the Imperator and the Prophet, and in the middle, the familiar, six-sided symbol now tattooed on Ben's wrist. All of it made him feel insignificant.

On either side of Davato were François Desroches, vice imperator of the Unitum Imperium, and General Eric Hofmann, head of the UI armed forces and the Ministry of Peace, of which Ben's Department of Science was a part. His department head, Director Wong, sat beside the general, and next to him was Grady Wilson, Davato's new personal secretary. Various military personnel and a dozen or more technical people, a few of whose faces Ben recognized, filled one side of the table.

When everyone was present, Davato laid both hands on the table, leaned forward, and focused on the newcomers. "Now, Ben Smiley and Jeffrey McPherson, will you please explain to me what, exactly, you found yesterday?"

Nodding, Ben stood and faced the screen at the small end of the room. Even before he'd arrived, the technical staff had taken his pictures, graphs, and calculations and made PowerPoint slides. "Two days ago—At least I think it was two days as we've been traveling nonstop—two objects appeared at two o'clock in the morning, blocking my view of M82.

Messier 82 is the spiral galaxy in Ursa Major where I've been seeking the existence of planets that might explain where the UFOs came from. It's only twelve million light-years away, perfect for my . . ." But by the looks on the faces around the table, he'd better skip further details.

Davato raised a hand. "You work where, again?" He read from a paper before him. "At the McDonald Observatory in Texas?"

"Yes, my lord"—he'd been strongly advised on how to address the Imperator—"I've been an astronomer there for twenty years. We're using the Harlan J. Smith scope. It was all we could piece together after the EMP attack."

Davato waved for him to continue, and Ben cleared his throat.

"Yes, well . . . when we changed the focal point, we discovered that both objects were asteroids. I watched them long enough to make some calculations and learned they were heading straight for earth. To cross-check what I did, I called Jeffrey McPherson at the Mauna Loa Observatory in Hawaii." Ben nodded to his friend. "Jeff verified what I'd concluded. Both asteroids will make direct hits on earth."

"When will they arrive?" asked an unsmiling General Hofmann.

"For the first one, my guess is . . . approximately twelve days. The second—three days later."

Feet on the opposite side of the room shuffled. Davato, Desroches, and Hofmann exchanged glances. Grady Wilson looked up from his laptop.

Davato whipped his head toward Director Wong. "Has anyone verified this? How confident are we in his estimate?"

Wong swallowed. "We have repurposed the Hubble, and I'm expecting confirmation within the hour. But I've reviewed the work of these two, and tentatively, I concur. We have less than two weeks."

Davato closed his eyes and rubbed his forehead. When he looked up again, he turned to General Hofmann. "We have a contingency plan for this, do we not?"

"We do. But it was for one, not two, small asteroids. I have already given orders to activate Project Interceptor."

Again, Davato waved a hand. "Please elaborate."

"We took over the project from the Americans. It's an orbiting platform carrying four rockets designed for just such an event. Anything we launch from earth would be too little, too late. Three of Project Interceptor's missiles carry a five-hundred-kiloton thermonuclear warhead attached to a self-activated rotary mining drill. The Americans retrofitted their LLRVs—Lunar Landing Research Vehicles—to carry the drills and warheads. When the missiles approach the asteroid, the LLRVs will spread out and land. Their rotary drills will activate, drill down as far as they can into the core. Then all the nukes will synchronize and detonate simultaneously. It's hoped this will split the rock into thousands of pieces that will simply burn up in the atmosphere. A fourth missile carries observation cameras to assess the result."

With that information, Ben began scribbling calculations on the notepad before him.

"That sounds promising," said Davato. "But can you not redirect their course? And, General, we're facing two asteroids, not one."

"Yes, but the Americans only planned for one, and I'm told it's the second we should worry about. We've run calculations, and, assuming the second one is not a planet killer—" He faced Director Wong. "It isn't, is it?"

"No. We don't believe so. But both are big. And when they hit, well—the planet will never be the same."

"Right." Hofmann stared at him before going on. "But to answer your question, my lord, we are unable to alter the course of an asteroid with current technology. All we can do is split one of them—"

An aide burst into the room holding a sheaf of papers, and everyone faced the interruption.

Davato was about to say something when Wong raised a hand. "My lord, this must be from the Hubble. I ordered him to interrupt when he had new information."

Everyone was quiet as Wong perused the papers. When he again raised his glance, his face was somber. "I regret to inform you that the work of Ben Smiley, Sally Stewart, and Jeffrey McPherson is correct. The first asteroid will hit twelve days from now. And the second, much larger rock, will hit three days later. That the second asteroid won't arrive for fifteen days is actually good. It gives us more time to prepare."

"When will you be able to launch the missiles from orbit?"

"It's unclear. I will have to confer with—"

Ben raised a hand, and Director Wong nodded for him to speak.

"I would suggest hitting number two no later than about four million miles out, or about three days away from earth. I assume the missiles will travel at an escape velocity of twenty-five thousand miles per hour. Is that correct?"

General Hofmann's eyes widened, and he nodded. "That is indeed their final velocity."

"Yes, well . . . then you need to launch approximately four days from now. But I have another concern about Project Interceptor."

"And what might that be?" Hofmann was frowning.

"Even if you split up the asteroid, gravity might just bring all the pieces back together, and you'll be right back where you started."

Again, feet shifted across the table, and the technicians exchanged worried looks.

Davato's eyes narrowed. "Can you suggest another solution, Ben Smiley?"

"Well, ah, no."

"Then that must be our plan. Hofmann, can we launch in four days?"

Hofmann laid both hands on the table and shot a glance at the techies. "What about it?"

A bald man wearing a bow tie and striped shirt swallowed. "It's not much time."

Davato speared him with a dark look. "But you *will* do it, will you not?"

"Y–yes, my lord. Of course." The man dropped his gaze, and one shaking hand grabbed the other. "We will do it."

"Very well." Davato rubbed his eyes again. "It seems we have a plan of sorts. For everyone in this room—your purpose from now on is to destroy the second asteroid with everything at your disposal. As for the first, well . . . we'll just have to ride it out."

Director Wong turned to Ben, Jeff, and Sally. "You three will work with the staff here to keep us advised on the asteroids' progress. We'll need precise coordinates for targeting."

The meeting adjourned, and Ben followed the others to the elevators. Their quarters were somewhere in the mammoth building below.

As they walked side by side down the hall to their assigned rooms, Sally turned a worried glance his way. "Is this the end of the world?"

"No, but maybe the end of the world as we know it." He'd said the words to calm her fears, but did he really believe them?

CHAPTER 51
BY THE LAKE

Lake Shetek State Park, Minnesota — May 6, Year 4

As gentle waves lapped the sand, Caleb grabbed the stick and tossed it far down the beach. Her tail wagging fast, Nika raced along the narrow strip of beach, grabbed the branch, and returned. A few yards before him, she slowed and pranced. As if it were a mouse that needed killing, she jerked the stick side to side. Then she dropped it at Caleb's feet.

"She'll do that all day if you let her," said Tanya from behind.

He turned and smiled. "Yeah, it's time to quit."

After Nika retrieved the stick once more, she dropped it. Panting hard, she looked up with eager eyes.

"Enough, dog." He reached down and patted her head. "Catch your breath."

Backing up to the boulder behind him, he sat and removed his sweatshirt. Tanya sat beside him. Nika sprawled on the sand nearby, her tongue lolling.

Above, the sun shone bright and clear. A slight wind drifted clouds across the sky, rippled gentle waves over the lake, and herded dark shadows along the gray-blue waters until they crossed overhead. Just to his left lay Loon Island where cormorants dove for fish in the calm beside the pedestrian causeway. But the only strollers using the causeway nowadays were Caleb, Tanya, Brianna, and Andy.

On the opposite shore, nearly all of the vacation houses were vacant. V-Day, the plague, the famine, and the gangs took many of them. Some never returned. That left only a handful of residents, most of whom Caleb knew from the church.

Tanya leaned back on the rock, closed her eyes, and let the sun bathe her face. "We'll never find a better day than today. And we'll never find a better refuge than this. I never want to leave this place."

Caleb frowned. "But you know what's coming. It won't stay like this. In a month or so, we should continue our search for the Sanctuary."

She opened her eyes and whipped her head toward him. "Why? What more can the Sanctuary offer that this doesn't? Here we've got a beautiful lake, friends in town, and plenty of game. You and Andy have been getting a deer whenever we need one. Brianna and I have a garden. Next fall, we'll have corn and wheat and barley and pumpkins. We've got water, plenty of space, and"—she reached over and laid a hand on his knee—"I've got you. I never want to leave."

Caleb smiled. "Maybe you're right. Maybe we should wait and see what the future brings before we leave the good thing we've got here."

Then she searched his eyes, and hers were so bright and smiling and eager, he grabbed her head, pulled her lips toward his, and kissed her. The kiss went on and on, and when they parted, he was breathing fast.

She smoothed her jeans, reached down, and patted Nika. Then she faced him. "I talked with Pastor Henry Adams last Sunday, and—"

"I thought he didn't want to be called that?"

"He's coming around to the idea. Anyway, he brought up the subject of marriage."

"Marriage?" He opened his eyes wide. "Whose?"

"Ours."

For a moment, Caleb was taken aback. Then he laughed. "What else did he say?"

"Well . . . he's looked up what's needed to perform a marriage, and he's willing to do it. And he says the church would love to have a wedding."

Caleb slapped his knee. "Then let's do it! Let's get married. Officially."

"Great!" She grinned. "Next time we see him, we'll set a date."

"But I haven't proposed, have I?"

She cocked her head. "Didn't we agree a while back that we might as well consider ourselves man and wife?"

"Yeah, but that wasn't an official proposal." He slipped off the rock and got down on one knee. Then he took her hand in his. "Tanya Baranov, light of my life, will you marry me?"

She gave him a mock frown, released his hand, and faced away. "Well, now, this is unexpected. Let me think. I'll have to weigh your proposal against all my other suitors."

"What can they offer you that I can't?" He tried not to laugh.

"You're right. I accept. Yes, I will marry you." Then she grasped his hands and pulled him up.

He searched her eyes, and again, he pressed his lips to hers. And when they parted, such a feeling of joy filled him, he picked up the stick and threw it far down the beach.

Her tail wagging fast, Nika raced after it.

As Tanya rose and stood beside him, he faced her. "Tanya, you're right. How could there ever be a better day than this?"

CHAPTER 52
BEFORE THE MASTER

New Babylon, Iraq – May 9, Year 4

In an hour or so, Grady would join the others in the Situation Room to watch the launch of Project Interceptor. But right now, he stood before the mystery room with Adam Turner and the Prophet as Davato punched numbers on the keypad and the door clicked open.

"Before we launch"—Davato laid a hand on the door—"we must bring an appeal to the Dragon himself. We will bow before him and ask for his intervention. Only he can ensure that our rockets destroy the asteroid."

"They're calling it Wormwood," added Turner, but it was the wrong thing to say.

"*What!*" His eyes wild as a windswept storm, Davato let the door shut and whirled to Turner. "Who gave it that name?"

Stunned by the Imperator's reaction, Turner dropped his gaze. "Jeffrey McPherson, one of the Americans."

Davato stood motionless, and his whole body shook. "Look at me, Adam Turner!"

Turner raised his glance, and now he, too, was shaking.

"Has he read the Enemy's book? Is he trying to mock me?" A black cloud swept across Davato's forehead. His eyes widened and speared Turner with a look so dark, even Grady turned away. "Tell your men to get rid of him. Immediately!"

"B–but he is contributing to—"

"I don't care. I want him gone. Today!"

"Y–yes, my lord." Turner summoned one of the CSA men standing by and whispered in his ear. Then the man hurried away.

No one moved as Davato stood silent, possibly collecting himself. Then he turned to Adam Turner and Grady. "When we come before the Master, say nothing and follow my lead. Let Sebastien and I do the talking."

Both men nodded. Grady was more than willing to remain silent.

"Now we go in." Davato reentered the combination and pushed through the door.

Grady swallowed. He wanted to be anywhere but walking through that door. Many times, he had passed it and felt what was inside—something dark and unworldly, something to be greatly feared. Now, they were forcing him to go in.

The room was twenty meters square. Climbing the walls were gray, white, and black swirls, mixed with red and yellow flames. At one end, a golden statue, vaguely phallic, broke out of the floor at an angle. Was it made of gold?

At first, the recessed ceiling lights gleamed off the gold, and Grady felt nothing like what had troubled him in the hallway outside.

Davato knelt and motioned for the others to do the same.

As Grady focused on the idol of shining gold, it morphed in his vision into a pillar of wavering red and yellow flame. Then it became a tower of flickering dark fire that sucked into itself all the room's light, even extinguishing the neons in the ceiling.

A swirling darkness, deep and chilling and without end, stole Grady's breath away.

"Oh, g–great Master," said Davato, and Grady had never heard such fear and submission in his voice. "We call on you today in our hour of need."

The Imperator bowed low, and his hands touched the floor. "The Enemy has sent asteroids against us, and we need your protection as never before."

"Great Master," added the Prophet. "Give our rockets the power to destroy what the Enemy has sent. Let our mission be successful."

The darkness in the room intensified. A hand of ice reached deep into Grady's chest, and icy fingers closed about his heart. He laid his face on the cold marble, and tears ran down his face. He wanted to be away from here, far, far away, but he was trapped.

The mark on his hand tingled—no, it burned—and he stared at it.

The words of the third angel came back to him, the one announcing doom for all who followed the beast. Grady thought he had followed

Davato, but now he understood he had really followed the Dragon, the one called Satan, the Master, the lord of the underworld.

And now, there was no undoing that choice, no going back.

Then someone, or some *thing*, was inside his head, laughing, telling him what a fool he was. And he was falling, tumbling, down a dark well from which there was no escape. His limbs wouldn't stop trembling. Below him opened a border between light and dark, good and evil, and he broke through to a place from which there was no return.

As Davato and the Prophet continued to beseech the Dragon, the one who ruled the dark, Grady realized there was something worse than starving to death, and that was to enter an eternal netherworld of dark shadows, perfect evil, and black fire.

Beside him, Turner was having a different experience. He was smiling, raising occasional joyful glances to the golden stone, and breathing heavily. Turner was possessed.

When it was over, every nerve in Grady's body was shattered. Fighting for balance, he rose. Still shaking, he walked woodenly after the Imperator into the hallway.

"Now," said Davato, "we go to the Situation Room and launch our counterattack against the Enemy."

Grady Wilson followed the others to the elevator toward the room where the monitors would show the launch of the four rockets—three to kill the comet, one to observe the results.

CHAPTER 53

THE FIRST TRUMPET

*Revelation 8:5, 7 (NLT): Then the angel filled the incense burner
with fire from the altar and threw it down upon the earth; and
thunder crashed, lightning flashed, and there was a terrible earthquake. . . . The first angel blew his trumpet, and hail and fire mixed
with blood were thrown down on the earth. One-third of the earth
was set on fire, one-third of the trees were burned, and all the green
grass was burned.*

New Babylon, Iraq — May 12, Year 4

It was three days after the interceptor launch, and Grady Wilson left the
World Casino around six o'clock. Overhead, jet engines roared west-
ward, taking revelers home. Twenty meters away, water jets gurgled, surrounding the statue of a naked nymph.

Someone had leaked what was happening. At first, the news channels reported the story of the two asteroids in breathless tones, hinting
of Armageddon. But social media and government censors squashed that
kind of talk. Now, official releases assured everyone that the Ministry of
Peace was sending three rockets to destroy the larger rock and make the
world safe for humanity.

So his plan tonight was to take supper in a favorite restaurant a few
blocks away then spend the evening in one of the pleasure dens and
smoke hashish. Like many others around him, he relied increasingly on
the pleasure dens to blot out his fears. Lately, even Davato seemed on
edge, snapping at subordinates, finding fault for no reason, and wearing
a permanent irritated expression.

There was one piece of good news. Scientists had calculated that the
first asteroid would fall harmlessly somewhere in the Atlantic. The con-
sensus was that, if it hit more than forty kilometers from land, unlike all
the movies about such disasters, the resulting wave would quickly die

out. There would be no devastating tsunami, and they could discount the first asteroid.

But the second object was worrisome. Amateur astronomers across the world were following both objects, and no one could squelch the air of panic and uncertainty sweeping cities, towns, and villages everywhere. Even the launch of Project Interceptor couldn't allay the public's or Grady's fears. Everyone knew that stopping the second asteroid wasn't a sure thing.

The sun hung low over the desert city, the evening was warm, and he had no reason to hurry. Strolling past dozens of couples of various sexes, he passed rows of dead saplings, now only scarecrow sticks, casualties of the drought that even the return of the rain couldn't revive. But tonight, everyone was outside, enjoying the pleasant weather, trying to forget what the coming days might bring.

Ahead was one of the fountains Davato had ordered for the pedestrian walkways. Water jetted from the mouth of a naked nymph, rose in a perfect ten-foot arc, and splashed into a pool. From six points along the basin, water shot in more arcs, crisscrossed, and drilled into the pool, joining the central jet.

Grady was still walking, admiring the water art, about to take a step. But while he had one foot still in the air, the ground rose to meet it.

He stumbled and fought to remain upright, but the sidewalk buckled and heaved. A ground wave rolled beneath him. A crack raced across the street, split the concrete ahead, and ruptured the fountain's base. The nymph toppled into the pool, and water gushed onto the walkway.

The earth jumped, and he found himself on all fours, reaching for a buckling, jumping planet. A torrent of water soaked his pants as the fountain emptied. Water rushed into the gaping crack in the earth only meters away.

Standing, he swayed then slipped on the wet pavement before regaining his balance.

Upright again, he sent a horrified glance to the noise from the skyline.

Someone on the walkway screamed, and hundreds of terrified faces followed his gaze.

Hundreds of lightning bolts played and touched and licked the tops of the buildings across the cityscape. Boom after thunderous boom echoed in a continuous, earsplitting volley as, from one end of the city to another, giant electric fingers torched the horizon. It seemed as though the sky itself roared in never-ending anger.

The lightning, the thunder, the shaking ground went on and on, and Grady rocked and swayed and fought for balance, afraid to go forward, yet fearful to remain where he was.

And then he wondered. The first asteroid was still many days out.

So what was this?

CHAPTER 54

MOUNTAIN RUMBLINGS

Kronberg Mountain, Switzerland – May 12, Year 4

It was three in the afternoon when Dylan reached for Margot's hand and helped her over the log. Above, the shrill chirping of Alpine chough birds drifted down from the treetops. At Jakob Huber's suggestion, they'd spent the day exploring a hidden route well off the public hiking trails.

Jakob and Emma had joined them at the warming hut at the end of the ski trail that was now their new home. Yesterday, Jakob, René, and Pasqual had trekked back to the Skihaus for the disabled van. They'd resurrected the vehicle, driven to the nearest village, and bought what supplies they could. It was a risky venture, but they needed food. And besides, once on the road, there was cell coverage, and they were desperate for news.

As everyone huddled around the woodstove, René told them about the asteroids.

"They must be part of the first three trumpet judgments," said Pasqual. "But if Davato thinks he's going to stop them, it's not going to work."

"There's nothing we can do about it, is there?" said Jakob. "Just keep on keeping on, as they say."

"That's the truth," added René.

When Jakob heard about Dylan and Margot's hiking plans, he told them about the hidden trail. "There was once a lodge tucked off that trail. If it's abandoned, maybe we could move there?"

Dylan offered to take him along as their guide, but Jakob smiled and shook his head. "I'm thinking you two should be alone tomorrow."

The resort was just where he had said it would be—one kilometer off a side trail in the woods, accessible only by snowmobile in winter or four-wheeler in summer. Few folks were vacationing nowadays, and it had been abandoned for years.

René was always on the lookout for another hideout, especially if it had more room, and the *Grünes Bergversteck*, or Green Mountain Hideaway, as the wooden plaque above the entryway announced, was perfect. It had eight bedrooms, a stone fireplace in a spacious living room, and a wood cookstove in a large kitchen. The storeroom held skis, snowshoes, walking sticks, and a hidden store of freeze-dried army food, good for another thirty years.

Since it was late, after they explored the resort, they skipped the hike to the summit and started back down.

They'd just crossed a bridge over a roaring mountain stream and a mountain meadow alive with purple and white crocuses. The trail switched back and forth as they descended through pine forests. It had been raining for the last three days, and the trail was muddy. A sheen of moisture covered every leaf, and all morning fog hovered in the valley.

"It's good to see life and flowers on the mountain." Margot stopped to catch her breath. "Today, I want to forget all about asteroids and prophecies."

Pausing beside her, Dylan cocked his head and grinned. "There is no more beautiful flower up here than the one beside me."

"Dylan Turner!" She landed hands on hips and frowned. "That is so, so . . . schmaltzy. But thank you."

"I mean it." He grabbed her hands and pulled her close. "I cannot think of another person I'd rather be with right now than you."

She blushed. "That's nice. And I feel the same about you."

He kissed her on her cheek. They separated and continued their descent.

At the overlook, they sat cross-legged on a bare rock ledge. A forested valley spread out below. Filling the vista were pine forests mixed with green meadows and an occasional village, now mostly abandoned or sparsely populated. High above, an eagle soared in circles, emitting random cries.

"It's so beautiful here. It's hard to believe it's real. It's been five months since I left the camp, and I still have nightmares about it. How people can be so cruel to one another I don't understand. I nearly despaired that you and I would ever be together again. The whole time I was imprisoned, I prayed to Jesus to get out, to see you again." She caught his glance and smiled. "And yet, here we are."

Below, hundreds of birds burst from the treetops and began flying south.

"Look at that!" she cried. "Did something scare them?"

"I don't know, but when you were in the camp, I, too, prayed. And I confess that at times I lost faith. I didn't know how or when or if we could ever find that camp. Even if we did, I didn't know how we would ever get you out. It was tearing me up inside."

"But I did get out, and what happened was a miracle." She laid a hand on his knee. "You came at the exact moment the earthquake hit. When I escaped, you were at the right place where you could find me."

"That was because, on the night before, Caleb called me out of the blue with a message from what he said was an angel. He told me where to go and what to do." Dylan shook his head. "It was all a miracle, wasn't it? God guided us every step of the way."

"He did." She faced the vista below. "But now what's in store for us?"

"I don't know. We're living in the end times. And last night, I prayed we would escape what lies ahead."

"Still"—she smiled at him—"we're not like those who have taken the mark. We've given ourselves to Jesus. And to each other. That's something, isn't it?"

"Yes, Margot. That's something."

Rising, they started across the rocky precipice.

But they hadn't taken three steps when the sky exploded.

The mountain shook, Dylan slipped on the rock, and he dropped to his knees. He struggled to his feet.

Beside him, Margot wobbled but remained upright.

Peals of thunder rumbled down from the peak, followed by lightning. The thunder boomed so loud and so continuously, he smashed his hands over his ears.

Out over the valley, lightning flashed and played and licked the tops of trees.

The ground heaved again, and Margot grabbed his hands for support.

Something was crashing downhill above them, knocking down saplings. Ten meters away, a boulder the size of a car rolled through the brush and sailed over the ledge, out into space. Long moments later came a crash as it hit the valley below.

"Come on!" he said. "We need to get off this mountain."

The lightning, the thunder, and a shaking earth followed as they headed down the trail toward home.

CHAPTER 55

MOUNT ETNA

Isaiah 24:4–6 (HCSB): The earth mourns and withers; the world wastes away and withers; the exalted people of the earth waste away. The earth is polluted by its inhabitants, for they have transgressed teachings, overstepped decrees, and broken the everlasting covenant. Therefore a curse has consumed the earth, and its inhabitants have become guilty. The earth's inhabitants have been burned, and only a few survive.

The Mediterranean, South of Sicily – May 12, Year 4

It was three in the afternoon, the salt breeze caressed Chelsea's face, and the waves washed against the hull. She relished her time outside as, behind her, seagulls cried to each other, following in the ship's wake. To the north, the coast of Sicily and distant snowcapped mountains rose over a blue-green sea. Rows of ancient houses climbed the cliffs and shoreline.

While in Chania port, Chelsea and Enzo had been locked in their cabins, not even allowed out at mealtimes. On the first day, she'd formulated a plan to escape and waited for Altin to bring her supper. . . .

She sat on the bed with the pistol behind her back and leafed through the Bible in her hands. But she was so nervous, she was unable to read. It was after six, time for him to come, but he was late. Was she too obvious, sitting here like this? Should she be at the desk? But no. That's where he'd place the tray, and then she couldn't hide the gun.

The lock clicked, and he opened the door, bearing the tray with her supper. As usual, a pistol was holstered at his waist.

As he headed for the desk, she tried to slow her racing heart.

She groped for the gun behind her back, but her fingers closed on the blanket. Where was the pistol she'd placed so carefully? Without thinking, she grimaced.

But Altin had already deposited the tray, and he'd turned. He saw her grimace, and he raised an eyebrow.

Even as her hand brought the gun around, he lunged. He grabbed her wrist. Strong fingers squeezed so hard she cried out and dropped the weapon. It clattered to the floor.

"What's this?" He bent down, picked it up, and grinned. "The little lady has a pistol?"

She glared at him.

Then he slapped her so hard she fell back across the bed and up against the wall.

"Get up!" He waved her own weapon at her. "Get down on the floor!"

She rose, fell to her knees, and watched while he again searched the room. This time, he found her box of bullets under the mattress. Before leaving, he stood before the open door and shook his head. "You can't escape, little lady. In Morocco, you're going to make me very wealthy, indeed."

He locked her in, and she didn't set foot on deck for the next three months. And that was the end of her escape plans. . . .

Then the engine parts arrived, and the repairs were completed. For the last three days, they'd been at sea, heading west.

Since they were no longer in port, she pleaded to be allowed some fresh air, and the captain relented. For two hours each afternoon, Altin brought the prisoners on deck where he handcuffed them to the railing.

Every day now, Altin insisted that they pipe the news through the ship's speakers to hear about the approaching asteroids. At first, the broadcasts were filled with dire warnings about planetwide catastrophe, but that changed to assurances on every media outlet that the Imperator had the situation well in hand, that the first asteroid would fall harmlessly into the sea, and that Project Interceptor would save the planet from the second rock.

But Chelsea wasn't so sure.

Flocks of seagulls burst overhead, heading south at a rapid clip, and when she looked, the gulls behind the ship joined their fellows from the north.

"That's odd," said Enzo cuffed beside her. "Something must have scared them."

In the pilothouse, Fabio was manning the controls, and Altin had just left for the bow.

She'd been waiting for this moment, and now it was safe to talk. She leaned toward Enzo and whispered. "We need another plan to escape."

"I know, but how?"

"Next time we land, what if we both go after one of them at the same time and try to take a gun?"

"I've never seen Altin without that pistol on his hip. It might be worth a shot." He scratched his chin. "But what if we don't go ashore until Morocco? I don't want to escape there with Marzuq waiting for us."

"Good point. What should we do?"

"Maybe we could force them to land sooner, perhaps in—"

Everywhere in all directions, lightning flashed on the horizon, accompanied by booming thunder so continuous, the sky itself seemed to be breaking apart.

A shock wave of sound rolled over them, and she shot a glance to the north. Angry dark clouds boiled and spread out and up from a distant mountain. Black smoke mixed with fire and lightning churned and climbed until it seemed to touch the roof of the sky. Rockets of flaming lava burst from the peak and shot out in all directions. It was as if God himself had set off an enormous Roman candle as the mountain threw up one ball of fire after another.

She shuddered and cupped her free hand over her mouth. What was happening?

Everywhere in all directions, lightning filled the skyline, followed by continuous, never-ending thunder so loud, it shook the boat.

"It's Mt. Etna!" Enzo pointed. "It's the first trumpet, and Etna's volcano has exploded."

Balls of flaming lava landed farther and farther from the mountain, and an angry red glare spread over the horizon as fire swarmed across the forests.

Fabio ran from the wheelhouse and stared north. He put both hands on top of his head and shook it from side to side.

Fireballs arced high, dropping still farther and farther from the mountain, some plunging into the sea on the shoreline. Some of the houses on the coast were now ablaze. A few flaming balls crossed high above the ship, heading south, leaving thick, roiling streamers of ugly black smoke.

A frightened Altin ran back from the bow, but Fabio ordered him into the wheelhouse.

Her gaze followed a flaming missile headed straight for them. Fabio, too, saw it, and he stood frozen as a ball of molten lava, possibly as big as a house, slammed into the sea less than a kilometer away. The jolting crack of the impact, followed by the hiss of quenching fire, raced across the distance.

Fabio joined Altin at the controls and turned the ship toward the receding column of water. Slowly, the vessel changed direction.

Then she saw why the captain made the turn. Coming fast at them, perhaps five meters high, was a giant wave. Her breath now came fast and ragged. She gripped the rail and held on.

When the wave reached the ship, the bow climbed at a forty-five-degree angle and topped the crest. Then, as spray washed the deck, the vessel plummeted into the trough. The impact jerked her to the deck with Enzo falling on top of her. The handcuffs cut into her wrists, but they kept her from washing overboard.

Enzo helped her regain her seat, and, where the cuffs had held her, the skin was now raw and bleeding.

The captain resumed their previous heading, and now everyone kept glancing north where the mountain's slopes were covered with an angry red, above which smoke roiled and churned in a never-ending, restless cloud, and where rockets of lava shot for hundreds of kilometers in all directions.

Then the clouds began raining what appeared to be blood. Red balls splashed with a hissing sound into the sea. Here and there, droplets splattered the deck. When Chelsea ran a finger across a puddle, she jerked it back. The rain wasn't blood, but hot, red mud.

Bearing a pistol, Altin climbed down from the bridge, unlocked the prisoners' restraints, and hurried them to their cabins. Before he locked the door on her, he stared at her bleeding wrist and shook his head. "You asked for time on deck, didn't you? And this is what you get."

Then he slammed the door and locked it.

CHAPTER 56

THE YELLOWSTONE CALDERA

Salt Lake City, Utah – May 12, Year 4

Just before seven in the morning, Randy Foster ended his walk from the dormitory apartments to the Department of Geology and Geophysics building. Even though he now had to carry a sidearm, he loved this early morning walk, especially when the sparrows cheeped in the treetops.

He almost reached the door when the sidewalk shook and lightning crashed all along the horizon. There followed continuous peals of thunder.

To the north, billowing black clouds, mixed with streaks of glowing fire and lightning, spread south. Transfixed where he stood, he stared at what could only be an eruption from the Yellowstone Caldera over three hundred miles away. The ground heaved and jumped, cracks ran beneath him on the sidewalk, and he fought for balance. From the north, balls of flaming lava shot in all directions, leaving behind thick, black steamers of smoke.

The ground shook again, and he flailed his arms to keep from falling.

When the quake lessened for a moment, he tried to push through the revolving doors, but they'd jammed. He took the side door, and, avoiding the elevator, he lurched his way up four flights to the lab. Inside, his seismographs jerked erratically, and the bank of screens recording the event held so much red and blue, they were opaque.

He tried to calm a racing heart. He needed to calculate a number—the Volcanic Explosivity Index—a number that would tell him everything he needed to know about what was happening under the Yellowstone supervolcano.

The number uppermost in his mind was seven. It couldn't, mustn't exceed seven. Some had estimated that around six hundred thousand years ago, the Yellowstone Caldera had exploded with a VEI of eight. It had been catastrophic, enough to violently alter life on the planet. He gripped his arms about his chest and tried to slow his racing heart.

Cameras, infrared cameras, and sulfur dioxide correlation spectrometers situated around the Yellowstone site would allow him to guess the volume of smoke, fire, gases, and ash being thrown into the air. They would also record the height of the smoke column. Seismometers and other detection instruments were already relaying information to a bevy of frantically jerking instruments on the long tables beside him. He wiped sweat from his forehead as he examined one device after another, writing down measurements. By switching cameras situated near the caldera, he could examine the eruption from different angles.

Suddenly, the entire building shook. His monitors jiggled toward the table edge, and he stopped recording. When the quake passed, he pushed all the equipment back where it belonged and continued collecting data.

Something bright flashed through the windows, followed by an explosion that rocked the building. He hurried over and looked out at a smoking trail that had fallen only a few kilometers to the west. Flames rose from the crash site, and before he turned away, yet another flaming missile dropped into the city to the north.

Ripping himself from the scene, he returned to his instruments.

He switched to yet another Yellowstone camera on a hill, but the quakes had dislodged it. Now it pointed at the forest below. A roaring fire was racing up the slope, consuming every green thing before it. He refocused the camera skyward as far as it would go and tried to measure the rising column of smoke. He did what he could before heat distorted the lens and melting plastic made further observation impossible.

Finally, he had enough data to make a guess. His fingers shook as he punched numbers into his laptop program that would calculate the VEI.

He held his breath as the progress bar crept across the bottom of the screen toward 100 percent.

It finished. The number was—

Six.

He breathed out and sat back in his chair. The planet would survive. The world might be ending, but Yellowstone wouldn't be the cause.

But his email was flashing, and he turned to look. Reports were arriving from all over the planet.

Yellowstone wasn't alone.

Volcanoes and earthquakes were erupting all over the world.

CHAPTER 57
SNOW IN MAY

Lake Shetek State Park, Minnesota – May 13, Year 4

When Brianna burst in from outside, out of breath and with wonder written all over her face, Caleb was still recovering from yesterday's events.

It had been a day when the ground had shaken so hard, it cracked the dining hall's concrete floor and felled trees outside.

It was a day when lightning filled the skies from horizon to horizon, flashing, striking, and lighting up the heavens as if God was pouring his wrath on every inch of the planet.

It was a day when thunder boomed and echoed so continuously and so loud and long it seemed the world was ending. While, in the distance, fires lit by lightning raged across the prairie, filling the skies with smoke.

It was a day he wished never to see again.

This morning before he returned to the cabin, clouds had rolled in, dropping a bit of fresh rain, and he had relaxed. Like a green shoot poking through frozen ground in spring, hope sprang again. Maybe things would return to normal. At least for a while.

Then Brianna burst in, and he knew they hadn't. "It's snowing some kind of white stuff," she said.

His muscles tensed, and he shot out of his seat. With Andy behind him, he left their checkers game and headed outside where snow was indeed drifting down all around them. He splayed his fingers then rubbed the flakes together, and they were indeed white. But they weren't cold. And they didn't melt. Instead, they made a smudge on his skin. It wasn't snow.

"It's ash, isn't it?" Andy craned his neck skyward.

"From the fires?" They'd lived through weeks of burning forest in the Northwoods, and they knew what kind of ash fell from burning trees and brush.

Andy rubbed the ash between his fingers. "It's white, and it's gritty." He brought it to his nose. "It smells of sulfur."

Caleb shot him a worried look. "Volcanic ash?"

"Yep."

They both looked to the sky as if it could explain what had happened. But the ash just kept drifting down, and the clouds revealed no secrets.

Tanya crossed the yard and waved a hand at the heavens' dark ceiling. "It was too good to be true, wasn't it? We're at the end of the world, and we can't pretend that everything will just go on as it did before."

Only then, did Caleb see the tears running down her cheeks and her shaking hands covered with ash. He drew her close and hugged her. "It will be all right. If we stick together, if we put our trust in God, everything will be all right."

She eased away, wiped her cheeks, and nodded. "I hope you're right."

He pulled her back and held her even tighter.

CHAPTER 58

PROJECT INTERCEPTOR

Psalm 2:1–2, 4–5 (HCSB): Why do the nations rebel and the peoples plot in vain? The kings of the earth take their stand, and the rulers conspire together against the LORD and His Anointed One. . . . The One enthroned in heaven laughs; the Lord ridicules them. Then He speaks to them in His anger and terrifies them in His wrath . . .

New Babylon, Iraq – May 16, Year 4

The New Babylon Situation Room was an exact copy of the one in Jerusalem, and Grady followed the others to the master electronics consoles where he was directed to a chair four seats down from the Imperator and General Eric Hofmann. On the floor below, thirty technicians sat at screens and keyboards. Twenty large monitors filled the far wall, below which were twice that number of smaller screens. But today, only a third of the monitors were active. Still, the room hummed with electronics.

As before, black-haired Marcia was there to help Grady understand what was going on. As he pulled on headphones with its attached microphone, they exchanged knowing smiles. Many times, both had gone together into a worship room in the World Temple, now fitted with a giant statue of Davato, to experience "sharing time" together.

"What you're seeing on the main screen," she said, "is video from an observation craft launched behind the three missiles carrying the warheads and rotary mining drills. It's following at a safe distance to assess results. There's about a twenty-second delay for the signal to reach us."

In the blackness of space, the screen showed three shining metal dots and the asteroid itself. A long tail of gases extended far behind the rock.

"The missiles are hard to see. They don't look very big."

"That's because the observation craft is far behind them."

"How long until they land?"

She pointed to a smaller monitor displaying the countdown: fifty minutes, thirty seconds.

As they waited, she pulled off her headphones, urged him to do the same, and laid a hand on his knee. "Later? My apartment?"

Grady grinned and nodded. But then a flicker of shame rose up within him. She wasn't the only one he'd slept with lately. How was it that he no longer even blinked at moving from one, to two, to three, to four different women—all in a matter of a week? It left him feeling soiled and empty. What was happening to him?

When the count reached twenty minutes, maneuvering rockets turned the missiles around.

At the same time, the observation craft fired its rockets to match the course of the others, and its camera swiveled to keep the asteroid in view.

Retrorockets fired on the landing craft, slowing their approach. They continued firing until each had aligned their speeds with the oncoming asteroid. By the time the countdown reached zero, all the landing vehicles had touched down on the surface, throwing up dust and debris around them.

Meanwhile, the observation craft stopped approaching the asteroid and matched its speed.

A loud cheer went up from the technicians as the mining drills began their work.

"Now it's just a matter of time until they reach the right depth," said Marcia.

"How long?" asked Grady.

"We're not sure. Until they can't make further progress, I suppose."

As they waited, the drills dug deeper. Lunch came, and Grady and Marcia ate together in the cafeteria. Around six at night, one drill stopped.

Around eight, a technician announced that those not directly involved in the operation were released for the night. If all the drills stopped, everyone would be notified to return before the thermonuclear devices triggered.

Grady went with Marcia to her room, and there they spent the night.

* * *

It was four in the morning when Marcia's and Grady's phones buzzed. Text messages alerted them that all the drills had reached their maximum depth. Both dressed and returned to the Situation Room where a new countdown was underway—

Five minutes to detonation.

But then they received unwelcome news—one of the devices had stopped communicating. Instead of the expected three detonations, there would now be only two.

The seconds ticked down. When the count reached zero, the observation screen filled with white light. They couldn't see anything. The technicians, the general, and even Davato froze in their seats, their gazes fixed on the screen as the nuclear blasts receded.

An electric tingling ran down Grady's back and up his arms. Would the explosions blow the things apart enough to keep the earth from disaster?

Finally, the view cleared. But instead of one asteroid, there were now possibly sixty. And instead of coming back together, as the astronomer Ben Smiley had predicted, they did an unusual thing—they separated even further.

A rousing cheer rose from the room. "It's a success!" came General Hofmann's excited voice. "We've destroyed it."

"No, wait!" cried Ben Smiley, the American. "Look at what's behind it."

Everyone focused on the screen. Indeed, hundreds, possibly thousands of smaller hunks of rock, previously obscured by the larger asteroid and its gas trail, followed in its wake.

"What does this mean?" Davato turned to Ben Smiley and General Hofmann.

"I'm not sure," said the American. "The debris is smaller. But there's so much of it. It's possible they'll all burn up in the atmosphere."

"Then it's a success?" The Imperator cast a withering gaze on the American.

A look of fear twisted Smiley's forehead, and he opened his mouth, but apparently changed his mind, closed it, and then spoke. "Yes." He swallowed. "Yes, I think it was a success."

The room exploded in clapping and cheers.

Grady wiped sweat from his brow and turned to Marcia. "I hope he's right. That was tense."

"Yeah, and you know what?" She checked her watch. "Though it's after four in the morning, I could use a drink to celebrate."

"What's open right now?"

"Are you kidding? It's New Babylon. Everything is open. Let's go!"

CHAPTER 59

TANGIER PORT

Tangier, Morocco — May 17, Year 4

When the *Am Albahr* chugged into Tangier's harbor, the moon was full, and Chelsea was close to despair. This was the first time since Crete that they'd docked, and she feared she'd lost the opportunity to free herself and Enzo. If some emir made her a prisoner in his harem, what chance would she ever have to escape?

When Fabio entered the harbor, he stopped first at a floating fuel depot. Using hard cash plus a bribe to avoid the paperwork, he refueled and resupplied the ship. They cruised deeper, passing the tumbled ruins of a Muslim prayer tower before landing at one of the docks reserved for private vessels. The Yacht Club building was only twenty meters away across a cement walkway. Though Fabio's was a fishing vessel, the Yacht Club was where he was told to meet the emir. This was an unlikely place for a man like Fabio and a ship like his to park. But since Marzuq ruled the city, Fabio said the man could dictate whatever terms he wanted.

Before leaving the ship, Fabio, armed as usual, locked Chelsea in her cabin with a warning. "I'll be just outside, and Altin will stay with the ship. After I call the emir, he will come aboard. Before he pays, he wants to see what he's buying. Be nice. Don't make trouble."

The moment he left, she opened her porthole and peered out to find Fabio pacing the sidewalk under the lights from the Yacht Club windows. It was well after supper, and beardless men and bareheaded women milled about beyond the second-floor windows, waving drinks and dancing to loud, pounding music. With the demise of Islam, people had abandoned Muhammad's restrictions and were making the most of it.

Someone crept along the shadows next to the building, heading in Fabio's direction, and he kept glancing behind him. Why wasn't he out in the open? Something was wrong.

She craned her neck to see better.

The mystery man stepped out of the dark and approached the captain. "Are you Fabio Caruso?" His voice bounced off the building and water, and Chelsea could hear everything said.

"Yes."

"Then I have bad news for you. Marzuq has been arrested, and you should leave here at once."

Fabio gasped. "Arrested? By whom?"

"By the CSA. How did you enter the harbor?"

"We motored in. No one stopped us."

"You're lucky. Most of Davato's goons are up there"—he pointed to the second floor—"drinking and partying. Hardly any ships come here anymore. They weren't expecting anyone tonight."

"G–government men?" Fear reverberated in the captain's voice. "What happened?"

"A few days ago, they landed in force, there was a quick battle, and they took Tangier back from Marzuq. Now they're making everyone take the mark. The emir refused, and he's in prison."

"I sailed all the way from Haifa for this deal."

"Deal?" The man laughed. "No Marzuq, no deal. Save yourself and get out of here—fast. I took a risk just warning you." Then the man melted back into the shadows and was gone.

Even as Fabio hurried back up the ramp, two men in green-and-white uniforms bearing rifles turned the far corner and sauntered down the sidewalk. CSA men patrolling the dock?

Fabio disappeared from view. Moments later, the engines vibrated, and the ship pulled away.

"Halt!" came a voice from the walkway. "Show us your papers."

The engines revved, and the ship gained speed.

More shouts followed, but the *Am Albahr* now broke every rule about no wakes in the harbor. There followed more rifle shots, and a few ricocheted off something metal. The engine revved higher, and the ship picked up speed.

Soon, they left the marina and were out in the open sea, heading for the Strait of Gibraltar, between the Atlantic and the Mediterranean.

Then Altin opened her cabin door. "The captain needs you in the pilothouse."

Surprised at the request, she followed him to the superstructure.

"I need your help tonight," said Fabio as she entered.

She cocked her head. "Why?"

"Look behind you."

She turned, and a patrol boat with searchlights was cruising a kilometer or so behind them. "Someone's following us?"

"The deal with Marzuq is off. The CSA has captured Tangier and the emir. When we docked, they spotted our ship. If they stop us, everyone aboard, including you, will be in deep trouble."

"What do you want me to do?"

"Keep the ship on this heading while Altin and I prepare a defense." He pointed to a number on the compass.

She glanced at the compass, at Fabio, at the approaching CSA vessel, and swallowed. "Okay. I'll do it."

Fabio nodded then raced down to the aft deck where Altin was dragging out a round metal stand with pintle mount. Behind it, Fabio lugged some kind of large machine gun and began bolting it to the mount.

Behind them, the CSA ship kept coming. Would there be an exchange of cannon or machine gun fire?

Then night became day, and the sea around them lit up as if the sun had risen.

She raced from the pilothouse. An enormous ball of blinding fire streaked down from the heavens, leaving a massive trail of flame and smoke.

An earsplitting sonic boom, as if a thousand cannons had fired all at once, rocked the boat, and she smashed her hands over her ears.

She followed the path of what must be the first asteroid. Hundreds of pieces plunged straight down, leaving trails of fire, smoke, and racing meteors. The clouds rolled away in panic, and lightning flashed away from the rock on all sides.

Transfixed where they stood, Fabio and Altin stared up.

Chelsea's glance followed the fireball until it dipped below the horizon.

CHAPTER 60

THE SECOND TRUMPET

Revelation 8:8–9 (NLT): Then the second angel blew his trumpet, and a great mountain of fire was thrown into the sea. One-third of the water in the sea became blood, one-third of all things living in the sea died, and one-third of all the ships on the sea were destroyed.

The Canary Islands – May 17, Year 4

The first asteroid plunged through the stratosphere at a speed of 42,270 miles per hour. Thirty-four miles above the earth, it burst into smaller pieces.

But it headed—not for the middle of the ocean as expected—but for a point four miles off the coast of La Palma in the Canary Islands.

The fireball's radius was eight miles, and as it approached, it burnt to a crisp everything on the island below.

When the asteroid hit the water, it plunged six hundred meters to the sea bottom, throwing up an eleven-mile-wide curtain of ocean that crashed down onto the island of La Palma. Winds approaching eight thousand miles per hour swept out from the center of the water column.

It created an earthquake measuring eight on the Richter scale.

A huge volume of water hit the Cumbre Vieja volcano. An initial tsunami swept out from the point of impact, but as expected, it dissipated. Forty kilometers away, it was spent.

But the damage had been done.

The quake and the huge volume of water crashing down on the volcano ruptured a nine-mile-long fault running the mountain's length. Slowly at first, then increasing, one and a half million metric tons of volcanic rock ripped away from the mountain and started down.

It gained momentum until, by the time it crashed into the Atlantic, it had reached a speed of two hundred and twenty miles per hour. The resulting landslide generated a one-thousand-foot-high tsunami that, in deep waters, would race across the North and South Atlantic at five hundred miles per hour. When, eight hours later, it reached the eastern seaboard of the Province of North America, the waves would be eighty feet high.

Cities on every coast of the Atlantic—north, south, east, and west—would be devastated.

Ships in port and on the coast would not survive.

But then a strange thing occurred, defying every scientific explanation. At the site of the initial impact, the sea began to turn red. The red tide spread in all directions. But it wasn't algae.

It was blood.

Two and a half hours after impact, when the tsunami entered the shallower waters in the Strait of Gibraltar, it would be sixty feet high and slow to thirty miles an hour.

In its path—two vessels heading east at nine miles per hour:

A CSA patrol ship mounted with a 127-mm cannon.

And a freezer trawler with a .50-caliber medium pintle-mount machine gun.

CHAPTER 61
THE TSUNAMI

The Strait of Gibraltar – May 17, Year 4

Chelsea stared at the ribbon of smoke and the thousands of meteors falling in the fireball's wake and trembled. On the aft deck, Fabio and Altin stood transfixed by the flaming horizon, their hands frozen on the machine gun.

But behind them, the CSA ship kept coming.

Moments later, the captain climbed to the wheelhouse. "If what they said was true, that asteroid isn't a problem. Continue on the course I've set. The patrol ship is still after us."

Chelsea nodded and turned her attention to the compass and the sea ahead. But she kept glancing back. The angry red glow in the southwestern sky, the way the clouds still roiled and churned, the lightning still playing all along the horizon—something warned her the experts were wrong. She'd read about the trumpet prophecies and feared the worst was yet to come.

As the minutes lengthened, the CSA ship gained, but she kept the captain's chosen heading. Two hours later, their pursuer had closed the gap to only five hundred meters.

The sound of a cannon boomed from behind, and she whirled to look back. A shell exploded in the nearby waters. The cannon shot again, and she followed its arc until it splashed into the sea only thirty meters away.

Down on the aft deck, Fabio left the machine gun and stared west. She followed his glance across the moonlit waters.

Something was racing toward them—a dark line on the horizon, stretching from one end to the other. It was growing in size.

Fabio said something to Altin, who began dismantling the gun. Then the captain raced up to the pilothouse. "It's a tsunami!" He took the controls but kept going east. "We have to head into the wave, but not until that ship behind us turns around."

She glanced back. The CSA vessel seemed oblivious of the approaching threat, and Altin was having difficulty dismantling the gun.

The advancing dark line rose to become a giant wall of water racing toward them, and she gasped. How could anyone survive such a thing?

Finally, the CSA ship saw the wave and began turning. An instant later, Fabio spun the wheel and headed the *Am Albahr* toward the onrushing threat.

It hit their pursuer first, but the vessel was still broadside and hadn't completed its turn. It struggled to climb, leaned to the side, then tipped. The superstructure went under, and Chelsea gasped. When the crest reached the hull, the ship rolled, once, twice, and disappeared under the foam.

But Fabio had the *Am Albahr* pointed at a ninety-degree angle toward the mammoth wall of sea racing toward them. On the deck below, Altin was still fiddling with the gun. Why wasn't he heading for cover?

Her heart beating fast, her focus on the oncoming wave, Chelsea grabbed a railing and held on.

The sea rose up to meet them.

Out the window, they rode a mountain of ocean, scaling its slopes.

The engine struggled and groaned as the ship climbed at a forty-degree angle.

Loose instruments and papers flew past, crashing onto the windows aft.

This couldn't be happening. It was an impossible nightmare. She tightened her grasp on the railing and held fast.

When they reached the crest, the sea broke over the ship, sending a wash of water and foam across the bow, rushing through the central passageway, pounding onto the pilothouse windows. Seawater smashed the door off its hinges, gushed into the wheelhouse, drenching her, knocking her onto the instrument console behind.

As Fabio gripped the wheel, they slid down the far slope and raced toward the trough. Faster on the downslope, the *Am Albahr* hit the valley. The prow dipped into a wave, water again washed over the bow and filled the pilothouse, and the ship climbed a smaller wall of surf beyond.

As the sea drained from the wheelhouse, they hit wave after wave, each smaller than the last.

Behind the tsunami, high winds, rough seas, and whitecaps churned the waters. But the worst was over. Wet and shivering, Chelsea released her grip on the railing and collapsed into one of the wheelhouse chairs.

Fabio wiped his brow and breathed deeply. His eyes wide with fright, he turned the ship east. "Take the wheel. I'm going to see about Altin."

She did as ordered and guided the ship through stormy waters after the giant wave.

Time passed. Then a long-faced Fabio returned. "He's gone. I can't find him anywhere."

"Was he washed overboard?"

"I fear so." Fabio plopped into the pilot's seat and dropped his head in his hands. "He was a difficult mate, but a good seaman."

"I'm sorry."

Then he raised troubled eyes to her. "I don't understand what's going on. The world is falling apart. The earth, the sky, and now the sea—everything is against us." He stood and stared out the window at the thin line of the tsunami, receding far to the east.

"All that's happened was prophesied." Her voice was low. "This is the judgment of the second trumpet. And there's more to come."

"Is it all true? Were the angels real?" His eyebrows scrunched together. "Is there really a God in Heaven doing this to us?"

"It's God's judgment on a world that has turned its back on him, that has despised and rejected the Son he sent to save us." She straightened her stance, amazed by the words spilling out of her mouth as though someone else were speaking. "How many times do you have to see the hand of God before you believe?"

He stared at her. Finally, he turned away. "Keep this heading, yes? I have to think." He left the wheelhouse and retreated to his cabin.

For the next hour, she steered the ship alone, wondering what Fabio would do. But she was soaked, shivering, and needing dry clothes.

When the captain reemerged from his cabin, he bypassed her and descended to the crew quarters. Moments later, he returned with Enzo.

Standing before his two prisoners, Fabio kept his eyes downcast. He unstrapped the pistol at his waist, laid it on the counter, and opened his hands as if in apology.

"Without Altin, I cannot run the ship. Now, I must ask your forgiveness and your help."

Enzo placed hands on hips and frowned. "Why should we help you? You were going to sell us into slavery."

"Please, please." Fabio opened his hands. "I have changed my mind, yes? I will take you both back to Italy as originally agreed. You want to go there, yes? But I cannot run the ship alone. We will land somewhere on the eastern coast. Perhaps the tsunami won't have reached there."

Chelsea crossed her arms. "A while ago, you seemed on the verge of believing in God. Do you now believe? Or are you going to take the mark?"

For long moments, he didn't answer. "I'm still thinking about it. Isn't it enough that I will take you to Italy?"

She sighed and exchanged glances with Enzo.

"All right, Fabio," he said. "We will help you get us back to Italy."

Fabio grinned and reached out a hand. Enzo shook it, then Chelsea.

"Thank you, thank you," Fabio said. "Soon, you will be on Italian soil, and all will be well, yes?"

She didn't answer but left the wheelhouse and headed to her cabin to change her clothes. He'd said the words, but would he ever stick with anything he promised?

CHAPTER 62

THE THIRD TRUMPET

Revelation 8:10–11 (HCSB): The third angel blew his trumpet, and a great star, blazing like a torch, fell from heaven. It fell on a third of the rivers and springs of water. The name of the star is Wormwood, and a third of the waters became wormwood. So, many of the people died from the waters, because they had been made bitter.

Above the Earth – May 20, Year 4

Nothing like the second asteroid had ever fallen to earth since the world began.

It would disobey every prediction, every law of science and logic. Like the first rock, it would plunge through the stratosphere at a speed of 42,270 miles per hour. But after that, it would break all the rules.

Defying gravity, the sixty loose chunks, separated by Davato's attempt to destroy it, and the hundreds of fragments of asteroid debris behind it would spread even farther apart.

The resulting meteors were guided, given a preset course. Defying every law of physics, they would spread out, circle the globe, and choose targets. They would head for major landmasses, concentrating on certain rivers, streams, and freshwater lakes.

From one end of the horizon to another, they would fill the sky with sonic booms, flashes of lightning, contrails of black smoke, and streaks of red, orange, and yellow fire. And somehow, again defying the laws of physics, none of them would burn up.

Each rock was composed of dense cadmium and arsenic trioxide. Millions of flaming missiles would rain down on the planet. But oddly, they were given an affinity for rivers and streams where the Antichrist's people drank, and they would avoid rivers and streams where the Christ-followers drank.

Wherever they hit, they would make the water bitter, and whoever drank of the bitter water would soon die. For this was their mission of divine judgment—to bring lethal toxicity to one-third of the earth's fresh water.

CHAPTER 63

AMBASSADOR DAY

New Babylon, Iraq – May 20, Year 4

It was Ambassador Day, an idea Adam Turner had strongly suggested Grady propose to the Imperator. The noise of jackhammers filled the air, and he walked with the ambassadors from the ten provinces and a few of their staff as they followed Davato beside the Euphrates River. But Grady held back, putting as much distance as possible between himself and Alex Reed, the Wilson family friend from Boston. Though it was Grady's job to escort these men and women, answer their questions, and issue the occasional boon, he wanted nothing to do with the man. No matter how much Grady tried to hide, Alex Reed seemed drawn to him. But every moment spent with Reed increased his risk of discovery.

Davato stopped the group on the riverwalk. "If some of you are wondering about the second asteroid today, have no fear. My scientists tell me the pieces will all burn up in the atmosphere."

Then he pointed east toward a mammoth construction project just getting underway. "Here, my friends, is where we are rebuilding the great hanging gardens of ancient Babylon. It will be twenty stories high, one layer of garden overlapping another, all of it lush with palms, vines, tropical shrubs, and trees. Escalators will take the visitor from one level to the next. Women and men, dressed as forest nymphs and satyrs, will be on hand to entertain folks in the bushes."

"Amazing, isn't it?" came the voice Grady was trying to avoid. He shot a glance to the side where stood Alex Reed. Despite Grady's efforts, he'd found his host. "Everything about this city is mind-blowing. And here you are, an old family friend, and we find ourselves together again in New Babylon."

"Yes, what a coincidence." Grady sighed. Was there no way to free himself of this man?

Cold eyes speared him. "You should know, Grady Wilson, that I've been digging around in the recently digitized paper records from the US military. Some relate to the USS *Avenger* and its crew. Apparently, there was a Jew on board reported to be your exact look-alike. Isn't that interesting?"

A flush rose to Grady's forehead. "Yes. The man was a total annoyance to me."

"I imagine he was." But as Reed turned away, Grady's heart raced. Was everything about his deception about to be undone?

The group followed Davato up an escalator to the first level, already completed, planted, and dripping with greenery. Smiling, half-naked women and men met them on top and thrust coconut-rum smoothies into each of their hands. "Welcome to New Babylon's hanging gardens!" they cried in unison.

Davato raised his drink and toasted the gardens, and the group followed his lead. After a tour of the hidden alcoves and secret nooks, obscured beneath the overhanging plants, they descended to the riverwalk where the Imperator gathered them again. "I hope you have enjoyed this part of the tour on this special day. We are bringing back the glories of Nebuchadnezzar, but a thousand times greater. Are there any questions?"

A woman raised a hand, and Davato nodded.

"What did the earthquakes—?"

But a sonic boom nearly burst Grady's ears.

Above, thousands of tiny fireballs streaked down, leaving dark trails of billowing black smoke. Red and yellow and white-hot flaming missiles screamed through the atmosphere.

Even Davato looked up with an open mouth.

A meteor crashed into the garden they'd just left, and the ground shook. Above, raging fire was fast consuming everything—palms, vines, cacti, nymphs, and satyrs—and a worrisome grinding of concrete rumbled from beneath the structure's base. Was the entire first level about to collapse?

Meteor after meteor dropped into the canal channeling the Euphrates. A half a kilometer distant, a large fireball quenched itself in the ancient river and sent a waterspout shooting hundreds of meters above them. There followed a fierce wind that knocked several of the group off their feet, accompanied by slanting, piercing needles of rain. Grady shut his eyes against the storm and fought to maintain his balance.

With Davato leading, the group broke into a run, heading away from the riverwalk toward the bus.

Behind them, missile after missile hit the Euphrates, exploding in the water, drenching everything for kilometers around.

When they gained the bus, the driver drove them away, windshield wipers flapping.

After they gathered again on the World Casino's promenade, Davato rose to his full height. "That clearly came from the Enemy. Tomorrow, I will order construction crews to start rebuilding the gardens. But if the Enemy intended to do me harm, all he did was give me a good drenching." He ran a hand over his wet clothes, and the group joined him in subdued laughter.

"In four hours, it will be seven o'clock." He checked his watch. "At that time, we will meet in the Dragon Dining Room for a feast in your honor."

But as Grady headed toward his apartment to change his clothes, he was troubled not only by the meteors that had narrowly missed the group. But also by the man who could bring the unmasking of Chaim Weinberg and the end of Grady Wilson.

CHAPTER 64

BAD WATER

New Babylon, Iraq – May 20, Year 4

On the second floor of the World Casino, the Dragon Dining Room was an intimate chamber intended for private affairs. As the ice clinked in their cocktails and the group stood around before dinner, Grady glad-handed, made small talk with the ambassadors, and maneuvered as best he could to avoid Alex Reed. But as luck would have it, when everyone was seated and he searched for the last empty chair, all that was left was the one beside the Wilson family friend from Boston.

He swallowed, closed his eyes, and sat.

As tuxedoed waiters and waitresses brought appetizers of caprese to each place, others filled water glasses and took orders for wine or cocktails. Smiling and bowing, the headwaiter appeared and made an announcement. "My deepest apologies and regrets, but this evening, we have a slight problem with the pipes. Please excuse the water's somewhat metallic taste. We are working to resolve it. However, I myself have drunk it, and I assure you it is safe. We will have it fixed shortly."

Davato frowned and waved him away.

Around the table, faces were flushed, voices were loud, and eyes were alight with inebriation. Despite Davato trying to make light of it, the incident at the Euphrates had shaken everyone. Two had even sent word that they weren't feeling well and wouldn't attend.

Alex Reed had also been drinking. His eyes too bright, he leaned toward his host and smiled. "I'm glad to be filling your shoes, Grady Wilson. You'll have to tell me your secrets. Like how to be an ambassador for the North American province."

"I am happy to oblige."

Alex drank from his water glass. "This is just like the old days, isn't it? And I'm sure you remember everything so well. When we were back in Boston, do you recall when we all went to the marina on the Fourth of

July and your mother got so drunk she fell into the harbor?" He speared Grady with an accusatory glance. "What was that nickname your father used to call her?"

Grady shrugged and picked up his water glass. Just then, a waiter brought him the whiskey he'd ordered. He set down the water and grabbed the whiskey instead.

Alex shot him a quizzical look. "You don't remember? But of course you do."

"The name escapes me right now. After the incident in the Taiwan Strait, I often forget things." He took a long draught of his drink and searched the room for an excuse to leave his seat.

"I bet you do. Well then, you must remember the name of your family's yacht—What was its name again?"

"I'm sorry." He waved a hand. "It's my memory."

A wicked thought crossed his mind. Even here in New Babylon, despite Davato's calm and untroubled assurances, anarchy and lawlessness often ran amuck late at night in the streets. And who, these days, wasn't staggering home late at night? For debauchery breeds debauchery. And lawlessness does, indeed, breed lawlessness. So wouldn't it be possible to hire someone to make an end of this man in the wee hours?

He surprised himself. Was he actually considering murder? He shuddered.

"Come on, Grady." Alex frowned and again drank from his water glass. "How could you forget such a thing?"

His face warming, Grady shrugged and turned away. "Let's talk about something else."

"I don't think so. When your ship sank, only you and a certain ensign survived. The paper records indicate that your doppelganger, this Chaim Weinberg—a Jew can you believe?—perished. But what if such a person switched identities with the real Grady Wilson?"

Grady's hands balled into fists beneath the table. His jaw muscles tensed. He whirled toward the man. "What are you implying? This is outrageous. You'd better be careful, Alex Reed. I am the personal secretary to the Imperator, and I have his ear."

The ambassador from the North American province wiped his forehead. "It's rather warm in here, don't you think? But for someone who's created such a fabulous work of fiction, I imagine things could get quite warm indeed."

Grady drained his whiskey and waved to a waitress for another. Alex flagged down the same woman, asking for more water and a glass of brandy, and she hurried over.

Two seats down, the woman ambassador from South America pushed back from the table and stood. Her face was flushed, her eyes glazed. She apologized to Davato, excused herself, then started for the exit. But she hadn't taken five steps when she collapsed to the floor and vomited. Waiters rushed for her, helped her to her feet, and hurried her from the room. Others cleaned up the mess.

"Sorry for the disturbance." A smirk lifted one side of Davato's mouth. "Here in New Babylon, we sometimes participate in too many pleasures—if such a thing is even possible."

Scattered laughter spread around the table, and conversations resumed.

Alex Reed wiped his forehead and again leaned toward Grady. "An unfortunate incident, that. But now I want to talk about the one thing that can prove who is who. Let's talk about the time you and I got so drunk we both went to that tattoo parlor and got tattoos on our arms." He smacked his brandy glass so hard down on the table that it slopped onto the man next to him. "What were they, Grady? What kind of tattoos were they?"

Men and women on all sides stared at the two. Alex was making a scene. What was wrong with him?

Grady's heart leaped. How was he going to get out of this? "I'm not playing this game, Alex. You're drunk."

"Drunk or not, tell me what kind of tattoo you and I both got!"

"No!" His heart racing, Grady looked away.

"You can't tell me because we didn't get any tattoos and you are not Grady Wilson." Then Alex stared into Grady's—Chaim's—eyes so long, that Cam knew he was undone.

"What do you want?" Cam lowered his voice. "Why are you doing this?"

Alex relaxed and lifted his brandy glass. He swirled it, held it to the light, and set it back down. He frowned and wiped sweat from his forehead. "It's getting really warm in here, don't you think? I've been terribly thirsty all afternoon."

"What do you want from me?"

Again, Alex focused on him, but his eyes seemed clouded. He lowered his voice. "Given what we both know, a man in your position—in your very precarious position—should be able to accommodate any wish from an old friend, no matter how outrageous, don't you think?"

So that was it. Alex was blackmailing him. Grady played along and nodded.

"Yes, I imagine a person in your position could make someone very—" But Alex stopped, his eyes unfocused again, and he shook his head. "It must have been something I ate. So much rich and strange food here." He waved a hand and stared off into space, and for a moment, Grady thought he might not go on.

"Yes, well, excuse me. I'm not feeling the greatest this evening. But as I was saying, a person in your position could make a person in my position very wealthy indeed, could he not?"

"I suppose he could."

"Good. Very good." But then his eyes unfocused again, he placed both hands on the table, and he pushed back. "But . . . we'll have to . . . continue this later."

Alex stood, grabbed the chairback for support, and scanned the room with vacant eyes. Then he vomited blood all over the uneaten caprese on his plate, splashing even the man across from them. Everyone stared, including Davato, who waved for assistance.

The waiters converged, and as Alex Reed collapsed in their arms, they hauled him away.

But they hadn't reached the exit with their charge when the headwaiter burst into the room, his face flushed, his eyes wild, his hands waving. "Don't drink the water! Something's wrong with the water. All over the city, people are getting violently ill. Some have already died."

Grady stared at his water glass. Had he drunk anything but whiskey since the visit to the Euphrates? No, he didn't think so. He breathed out.

In the eyes of the ambassadors around the table, he saw mostly relief except for a man with flushed cheeks, sweating forehead, and widened eyes, as he stared at the empty water glass before him.

Davato waved the headwaiter away and shot out of his seat. "This was obviously the Enemy's doing. I'm sorry, but in the present circumstances, I think it best that we postpone this dinner for another, more convenient time." Then he stormed from the room.

As Grady headed for the elevator and his apartment, he hoped that Alex Reed, above all others, would soon succumb to whatever poison he'd drunk.

$*\ *\ *$

In the following twenty-four to forty-eight hours, forty thousand people out of New Babylon's population of one million two hundred and fifty thousand would die of the arsenic they'd drunk from water fed by the Euphrates River. Twice that number would later become so sick they would die in the weeks ahead.

Across the globe, some who had taken the mark or were in sympathy with the Antichrist would drink the water and die.

Only those following the Son of God would find water that was safe to drink.

Henceforth, whenever someone turned on the tap or lifted a glass of water to their lips, they would stick their tongue in the liquid. And if they found any hint of metallic taste, any question of taint, they would pour it out. For all who drank of the poison water would die.

This, then, was the judgment of the third trumpet.

CHAPTER 65

THE FOURTH TRUMPET

Revelation 8:12 (NLT): Then the fourth angel blew his trumpet, and one-third of the sun was struck, and one-third of the moon, and one-third of the stars, and they became dark. And one-third of the day was dark, and also one-third of the night.

Joel 2:10–11 (HCSB): The earth quakes before them; the sky shakes. The sun and moon grow dark, and the stars cease their shining. The Lord raises His voice in the presence of His army. His camp is very large; Those who carry out His command are powerful. Indeed, the Day of the Lord is terrible and dreadful—who can endure it?

Lake Shetek State Park, Minnesota – May 22, Year 4

It was around noon, and Caleb clutched his M16 as he followed the forest's edge beside the field. Barely above a whisper, his boots squished mud and leaves below. Above, a dull gray orb hung over the land. Since yesterday, the sun's light had dimmed so much that sunset had come two hours earlier. And last night, the moon and stars barely shone. And this morning, the sun rose two hours later.

To his left, weeds and volunteer corn stalks dotted the field. Ahead, deer tracks entered the border between field and forest.

If he got a deer today, they'd have meat for the next two weeks. He had about four hours before dusk.

Two days ago, when the meteor storm crossed the sky, it had spared the lake. He had read the prophecy of the trumpets, and he was grateful they still had fresh water to drink—especially since Tanya was adamant about staying at the park. She was planting a garden, talking about dividing the cabin into rooms for Andy, for Brianna, and for her and Caleb. She wouldn't hear any more talk of the Sanctuary.

But Caleb wasn't so sure.

With the shortened days and longer nights, how cold would the winters be? There was still game here, but what would happen without enough sun? The prairie had burned up. Would the rains bring it back? Would the animals and plants start to die? Already, finding feed for the horses was difficult, and they were getting thin. And what about the Pipestone squaddies? What if they came in force to stop the Currie church from worshiping the Son of God? What if they tried to take away their weapons? And what if the demon Morgoth returned?

He shuddered.

Yesterday, it had rained black rain, probably the ash and soot from whatever western volcanoes had brought the ash two and a half weeks ago. Maybe that would help, not hurt, the garden.

For now, they had no reason to leave. But there were so many unknowns, so many dangers—he shook his head.

Something rustled the branches in the trees to his right, and he froze. He peered through the nascent buds, just sprouting, and heard it again—stronger, heavier.

There! Something black and large. Not a deer, but a bear!

What was a bear doing this far south? But, of course, when the Northwoods burned, the fire would have chased many of them far from their normal habitat.

It rumbled behind a clump of pines and disappeared from view.

He raised his rifle and crept between oaks, hoping to get a shot. Slowly, he put one foot before the other. Surprise was the key.

But on the other side of the pines—nothing. The bear was gone. He relaxed. He'd missed the opportunity to—

The thud of something heavy behind him, and he whirled. The bear was standing on hind legs, paws out, advancing, ready to attack. Then it roared.

Taking a step back, he shouldered the M16, aimed for the chest, and squeezed the trigger. The crack of his shots echoed through the woods—one, two, three . . . four.

Unfazed, the creature dropped to all fours and lumbered toward him.

Caleb spun and began running. Twigs scratched his cheek. He

jumped a log. Branches snapped under his feet. The ground thundered as the bear kept coming.

A glance behind convinced him the beast wasn't stopping. He turned away. But something—a hidden rock? a limb under the leaves?—caught his foot, and he tripped.

He sprawled face-first into the dirt. The M16 flew from his hands.

Twisting around, he lunged for his weapon, but it was out of reach.

The bear was taking long strides, racing for him, only fifteen feet away.

His heart pounded in his stomach.

Then the beast dropped with a thud and a whoosh of dried leaves.

Pulling himself to a sitting position, Caleb retrieved his M16 and tried to slow his racing heart. He kicked the beast with his foot, but it didn't move. Black bears weren't supposed to attack humans like this. But of course, this was the work of the fourth seal, bringing death by wild animals. Only, he'd escaped. And now they had bear meat to eat.

He must return to the cabin and get help. He couldn't cut up this monster and haul it back alone before dark. But he wouldn't tell Tanya about his close call. It would only worry her.

Something wet hit his face, and he looked up. A cold drizzle fell from an ashen-gray sky, and he laughed.

Not so long ago, Caleb Turner had spent his days writing unpublished novels on his laptop, running out for a vanilla latte in midafternoon, and wondering whether the cute blonde in the upscale apartment next door would go out with him.

Now here he was—a caveman with a rifle, hunting bear in the rain, fighting for his very survival at the end of time.

CHAPTER 66
ENGINE TROUBLE

In the Mediterranean, South of Palma de Mallorca,
Spain — June 6, Year 4

Rain splattered against the pilothouse windows as the wind screamed through the ship's superstructure. It was Chelsea's turn to steer the ship, but after surviving the tsunami and heading northeast in a line for Italy's western coast, they now battled high winds and rough seas. Fabio had them on a course to intercept Palma de Mallorca, a resort island off the coast of Spain. "The engine is acting up," he reported with a dour face. "Once again, we have to put in for repairs."

What should have been a quick, three-day trip had become a two-week ordeal, fighting the storm's headwinds with the engine barely moving them at times. Worsening their plight, day was now a dim twilight of shadows. For all the good it did, Fabio kept the searchlights on all the time.

Chelsea peered through the slanting downpour at the next four-meter wave. The ship climbed the slope, topped the crest, then dropped into the trough on the other side. Again and again, the ship labored against wind and rain and wave.

A glance at the GPS convinced her they were about three nautical miles off the coast of their destination. She flipped on the loudspeaker and reported it to the captain.

Moments later, sleep still in his eyes, a disheveled Fabio entered the pilothouse and took over. He waved at the rollicking seas beyond the rain-drenched windows. "Once we pass the breakwater and enter the harbor, we'll be out of this."

Exhausted by her stint at the controls, she plopped into the seat beside him.

"It won't be long now," he said.

"What about the CSA?" she asked.

"I'm told that in Mallorca there are few of them, and they'll take a bribe to look the other way. But we need to keep anyone from seeing that we don't have the mark, yes?"

"If we get the parts you need, how far are we from La Spezia?" La Spezia, a small village on the western Italian coast, was now their destination. Fabio hoped there would be no squaddies there.

"From Mallorca, it's only a three- or four-day trip."

In less than a week, she'd be back in the family villa in Tuscany with Bettino. She couldn't wait to eat his pasta and sleep until noon in a soft bed that didn't rock with the waves. But most importantly, she could get Dylan's phone number, call him, and find out where to meet him.

It took another hour before they saw the beacon and the entrance through the breakwater. Fabio steered the ship into the harbor's calmer waters, still choppy, but without the wildly bucking seas. As they neared the marina, he throttled down the engine, pulled alongside an empty berth, and docked. The tsunami, they'd learned, had been only a meter high when it poured over the breakwater, and they were still cleaning up. It had piled a few boats against each other on the far side of the harbor.

"I will meet the harbormaster." He pointed to a man heading toward the ramp. "You should go to your quarters until I fill out the paperwork for supplies, repairs, and a docking permit."

She did as told but opened her porthole so she could listen to the official exchange. Most of it was boring bureaucracy until they came to Fabio's request to have the engine repaired.

"What kind of engine?" asked the harbormaster.

"A Mercedes-Benz 484 kilowatt."

"Señor, unfortunately, you are not the only one requesting such engine parts. There are others ahead of you, who have been waiting for months. The factories are not prioritizing marine requests." He threw up his hands. "Nothing works as it should anymore, and my guess is you will be unable to fix your engine for two, three, maybe even four months."

"Four months? Unacceptable! We cannot be stranded here for four months."

"I am sorry, señor, but it is what it is." He opened his hands in apology.

Chelsea closed the porthole and plopped back onto her bed. Four months stranded in port again? Had they not already been through this in Crete?

Fabio was right. It was impossible.

How long had it been since she'd seen Dylan? Had it been two years ago when she met him at the Paris restaurant? She wiped a tear from a cheek, pulled the pillow over her head, and buried her face in the mattress.

Please, dear God, she prayed to herself. *Let me return to Bettino. Let me see my brother again one last time before the end.*

CHAPTER 67
AND THEN IT SPOKE

New Babylon, Iraq – July, Year 4

Grady clutched his empty twenty-liter plastic can and walked outside the ropes, past a seemingly endless column of people snaking half a kilometer around the corner. Beside him, inside the ropes, two women screamed and shoved at each other. Further on, he veered far away from three men intent on beating each other senseless. CSA troops, on hand to keep order, rushed to break up the fight.

As he held his pass and walked outside the ropes, people stared at him. Some even shook their fists. Others just turned their heads away in disgust, for he was one of the elite, one of the privileged, one for whom the ordinary rules didn't apply. Wasn't it always thus?

He could empathize with their anger. They'd been waiting in line for hours for the privilege of filling one container with fresh water. And here he was, holding a pass allowing him to skip to the front ahead of everyone else.

He avoided the ugly glances and walked on. No way was he going to wait in that line.

Overhead, an oppressive gray shroud hung over the city. Sunset now came at four o'clock in the afternoon. As much as anything, the short-ened days contributed to the foul mood infecting the city.

At first, the news media warned that all the ash and dust thrown into the sky by the volcanoes and asteroids would cool the planet. Scientists expected the coming winter to be harsh, and everyone bought blankets, portable heaters, vodka, and brandy.

But it didn't happen. The planet didn't cool. And the scientists changed their minds. Water was by far the greatest contributor to green-house gases, dwarfing by 2,500 percent the carbon dioxide everyone had feared for decades. The first asteroid had thrown such an enormous vol-ume of seawater into the troposphere that scientists believed its greenhouse effect more than compensated for the lack of sunlight reaching the earth. So they changed their initial assessment to match what everyone was seeing with their own eyes. Temperatures would remain unchanged.

When Grady heard the news, he simply shrugged. The scientific "experts" had been wrong on so many things for so long that he stopped listening to their pronouncements.

Beside him, one of the death trucks lumbered down the street, gears clanking. People called them death trucks because they were painted black, without insignia, and government women went from apartment to apartment collecting those who never showed up for work, who had maybe drunk the poison water in the days after the second asteroid's meteor shower.

Now, the city took its water from the Tigris, which the asteroid had spared.

Grady had sat in meetings discussing how to pipe water across the desert to New Babylon, but it would take months to complete the task. Meanwhile, trucks arrived hourly with fresh water, rationing it in a slow, meager, and time-consuming process, while the populace grumbled and shook their fists.

Suddenly, everyone began to look up.

He stopped and craned his neck to the sky. Far above soared an enormous bird with an impossible wingspan. It shone with an ethereal, golden light as if it had come from Heaven itself.

It was an eagle, and its dark, piercing eyes speared the inhabitants below.

With the bird's appearance, all of Grady's doubts returned. Davato had surely risen from the dead, so there was no question he was a god. But here, again, above him, was a reminder that there existed another power, one who sent heavenly creatures to warn him and pass judgment, one who shook the planet, blackened the sun and moon, rained down meteors, erupted volcanoes, and hurled asteroids to earth. And if that power existed, it reminded him of the angels' appearance and their warnings of doom.

Grady raised his gaze to the mammoth bird soaring far, far above, and he cowered.

And then it spoke.

* * *

Kronberg Mountain, Switzerland

THIS MORNING, THE NAZARENE FRIENDS hauled the final load up to the resort. Seeking a break, Dylan and Margot left the unpacking to the others and went to the porch where they dropped onto wooden rockers.

"That was the last of it." She leaned back, squeaking her chair.

"Yes." He rested his head on the high wooden back. "And I need a rest."

Two kilometers down the trail was a dirt access road and a pull-off in the trees where René and Pasqual had hidden the van. They'd hauled everything from the warming hut across the mountain to the nearest road, filling the vehicle with everything they'd left behind. Four trips up the trail had brought what they needed to make the Green Mountain Hideaway their new home. "It's fortunate the fires skipped this section of forest. When we left two months ago, I was worried about the lightning."

"All that rain helped."

"Yes, but the meadows are nothing but stalks of charcoal." He pulled his phone from his pocket. Though it wasn't a solar phone, Victor had figured out how to work with the new signal they were broadcasting. But it didn't work as well as before, and they kept losing the connection every few minutes.

"Are you going to try again?" Margot shot him a glance.

"I keep hoping." Unlike their last hideout, this one was near a cell tower. He punched in Chelsea's number and held his breath. So many things could have gone wrong with her phone and with her, but he kept hope alive that somehow, he'd get through. Of course, if she'd received a new solar phone, she'd have lost her old number. Still, he kept trying.

Once again, he received an automated recording. The number was out of service.

Next, he tried reaching Caleb. It rang, but he received no answer. Of course, Caleb had said he was moving, and with cell service in the center of the continent so unreliable and spotty, that wasn't surprising.

Finally, he called Bettino in Tuscany. Bettino had a solar phone with a new number, and last week, Bettino hadn't heard from either Caleb or Chelsea. Maybe today, he'd have better news.

But instead of the old Italian's friendly voice, another automated recording came on the line. Bettino's number, too, had been disconnected.

Dylan stared at the phone. This wasn't good. Had something happened to him? Bettino was his only connection with Chelsea. If his sister was okay, and if she ever tried to contact him, it would be through Bettino.

Dylan stood and paced the length of the porch.

"What's wrong?" asked Margot.

"Bettino's number is disconnected."

"Did they get to him?"

"I don't know." He stepped off the porch onto the yard and cupped his hands behind his neck. This changed everything. Maybe he should go to the Tuscan villa to see for himself if Bettino was all right? While there, he could also leave a note for Chelsea.

Margot stepped off the porch and stood beside him. "It's worrisome. Everyone is on the run all the time."

"It seems like it."

A great shadow darkened the forest clearing surrounding the resort, and he looked up.

Below the cloud ceiling, yet still far, far above them, soared an impossibly large bird. Its feathers glowed with a glorious golden light as if it had flown down from Heaven itself.

It was an eagle, and its dark, piercing eyes speared the inhabitants below.

Dylan knew instantly it was another messenger from God and that more trials and tribulations lay ahead. And now he also knew, as if through some sixth sense, that the Nazarene Friends couldn't stay in the Appenzell Alps, that it wasn't safe here, but that before they moved, he must find Chelsea. Yes, he must go to the family villa and contact Bettino, for that is where Chelsea would go.

He looked to the sky, to the massive eagle soaring far, far above him. And then it spoke.

* * *

Palma de Mallorca, Spain

Since they were stuck in port possibly for months, Fabio had relented, and as they had for the last several weeks, Chelsea and Enzo left the ship for a walk through town. It was Sunday, and from somewhere, they heard singing so beautiful, it drew them on. She turned to Enzo. "Shall we investigate?"

He nodded, and they headed off toward the sound.

Above, the sun burned dimly through a layer of dark, churning clouds. The days had been shortened by a third, and the nights seemed darker yet.

Stately houses, half of which now stood empty, rose beside palm-lined avenues. Belying a hint of old-world Spanish wealth, two teenage girls in ragged dresses accosted them, begging for food. Chelsea gave them each a euro.

If the singing was coming from a church, wouldn't it soon attract the CSA? But the plague had been especially severe and long lasting on the island, and the Unitum Imperium had only recently arrived. The CSA had only a single headquarters with four Truth Squad members, and, like elsewhere, rumor had it they could be bribed.

They'd passed the town's massive cathedral days before, and as they neared it again, singing came through the broken windows of the clerestory high above the street.

Exchanging a puzzled glance with Enzo, she mounted the steps and pushed through the massive wooden doors into the narthex. From the sanctuary echoed the voice of an angel, from a woman of about thirty, wearing a thin blue dress, dirty and worn. She sang in Latin, and her voice filled the chamber, bounced off the frescoed walls, trilled around the crystal chandeliers, and escaped, high above them, through the broken windows and into the city beyond.

Chelsea recognized the song as "Ave Maria", and though she didn't know what the words meant, right now it seemed like the most beautiful song she'd ever heard.

A young man and a woman sat before the singer.

Standing in the nave at the cathedral's far end, Chelsea stood transfixed.

"She has a beautiful voice, no?" Startled, she turned to find a black-haired older man appearing from behind a pillar. But he wore the green-and-white uniform of the CSA, and when two other uniformed officers followed, she tensed. "It's a shame we have to end this, but we have our orders. If I were you, I'd take your friend and leave now."

She hid her wrist, grabbed Enzo's hand, and, as the CSA men stomped toward the sanctuary's front, she hurried toward the exit.

But at the doors, she stopped to look back.

The CSA men spread out before the front, and the woman stopped singing. Her young man rushed forward to block the way.

Voices rose as the woman's protector argued with the Unitum Imperium agents. One of the CSA placed a hand on his pistol, but the black-haired older man waved his younger counterpart away. Then came a quieter discussion, after which the singer's protector passed a series of bills to the agents.

Disgusted but also relieved, Chelsea pushed through onto the street and turned to Enzo. "At least they won't take her to jail."

"Yes, but they didn't let her sing. I don't know what the words said, but the music was heavenly."

Then a shadow, as of a large cloud, darkened the street, and she looked up.

Far above, an enormous bird soared below the cloud ceiling. Its wingspan was impossibly large, and from its feathers came a golden glow, as if Heaven itself had sent it to earth.

It was an eagle, and its dark, piercing eyes speared the inhabitants below.

Instantly, tears filled her eyes, for she knew it was yet another messenger from God. And its presence reminded her that many dark days of trial lay ahead, and she regretted what she'd done so far with her life. What a fool she'd been to follow the man of lawlessness, the son of destruction, the Antichrist. Too late had she come to faith, and now she was stuck in Palma de Mallorca, waiting for engine parts that might take months to arrive. She wanted with all her heart to leave this very instant and be with her brother Dylan. And with Margot. And with all of Dylan's friends. For they were the only family left to her on this earth.

She fixed her gaze on the eagle, this impossibly large, heavenly creature soaring far, far above her.

And then it spoke.

$$* * *$$

Currie, Minnesota

As they left the American Legion Post, Caleb held Tanya's hand and beamed. The congregation spilled out the doors, shouting congratulations and throwing dried flower petals over the newlyweds. The churchwomen had set up tables in the street, and now they carried out trays piled with boiled corn, still steaming; jars of molasses; and corn muffins. Someone had butchered a hog, and as the meat rotated on a spit over a fire in the parking lane, women were slicing meat onto plates. Others served apple pie and homemade beer.

"Let me be the first to kiss the bride." Andy rushed forward then stopped, a question on his face. "But only if it's okay with her husband?"

"Go ahead." Caleb grinned. "But be quick."

Andy hugged her, gave her a peck on the cheek, and stepped back.

Then Brianna held up the bouquet of dried flowers she'd picked and asked, "Can I kiss the groom?"

Laughing, Caleb nodded. But instead of a kiss, she hugged him. "Thank you, Caleb," she whispered in his ear, "for all you two have done for me."

When they separated, Henry Adams, who'd performed the ceremony and finally agreed to be called Pastor, approached with hand extended. "It's good to have a wedding for a change. There've been way too many funerals around here. I know you two will be happy together."

"Thank you." Caleb pumped Henry's hand. "You folks have been like a family to us."

Henry then ushered them to seats in the center of the table, and Caleb feasted his eyes on his bride. She wore a yellow flowered dress one of the women had lent her. Her hair, washed and falling in reddish-blonde curls around her breasts, now held a petunia Brianna had stuck between her locks. Around Tanya's neck hung a string of purple cornflowers. But today, her eyes were so bright, it was as if the light of Jesus himself shone through them.

At no time in his life could Caleb ever remember being as happy as right now. If happiness could explode a person, he was on the verge of popping.

Someone struck a fork against a glass. Up and down his table and the table behind, eager, happy faces turned to the newlyweds, tapping a symphony of clinking glassware.

Caleb smiled, stood from his seat, and took his bride in his arms. Then he dropped her in a dramatic embrace, and his lips found hers. Cheers and clapping followed as the kiss lingered. Energy shot through him. He dropped the drama and brought her upright as their lips, their faces, even perhaps their souls, merged as one, refusing to part. Oohs and aahs rose around them.

Finally, they separated.

He was breathing fast, and she raised a hand to the back of her head as if to keep herself from flying away.

"Here's to the bride and groom." Andy raised a mug of beer, and everyone found their drinks. "May their lives together be as happy as anyone can expect, given the times in which we live."

People raised their mugs, glasses, and cups to the toast and drank, followed by an impromptu cheer.

A shadow covered the length of the street, and Caleb looked up.

High above, a massive bird—too big for any earthly creature—soared across the sky. Its wings shone with an ethereal, golden glow, as if Heaven itself had sent it to earth.

It was an eagle, and its dark, piercing eyes speared the inhabitants below.

Its presence broke the joy of the moment, and it told Caleb that here, again, was another messenger from the One who created the Universe. It reminded him that many dark and terrible days lay ahead and they wouldn't be able to remain in the relative safety of a park by a lake. For God's judgment would eventually fall even upon that place of refuge. And he knew, as if through some sixth sense, that one day soon, they must leave for the Sanctuary.

The eagle, so large and bright and heavenly, soared far, far above, and he couldn't take his focus off it.

And then it spoke.

CHAPTER 68

THE EAGLE

Above the Earth — July, Year 4

The eagle soared high above the earth on wings of shimmering, rippling gold.

It traveled from one end of the planet to another, drawn to wherever the people lived.

It passed over burnt stick forests where, hundreds of miles from the volcanoes, missiles of lava had set the land ablaze.

It hurried over vast grasslands and prairie, now blackened, charred, and lifeless.

It passed over cities toppled into ruin and churned into rubble by earthquakes.

It sped over the Atlantic where a toxic red tide spread out from the east, where seawater had turned to blood, killing every living thing and breeding an ocean of squirming white maggots. From the spreading blood-sea issued an overpowering stench of death and decay.

It crossed over shores where tsunami-ravaged boats, cars, and debris piled helter-skelter in a chaotic jumble against the skeletons of buildings.

It soared above endless lines of cars, bicycles, and panicked pedestrians fleeing inland from the ravaged coasts.

But to the carnage below, the eagle was oblivious, for it carried a message of divine judgment.

The people had turned their backs on the God who created them. The Lord of Heaven and Earth had given them the ability to choose. They'd had chance after chance. But again and again, they chose the darkness over the light, the wrong over the right. And then—horror of horrors!—their thinking became so twisted and evil, they believed that evil was good, and good was evil.

The light shone in the darkness. But the people rejected the light, and now they worshiped the darkness.

Some had taken the mark of the beast. They'd made their choice. Their doom was forever sealed.

For the undecided, there was still time. But few were the grains of sand left in the glass. For the time of final judgment would soon be upon them.

So the God who created all that was, that is, and that is to come sent a messenger, an eagle to which he gave life and breath and words with which to speak.

And this was what it spoke: "Woe! Woe! Woe to those who live on the earth, because of the remaining trumpet blasts that the three angels are about to sound."

The fifth trumpet would release a horde of demon locusts with scorpion tails that, for five long months, would torture the unsaved.

The sixth trumpet would send forth a demon army to kill one-third of all who had rejected the Son of the Living God, the Lord of Lords, the King of Kings.

And the Seventh—oh, the seventh trumpet!—it would bring the final terrors of the seven bowl judgments.

"Woe! Woe! Woe to those who live on the earth," cried the eagle.

And all who heard its voice—echoing and piercing and tearing across the seas, mountains, and valleys—trembled with fear.

The shadow of the Tribulation already darkens our world. Know what's to come, stay true to the faith, and seek refuge in Christ. Subscribe to Mark's newsletter and receive two free gifts:

1. 10 Reasons Why the End Times Could Come Tomorrow
2. How the Green Agenda Prepares the Way for Earth Worship and the Antichrist

Go to: www.MarkFisherAuthor.com/newsletter

AUTHOR'S NOTES

THE GIANT IS NOT FICTION!

In 2021, the Giant Company unveiled the world's tallest moving statue with plans to erect others in twenty-one cities around the world. Its goals are to create community centers, seek advertising, and become "a beacon for sustainability", promoting a climate change agenda. It is a one-hundred-foot-tall monument to mankind, a mammoth idol celebrating humanity, and a perfect vehicle for the Antichrist when he comes to power. (Search on "giant statue" or "world's tallest moving statue".)

DOES THE ANTICHRIST REALLY DIE?

Satan cannot create life. One sees this in Exodus 7–10 when Moses stands before Pharaoh and announces the ten plagues against Egypt. Through magic, Pharaoh's magicians turn a staff into a snake, but Moses's snake swallows it. But when Moses created a plague of gnats, the magicians could not repeat the deed. Satan cannot create life.

Yet in Revelation 13:3–4 and 17:8, we're told that the Antichrist is killed and that he comes back to life. There are two views about this. The first is that Satan does not have the power to resurrect anyone and that the Antichrist didn't really die but was only wounded. Yet the text strongly suggests the wound was fatal.

The second view is that the Antichrist does die and that God will permit Satan to resurrect him in order to fulfill biblical prophecy. This is the view I have taken to match Scripture.

THE ANTICHRIST'S TWO FALSE RELIGIONS

Revelation 17 describes the two false religions that the false prophet will administer. But in Revelation 17:16–17, the Antichrist rejects the first religion and implements a second in which the world worships only himself.

As we see the gathering signs of the end, one can only conclude that the seeds of the first false religion are already in place in the climate change agenda.

The World Economic Forum and the United Nations, supported by nearly every government and corporate leader on the planet, are preparing for a New World Order, a Great Reset—their very words. They call their plan "Agenda 2030", and, according to them, by the year 2030, the world will be an alarmingly different place. Yuval Noah Harari, principal advisor to Klaus Schwab, the founder of the WEF, is the architect for much of it.

The people behind this are climate fanatics, elitists who know better than everyone else, who want to control every aspect of everyone's lives, all to stop the boogeyman of "climate change". They are godless enemies of Christ and all that Christ stands for. Included in their supporters are a host of high-profile leaders.

Across the world, they are reducing the acreage of farmland devoted to cattle and dairy cows. In their view, bovine flatulence creates too much CO2. Thus, they want to control all private property, especially farmland. Supported by woke billionaires, they are already, right now, preparing vast cricket farms as a protein substitute. To foster one world government, they want open borders. They ascribe to all the goals of the godless woke—gender fluidity, homosexuality, abortion, atheism, destruction of the nuclear family, and a new kind of socialism one might call woke fascism.

And their solution? Restructure every facet of life, upend economies, change lifestyles, impoverish everyone, and impose draconian, totalitarian government control across the world.

But please note: *This is not some wild-eyed conspiracy theory. It's a fact. These are their goals, stated loudly and publicly, and they are actively working to accomplish them now!*

They've convinced almost everyone that some future climate catastrophe will destroy the planet and that we must alter everyone's lifestyles, government, and the entire social order to stop the threat of global warming.

They have an atheist worldview that mankind, not God, is in charge.

Their rabid fixation on global warming and saving the earth is preparing the world to worship the planet.

Thus, it seems clear: Earth worship will be the first of the Antichrist's false religions.

Filled with jealousy and ego, the son of destruction will eventually rebel and make himself the object of worship.

To learn more about this subject, please visit my website and subscribe to my newsletter, where you will be offered a free copy of "How the Green Agenda Prepares the Way for Earth Worship and the Antichrist." There you will learn:

1. Why thousands of scientists, in opposition to the woke organizations to which they belong, disagree with the notion that carbon dioxide poses a catastrophic threat to the planet and is causing global warming,

2. Why the green agenda is impossible to implement and destructive to the environment and society, and

3. More about the way the green agenda prepares us for earth worship and the Antichrist's two false religions.

LOOK TO ETERNITY AND HAVE HOPE!

Though we live in the shadow of the Tribulation, though the world spirals ever downward with each passing week, we have a hope and a certainty that nonbelievers do not. Before the terrible events of the Tribulation, Christians will be raptured away. That is our great hope. Paul describes this in 1 Corinthians 15:51–52 (NLT):

> But let me reveal to you a wonderful secret. We will not all die, but we will all be transformed! It will happen in a moment, in the blink of an eye, when the last trumpet is blown. For when the trumpet sounds, those who have died will be raised to live forever. And we who are living will also be transformed.

And in 1 Thessalonians 4:16–18 (NLT):

> For the Lord himself will come down from heaven with a commanding shout, with the voice of the archangel, and with the trumpet call of God. First, the believers who have died will rise from their graves. Then, together with them, we who are still alive and remain on the earth will be caught up in the clouds to meet the Lord in the air. Then we will be with the Lord forever. So encourage each other with these words.

We who are Christians, who have put our trust in the promises of God, are *not* destined for wrath. It is God's promise that, though the world heads ever closer to destruction and judgment, Christians will be spared the time of testing in the seven years of Tribulation. In Revelation 3:10 (NLT):

> "Because you have obeyed my command to persevere, I will protect you from the great time of testing that will come upon the whole world to test those who belong to this world."

And in 1 Thessalonians 9:10 (NLT):

> And they speak of how you are looking forward to the coming of God's Son from heaven—Jesus, whom God raised from the dead. He is the one who has rescued us from the terrors of the coming judgment.

So look not to this life or to the flawed, sinful leaders of this world for salvation, but to Jesus, King of Kings, Lord of Lords, to the God who came to earth as a man, whose love for us knows no bounds. For those who believe in Jesus, look upward, to the blessed eternity he has promised us.

SCRIPTURE REFERENCES

- Preface:
  - God's response to rebellious nations. Isaiah 2:12, 17–19, 21b–22 (NLT)
  - Jesus warns about the signs of the times. Matthew 24:6–8 (HCSB)
- Chapter 2: On the Day of the Lord, fire will consume the wilderness and forests. Joel 1:15, 19–20 (HCSB)
- Chapter 4: A warning about participating in Babylon's evil deeds. Revelation 18:4–5 (NLT)
- Chapter 7: After the Battle of Gog and Magog, the house of Israel will spend seven months burying the dead. Ezekiel 39:9–16 (HCSB)
- Chapter 9: Christians will be persecuted in the end times. Matthew 24:9–10 (NLT)
- Chapter 17: A symbolic depiction of Israel as a woman clothed with the sun, the moon at her feet. Revelation 12:1–2 (HCSB)
- Chapter 20: The breaking of the sixth seal, bringing an earthquake, darkening the sun, and making the moon blood red. Revelation 6:12–14 (NLT)
- Chapter 21: An Old Testament prophecy that parallels the opening of the sixth seal. Joel 2:30–31 (NLT)
- Chapter 23: In the end times, there will be false prophets and messiahs. Matthew 24:23–24, 27–28 (NLT)
- Chapter 25: The false prophet will give a spirit to the image of the beast, causing it to speak. Revelation 13:15 (NLT)
- Chapter 28:
  - An Old Testament prophecy that the Antichrist will make a treaty with Israel for three and one half years, then break it. He will put a sacrilegious object in the Temple. Daniel 9:27 (HCSB)
  - A New Testament prophecy about the false prophet, who will put a spirit into an image of the beast, then he will require everyone to receive the mark of the beast. Revelation 13:11a, 12a, 15–17 (HCSB)

- Chapter 29: The false prophet will perform signs and wonders. Revelation 13:11–12a, 13 (HCSB)
- Chapter 30:
  - When the sacrilegious object is in the Holy Place in the Temple, Judea must flee to the hills. Matthew 24:15–16 (NLT)
  - A prophecy detailing those will escape the Antichrist, including Edom where resides the fortress of Sela. Daniel 11:40–41 (HCSB)
- Chapter 33: Christians will cast out demons in Jesus's name. Mark 16:17 (NLT)
- Chapter 38: The Antichrist will rule a kingdom that will devour the whole earth. Under him will be ten rulers. Daniel 7:19–20, 23–24 (HCSB)
- Chapter 40:
  - Three angels will circle the earth, warning people that they must turn to God, that Babylon will fall, and that anyone who takes the mark of the beast is forever doomed. Revelation 14:6–12
  - The account of Jesus feeding the five thousand. Matthew 14:15–20 (HCSB)
- Chapter 42: After the Antichrist is killed, he will descend to Hell then be resurrected to life. Revelation 17:8 (NLT)
- Chapter 44: Another prophecy declaring that the Antichrist's fatal wound was healed, after which the people worshiped him and the Dragon. Revelation 13:1, 3–4 (NLT)
- Chapter 47: The opening of the seventh seal, bringing silence in Heaven and the beginning of the trumpet judgments. Revelation 8:1–5
- Chapter 53: The first trumpet judgment brings an earthquake, lightning, and thunder. Hail and fire and blood falls upon the earth, burning up a third of the trees and all the green grass. Revelation 8:5, 7 (NLT)
- Chapter 55: God's judgment on a people who have turned from him and his word. Isaiah 24:4–6 (HCSB)
- Chapter 58: God sees the rebellious plans of the nations and laughs. Psalm 2:1–2, 4–5 (HCSB)

- Chapter 60: The second trumpet judgment sends a mountain of fire into the sea, and the water turns to blood. Revelation 8:8–9 (NLT)
- Chapter 62: The third trumpet judgment sends blazing fire to earth that poisons a third of the fresh water. Revelation 8:10–11 (HCSB)
- Chapter 65:
  - The fourth trumpet darkens a third of the sun, moon, and stars, and shortens the day by one-third. Revelation 8:12 (NLT)
  - An Old Testament prophecy describing the fourth trumpet. Joel 2:10–11 (HCSB)
- Chapter 68: An eagle circles the earth, bringing a message of woe from the next three trumpets and the bowl judgments. Revelation 8:13.
- Author's Notes:
  - First description of the Rapture: 1 Corinthians 15:51–52 (NLT)
  - Second description of the Rapture: 1 Thessalonians 4:16–18 (NLT)
  - First promise that believers are spared the Tribulation: Revelation 3:10 (NLT)
  - Second promise that believers are spared the Tribulation: 1 Thessalonians 9:10 (NLT)

MARK'S BOOKS

Christian Historical Fiction:

- The Bonfires Of Beltane: Following St. Patrick Across Ancient, Celtic Ireland
- The Medallion: An Epic Quest In A.D. 486
- The Slaves Of Autumn: A Tale Of Stolen Love In Ancient, Celtic Ireland

General Market Historical Fiction:

- Death Of The Master Builder: Love, Envy, and the Struggle to Raise the Greatest Cathedral of the Italian Renaissance

Days of the Apocalypse, a Series of Christian End-Times Thrillers:

- Book 1: The Day They Vanished
- Book 2: Days of War and Famine
- Book 3: Days of Trial and Tribulation
- Book 4: Days of Death and Darkness (coming soon)
- Book 5: Last Days of the End (planned)

The Scepter and Tower Trilogy, an epic fantasy for young adults of all ages:

- The Stolen Scroll, a novella prequel (eBook only)
- Book 1: Quest for the Scepter
- Book 2: Into the Druid's Lair
- Book 3: Return to the Tower

To learn more about Mark's books, please visit:
MarkFisherAuthor.com

www.ingramcontent.com/pod-product-compliance
Lightning Source LLC
Chambersburg PA
CBHW060857210726
48293CB00006B/1841